The
CHASE

LORNA
FERGUSSON

To Jane,
best wishes
Lorna Fergusson

FICTIONFIRE PRESS

The Périgord, they said, is life itself. The cradle of man. A festival.

'*The Chase* is, among other things, an expression of love for France and for a special time in my life. For several years, my husband and I were part-owners of a house in the Dordogne. Le Périer stood on a hillside overlooking a vineyard. We had no mobile phone – no phone of any sort – no computer, no TV – no distractions, except long lunches with friends, French acquaintances who would drag us away for *apéros* and, for me, too much gazing out at the vineyard and the hills when I should have been writing. Wild creatures stirred in the garden outside and at night gave us the heebie jeebies by scuttering about in the roof-space. In the evening, to wander away from the pool of light cast by the open French windows was to wander into a world of darkness where the stars had true liberty to shine – and unnerve...'

Lorna Fergusson

Revised edition 2013
Published by Fictionfire Press

Originally published by Bloomsbury Publishing 1999 and 2001
The moral rights of the author have been asserted.

For permission requests, contact lorna@fictionfirepress.com
Cover Design: JD Smith Design

www.fictionfirepress.com

ISBN: 978-0-9576474-1-1

In memory of my parents George and Elizabeth Fergusson

What shall assuage the unforgotten pain
And teach the unforgetful to forget?
Dante Gabriel Rossetti, 'The One Hope'

Contents

Cave

He swiftly draws a broad line downwards: the dipping backbone of a bison. Two quick dashes forward: the eager horns. Russet and brown and blood-orange fill the flanks. He gasps at his own skill, half-expecting the animal to turn, to breathe, to bellow.

In the flickering light cast by his tallow lamp, he populates ghostly plains with magic beings. He draws sharp black men and even sharper rows of spears and arrows, plunging into the spirit creatures. On a whim he outlines the face of the wild boar, subtle master of the undergrowth. His blood surges and power flows into him. He stamps and crows, dabbling at himself with his pigments. He places his palm against the limestone and blows red ochre through a tube, stencilling the outline of his hand, again and again.

Sinking down at last, panting, he hears the sound of dropping water and his heart hammers. A ripple runs through the ground and the stony spears which hang from the roof shiver with a lapidary chime.

As the earth begins to heave, he forgets his precious cups of colour and throws himself on his belly to worm back through the tunnel. Rock bites and his blood paints him from scalp to shoulder. The earth shudders again as he scrambles out and slips down the slope through wet vegetation. Wide-eyed, he looks back at the pebbles bouncing and splintering, at the slurry of red clay sealing the entrance.

He lies, retching. The others are waiting: tomorrow's hunt will be successful, for has he not created strong magic? And his creatures will lie eternally, glowing colours in a tomb of darkness, forever hunted, forever killed, forever alive again.

Voyeur

1987

It was the dog's fault that she saw what she saw.

Claudine Bellenger set off to walk through the woods with Patapon.
The dog's fluffy name did not suit its breed. It was a beagle, and in
England it would have been called Ben or Sam. Madame Bellenger
loved all things English; indeed she had been given the dog by her
friends, the Lukers, when she had last visited them, just after Henri's
death. Felix and Deirdre had moved to a large apartment in one of
those newly renovated Victorian warehouses in Wapping. They'd
paid a substantial sum in order to have a view over the river. Claudine
could see it was an astute investment: the whole Docklands area was
buzzing with development. However, she had thought the industrial
architecture and treeless cobbled streets bleak. Depressing.

At the time, though, there had been more to depress her than
unfriendly architecture. Her beloved Henri had died of a heart attack
just a month previously. He had died right in front of her, keeling
over in the course of a fine dinner she had prepared for sixteen
guests. He had, apparently, been dead before he hit the floor: no time
for farewells.

Henri had been a good man; theirs had been a good marriage,
cerebrally and sexually. Now she had been cheated of the years of
companionship to come. *Voilà*, she thought, there it is, it is finished.

Not for her to be a predatory widow haunting other people's parties in search of a second mate. A part of her life was over, and so she settled her affairs, shut up the apartment in Paris, and after her trip to London, retreated to the château in the Périgord she and Henri had owned for fifteen years.

The Lukers gave her their dog because they felt guilty about locking him up all day in their flat with nothing for the poor creature to look at but the grey Thames and the cranes and half-finished buildings across the water. 'He'll keep you company,' they had said. 'You'll need company. Don't you think you should stay in Paris? Or why not London? You should be with people.' But Claudine had shaken her head, stating that she was quite happy with her plan for the future. And she *had* been happy. A year had passed, of a kind of serenity she had scarcely expected to achieve, so soon after Henri's death.

It was a humid August night. The heat had been too intense during the day for Madame Bellenger to wish to venture out. Heat enervated her, and besides, she liked to keep her skin pale; it kept her young-looking for her fifty-eight years, and made a striking contrast to her sleek black hair, pulled back in a chignon from her rather hawkish features. Only when the air had cooled somewhat did she call Patapon and venture out into the dusk.

She climbed the hill, following the sinuous paths through the woods by the light of the half-moon riding the sky above her. She knew her territory so intimately by now, there was no need for a torch. Well, strictly speaking, it was not all her territory. Of the hill she was climbing, she possessed some ten hectares of woodland, rising from behind her château, Bel Arbre, to the crown of the hill. Over the crest, the land belonged to an old country house called Le Sanglier, which was placed higher up the slope than Bel Arbre and looked down into the valley of the Meuron and the village of Malignac. Whereas Bel Arbre stood a few hundred metres beyond the fringes of the forest, Le Sanglier was buried in it: for this reason Madame Bellenger had never been attracted to that house: she would feel too hemmed in, having the trees in such proximity. She preferred the symmetry and dignity of Bel Arbre and the neatly trimmed lawns and box hedges around it, in imitation of the gardens of classic English country houses.

It had often amused her to think of herself adopting *le style anglais* while the English themselves — like, for example, the recent purchasers of Le Sanglier — were flocking to France in ever-increasing numbers in search of some dream of lost rural contentedness. They might be mad and misguided, but *bof!*, they took care of the buildings they bought and at least they restored them with taste, which was more than you could say for the Germans.

The thought of this made Claudine smile, as she reached the bare knoll at the top of the hill. It was such a lovely night, she almost unconsciously headed down through the dark woods on the other side, with Patapon scampering ahead. For some reason, the air was thicker and heavier on this side of the hill, redolent with late greenery and rotting vegetation. After a few minutes of this, Claudine felt oppressed, but as she was now nearer Le Sanglier than the top of the hill, she plunged on, deciding to by-pass the house, and follow its drive down to the base of the Colline Nemorale, to join the lane near the foot which curved round to the approach of Bel Arbre.

As the trees thinned and they emerged into the silver moonlight again, Patapon gave a short excited bark and dashed off towards the house itself. In a low voice she called him back, but he ignored her, which was most exasperating. She had not met the new owners properly; they had only lived at Le Sanglier for three or four months, and although she normally loved to associate with the English, she had not found the energy to make contact.

It would be highly inappropriate, she felt, and would spoil any future acquaintanceship, if she were to be found like this, as a common trespasser on their land. How embarrassing. So she quickened her pace to follow the heedless dog, hissing at him, and slapping his leash sharply against her leg.

The last trees gave way to scraggy bushes and the overgrown garden at the back of Le Sanglier. Claudine clicked her tongue in disapproval of such untidiness; surely the owners, recent arrivals as they were, could have done more to discipline their environment? Strands of briar snagged at her, twigs jabbed at her, dew on the long springy grass drenched her shoes. Tall hollyhocks seemed to lean towards her, their flowers, monochrome in the strange grey light, like so many ear-trumpets straining for a word.

Claudine was becoming seriously angry with the dog, but dared not raise her voice. The house loomed up in front of her, a long dark silhouette. All at once, Patapon scurried out of nowhere, towards her and away, the sound of his quick excited panting leading her as she followed, round the side of the house and along the paved space in front of it. His claws clicked on the paving as he scampered along.

As often at night, every noise seemed magnified. Claudine saw to her left the drop of the land away down to the evening lights of Malignac, more than a mile distant. She looked up, and the fringes of the forest seemed for a moment to shift and heave before the stars. She put a hand to her bosom; imbecile, she thought, to hurry like this after a *méchant* dog. Her heart was thudding and she felt sweat prickle under her armpits and between her breasts.

She looked towards the house and her fear of discovery increased, for it was clear that the occupants were still awake. The central door was closed, as were most of the shutters, but those at the far end were open, and an amber-yellow stream of light flowed out onto the terrace. It was over there that she could see the solid little silhouette of Patapon. She crouched down to throw her whisper the twenty metres between them: *'Patapon, viens ici! Viens!'*

To her relief, the dog came rushing up, tail wagging. She reached out to grasp his collar, the leash at the ready, but he would not come close enough to be caught. Frustratingly, he pranced and darted about, just out of reach. She toppled over onto her knees, cursing him, reaching out but just missing. For a moment she felt his hot breath on her hand and near her face, and then he was away again, just a few feet, looking at her with moist happy eyes.

The thudding of her heart had increased and now there was a pounding in her head, too. She could feel the rhythmic passage of each pulse of blood down every artery, up every vein, to the tips of her fingers, the pads of her toes. The house as she looked towards it tilted to and fro, as if her blood, the earth, the trees and the house itself were all involved in a crazy dance. And there was music, flowing with the light from the open window, strange haunting piping sounds, woeful, yet charged with vigour.

The dog jumped from paw to paw. Then he made distracted little rushes towards that beckoning window. Half on her hands and knees, she found herself following. Patapon was giving increasingly excited little yelps and whimpers. Claudine's breathing quickened and she found herself keener to peer in through the window than to catch the errant beagle.

The last remnant of cool sanity within her was shocked at her behaviour. She had always prided herself on her detachment, her dignity, her self-containment. Yet now she was eager to spy into the lives of people unknown to her; she could not help it, she could not. It was as if an invisible hand were pushing her from behind, or an unseen cord tugging her towards the yellow window; skeins of music winding her in.

She reached the wall of the house to the right of the French window. Her dizziness still on her, she flattened herself against the warm gritty stone. Patapon stood beside her, his muscles quivering, his nose twitching. Then with a yelp, he leaped up at her repeatedly, trying to bury his nose in her groin, sniffing vigorously and panting. She attempted to brush him away, but still he leapt, and only a sharp switch with the leather leash drove him off. He stood a few feet away, tongue hanging out, staring at her. Eyeing him nervously, she edged along and from the shadow cast by the shutter, she gazed into the room beyond.

It was a bedroom. Red tiles gleamed softly in the light of fat yellow candles which seemed to have been placed on any surface available, including the floor itself, where they trailed molten tails of wax.

In the flickering, uncertain light, she saw articles of clothing strewn about in crumpled heaps. By a cane chair lay a pair of the most extremely high-heeled shoes she had ever seen, their heels sharpened to points. On the chair lay articles of lace and corsetry. On the floor some male clothing and — for a moment she drew back with a gasp — it looked like a snake, dark and shining on the tiles. But no, not a snake — a coiled whip.

She should leave; take the dog and leave. Here she was, in the depths of the rural Périgord, with a scene in front of her like a peep-show in Pigalle. But she could not leave. The eerie flute music entangled her and she leaned further forward to see the lovers on the bed. Moving bodies gleaming, soft drums beating in and out of the flute music, gasps and groans as limbs twisted and turned. Their faces were in shadow. The woman was tawny and full-breasted, the man stocky and covered in black hair. A flailing arm knocked over a glass on the beside table. A dark stain spread across the sheet. The lovers ignored it. The woman writhed and twisted until she sat astride the man; she bent repeatedly to let him nuzzle her breasts. They muttered and groaned, no words distinguishable.

Animals, thought Claudine, her lips dry, but hot wetness between her legs, a sensation with which she had long been unfamiliar. Memories of herself and Henri came back to her in sharp flashes; how they had indulged their mutual taste for clandestine love-making in taxis, at the theatre, wherever the risk of discovery would lend an extra *frisson*. The man on the bed, now flinging the girl under him, was coarse and repellent compared with her elegant long-boned husband. The hair on his back and shoulders and straining thighs was like the pelt of a goat. The girl began to whimper like Patapon, still jumping beside Claudine; the man's grunts became gutteral, louder, rising to a bull-like roar. Claudine gazed, wide-eyed, as he thrust into the woman, his squat hands at her neck, wrenching at her. The breathy flute music became shrill.

Claudine backed away and fled into the darkness and Patapon, tail between his legs, followed her meekly.

Arrivals

1989

The last part of the approach to the house reminded Netty of the old film of *Rebecca:* the long twisting drive through gnarled trees and thick bushes, the endless series of bends and corners, the delayed revelation of the great house itself. But the first view of Le Sanglier was more like the heroine's dream of Manderley in later years: the house and grounds wrecked and overgrown.

'It's a bit tatty,' she remarked to Gerald.

Gerald snapped, 'Well of course it's a little run-down — what do you expect? It's been empty for more than a year.'

Netty sighed and bit her lip. It had been a long journey, he'd been waiting to show her the house for months — and she'd spoiled the moment for him.

'I'm sorry. It probably just needs a bit of cleaning up. And you were right, the view is great.'

The sulky look on Gerald's face remained for a few moments. She could almost see him thinking 'Bloody woman'. He drew the car to a halt in front of the shuttered main door, leapt out with an energy surprising for a man of his bulk, and came round to open the passenger door for her. 'Your château awaits, madame.'

'Château' was too strong a word, but she responded to his pride with a little surge of excitement of her own. While Gerald struggled with the heavy weight of the front door shutters — the recent rain having swollen the timbers — Netty stood by the car and looked down the hillside. Behind and on both sides of the house were dense woodlands; the narrow weed-covered drive had meandered its way up through the gloom to the left. But directly in front of the house the land was open to a flood of sunlight. First there was the lawn belonging to the house, though it could hardly be termed a lawn when it was so overgrown with nettles and hollyhocks and all manner of unnamed weeds. Beyond it, some gentle pasture-land belonging to the farm further down the hill. Six pale toffee-coloured cows were lying down there, ruminating in the midday sun. The terraces of vines beyond also belonged to the farm. Blurred in the haze of distance were the red roofs of the nearest village, Malignac.

Behind her, the straining and swearing stopped; with a violent wrench and an ominous cracking of wood, Gerald succeeded in tearing the shutters open. He peered into the shadowed darkness of the doorway, selected a key from the weighty bunch he carried, and turned it in the lock of the glass-paned inner door. It opened easily. Stale air came flowing out: odours of damp and dust and crumbling paint. Before he entered, he turned to call Netty to join him. She came out of the sun towards him, her hair a pale gold aureole, and for a moment he was dazzled by her, his eyes unable to adjust from the dimness of the interior.

He held out his hand, sorry for his earlier bad temper. She had been right, the place did look a bit seedy just now. But he'd put it right. He just wished sometimes that she'd see the positive side of things first, instead of the negative.

'Come here, love,' he said, and as she approached, a silly notion took him, and with a grunt and a heave, he swung her up into his arms, staggered over the threshold, and dropped her gratefully back to earth.

She was giggling like a shy girl. 'You daft bugger, what are you playing at? At your age ...'

'Begorrah, you're just a foine little slip of a lass,' he answered, 'and isn't this the start of our new life together — a new honeymoon?'

She looked around her.

Of course, Gerald had described the house to her many times, and she had seen the details of it in the estate agent's handout. The typed description there had been in French, but the English firm acting as intermediary had translated. Gerald had seen it twice previously himself: once in February when he had first flown out to look at the properties on the list drawn up by Monsieur Lupin from the Agence Lupin, and again in April to finalise the contract.

Gerald had fallen for everything about the house: its location, its stunning view, its name, its age. He had talked ceaselessly about it at home and on the journey down through France: how it had been built by the Comte de Saint-Eymet back in 1788 as a hunting-lodge; how 'Le Sanglier' meant 'wild boar', which was one of the animals the Comte had liked to hunt; how only one room, the Salle de Chasse, survived from that time, but what a great room it was: she'd love it. It had been hard, whatever her doubts, to resist his enthusiasm. But now she was here, and seeing it for real, and disappointed.

They were standing in a sort of reception room and hall. Immediately opposite was another set of floor-length windows barring the way to the rear garden. When Gerald had succeeded in opening the inner doors and pushing out the heavy wooden shutters, swollen with damp and protesting all the way, light percolated into the hall to reveal a quarry-tiled floor, with a few worn mats lying around and a tipsy sofa in the corner. To the right, a staircase angled its way upwards. Dust lay everywhere, but also worse than dust. As Netty walked into the centre of the room she could see out scuttling movements into the corners and up the walls. Spiders, what seemed like hundreds of them, resentfully scrabbling off into hidey-holes, winding up their threads high into the ceiling. Netty jumped sideways, clashing into Gerald as he passed.

'Oh Gerald — look at that one! Bash it or something!'

'For God's sake, Netty, let go of my arm! It won't hurt you — it's more scared of you than you are of it.'

How many times had that been said to her? It irritated her beyond measure. Besides, that brute didn't look in the least bit terrified of a pale, skinny Englishwoman: it crouched there on its anglepoise legs, ready to fight for possession of its territory.

As a temporary escape Netty ventured a step or two out into the garden, which was buzzing with insect life, throbbing in the afternoon heat. It was overgrown almost beyond description. She sighed, quietly, thinking of her garden back in Oxford: the square lawn with the islands of paving stones, the neat hedges, the flowering cherry, the bulbs in springtime. Gerald came up behind her, swelling his chest with pride and taking deep breaths.

'Smell that air, Net. Bloody wonderful. Clean. Lot of work to do here too, but it'll be worth it. It'll look great when it's done.'

He looked at her. Netty made an effort to square up her shoulders and look keen, but it was too late.

'For God's sake woman, will you stop looking as if you've come to a concentration camp or something. Why do you always have to look on the black side of everything?'

'Don't I have reason?' she fired back.

For a moment they stared at each other. Netty drew breath to say more, but Gerald stepped forward, that determined cheeriness plastered on his face again. He grasped her upper arms. 'Netty. Let it go. We agreed we'd let it go. This is our new life — doesn't that excite you? Doesn't it?' She nodded, hypnotised, and he pulled her close.

They re-entered the house, back through the hall and on into the giant kitchen at the end of the house. It had windows looking out to the front of the house and to the side where the forest came quite close. There was a side-door out onto a paved terrace, with a couple of poles standing there, presumably to carry a washing line, and a few large terracotta pots. Grasses and weeds had pushed their way up between the paving stones, tilting them. Gerald took a small notebook from his trouser pocket and added that to his Things to Do. He was already on the third page of his list.

The kitchen was a mixture of old and new: some white units hung on the wall, and there was a marvellous slab of marble embedded into the long worktop, just right for making pastry. But the immensely deep china sink was cracked and stained, the walls were greasy and the stove antediluvian.

Still, Netty perked up at the sight of it: it was a lovely, airy room, and with pans and bunches of herbs and strings of garlic hanging from the hooks in the beams, and a big oak dining table, some straw mats and lots of blue-and-white pottery such as she'd seen in magazine articles devoted to Provence, she could be proud of it. She made Gerald jot down these things on The List, and he was pleased to see her taking an interest at last.

They retraced their steps to the hall. The arachnid life there had now mostly made itself scarce. Netty still felt, though, as if one of the hairy monsters would swing in on gossamer, like an SAS paratrooper, to land on her hair. It was an uncomfortable thought.

Gerald ushered her into the Salle de Chasse itself. It was dim, with small shuttered windows high on the thick stone wall which Gerald strained to reach. Eventually the wooden boards creaked open and light fell on the massive fireplace opposite, set into the rear wall. Netty gasped.

'This is like something in a castle, Gerald!'

'It's grand, isn't it? I fell for it on the spot, back in February. I want us to sit here in winter by a roaring fire. You could roast an ox in that, if you wanted to.'

Netty, gazing round, couldn't envisage cosy evenings of the sort Gerald was picturing. There wasn't enough light. Those tiles weren't that nice browny-red, as in the rest of the house. No, they were dark red. There was a border of ornamental wall-tiles at shoulder height, depicting scenes of leaping deer, bouncing hares, fluttering partridges and charging boar, all portrayed with great animation in oxblood tints on a pale cream background. However, when she looked more closely, she saw the arrows piercing the birds, the nooses round the hares' necks, the spears embedded in the flanks of the boars. The room of the hunt, indeed.

Beyond the Salle de Chasse, there was a dark little anteroom with doors leading off to two bedrooms. It amazed Netty that there were so few bedrooms in a place that looked so large. The first door led to the master bedroom, huge and L-shaped, with tall French windows looking out to the front of the house.

The second bedroom was tucked into the nook of the L, and stuck out into the back garden slightly, obviously tacked on later to provide more accommodation. Its side window gave a view along the back of the house. Ivy had poked its way through the shutters.

The house had two bathrooms: one *en suite* in the master

bedroom, one by the kitchen, and both with plumbing which looked ominously creaky, setting Gerald's pen scribbling down several more pages.

And where did the stairs off the hall lead? Clattering up them, Netty came out into a cream-painted room with windows looking in all four directions, although only the one to the east was any use, down to Malignac. The rest seemed only to confront the green wall of the woods, as the tower, with its square Périgordine roof-cap, was not high enough to rise above them.

Netty's heels and Gerald's heavy tread echoed on the bare floorboards. Netty smiled at him. This was the room that excited her most; better than the elegant bedchamber, better than the soon-to-be welcoming kitchen. This was to be hers, and hers alone, and she wanted to make that clear before he laid any claim to it. Let him keep the gloomy old Hunting Room; she would sit up here in the sunlight, and sew.

She turned to her husband and for the first time her smile was filled with a pleasure that was totally genuine, an anticipation of future happiness which matched his own. For the second time that day, he caught his breath at the sight of her: her pale skin glowing in the creamy room, her glinting hair, the look of youth on her in the soft light. He held out his arms and hugged her tight. He knew he had done the right thing in bringing her here, he knew it. Close the door on the past. Open up to the future.

'Netty, sweetheart, I know it's a bit of a dump right now. You were right. But I'll make it so cosy for you, so comfortable. Forget the old house: this will be home for you, honest it will. You won't regret it.' He kissed the top of her head as she nestled close to him.

Their new-found feeling of unity and contentment lasted the rest of the day. With a sigh Gerald locked the house up again: to an impatient man like himself any delay was intolerable. Even Netty felt some slight regret as the car crunched over the gravel and dipped down into the winding obscurity of the lane through the woods, to emerge some minutes later at the junction with the D-grade road to Malignac. They dined that evening at the Coq d'Or, their pretty little hotel overlooking the Rue Jusserand.

Encounters

The next five weeks were a blur of activity, a whirlwind at the centre of which was Gerald, notebook in hand, striding about, directing this and that, barking down the phone.

Netty truly believed that no other man could have done so much in so little time. At the end of each day he would eat a gargantuan meal at their hotel or the nearby restaurant, L'Ail en Chemise, gulp down a bottle of Pécharmant, and tumble into bed and instant slumber. She would lie in the stillness of the night, her hands twitching, her eyes so wide that sometimes she wondered if her blink reflex had entirely gone. She thought of the trees rustling round Le Sanglier, of the silent house waiting for them to move in. She didn't relish the prospect. She thought of Oxford: the openness of Port Meadow with horses grazing amidst the buttercups. She thought of the view from the Wittenham Clumps, remembering how she and Gerald used to take Lynda and Paul there, cycling down through Nuneham Courtney to Long Wittenham, where they left their bicycles by the church and climbed the steep hill, the children excitedly pointing out Dorchester below, and Didcot power station and away in the distance, Oxford itself. She thought of all that they had left behind — and all that had come with them. *You can't ignore what's happened, Gerry. It's too big.* She was good at making speeches in her head, speeches she would never utter, knowing he would never listen.

All this while Gerald would snore beside her, an arm flung out across her stomach, pinning her to the bed. She would sigh, gently, and watch the curtains filter the early light of another French dawn.

Gerald was fast becoming a character in the village. The

Malignacois were well-used to the English, of course, and were both in awe of and amused by him. They were pleased that Gerald made the effort to speak French, however rough and ungrammatical it might be. At breakfast, out on the terrace at the back of the hotel, he would put on his headphones and plug another language cassette into his personal stereo. In between mouthfuls of croissant would come requests for directions, comments on the weather, lists of dishes on menus, all in a voice made loud by the insulating headphones. Gerald in his world, Netty in hers. She would nibble at a *chocolatine* and play with the hotel cat, Fripon.

The people of Malignac saw Gerald's potential as a one man boost to the local economy. They all knew of Le Sanglier and several of the older villagers, remembering the time before the war, could recall it having been a happy house. Old Bertier the tobacco-farmer, he'd owned it in the twenties and thirties, hadn't he? Retired there, with his fat wife and his grandchildren, who compensated for the loss of his only son in '16, up at the Somme. But then the next war came, the grandchildren had gone, some joined up perhaps, and Bertier found the house too big. What happened to him? No one knew. There were the Nazis to think about then, so they'd lost track of him. Besides, since then there had been that other business. No one in their right mind would want to live there after that.

After breakfast, Gerald was like a king holding court. Plumbers, electricians, carpenters and gardeners would arrive at the Coq d'Or and await orders. Gerald drew sketch-plans and waved his arms around expansively. When things reached an impasse, the hotel manager Monsieur Quiberon would appear with a tray of tall glasses, ice, water and Ricard. They would all sit down and Monsieur would endeavour to translate for the English *propriétaire*. The workmen would shrug doubtful shoulders, but two or three Ricards would usher them into a more positive frame of mind; they would pile into their cars and disappear in a flurry of dust up the main street, hard left, and into the forest.

The last time Netty had seen Gerald like this had been twenty-seven years previously, when he and Roy Benson had begun setting up Feldwick & Benson Boiler Systems. A hard struggle, long since won, more by Gerald's energy and flair than by Roy's efforts. Roy was steady, the anchorman, but he lacked the charisma to attract sales, to make the product stand out from all the others in the market. Netty wondered how he would cope now that Gerald had sold out of the business. No doubt he'd keep it all ticking over nicely, but it would be a business treading water.

How lucky they were, to have such good friends. No doubt Roy and Sheila would be over to visit, as soon as Le Sanglier was fit to receive them. Sheila had often talked of how she envied Netty her new adventure. But Netty knew she didn't really mean it. She had seen in Sheila's eyes the criticism of Gerald's heavy-handedness.

The shops in Bourdonne welcomed Gerald and his Visa card. They visited 'BUT' *(Vraiment pas cher)* and 'Cash Distribution' *(Le client est roi)*, 'Mobis' and 'Nouvelles Galeries', *brocantes* and *antiquités*. All of their purchases were to be added to the van-load of possessions coming over from England in early July.

By the end of June they were ready to move in, or at least Gerald was. Netty had grown fond of the airy, pine-floored room at the Coq d'Or, and the vine trellis outside the window, on which miniature grapes were hanging in pale splendour. She liked Monsieur Quiberon and his wife Isabelle, who were concerned for her health. They said she was far too pale and lethargic, and told her to drink more red wine. She liked the local gutsy Pécharmant and the smoothness of Montravel or Saint-Emilion, produced fifty miles away on the rolling terraces halfway to Bordeaux. They plied her with coarse goose pâté and crusty bread. They made walnut dressing for salads and poured sweet cold Monbazillac wine, fluid honey, into half-globes of Charentais melon. Eat! they said. Drink! The Périgord is life itself. The cradle of man. A festival.

The day came when she promised their hosts that they would return often to dine in the hotel restaurant, she chucked Fripon under his furry chin one last time, and got into the car with Gerald. She felt the pressure of his desire that she should make the best of her new life. She felt him glance towards her several times as they wound their way up the hill. Her neck muscles went rigid and she could not return his look.

Near the last bend of the long driveway, a tall, slouching figure stood back off the road to let them pass. She caught a glimpse of a hat low on the man's brow, a loose jacket and sagging trousers. His face turned in the arboreal gloom to watch them as they passed.

'Who was that?' she asked, not recognising the man from the droves of workers who had visited the Coq d'Or daily.

'Him? Oh, that's Norbert Lelouche. He's been doing some gardening for us. Doesn't have much to say for himself, and the others don't seem to have much time for him, but he's a worker, I'll give him that. He's the son of that old dragon Mathilde — ever seen her in the village? Not a person to be messed with, apparently. God knows why — she doesn't look any more fearsome than any other old French bat in black. Anyway, Netty, what do you think? We've made quite a difference, eh?'

They swept onto the sunlit plateau in front of the house, and drew up at the door. It was like and yet totally unlike their arrival of a month ago.

The tennis-court-sized rectangle of grass had been mown. Great banks of cut grass, teazles, hogweed stems, withered hollyhocks and dead leaves lay off to the right, ready to be burnt. Netty strolled to the outer edge of the lawn and looked down the hill. A couple of the cows in the lower field looked up. The rest kept their heads down, wrenching at the grass, ears flicking constantly under the barrage of flies. The day was humid. Down in the valley lay the red-brown roofs of Malignac. She could pick out the square church-tower, and the long roof of the Coq d'Or almost opposite the pretentious Hôtel de Ville, with its three tricolours over the grand double doors.

Malignac throbbed in the midday heat. She thought she caught a gleam of water — the thin but lively Meuron, on its way to meet the broad and lovely Dordogne, some five miles away. She shaded her eyes, peering out across the rippling landscape and thinking longingly of paddling her feet in cool water. The minor D-road out of Malignac crested the limestone ridge a mile and a half beyond the village; she saw its dark thread stand out against the bare bone-white of the scree. A yellow post-van rose up like a little lifeboat cresting a fossilised wave and then vanished from sight.

Off to the right, the Colline ended in a couple of subsidiary hills, like children crouching at their mother's skirts. At the base of the nearer one lay a pretty little cottage, typically Périgordine. It seemed to be very old — there were greenish *lauze* tiles on its roof. Small dormer windows projected and there were some chairs and an umbrella-canopied table in the courtyard in front of it.

'Netty!' called Gerald from the front door. 'You'll fry out there — come on inside.'

Turning from the glorious view, Netty walked back across the lawn to the house, fanning herself with her hand as she did so. Her dress was sticking to her.

The hall was cool. Gone were the webs and the dust and fragments of dead leaves. Gerald proudly showed her how the shutters and doors, gleaming now in deep green livery, opened and closed without a squeak. The walls were fresh and white. The whole house stank of paint.

'I thought, Netty, you could do some of those embroidered pictures of yours — there's a lot of wall-space to fill.'

Her eyes slid upwards, up the square well of stairs leading to the tower room. She longed to go there, but first she had to follow Gerald round the place and praise his efforts at every stage. It wasn't hard to do: the house looked so much better now. The local carpenter, Monsieur Charbis, was busy in the kitchen, installing solid chestnut cupboards. Netty smiled at him; he nodded and went on working. Her spirits lifted. It really was the kitchen she had always dreamt of: airy and large with sunlight streaming in from the kitchen garden beyond, and the new blue-and-white Delft tiles gleaming and pale beige tiles on the floor toning with the warm wood.

Beyond the Salle de Chasse the bedroom was sunshine yellow and felt as large as something from Brobdingnag. The French doors at the front went all the way to the ceiling. A couple of sheets were pinned up there, for privacy's sake. Netty intended to sew the most flamboyant curtains and hang them from a golden curtain-rod with golden finials.

Hoping to create a Napoleonic atmosphere, they had tracked down, in a huge warehouse selling antiques out on the Bordeaux road, some refugee furniture from a château. They were lucky to have a room high enough to cope with the towering walnut wardrobe with a huge oval mirror set into the central door — slightly spotted, but with the most beautiful mistiness about it because of its ancient silvering. Netty's reflection looked blurred and grey, as if she'd vanished down a corridor of time.

There was the tallest of tallboys to match, an elegant dressing-table, a couple of mahogany chairs and a magnificent walnut *lit bâteau*. Its mattress was carried high, its head and tailboards swelled outwards like waves poised to break. She sat on the edge of the dramatic bed and looked around, half in awe, half in amusement. It was a stage set for the Empress Josephine, not Netty Feldwick of Cowley. Oh, but it was *so* lovely.

The workmen had packed up and gone, leaving bin-bags full of shavings and woodchips, peeled plaster and copper wire and plastic insulation. Two-core wires hung from holes in the wall, ready for lights to be attached. The wires were encased in corrugated white plastic tubing like petrified caterpillars. She and Gerald ate at a folding garden table set up in the still fairly empty kitchen. Gerald chuntered on about his plans for the next day and waved his fork about. It was unsettling to be alone with him. She'd grown used to the hotel dining-room and the inhibiting presence of other guests.

Now there was no one. Just Gerald, and the house, quiet and still, sitting in judgement perhaps of its new proprietors. How many others had it seen come and go, she wondered, down the years?

'Tomorrow, Net, I'll run you into Bourdonne, and you can buy all the material you want; get going with your needle. Or do you want to wait for your sewing-machine to come out from England? Not long now. Anyway, what you say goes, and you've got all the time you want now, eh? Take all the time you want.'

Netty tore off another hunk of springy bread. 'Sounds great,' she said. 'I'd like a little visit to Bourdonne. I think I saw a fabric shop just past the post office last time we were there.'

'Tell you what else, Net, we need to get a TV. It's bloody quiet. Too quiet, like they say in the Westerns, just before the guy gets the arrow in the throat!'

Two hours later he flung back the double doors in the entrance hall and they strolled out onto the lawn, his arm round her waist, hers round his. It was a warm night, with only the gentlest breeze. Malignac twinkled at them, and a sickle moon rode high in the sky, looking as if it could tilt to and fro like a see-saw.

She turned to look back at the house. It was ghostly and grey, that strange non-colour the night can lend stone. Golden light flowed out through the door and seeped through the cracks at the sides of the shutters.

'Oh, Gerald, it's lovely. You were right. We can start again here. But you're sure it's not too expensive?'

'Don't you worry about that, Net. With the price Roy gave me for my share of the business and the money from Number 143, we're OK. We're very OK. Ha!'

Netty hugged him. 'That's good to know.'

He looked down at her upturned face and kissed her. His breath tasted of wine. The kiss was familiar — nearly three decades of marriage in it. Kisses, back seats of cars, beds, children, fights, makings-up, laughter, grief.

His kiss grew more searching, his hand felt for her breast. Netty jerked away.

'Must go in, Gerry. There could be a night-chill. Anyway, I really need a good old English cup of tea.'

She returned to the house. Gerald sighed heavily, stood for a moment, then tramped after her. Malignac twinkled on.

At some time during the godless hours of night, Gerald's heavy body was on her. After he had rolled away she lay there thinking what a sad christening it was for the Napoleonic bed.

In the morning they had just finished drinking steaming bowls of coffee when the workmen arrived. Netty sat at the folding table in the kitchen, making out a list of her own this time and trying to concentrate while Monsieur Charbis hammered and sawed and planed. Monsieur Lacombe, the electrician, attached uplighters to the wall and Monsieur Dusseau, the plumber, clanged away in the bathroom next to the kitchen. The sporadic gush of running water and the occasional ferocious flush of the toilet punctuated his labours.

Gerald came in. 'Done yet, Net?' he asked. 'Come on. Let's go visiting some neighbours, before we head off to Bourdonne. We'll take a stroll down to the farm. See what's what.'

'Gerry, I'm not sure. I don't feel up to it. Surely there's lots of time for stuff like that?'

'Rubbish! You've got to face them sooner or later. Anyway, we want to get off on the right foot, if this is where we're going to live. They're a sociable lot. Nosy, too, I'll bet. We'll be the seven days' wonder round here. You don't want to disappoint them, do you?'

Netty rose and followed him. They skirted the lawn to the right. The woods bent closer to greet them. At the bottom of the lawn a track opened up, following the borders of the trees and going quite steeply downhill, past the field of cows, down into the dip between the Colline Nemorale and the next little hill. Off to the right she could see the roof of the cottage she'd spotted the day before. A strange bird was sitting on it, a bird with a curved bill and a crest on its head. She pointed it out to Gerald before it took off on a wide arc, up to and into the forest.

'A hoopoe,' he said. 'Nice, aren't they? I'd heard that they got them round here. Nature's wonderland, this is. Unspoilt. No industry. Just tourists, tobacco, and grapes. Oh my, just look at those! Another reason for keeping in with the neighbours, I'd say.'

He pointed downhill, past the cottage, and Netty saw field after curving field of vines. In the distance, the ranks of vines seemed to draw closer to one another, looking like green corduroy on an appliqué collage. She had an idea that it would be nice to design something like that; a challenge to find the fabrics that would match the textures of the landscape.

'Let's hope that farm owns those vineyards. We could be onto a good thing here.' Gerald strode on. Down at the foot of the hill the heat was quite stunning, deprived as they were of the light breeze that aired Le Sanglier that morning. She could hear voices in a nearby field, and the distant throaty prowl of a tractor.

Gerald turned into a wide opening to the left, which led immediately into a large farmyard. A cockerel rose on his toes to stare at them, his coterie of hens pecking mindlessly in the dirt around him.

Ahead of them was a neat plain farmhouse, crowned with smooth grey slate. Geraniums grew in terracotta pots at the base of the little flight of five steps leading up to the central door, which stood open.

There seemed to be no one about. *'Bonjour!'* shouted Gerald. *'Est-ce qu'il y a quelqu'un ici?'*

No answer, just the mournful tucking of the hens, and the puttering of some farm machinery nearby.

Then a figure, all in black, appeared in the doorway, so suddenly that Netty clutched at Gerald's arm.

Even Gerald seemed nonplussed for a moment, but then he strode forward, hand outstretched, prepared phrases at the ready.

'Ah, madame, bonjour. J'espère que nous ne vous dérangeons pas. Nous sommes vos nouveaux voisins, de la maison en haut — Le Sanglier — vous la connaissez?'

As she came forward, the harsh light revealed the woman's age. She shook Gerald's hand ceremonially, then Netty's hand, with a quiet *'Bonjour'*. When she spoke, her accent was virtually impenetrable. Gerald concentrated hard. 'I gather the rest of the family's out in the fields,' he relayed to Netty, 'but she's inviting us in for a drink, an aperitif.'

'But it's hardly ten a.m., Gerry!'

'I know, Net. Don't worry, we'll go easy. We can't refuse — it would cause offence. Hospitality's very important to these people.' He kept saying 'these people' as if he were a box-wallah in the days of the Raj.

The woman ushered them into the house. In the kitchen they sat at a square table, Gerald and Netty side by side. Their hostess, after fetching a tray on which she placed, with slow and methodical precision, three glasses, a tumbler of ice and a tall brown jar, sat facing them. Formality still prevailed. Netty couldn't think of a thing to say as Gerald made stilted conversation. It was as if he and their hostess were on parallel streets, close but never meeting. Netty gazed around the neat but shabby room — the ornamental nets hung from café rods on the backs of the windows, the worn lino, the massive boxy fridge, the faded oilcloth on the table. Then she caught the woman's name, and sat up to pay more attention. So this was the 'old bat', Mathilde, Lelouche's mother.

Her blouse had a high neck, with a small cameo brooch pinned at the throat. Her shoulders were rounded, but she held her head high, as if pulled back by an invisible hand. Her hair was white and coiled into a tight bun covered with a net. There were liver-spots on her olive-coloured face and great archipelagoes of them on the backs of her hands. Netty noticed that her wrist bones were delicate and there was an element of grace in her movements. She was probably in her seventies, she estimated, but in her day there had been attractiveness there.

Netty nodded when Mathilde asked her something, and as the old woman crossed the kitchen to fetch a large tablespoon from a drawer, Gerald leaned towards her and said, 'She offered you some plums in brandy, Net. You'd better get them down the hatch!'

Some elevenses, thought Netty, with a sinking heart.

Mathilde opened the large jar, extracted a large, very dark brown plum and put it into a tall glass. She then ladled brandy from the jar, over the plum and courteously offered it to Netty, along with a long-handled teaspoon. The same ritual was followed for Gerald, then herself. They watched her spoon out pieces of plum, then drink the brandy, and they followed suit. The liquid tasted white-hot, raw, burning, but wonderful. Netty felt tears start to her eyes.

'*Vous en voulez une autre?*' Mathilde asked.

'*Ah non, non, merci,*' Netty said, then felt the surprise of having spoken in French.

Gerald had another saturated plum and complimented Mathilde. She seemed pleased. She explained that her brother Augustin ran the farm and that she acted as housekeeper for him. Augustin had five children, but only one, Albert, showed any real interest in farming. Albert and his wife Solange lived here at Grand Caillou, the rest had all dispersed — this said with a 'Ftt!' and a wave of the hand that took in Bourdonne, Périgueux, Bordeaux, even Paris.

'I apologise,' she said in French, 'that there is no one here but farming is you understand hard work, all the time. It leaves one little leisure. We had heard of your arrival ... there are many feelings of friendship for the English in this area ... we who saw the war ... you understand.' She broke off to reach forward and shake Gerald's hand, warmly this time. Gerald, who had been straining every linguistic muscle to follow what she said, pumped her hand vigorously and beamed back at her, as if he had fought shoulder to shoulder with John Wayne in the liberation of Europe.

'We have met your son, Norbert,' said Netty. Mathilde looked at her, a slight shadow in her eyes.

'Ah yes?' she said politely. 'And does he work well for you?'

'Indeed he does,' answered Gerald.

'Good. He is too much alone, Norbert.' With that cryptic remark she rose and went to the door. It seemed to signal that the visit was over.

During prolonged farewells she invited them to dine at the farmhouse some night the next week. They would be delighted, they said.

The sun dealt them a heavy blow as they emerged into the farmyard. The combination of UVA, UVB and plums in brandy made Netty's temple throb.

'There now, Net, that wasn't so bad, was it? She was a decent old stick in the end, wasn't she?'

Netty remembered how Mathilde stood tall, in spite of her years, as if she was determined to challenge the world by looking it in the eye.

The Feldwicks didn't immediately go into Bourdonne. It took a little siesta at home for them to recover sufficiently from the brandy to brave the combination of heat and light again.

It was a happy afternoon. Netty found her haberdashery and bought yards of curtain material. Gerald stood by, agreeing whenever she asked if he liked her choice. He smirked at the overly polite assistant, who was plump and obviously gay, but very helpful.

It was an afternoon of errands: they visited La Poste and sent some duty postcards to friends in England and an airmail letter, off to Virginia, telling Lynda how things were going. Netty knew her daughter disapproved of the whole affair, so she'd been very careful in her letter to cast the best possible light on everything. She could just hear Lynda on the phone that last time before they had left Oxford.

'Mother, why do you let him drag you all that way? It won't solve anything, you know. If you have to go abroad, why not come here? You know Bradley and I would love to see you. And the kids, they're always asking for you. You don't just have a duty to your husband, you know. You have a duty to yourself as a person.'

Netty knew all too well that if she went to stay at her daughter's white-columned pseudo-Georgian mansion in Richmond she'd end up, as she had on every previous trip, being the unpaid skivvy and babysitter there. Lynda herself seemed unaware of how much of her father's forcefulness she had inherited, along with an expectation that everyone should think exactly the way she did, as it was so patently clear that only she could be right. The slightest contention led to an air of wounded bewilderment.

Another, briefer, letter to Paul. It might as well have been a postcard. She could never think of anything to say to him. Paul had been an industrious, cryptic child; he was now a successful financial trader. She supposed he had a good social life; his heightened colour and increasing corpulence around the middle was evidence of that, along with his inability to come home for a visit very often. And when he did, he never brought a girlfriend. His flat was like a museum; she was always afraid of knocking into things on the few occasions she visited him and half-expected to see a sign somewhere saying 'All breakages must be paid for'. Everything was concealment with Paul;

never a stray sock on the floor or a drawer half-open to spill out a jumble of garments.

Every time they visited, they had to give him lots of warning. Did he live with someone, she wondered. She hoped he took care. He thought that he'd concealed that part of his life.

'Camper than a row of tents,' Gerald had said dismissively of the assistant at Beautissu. It needed to be that obvious for him to notice. God help Paul if his father ever found out about him.

So, the duty letters were sent off along with the postcards. They stopped at a bar for a quick drink, then on to the EDF where Gerald was conducting a guerrilla war with the authorities of the electricity company.

Finally to Leclerc, by now their favourite supermarket. After trailing round congested aisles, Gerald went on ahead to open up the car, and Netty wearily pushed the trolley after him. A woman came rushing up to her. She was well-dressed, in tapering white trousers and a navy-and-white-striped top. She uttered something in French. Netty gathered that she wanted the use of her trolley when she was finished with it. Netty stumbled out an awkward reply. The woman smiled.

'You're English,' she said, perfectly Home Counties.

'Yes.'

'My dear, what a relief! I'd forgotten how rusty my French has become. No doubt it'll come back to me. It always does. It's like riding a bike, you know. Thing is, I don't have a ten-franc coin on me, and you know you can't free one these dratted *chariots* without one, so can I steal yours when you're done? Here's a couple of five-franc pieces.'

'Of course you can,' Netty answered, relieved to hear an English voice after more than a month of struggling with her inadequate French, and pushed her trolley over to the car where Gerald was waiting, the boot already open to receive the groceries. Her companion strode forward, hand already out.

'Hello, I'm Deirdre Luker. I've just waylaid your wife. I want to hijack your trolley!'

Gerald shook her hand. 'Gerald — Gerald Feldwick. And this is my wife Netty. You're welcome to the trolley — I just hope you have more luck steering the thing than we've had!'

Deirdre laughed. 'Oh, don't tell me — another of the Trolleys from Hell! Who designs the things?' A slight pause, then, 'Are you on holiday?' The standard question, begging the standard reply.

'No,' said Gerald, preening himself very slightly. 'We moved here just over a month ago.'

'How marvellous! You lucky things! Felix — that's my husband — and I have often toyed with the idea. It's so tempting, but we really haven't had the nerve to make the final break. Oh, Mrs Feldwick, do let me help you with that.'

Bright painted fingernails descended on the trolley. Mrs Luker grasped a four-pack of Danone Bio yoghurts and placed it delicately in the boot of the Rover, while Netty continued to struggle with the litre bottles of Evian and the multi-packs of Kronenbourg. Soon the trolley was empty and Deirdre insisted on handing over the two five-franc pieces.

'Where do you live? Is it nearby?' she asked.

'Yes,' answered Gerald. 'It's a house that used to be a hunting-lodge, about ten miles from here. Up a hill. Le Sanglier, it's called. Not the hill; the house. It means "The Wild Boar".'

'Why, *quelle coincidence*! Felix and I are staying with a very old friend of ours, Claudine Bellenger. She lives near you — isn't that amazing? Bel Arbre — it's on the other side of the hill, have you seen it?'

'No, I'm afraid not.'

'Oh, it's *gorgeous!* You must come round for tea. Claudine would love to see her new neighbours, I'm sure. God, I'm running late. Felix'll throw a fit. Must dash — so nice ...'

Casting her last words casually over her shoulder, she tripped off to the plate-glass sliding doors of the supermarket. Gerald slammed the boot shut. Netty was gleaming with sweat. Leclerc's car-park was a blistering sun-trap.

'Typically English,' said Gerald, getting into the car and fastening his seat-belt, 'to ask you for tea, and *not* ask you for tea. No date, no time, no phone number asked. Hypocrisy. God knows, we had enough of that in Oxford. 'Oh, you *must* come to tea sometime' — '*Do* come for sherry' — and what they really mean is that if they ever set eyes on you this side of Judgement Day it'll be too soon. Why can't people say what they mean?'

The evening. *Merguez,* salad. Pistachio ice-cream. Wine. Gerald's desire. Netty, wide-eyed to the night again, hearing an owl outside, and the creak of branches and the scuttering of tiny creatures in the roof-space. She wondered if she'd ever sleep properly again.

The next afternoon, she was standing on a chair in the bedroom, measuring the height of the French windows. She had bought cream silk brocade for the curtains, with a design of honeysuckle, lilies and pale-yellow cabbage roses on it. It was exuberant but justified in such a large room; it would have been far too powerful in their boxy bedroom in Cowley. The ivory of the lilies and the pale green of the leaves and stems echoed the paintwork of the room and helped to lighten the effect of the heavy walnut furniture. Any left-over fabric she would use to make cushion covers and other soft fripperies. A woman's touch, as Gerald said.

Poised there on her chair, she saw the man appear. People who visited the house tended to materialise out of the gloom of the overshadowing trees quite suddenly, as if they had been waiting in the wings for their cue to step on stage, into the light.

The man was tall, with a slight stoop of the shoulders. His hair glinted silver in the strong light. As he ambled up towards the front door, Netty saw he was carrying a bottle. She heard his knocking resonate in the hall. Hastily she got off her pedestal and brushed her skirt down. She saw the pale ghost of herself in the oval mirror as she passed. Gerald's voice boomed out in greeting.

She scurried through the Salle de Chasse and out into the bright hall. The two men were just shaking hands as she came up to them.

'Netty, you'll be glad to hear we've got a compatriot near us, so you don't have to struggle with your French all the time.'

As Gerald introduced her, her hand was taken in a firm dry grasp.

'Hello,' he said, 'I'm Rutherford — Professor Rutherford Appleby, to give it the whole works. I live at the bottom of your hill.'

'Oh, yes, Professor.' She felt awkward; they might have lived in Oxford all those years but they'd never had much to do with the academic community. 'I've seen your house, I think — is it that pretty cottage with the stone tiles?'

'Well observed. Yes, it is. I've rented Petit Caillou for donkey's years, but usually I spend the winters back in Cambridge. Yes,' he said, laughing slightly, 'yes, I have to admit it. I'm from the Other Place. I gather you're Oxonians yourselves.'

'Well,' said Gerald, 'town, not gown, that's us. Cowley.'

The Professor smiled disarmingly. 'Good,' he said. 'I've retired now, myself. Academic rivalry is the last thing I need to run into out here.'

'Anyway, do come in,' said Gerald. 'Let's have a drink.'

The Professor held out the bottle he was carrying.

'A little offering,' he said, 'some of the local wine from the farm. It's a bit rough but hale and hearty. To welcome you.'

They installed themselves in the Salle de Chasse. Netty fetched glasses, Gerald uncorked the bottle, and they drank a toast to British solidarity.

Settling back in his armchair, Gerald said, airily, 'So, Professor, just what did you profess, before you retired?'

'I was Windlesham Professor of Comparative Mythology at Harley College. That's partly what brought me out here — even now that I'm officially retired, I'm thinking of producing another book. Life in the old dog yet, you know.'

Netty leaned forward. 'Would it be a book about this area, then?'

'Yes. I have a particular interest in the Gallo-Roman background.'

'Gallo-Roman ... ?'

'It means the cultural blend that existed here when the Romans ruled Gaul. There are lots of reminders of it in this area, Périgueux being the most striking example. Have you been there yet?'

'No.'

'Vesunna, it was called. Lots of goodies left over: villa, amphitheatre, huge cylindrical tower which was part of a temple dedicated to Vésone, a Celtic manifestation of the mother goddess. Quite a remarkable edifice, actually. Good museum ... don't know if you're interested in that sort of thing?'

Netty felt she might be. Gerald's face had closed. He looked the way he had when she'd tentatively suggested taking up an Open University course.

'Nice wine, this,' he said, pouring some more into his glass.

'Well, it does the job, doesn't it?' said the Professor, pleasantly. 'Anyway, to cut a long story ... there's a fair amount of Roman stuff in the immediate area. There was a villa down by my little place. At Grand Caillou they still turn up coins and potsherds in the vineyards and maize fields. And up here on the hill, there was a temple.'

'A temple?' Netty was genuinely interested. Gerald snorted. She ignored him. 'What was the temple for? I mean, what — what god?'

'What god was it dedicated to? Well, I believe it might have been Bacchus — Bacchus or Dionysus. The God of wine.'

Gerald tossed back the last of his second glass. 'Here's to the bugger,' he said.

The Professor set his glass down with a clink and stood up. He was very tall for an old man.

'Well, I should be getting on. You must come to dinner, soon. Next week, perhaps. I'm not much of a cook, myself. Tend to grab something on the hoof, as it were. Sandwich, that sort of thing. But the woman who comes in and "does" for me, she'll come and cook a dinner for us. She's really very good, Mathilde.'

'Oh yes, we've met her,' said Netty. 'Mathilde Lelouche, was it?'

'Yes, that's the one. Not a barrel of laughs, not by a long chalk. But salt of the earth. Salt of the earth.'

They were at the door; he was gone, ambling lazily down to the tree-line, dappled light on his white head, then on into shadow and darkness.

'Snooty git,' said Gerald. 'Thought we'd left his sort well behind back in Oxford.'

'Oh Gerald, really! That's totally unfair. He was as nice as pie. He didn't have to bother with the likes of us at all. People like him come here to get away from the English, not to find they have to hob-nob with them.'

'Netty, for God's sake listen to yourself! "The likes of us"! He comes here, spouting all that history guff — "Have you done this, have you seen that" — like a bloody cultural sheepdog, snapping at our heels. Did he show the slightest interest in *us*? No — and I'll tell you why: he's got us marked down as ignorant peasants. He'll take the piss whenever he can — and half the fun for him will be that we don't know *when* he's taking the piss, because we're so bloody ignorant! God, I need a whisky. That wine was bloody vile. Wasn't going to waste his best vintage on us, was he? Where's the Glenfiddich? It's never sodding well around when I need it.'

Off stormed Gerald, successful businessman, retired.

Sales Talk

Two weeks later, Netty and Gerald spent the afternoon at the Salle des Ventes in Bourdonne. People crowded the brimming sales-hall, piled high with the biggest hotchpotch of the old, the antique, the kitsch, the stylish, the useful, the beautiful and the grotesque that Netty had ever seen. Little labels bearing numbers were stuck on all the articles, but the whole affair was chaotic: the numbers bore no relation to the order of sale that afternoon or even to whether the item would be on offer that day at all.

Netty and Gerald were lucky enough to find two deep armchairs in which to ensconce themselves. It was going to be a long haul. The chairs smelled musty and Netty tried not to think about whether there might be little denizens inhabiting the stuffing. The salesroom was very high, painted originally duck-egg blue, now stained and dingy. On a platform at one side stood the figure of authority, the auctioneer, with two moustachioed and muscled henchmen who darted up and down the room, pouncing on objects apparently at random and hoisting them up to the view. Two young women sat nearby, taking down the buyers' names and accepting payment. None of the goods could be taken away until the end of the sale itself. This took stamina: three to four hours in an atmosphere of sweat and dust. Around the walls hung various unappealing daubs and drawings. One, which Netty found particularly distasteful, was of a naked woman engaged in sexual congress with an octopus.

'*Vingt francs pour l'honneur!*' barked the auctioneer. It went for thirty. A three-legged, or rather three-hoofed stool made of deer-skin, each of the three hoofs pointing in a different direction, (what had happened to the fourth leg, Netty wondered), went for fifty.

The sale progressed, jumping from sofas to cigarette-card collections, from Foreign Legion shakoes to bunches of silver cutlery, from dog-eared editions of Hugo and Balzac, to worm-eaten *chevets* and coffee-tables.

At the front, in a row of seats which they seemed to regard as their especial property, sat a line of harridans dressed in black and sporting moustaches almost as luxuriant as those of the men. They pointed and commented in harsh and critical tones, they demanded that objects be displayed better, and they scarcely bought a thing. The auctioneer didn't seem to mind. They reached out to pick over the jewellery, dishes and cutlery laid out on trays on the front table, like vultures picking over the bones of the dead. In this bicentenary year of the Revolution Netty could imagine the forebears of these women knitting furiously at the base of the Guillotine. In another few years, when they were dead, it would be their possessions being picked over in this way, in an endless recycling of individual lives and tastes.

Lurking at the sides of the room were the dealers, out to find bargains which they would sell at a huge mark-up in their *brocantes* and *antiquités* shops in Bourdonne, Périgueux, Mont-de-Marsan. They would give the private wink to the auctioneer and somehow the article was theirs, all other bids ignored.

'Bloody scam,' muttered Gerald. 'The best things are going to those bloody dealers. They've got a good little game going on here.'

One of the techniques of the salesroom was to offer assorted boxes of items at very low cost. It was a lucky dip; customers hoped there would be something decent among the dross. The English fell for it every time. Gerald bought a tray of glasses for thirty francs: twenty tumblers, snifters and wine-glasses, some chipped, some stained, about seven really presentable. A box of books: obscure spongy yellow paperbacks, but also a couple of nice leatherbound efforts that he said would look good in the Salle de Chasse.

People came and went, in search of friends, relatives, air, refreshment. It was during one particular melée at the back of the room that Netty caught sight of her: Deirdre Luker, the woman from the Leclerc car-park. Their eyes met. Deirdre waved red fingernails at her and mouthed, 'Drink afterwards?' Netty nodded. Deirdre mimed, hand to brow, 'Phew! The heat!' and laughed. She turned to twinkle upwards at the man beside her.

At six p.m. Netty emerged, blinking, into the light. Gerald remained behind to sort out payments and load their car with the day's trawl.

'You go on ahead, Net — take them to the La Gabare, they'll like it there. See you there — won't be long.'

'Netty! Delightful to see you again! This is my husband Felix. I've told him all about you and Gerald. He's like me, he envies you both being able to live here for ever — don't you darling? We love it so much — it's hell every time we visit Claudine, absolute hell to go back to grey old London.'

Felix was blandly good-looking, clad in flawlessly white trousers and a cornflower blue polo shirt. Netty hated seeing men in white trousers, but she decided he was thin enough to get away with it. Nothing worse than pouchy buttocks under white polyester.

'My wife,' he said with an ironic smile, 'likes to fantasise about being a country mouse from time to time. Hello Netty, I'm pleased to meet you. How are you settling in?'

Before Netty could answer, Deirdre interrupted. 'You know, I had the feeling when we met before — I mentioned it to you, didn't I, Felix? — are you sure we haven't met somewhere? I could swear your face is familiar.'

'That's the kind of line men give women in nightclubs!' chaffed her husband.

Netty looked Deirdre in the eye.

'No, I'm sure we haven't met — I'm sure I'd have remembered you.'

'Yes you would!' said Felix. 'Deirdre makes her mark on people.'

Deirdre smiled at him, gave a slight shrug and dropped the matter.

Netty decided she liked Felix. In the bar he took charge, buying *pressions* for himself and Gerald, kirs for herself and Deirdre. To give him credit, he did make an effort to prevent his wife from monopolising the conversation, but it was an uphill struggle.

When he arrived, Gerald took to him immediately. Felix was nothing like that smug Professor. Felix was a businessman. At the start of the eighties he'd been nothing but under Thatcher he'd seen his chance and made his mint. He was a property developer, with various schemes underway in the south-east: in Reading, Chippenham and Basingstoke, but his main and most successful venture had been in Docklands.

'Gerald, it's been the thrill of my life to take those old warehouses in Shadwell and Wapping and bring them to life again. We had to gut them more or less, and of course bring a bit of light in — but within the constraints of the original Victorian architecture. My company, DeLix Estates, aims for the best of both worlds. What you get in the end is tradition *and* comfort: real Victorian brick and cobble, view of the Thames, cranes and wharves and so on, but with hi-tech luxury: heating, glazing, security systems, self-irrigating plants, ambient air-conditioning, the lot. Quality, that's what we aim for and that's what we find our clients choose to pay for.'

'Sounds rewarding, Felix.'

'It is, believe me. Deirdre and I even made the move ourselves: we've got a stunning place: a penthouse apartment in an ex-tea-warehouse in Wapping. River frontage, roof garden, all that. Great for access to the city, nice open views of the river.'

'Our son works in the city,' said Netty. 'Our son Paul. He was involved in that Big Bang business in the Stock Exchange.'

'Yes, he's doing very well for himself,' said Gerald. 'We're proud of him. Working with money fascinates me. I mean, you and me, Felix, we work with something tangible. With me it was boiler systems, with you it's homes. But Paul, our son, well, he just sits in front of a computer screen with a telephone at his ear all day and he watches figures and graphs and at the end of the day he's traded in millions of pounds' worth — of what? Futures, options and the like. Nothing tangible — nothing you could put your finger on. He's bought and sold money itself and the *idea* of money, more money than you or I will ever see.'

'The stresses of that sort of job must be quite something.'

'Well, yes, I suppose they are. But are they any worse than what we've been used to? I don't know. I think, really, that the big difference is the speed of it all. Paul has to make split-second decisions and a hell of a lot depends on each of those decisions and God knows how many of them he has to make in the course of a day. You and me, oh, you know, take the client out to lunch, few bottles of good wine, light up a cigar. You still might get an ulcer but you get it when you're fifty, not when you're twenty-five or less. These lads, they just burn out. It's cut and thrust, dog eat dog. For our own peace of mind, Netty and I don't ask too much about it. Do we, Net? We don't know what our lad gets up to, to compensate for a hard day on the financial highwire!'

Netty glanced at him, wondering if he was really joking, or if perhaps he knew about the kind of place Paul was likely to frequent in the predatory evenings.

'Actually, Gerry, I think Paul copes really well. I mean, well, he's never been the sort to come running to Mummy, but there's no sign that the pressure's getting to him. He was the same all through school and college. He knows how to keep things in perspective.'

Deirdre signalled sharply to a nearby waiter and ordered another round of drinks.

'What about you two?' Netty asked. 'Do you have any children?'

'Goodness, no,' answered Deirdre. 'We simply haven't had the time, what with Felix building the business up, and I help him, of course.'

'Secretary, PA?' asked Gerald.

'Gerald, you old-fashioned thing! I hope I contribute a good deal more than *that!* Don't I darling?' Felix smiled and squeezed her hand in reply. 'I've never been one for thinking a woman should just sit in the background. It's down to me to look after presentation and organisation. Of course that involves the usual share of wining and dining and showing a bit of leg if necessary, but I'm essentially concerned with corporate image. I came up with the concept of DeLix and the logo, didn't I, dear? And I design the interiors of the show flats: the whole *look* of the company is down to me.'

And you're bloody good at blowing your own trumpet, thought Netty, looking down at her glass as the lazy bubbles rose through the rosy liquid.

'And you, Netty, what do you do?'

'Me? I'm just a housewife, I'm afraid.'

Just.

'Netty, for God's sake, don't do yourself down.' Gerald's arm came round her shoulders, pulling her sideways towards him. He punctuated his clauses with repeated sidelong hugs. 'Netty's my sheet anchor. Don't know where I'd be without her. She's done a bloody good job of bringing up the kids. She had to: I was never there. You know about that, don't you, Felix? Up and down the country chasing sales, burning the midnight at the office. Netty here was a saint. Never complained. And look at our kids — turned out well. One in the city, the other married in America — you should see the house she's got over there! No thanks to me; I just opened the chequebook. Netty did the hard graft. Our house — it was like a palace — and she'll soon have the new one looking brilliant. She's good with her hands — aren't you, Net. She's a marvel with a needle.'

One final squeeze and he let her go, reddening. She wished he wouldn't call her 'Net'. That wasn't her name, nor was 'Netty'. Her name was Annette; it was soft and romantic and a little bit special. 'Netty' was like something out of *Coronation Street*. 'Net' was a curtain you twitched to spy on that lot across the street. Was that what she was to him? A transparent person? He looked at her every day and he never really saw her. 'Net'. 'Netty'. She'd always hated it. She'd never told him.

She muttered something deprecatory. Deirdre said: 'Well that's just it. That's my point. If you have children and all that malarkey, how can you have a career? I mean, it's all right once you've made it and you can pay for nannies and so on to take the burden, but when you're young and struggling, just starting out — we've all been there, haven't we? — well, you have to make a choice. Netty went one way and I went another, but on both counts we proved we were one hundred per cent behind our men.'

Netty thought Deirdre would have made an excellent politician's wife.

'Absolutely, darling. Without your chutzpah, I'd have got nowhere fast.' Another mutual squeezing of hands from the husband and wife team. 'I'd never have got off my backside if it hadn't been for Deirdre,' Felix said to Gerald, who was trying to work out what 'chutzpah' meant.

'Darling, of course you would — eventually. You just didn't have any faith in yourself — you just needed a little pushing.'

Netty could picture it.

'Anyway, now that we're pretty well established we can maybe think of having children. It would be delightful, although we'd probably have to move; I'm not sure the apartment would be big enough. Something in Hampstead, perhaps.'

'Darling,' said Felix. 'Look at the time.'

'My goodness!' cried Deirdre. 'We really must love you and leave you. We're off out tonight with Claudine — our hostess —and she'll be wondering what happened to us. Drink up, Felix. Oh, and that reminds me, I told Claudine about running into you the other day, and she said she'd very much like to meet you and that she'd been meaning to call round. She knows your house. So if you give us your number, we'll give you a ring to arrange something.'

While Gerald wrote down their telephone number, Deirdre signalled for the waiter to bring l'addition. The Lukers insisted on paying.

'No, no,' said Felix, waving away Gerald's wallet. 'We invited *you*. It's been a delight. We were curious, really — you two seem so young to be thinking of retirement. You must have made a packet with your business, Gerald.'

'Well, yes, we did all right. Sufficient unto the day — and quite a few to come.'

'But why give it up? I mean, I know Deirdre and I rave on about the Dordogne; God knows it is gorgeous, and we whinge about the Big Smoke, but when all's said and done, you are rather burying yourselves down here. It just seems a bit previous, that's all.'

Gerald's hand tightened slightly on Netty's. She bent down to pick up her handbag.

'No special reason,' he said casually. 'As you said, it's gorgeous here. I was looking for a little holiday home, saw Le Sanglier, fell for it hook, line and sinker. That's all.'

Outside, the sunlight glared on the pavement and through the car windscreen as they drove home. It made Netty's eyes water.

SPQR

A.D. 220

Aurelianus could see the messenger approaching from a long way off. The last heats of summer had gone, two days of drizzle had laid the dust and now, in the red light of the setting sun, Aurelianus stood beyond the eaves of the forest and let his shadow be cast giant-like down the slope before him.

The day had weighed heavily on him from the start. Waking uneasy in the cold before dawn, he had felt the breath of the divine, of the god passing through the woods, of mighty shoulders brushing the trees aside. Aurelianus had sensed the tightness of furred throats, the bulging of frightened eyes, as the beasts of the woods acknowledged the presence of their Lord.

Lighting a bronze lamp, he had bowed himself before it. Into his mind had come the vision of the great altar in Vesunna. Then he remembered: the altar was to Cybele; the Lady, the Mother. Not to his acknowledged Lord, Dionysus. Was this presence, this cold emanation of the supernatural, hers too?

Confusion beset him as the day unfolded. It was not new to him. The temple at the heart of the woods, over whose construction he presided, rose, grey stone upon grey stone. Sculptors arrived from Divona. The fashioners of mosaic laboured at the arrangement of tesserae; Dionysus and his leopards sprang to fierce coloured life.

But, ever since the task had been laid upon him, in spite of the honour and the devotion he felt, Aurelianus had been oppressed by the burden of it. Long before his Lord had come, chariot-drawn from the shores of the Aegean and beyond, the Lady had been here. Perhaps she was indeed that Cybele they honoured in Vesunna to the north-east: far-travelled Asiatic Cybele. Perhaps some ancient sister of Cybele, revered by the tribes of Gaul before the Romans came. A Lady of life and death; daughter and crone; giver and taker.

He sensed her displeasure. The people here told him that this hill was sacred to her: springs and caves were hallowed to her presence. What was he to do? What was he himself? His pride lay in Rome and what Rome had done: the great roads, arrow-straight, to Burdigala and to Aginum; the memorials in Vesunna, the games, the frescoes, the wondrous heavy tower planted like a folded fist on the earth, marking Rome's possession.

Yet he was of the blood of the Petrocorii, he was a creature of these woods and caves, he bore the memory of resistance against the might of Rome.

He was at one with the Empire, he was not. And this hill was not the Capitoline Hill, this goddess would not share her shrine with other gods. As he oversaw the labourers day after day, as he drank his wine in the evening, he sensed the Lady and the Lord prowling in the darkness, circling like dogs before a fight, and his own skin crawled.

His heart was heavy with the pressure of the long, anxious day as he stood on the natural rampart at the brow of the hill and watched the messenger approach. He knew it was a messenger, not just a beleaguered traveller or tradesman making for Burdigala to the west. He knew. His eyes became as sharp as an eagle's; it seemed as if from miles off he could see the sweat and dust on the man's face and hear him curse his unwilling horse. His was a seer's perception; he knew the man was weary in body and spirit, longing to arrive yet reluctant.

Aurelianus' shadow turned and dwindled, died into grey. He heard the laboured breathing of the man as he toiled up the hill. The horse jibbed; the man angrily dismounted and led it. They were beyond the huddle of huts at the hill's base. They were passing through the shadows of the beechwoods. The spirits of the forest watched their passage; the horse rolled a white eye and jibbed again. The man was too wrapped up in frustration and exhaustion to notice.

Aurelianus Felicianus — woe to the name — waited. In the deepening dusk the messenger stood before him, his face white with dust. In the heart of the woods behind, the labourers sat on tumbled stones and sang at their evening meal.

'Aurelianus!'

'Caius, my brother. You have brought news of Julia?'

'Aurelianus ... her time came upon her two mornings since.'

He waited. His brother stumbled for words. 'We did what we could ...'

'She is dead then.' Julia. Graceful, vivacious, kissing him farewell in the courtyard of their villa, proud of him, proud of his task, content to be separated if separation had a purpose, glowing with hope and expectation.

'She is dead.'

'And the child?'

'With her.'

Aurelianus turned and walked swiftly towards the darkness under the trees. He could not tell if the Lady or the Lord were responsible, but he had been struck in punishment — that he knew. Julia, he said in his mind, but could not reach her spirit.

Caius was at his shoulder. 'It is as the gods will,' he said.

'It is as the gods will,' Aurelianus echoed, as they entered the shade.

RSVP

1989

Less than a week later, on the eighteenth of July, they were on their way to Bel Arbre. Madame Bellenger herself had rung them.

'More like a bloody summons than an invitation,' Gerald said.

They had had to postpone the invitation from the Lelouches down at the farm. Aristo beats peasant.

They drove down to Malignac and skirted the broad base of the Colline, passing through Vergt de Meuron and Figueil, a drive of some five miles, before curving upwards to the great iron gates of Madame Bellenger's estate.

'Oh, Gerry, just look at it — it's so elegant!'

'It's bloody vast, too. This is big money, Netty.'

The driveway broke into a double curve, like arms reaching to embrace Bel Arbre. The house was built of the palest silver-gilt limestone and was of an absolutely severe symmetry. A sweep of grey steps led up to a high, classically-pedimented door. No geraniums, no pottery; nothing was allowed to blur the pure architectural lines of the place. To either side of the door, tall windows, three sets each side. Above, more tall bedroom windows; above that, round glazed portholes under dormers, marking the attics.

They were ushered into a lofty marble-floored hall where a shallow cantilevered stairway, bordered with iron wrought into curlicues, swept upwards to the right. Their hostess came to greet them. Netty's first impression of her was that she looked like a waitress, because

Claudine was wearing black, relieved only by a small white collar. However, this was deceptive; a closer look revealed that she was wearing a cocktail dress of the richest black velvet and its white spotted voile collar was a clever little piece of whimsy, lightening and yet at the same time emphasising the severity of the outfit.

'*Monsieur ... bonsoir, Madame.* It is indeed a pleasure to make your acquaintance. I am Claudine Bellenger. Do come through. I have a little gathering this evening. There are several people I am sure you will be pleased to meet.'

Her English, along with her manners, was faultless.

Netty was awestruck as they entered a high south-facing salon. There were tapestries and paintings on the walls, eighteenth-century chairs and sofas — the real thing — they had to be. A group of people stood by the open windows, idly conversing in the desultory way of people who know each other well and yet not well enough; beyond the empty platitudes of polite exchange but not as far as the intimacy of true friendship.

They looked curiously at the Feldwicks as they approached with their hostess. Netty felt for a moment like a butterfly on a pin. Then a figure detached itself from the group and stepped quickly towards them.

'My dears, how delightful that you could make it.' Deirdre's carrying tones announced their welcome. It was as if Mrs Luker, not Madame Bellenger, were their hostess.

Deirdre was wearing a bronze silk dress which set off the fiery quality of her hair. Gold chains draped her neck, heavy gold bracelets manacled her wrists. Giorgio Beverly Hills, liberally applied, swamped the white scent of lilies that Claudine wore. She kissed the air by Netty's ear, draped an arm round her shoulders, flung a kiss at Gerald, and swept the couple towards the waiting group. Looking at Madame Bellenger, a slim black pillar of the community, Netty wondered how on earth the Lukers could claim friendship with her. The answer was, of course, money. Old versus new, but still money.

Deirdre ushered Netty towards a tall youngish man. Netty felt her heart sink at the prospect of all the introductions. At the best of times names tended to vanish from her consciousness even in the moment of hearing them

'Here's Felix, Netty, but don't mind him!' Deirdre said, coquettishly, as they passed her handsome husband, wearing a white silk shirt and very well-cut black trousers. Netty gave him a shy smile as she was whisked by. 'Come and meet Edouard. Edouard, darling, here's yet another English person for you to meet!'

The man bowed over her hand. Netty caught her breath. He was a beautiful specimen.

'Isn't he gorgeous! Edouard, this is Netty, Madame Netty Feldwick.'

'Annette,' she heard herself saying, conscious of Gerald behind her, exchanging jovial greetings with Felix.

'Annette,' he replied, and gazed directly into her eyes. My God, she hadn't felt that sudden startled rush of blood to the heart since she was at school.

He was not as young as he looked at first glance; flecks of grey were in the black hair, and there were faint lines by his eyes and at his mouth. His eyes were richly brown with faint speckles of green.

'Annette, it is a pleasure.'

'Netty, this is Edouard Chevalier. He lives in Vergt de Meuron, and nobody's quite sure *what* he does for a living, but whatever it is, he does it beautifully!'

Gerald appeared by Netty's side, just as Edouard smiled dazzlingly at Deirdre. Netty felt a sudden urge to shake her husband off. Usually she enjoyed the sense of his protection, a bulwark against social fire and flood. Now, seeing him stand near the beautiful Monsieur Chevalier, she was conscious of how clumsily *English* he looked, his shirt buttons pulling just a little across a torso replenished by too many patisseries. His stance, round-shouldered, slightly thick-necked, head thrust forward, was in contrast to the stag-like grace of the Frenchman.

The two shook hands. She, who knew Gerald so well, saw the distaste, the suspicion he always felt when near a man to whom the epithet 'beautiful' could be applied. Men weren't supposed to have looks unless they were matinée screen idols or nancy boys. Edouard, in return, was charming, but she sensed that the hostility was mutual.

And God knows, in this elegant damask-dressed salon Gerald did look even more bull-in-a-china-shop than usual.

A round silver tray appeared at Netty's elbow. She half-expected a flunkey in full fig: embroidered waistcoat and white corrugated wig, but instead there was a demure maid in a black dress and a tiny white apron. Netty took a tall fluted glass at her hostess' behest, Madame Bellenger having quietly joined the group. She sipped quickly as other people gravitated towards them as if they were at the centre of a vortex, and were in their turn introduced, this time by Claudine, Deirdre being now lost in an animated monopolisation of Monsieur Chevalier, during which she frequently laughed and prodded him on the arm with her forefinger.

Felix winked at Netty. 'Don't mind Deirdre,' he said, 'she's a shocking flirt. Always has been. Man-mad, aren't you, my darling,' he added, loudly so that his spouse could hear. She laughed again.

In quick succession they met a doctor and his wife from Figueil, a banker from Toulouse — 'a friend of my own dear Henri,' said Claudine — two lawyers, and a gallery owner. Conversation was civilised but plodding. The hour for aperitifs seemed to be going on for an inordinately long time. Netty began to see what attraction the Lukers held for Madame Bellenger. They were like a breath of fresh air in a stuffy room. They might not always be in the best of taste but they had energy, brash confidence, *joie de vivre.* Of the other guests, the doctor looked bathed in flesh and sweat, like a *confit d'oie* preserved in its own fat. The lawyer was desiccated, the art gallery man attenuated and weary, the banker piggy-eyed, solidly encased in the hide of his own opinions. He held his glass of wine close to his portly breast, like a gambler unwilling to reveal his hand.

Claudine herself was like a Toledo steel blade or finest crystal. Her voice was quiet but had a piercing edge to it. She was the perfect hostess, her sense of timing acute, her ability to drift in and out of other people's conversations subtle and tactful. Yet, as Netty watched her, she gave the impression that part of her was not there at all, that she played the role of the châtelaine like an automaton. What was she really like, what did she really think? Netty felt she was just about the only person in the room whose thoughts she really would like to know, and yet this would probably be denied her.

She noticed, while nodding and smiling at the banker's peroration on the blessings of the new computerisation of the financial markets of the world, (Gerald trying to interject with 'My son Paul ...' every so often but never getting any further), that their hostess glanced every now and then at an exquisite little ormulu clock on the high marble mantlepiece, and each time there was the tiniest compression of her lips.

Felix glanced at his Rolex Oyster. 'Time's getting on, isn't it? We waiting for someone? Well, what the hell — have another — you too, Gerald.' He seized two glasses from a passing tray.

The double doors opened. Two men came in; one in a rush, eagerly launching himself at his hostess, the other in a slow amble already familiar to Netty. Professor Appleby glanced around. His eye lighted on her. He smiled, nodded slightly, would have made his way to her, but had to wait his turn to greet Claudine. This took some time, as the first man's apologies for lateness were profuse. Netty stared at the shabbiness of his clothes and his tousled gingery hair. Having boarded and disarmed Madame Bellenger, he fired himself across the room at the other guests.

'*Monsieur, Monsieur, Madame,*' he dispensed greetings and handshakes with vague abandon, trawling through the group for someone interesting. 'Ah, Edouard!' he said in English, 'Night off from the Casino? Bit fogeyish though, eh?' Edouard's smile was non-committal, his attention drawn back to Deirdre by the sheer force of that lady's magnetic will.

Unabashed, the Englishman ricocheted onto the art gallery owner. 'Yves, old man, how's business? Heard it was flagging a bit. *Do* hope not! Sorry I'm fully booked myself or I'd shove a few pieces your way. What it is to be in demand!'

The exhausted-looking Yves summoned up inadequate reserves, bristled slightly, replied faintly, retired *hors de combat.*

A final volley, directed at the whole assembled company:

'Sorry I'm late. Had a meeting in Bourdonne, ran on rather. Hope I haven't ruined the whole shooting-match! Claudine will kill me if the meat's overdone! The French like it still kicking!' Head thrown back, bark of laughter. Netty was transfixed. 'Anyway, ran into the Prof on the way, so I'm not the only one in the doghouse. Who've we got here? Not more *English* people!' (fake groan) 'We're taking over the whole bloody Dordogne! More chance of meeting an English person here than in Brixton, anyway! *Deirdre,* sorry darling, didn't see you — how can that be possible, you'll ask.' Kiss, kiss. 'Introduce myself to these new faces.' Gigantic coarse-knuckled hand held out. 'Peter Rettlesham-Carey. Yes, oh God, with a hyphen — I *know.*'

Gerald took the proffered hand cautiously, as if it might bite. 'Gerald Feldwick. This is my wife, Netty.' *Annette,* she thought again.

'Brilliant. Glad to meet you. More the merrier. What brings you to these parts?'

Gerald was just about to launch into his by now set-piece explanation when Claudine sailed serenely by. 'Dinner is served — do come along — it's much overdue,' she said, with a mock-stern glance of reproof at Peter. Netty still hadn't had a chance to say hello to the Professor.

She was in luck though; she was seated by him at the dining-table, a table so long that the doctor and his wife at the farther end looked quite shrunken. The china was pale turquoise and edged with gold. There was an escutcheon on every plate, small but significant, out by the northern circumference. 'Like an Oxbridge college,' murmured the Professor, before raising his eyes and smiling at Netty. 'Well, Annette, how are you settling in?'

Deirdre's piercing laugh caused him to raise an eyebrow before Netty had a chance to answer. Mrs Luker was seated between Edouard and Gerald, like Beauty and the Beast on either side of a siren. She was extracting fulsome compliments from each. The banker and the lawyer were conversing in low tones, the doctor and his wife were staring into space and ignoring one another and Claudine was trying to cheer up the drooping figure of Yves Daubier, the art gallery man. It was hard work: her determined animation versus his disconsolate defeatism.

'Well,' Netty answered, 'it's been a bit mixed. It's exciting of course, but, well, a bit tiring too, really. So much going on.'

'I'm sure that's so. There's a world of difference between having a two week holiday somewhere and starting a whole new life. Even if the place does seem to be populated by ex-pats!'

This was said with a jerk of the head towards Peter Rettlesham-Carey.

'Who *is* he?' asked Netty.

'Peter? I've known him for years. He's the scion of a very blue-blooded family. The Rettlesham-Careys have been around time out of mind, ever since Hugo Rettlesham married Elizabeth Jane Carey back in seventeen oatcake. He's the latest black sheep in a whole flock going back to the Conqueror, I should think. It's obligatory for every generation of the family to produce its ne'er-do-well, and he's it this time round. His elder brother — Hugo naturally — runs the estate and Rettlesham Park, back in England. Fine Queen Anne mansion. It's for his antecedents that Claudine stands having him around, I think. Maybe he amuses her, too.'

'What does he do? Anything?'

'He's an artist, would you believe. Fell into it by accident and he's become a great success, and may well remain so, until the fashion changes. Pardon me for being an old cynic, but I'm afraid I have trouble putting up with him. You'll have noticed already that he's rather overpowering!'

Netty looked along the table to where Gerald seemed to be suffering Peter very gladly. The two seemed to have hit it off. Peter was gesturing in an 'it was *this* big' manner, and Gerald was looking on admiringly, then encouraging him with questions.

'Are you still on for coming to dinner?' asked the Professor.

'Why, of course, anytime. I mean, whenever would be best for you.'

'Oh, it's open house with me. Just stroll in, though I can't promise you such palatial surroundings as these!'

He waved a fork at the dining-room, whose chief glory was a painted ceiling larded with overstuffed clouds, overstuffed goddesses, overstuffed cherubs.

'Bel Arbre was lucky to survive the war,' he continued. 'Lots of châteaux and *manoirs* were burnt down by the Nazis in reprisals against the Resistance. This one escaped because they flushed the Maquis out round here. Some, in my opinion, are so florid, the Nazis would have been doing us a favour if they *had* burnt them down! This place is just this side of my taste barrier. Do you like it?'

'It's magnificent! A bit overpowering, though, and, well, just not very *homey!*'

'*Not* one of the virtues Claudine looks for in a house! *Presence,* that's what she wants. Bel Arbre was in the hands of her forebears during the first Empire. I gather that it was a reward from Napoleon for services rendered in the conquering of Europe. The family lost it later and it had got very run-down, before Claudine had the wit to marry 'her Henri', a banker rich enough to pour money into buying and renovating the place. You have to admit, she's done a sterling job.'

'What happened to her husband, her Henri?'

'Heart attack. She was devastated. So, her Henri is gone, but Bel Arbre remains, to comfort her. Along with her dear friends, of course. Tcha! What a shower!'

'If they're so bad, Professor, why are you here?' asked Netty, then clapped a hand over her mouth, aghast. 'God, I'm sorry! That sounded so rude!'

'Not at all, not at all,' he chuckled. 'You're quite right: I'm an old hypocrite with no right to set myself up as any better than the rest of the crew here. For all I know, Rettlesham-Carey has the soul of a saint.'

At that precise moment the said aristocrat was sketching in the air the silhouette of a curvaceous female; guffaw of laughter from Gerald. Netty's smiling eyes met the Prof's.

'Somehow I don't think so,' she said. 'We'll let your first assessment stand. But really, I did want to know — why socialise with people you don't like?'

'We all end up doing that, don't we? It's partly out of friendship for Claudine, partly the basic human need to find one's position in the local social hierarchy. I do quite well on that score: I have, if not blue blood, a kind of cerebral aristocracy: retired Professor, Cambridge, etcetera. It's the kind of thing that gives you an entrée to all sorts of places, but the penalty is that you have to wear your learning fairly lightly, in case people judge you as an overbearing clever dick.'

He looked significantly at Gerald. Netty was glad that a servant at that moment chose to remove the hors d'oeuvre and put in its place some *truite farcie*. She looked down at the table, picked up her fish fork, put it down again to wait until all the guests had been served, looked at the Professor, who gazed back calmly.

'Professor, I don't think — that is — Gerald really didn't mean — that is — he likes you, honestly.'

'Annette, you're digging yourself into a hole. Best leave it, eh? Don't worry, and don't apologise for your husband. Let him apologise for himself, if he feels the need, which he doesn't. We're a bit different, he and I, that's all. It doesn't signify. We'll rub along all right, if you stay.'

'Oh, we'll be staying, Professor, I'm sure of that.'

'You don't seem to be overly delighted at the prospect.'

Netty took another swig of some deliciously cool Pouilly Fumé. It had a smokey tang that counterpointed the fish beautifully. A chorus of tiny *tchings* echoed in the high-ceilinged room as the guests tackled the fish. The trout all lay sidelong, gazing glassily at the fat cherubs as their flesh was torn away and their slender white bones peeled off and put delicately to the sides of the plates.

'I'm not,' said Netty. 'It wasn't my idea to come here. I'm as much of a fish out of water here as this poor thing on the plate.' She stabbed downwards and her fork made a louder *tching* on the Sèvres than the others. She saw Gerald look quickly at her, but then Deirdre's hand was on his arm, pulling his attention away. She saw Claudine look at her dispassionately then turn her poised head to converse with the languid Yves who seemed at least to have gained some colour in his cadaverous cheeks. She felt the swirl of the wine in her veins, she felt the old man facing her would understand and not judge. It all came spilling out.

'It was all Gerald's idea. He came to France in February and he got this agent to show him round a few properties. He was just having a look-see, he said, that's all. Maybe we could buy a nice little holiday home, somewhere to get away from it all, and we had the money to spend because he was taking early retirement. He saw Le Sanglier and he says he just fell in love with it. He came home, told me about it.'

'You discussed it?'

'No, he *told* me about it — and the next week he was back out here with a banker's draft, got hold of someone to act as interpreter, he was off to the *notaire* as quick as spit and the thing was bought. It was last owned by some English people, we heard.'

'That's true,' said the Professor, looking down at his plate.

'Well, I don't know what put them off, or if they went back to England, but for two pins I'd be scuttling off back home too. These people ...' Netty signalled vaguely with her fork, 'they're not *us*.'

Another loud cackle from Rettlesham-Carey, who'd been wolfing down his fish as if half-starved.

'And *him*. What does Gerald think he's at? We see enough of that type round Oxford.'

'And Cambridge, I assure you,' added the Prof.

'And the house ...' Netty went on, her litany of grievance a performance Gerald might well have benefited from but was never likely to because, when it came to a conflict of interest, it was always Netty who backed down, '... the house — the work we've had to put in, and still so much to be done, and it's still a house. It's not a home. Number 143 was a home. It felt real. We had all those years. It was like a second skin. Oh, I do all the work I can in Le Sanglier. I like to have something to occupy me. The bedroom's looking lovely now and the kitchen's coming on.' She glanced at the Professor. 'No doubt I'm boring you to death with all this women's stuff.'

'Not at all, not at all. Environment matters — I understand exactly. People need a sense of self, of at-homeness.'

'That's the point, though. No matter what I do, I can't imagine ever making that great lumbering place feel like home. It isn't me, it just isn't me. And it isn't *him* either.' Jab of angry head towards Gerald. 'If only he'd admit it.'

'You must give it time. It's a big move. Don't expect to feel at home overnight.'

Netty's mouth was in a tight, stubborn line.

'I just won't, I know I won't. Not ever.'

'Then tell him.'

'Gerald? Tell Gerald? It's just not on. Believe me, we've been through it all. I just can't win.'

More wine went down the hatch, and the main course arrived. Netty was aware of the Professor's sympathy and his bewilderment. It was no use going on with this. It had helped to have said what she'd said, but any more of it and she'd be like a hamster in a wheel, going round and round to no purpose. Let it be. Let it go. The wine was excellent, so was the food. What the hell. What did the hosts of the Coq d'Or say? *Festoyez.*

She cut into the *Châteaubriand aux trois poivres* in front of her. It bled all over the plate. She grabbed at her glass of wine, red as the blood, and downed a couple of great gulps. The wine was warm velvet.

'Careful, my dear. That's a Pomerol '85 — la Fleur Petrus — and you've just swallowed about fifteen quid's worth. Take your time. Savour it.'

She felt like a guilty child guzzling at a party. The afterglow of the wine was a reminder of its quality. He was right: it was a shame to waste it. She took a sip and let it linger on her tongue, dispensing largesse.

'God, it *is* good, isn't it? I really shouldn't rush it. It's just that the meat ... well, I expected to find signs of life.' She prodded at it with her fork. 'How can they eat it like this?'

'I know. The French like their meat bloody: *saignant* or *bleu.* I once ordered a steak *très bien cuit* in a restaurant and a French lady of my acquaintance told me that it was like *une vieille semelle:* the sole of an old shoe!'

'Cheek!'

'Ah well, it's just the custom. It's just what you're used to. If you're Hindu beef revolts you, if you're Moslem it's pork. Where do you draw the line? Where's the morality? It's what your culture says it is.'

'When Gerry and I were in Leclerc the other day we saw this lovely drawing of a pony, bridle and all, and it said *Mangez du cheval* and underneath it were all these deep red joints of horsemeat. We were horrified. But I see what you mean — we've been brought up to see horses as — well — not to be eaten.'

'Exactly. But where's the difference, on a plate, between bits of horse and bits of cow or lamb or pig?'

'I know, I know. I do think of it, but then I pull myself away from thinking of it, I suppose. As long as it comes in nice clingfilm and polystyrene packages in the supermarket it's easy to forget what it originally was. I used to hate going into the Covered Market in Oxford. The smell of blood, all those dead creatures hanging up, with their heads still on.' She shuddered. *'God* — what am I going to do with this? I simply can't eat it.'

Tching went knives and forks on plates, as the other guests tackled the meat.

'It's like a banquet of vampires,' said the Professor with a wry grin. 'Look, just eat the edge-bits that are done, cut the rest up, shove it around the plate a bit. There's a bit of green stuff there, *frisée* or something; tuck it under that. Don't worry. No one will notice. Claudine won't mind: she's familiar with the English and their gastronomic cowardice.'

'We've been asked down to the farm — the one near you — to dinner. I just dread it: I have nightmares at the thought of blood pancakes and chickens' feet!'

The Professor laughed. 'Ha! Don't worry — they're not likely to serve you anything of the sort. You've been watching too much Keith Floyd. But *gizzards* now — that's a distinct possibility. I'd give them warning that gizzards would, well, stick in your craw!' He laughed again at Netty's face and she joined in. The banker lifted his snout from the trough for a moment before rootling appreciatively once more. Yves *le maigre* twiddled the stem of his crystal glass and raised a withered eyebrow. Even Deirdre turned her fiery head away from the smouldering Edouard for a moment and laughed merrily. 'Wonderful meal, Netty dear, isn't it?' she chirped down the table. Netty thrust another bloody cube of meat under the shroud of pale lettuce. 'Oh yes, absolutely!' she answered.

'Divine! And Felix, you brute,' a mock pout at her husband, who was floundering in quicksands of mutual incomprehension with the wife of the banker, 'you have to drag me away from all this at the end of the summer. *Isn't* he a brute?' she asked Gerald, who nodded.

'Never mind, Deirdre. Come and stay with us. Plenty of room. Lots of fun. Don't blame you for not wanting to go, do we Net?'

Netty smiled weakly.

'There now!' said Gerald. 'Problem solved. Stay on — let that boring old fart of a husband go back to the city.'

Felix appeared not to hear this judgement of Solomon, being engaged in trying to explain the concept of property development to the banker's wife, whose English was not even *comme ci comme ça.*

Gerald was appreciating Deirdre's proximity. He found her perfume heady, her ebullience infectious. He felt as if he could really let go with her, say what he liked, brush casually against her, lay his hand on her knee for a second and there would be no rejection — just a challenging, flirtatious laugh. He didn't know how much of it was all show: he didn't know the Lukers well enough to understand what their ground-rules were. Did they play away from home, as Deirdre's flaunting behaviour implied? Or was it all a well-rehearsed routine by which to disarm potential business associates? If so, why do it here? Perhaps it had become an automatic response. Whatever the reason or significance it was surely preferable to his wife's eternal frigidity, the tensing of the muscles, the rigid submission that was no surrender, whenever he laid a finger on her. He was sick of it. Better to bask in the heat that seemed visibly to radiate from Deirdre's bronzed skin. For a moment he visualised her in leather ... the vision was like a galvanic shock, charging one part of his anatomy with enormous potential. Not comfortable in Claudine's dining-room. He took the mental equivalent of a cold shower and gazed at his wife, dressed in pale turquoise like a sea-nymph. To his surprise, for he'd caught her looking, as ever, tense and uncomfortable not so long ago, she seemed unusually animated. She was laughing — again — with the Professor. What on earth had happened to make her so relaxed? Ah, the red wine, that would have been it: gutsy stuff. It wouldn't have taken much to get her going. He hoped she'd have enough sense left to cut back. He hoped she wouldn't embarrass him. He watched her laugh again, and then glance at him, warily. He smiled, to encourage her. She was looking good. He didn't really want the overbright redhead on his left, too brassy by far, to be honest. He wanted Netty's sweetness, her tenderness, her yieldingness. Maybe she should drink more wine. Maybe tonight ... He cut a perfectly ripe slice of Camembert and watched it ooze all over the bread.

'Professor ...' said Netty.

'Oh, for goodness' sake, you mustn't be so formal — I'm not royalty.'

'Mr Appleby ... Rutherford ...'

'Won't do either, will it? Too much of a mouthful. My wife felt the same way. Used to call me Fred instead. I do wish you would too.'

'OK then ... Fred. Your wife. Is she ... ?'

'Dead? Yes: five years ago.'

'I'm sorry.'

'Hmn. Yes. People are always sorry, aren't they, when you say someone's died. As if it's their fault, somehow. Daft, really.'

'I'm sorry. I mean, I'm sorry to have said I was sorry. I didn't mean it to sound empty. I don't think it is. People are so uncomfortable, I suppose, that it's all they can manage. It just means sympathy, really — that we're all in this together. At least it does if it's said by anyone who's ever felt grief themselves. Then it's meant sincerely, because you know nothing can really help, no amount of words in the world.' The Professor opened his mouth to speak but Netty continued, 'Do you miss her very much?'

He sighed. 'Yes. We had about as good a marriage as any two mortal characters on earth could ever hope for. She was my best friend. She'd been through a lot, had Miriam, before I met her, but it didn't darken her — quite the opposite — she just revelled in life and somehow managed to give it up with dignity. I was the one who made all the fuss about it.'

'Was it ... I mean, how did she ... ?'

'Cancer,' he said shortly. 'Still, mustn't dwell on it. Miriam never did. Ah, here's dessert.'

Netty knew better than to pursue the subject.

The light raspberry sorbet on a *coulis* of blackcurrant slid down sated throats, melting as it went.

Eventually Claudine rose. 'Let us return to the salon for coffee: it will be more comfortable.'

'But Claudine, darling, I'm quite all right as I am, with these two lovely men!' cried Deirdre.

Claudine smiled. 'Deirdre, *cherie,* I'm sure you can keep them if you wish, only exert yourself! The rest of us want to *mingle.*'

In the salon Netty tried to stay close to the Professor, sitting by him on a spindly-legged damask-covered couch as a servant poured out coffee for them. With a sinking heart she saw Gerald approach, his arm round the shoulders of the Hon. Rettlesham-Carey.

'Net! Great meal, eh? Drop of cognac — don't mind if I do, thanks Prof. Peter's been telling me all about life here: sounds bloody good too. And you were so worried we'd be out on a limb. Pete tells me that over Eymet-way they've got seventy per cent English residents. Little England, this is, little England.' He flopped down onto a *bergère* chair whose fragile appearance fortunately belied its strength; it reverberated a little with the force of his descent, but held firm.

Peter sat almost as heavily, already nursing a very large glass of Armagnac. 'Coffee, thank God,' he said. 'Start working on negating the morrow's hangover, shall we?'

'Pete — tell Netty what you were telling me during the meal. Netty, you'll never believe it! It's porno-corner round here, I tell you. Go on, Pete, tell her!'

'She'll be shocked.'

'I know! Ha! Net — there's a cocaine-snorting duke about five miles Bourdonne-way. He holds orgies — three girls to a bed, apparently, and there's a couple of dykes living blatantly in Figueil, strut around starkers half the time Pete says, hands all over each other he says, and there's ...'

'Gerald, don't be so revolting.'

'See, Pete, I told you. My wife the prude. Good God Netty, loosen up! I'm not asking you to go wife-swapping, keys on the table, that sort of thing, am I? It's just a bit of fun. Jesus!'

'I think you'll find a lot of these tales are exaggerated,' interposed the Professor, gently.

'Ah no, Professor, I don't *think* so,' said Peter Rettlesham-Carey, wagging a finger at him. '*En retraite* as you are, I do not think you get the whole picture. As it were. But those of us in the, ah, *swing* of things ...!'

He and Gerald burst out laughing, like two schoolboys.

'How did you come to be living here, Mr Rettlesham-Carey?' asked Netty, conscious of the proximity of Claudine a few feet away with Edouard, Felix and Deirdre.

'Peter, my dear, Peter — don't be formal. After all, we're virtually neighbours and you'll be seeing a lot of me.' Perish the thought, Netty said to herself. 'Well,' he added, 'I came out here, when was it? Six years ago. Our aforesaid Duke invited me to a house party and to kill a few beasties that October. Well, I was sick of hunting in Perthshire, it made a change. And I had such a *rollicking* good time and the climate suited me and the wine was good, and I was far from the clutches of my worthy but insufferable family. Only question was, how to make a living? Aforementioned family being rather tight-fisted, you understand.

'Well, I dabbled in a little bit of this, little bit of that. Antiques, wine, and so on ... Nothing turned out to be very reliable and there was too much competition. Then I hit on the very thing. Art!'

He sat back, smiling.

'Art! Well, I'd dabbled in that too, years ago. I had the right contacts — a necessity, that, if one is to make one's way in this worldly world. As for this area, it just inspired me! I took off! There's one of my pieces out in the hall. Come along and see it.'

He swept them out to the marble hall. On an ebony table closely tucked under the staircase, stood a fat, swollen pot. On a background of red ochre, spindly black figures were drawn, wielding pointy spears and arrows. The spiky men arabesqued their way round the pot and underneath their sharp feet lay stags and bison and reindeer, geometrically executed, like parallelograms with heads and legs and tails and horns.

'This is quite an early piece,' said Peter, 'when I was still reeling from the shock of seeing Lascaux. Well, Lascaux II, the replica they had to build because all the visitors had affected the environment so badly — but it's as good as. I blended the style of Greek urns with the style of the cave-men and I played up the killing: one assumes those old aborigines were trying to make their hunts successful — there's one picture of an eviscerated bull in Lascaux. In the Font de Gaume caves, for some reason, they've got reindeer being all lovey-dovey, licking each other's noses. *Savage Visions of Prehistory* went down very well at the Mnemosyne Gallery in London and Claudine with her usual *marvellous* taste, was one of my first customers, much as I hate such a commercial word, but then, one has to live, hasn't one?'

Does the man ever pause for breath, wondered Netty, trying to look interested in the little black men on the bloody pot. Gerald was nodding sagely, as if he'd been a connoisseur of Art all his days. The Professor raised an eyebrow. 'My impression of cave-art is of roundedness, of life and contour, not 2-D straight lines.'

'Yes, but Prof, art is *interpretation,* not *imitation.* I decided to apply the style of the tectiforms to the figures themselves.'

'Netty, my dear,' said Deirdre, on their return to the salon, drawing her down to sit beside her in her miasma of scent, 'I've just been saying to Claudine what I mentioned to you that day at La Gabare. Are you *sure* we haven't met before? I mean, I keep having that feeling. Isn't it strange? Have you felt it, Netty?'

'Not at all, I'm afraid.'

Deirdre looked at her, closely. 'But I'm sure, the face ... maybe the hair was different.' She surveyed Netty up and down, then sighed and gave a shrug. 'Oh well, what does it matter? Where's the coffee? Edouard my love, do get me some more coffee. I'm parched. I don't know, I must have had *déjà vu* or something. Felix, my darling, maybe you married a clairvoyant, maybe I have influence on the Other Side! Maybe we're in the wrong line of business altogether!'

She broke into a peal of laughter so infectious that the rest of the guests joined in. Claudine passed round a small tray of Belgian chocolates. Gerald and Netty selected one each and sank their teeth into the confectionery, thoughtfully.

Ten, twenty minutes passed, then Deirdre, trying to engage in some sparkling repartee and chew on a praline at the same time, choked quite violently on the sweet. Volunteer hands slapped her hard between the shoulder-blades. When eventually the chocolate was dislodged she looked up, wheezing and with streaming eyes, straight into Netty's concerned face. She gasped.

'My God, I *have* seen you! In the newspapers! Oh my poor love, it was you, wasn't it? I *knew* I'd heard the name Feldwick before. I said so, didn't I Felix? It was your little boy, wasn't it? It was your little boy that was murdered.'

Fête Champêtre

Later.

'How could you, Gerald? How *could* you?'

'It wasn't my fault.'

'It wasn't your fault. Nothing's ever your fault. How *could* you?'

'It wasn't my bloody fault! How was I to know the bloody woman would recognise us? Jesus! I'm not in charge of people's memories, am I?'

'You know that's not what I mean. Recognition — well, that was on the cards, ever since we realised that half the population of England seems to have come out here. I'm used to that — I've had five years of it, for God's sake. We'll get away from all of it, you said. We'll start again. And I went along with it! God, I'd rather be back in Oxford where everyone knew, where everyone had had their fill, where there was nothing more to be said. But to meet that curiosity again, that *greed* that calls itself concern, and you to be feeding that greed — Gerald, how could you.'

'I don't know. I'd ... I'd had a few, Net — it all came out, I can't help it. It just has to come out. They *did* care, they weren't just vultures — you're too cynical, I've said it before. People can't hear about it and not *care*. They're human. I respond to that — a bit of human sympathy. God knows I bloody need it. I can't talk to *you*, can I. Oh no. You nurse it like it was private property.'

It is, it is, she cried in her heart. It's all mine, this grief, as he was all mine. The moon dipped and fled and nodded through the trees as the car was wrenched along the country lanes. They reached Le Sanglier. Gerald got out, slammed the door, went into the house, leaving the air shuddering behind him. She saw lights go on. She leaned back in the car seat and breathed out. She opened the door and craned out to look at the sky. A million more stars than could ever be seen from Oxford. Pure and silent and still. How small she was, how small her grief was, and yet how large, it filled the heavens. The moon grew larger and wobbled and brimmed over. In time she'd be calm again, in time she'd go into the house, and, somehow, she'd talk to her husband.

Inside Le Sanglier, the phone started ringing. Gerald picked it up with a not entirely steady hand. He'd been walking up and down the Salle de Chasse, blustering to himself in self-defence. But he found he couldn't blame Netty for her aggression. She was right. He'd said too much and at the time it had felt better, but now he felt rather sick.

The warble of the telephone was a relief. For a moment.

'Gerry?'

'Roy! Great to hear from you, mate! How's tricks?'

'Not too good, I'm afraid. I've been trying to get hold of you all evening.'

The conversation was over by the time he heard Netty come in. She looked pale and drained, and was constrainedly polite. They slept together in the same bed but might as well have been on different planets. Or rather, they didn't sleep. They stared at the white ceiling while outside the creatures of the dark set about their nocturnal exploits. Gerald rose several times, feeling nauseous. He didn't know how he was going to tell her about Roy's phone-call. His last memory before eventually succumbing to hot, unrestful slumber was of Deirdre's long fingers, red-tipped, on his arm, squeezing, and her voice saying 'Gerry, oh Gerry, how *awful* for you, how *awful*. Words fail me, Gerry. I know Felix and I couldn't imagine, not in a thousand years ...'

The moon bowled its way up and down the sky, heading for the horizon as the imminent sun cast rose-tints in opposition. An early woodpecker rattled an alarum to the creatures of day.

Netty had not slept. From time to time she turned her head to look at her husband. Gerald snored, puttering like an aged Triumph motorbike. His mouth was slack and the uvular vibration of his snoring revolted her. The flesh of his bare arm as it touched hers was clammy and repelled her. The smell of stale booze, stale cigarettes, stale sweat, made him seem animal and degraded to her. A heavy, stinking thing. A pig. The only time she closed her eyes was when he hoisted himself out of bed and lurched to the toilet.

She lay there, breathing shallowly, feeling herself becoming light, as if she could levitate from the bed. She saw Deirdre's talons on Gerald's arm, heard those words: 'Oh Gerry ... I just couldn't imagine, not in a thousand years ...'

Not in a million, she thought. Not in a thousand million. Not in a million million million.

You are not a mother, you tarty bitch.

Fred would understand. He knew death. He'd met it.

Could she talk to him?

Could she, ever, talk to anyone?

'Mrs Feldwick, have you considered counselling? Bereavement therapy? It might help, you know. It doesn't do you any good to bottle it up.'

'Well, Netty, I'll give you another prescription, but this is the last. These pills are just cotton wool. You're wrapping yourself up against life and you'll have to face it sooner or later.'

'Mother, see a therapist. Bradley's found the past decade so much more tolerable with analysis, and he's been a changed man since the Rebirthing Program. You're needy and you're hurting. If you want to shrink the pain, pay for a shrink — that's what Doctor Klugman always says.'

'Net, what should the wording be — "dearly beloved son" or "much-loved son"? The first sounds a bit too biblical, doesn't it? What do you think? Net? Net! Don't leave the room ... Net, for Christ's sake, he was my son too ... TALK TO ME!'

No, she couldn't talk. She wouldn't prostitute her grief like Gerald did. She was on her own, with her son, inside her head.

Even Rettlesham-Carey had been knocked out of self-absorption. Even Claudine's patrician features had displayed emotion. Deirdre had melted all over the rug. Too awful. Not in a thousand years.

There had been a ghastly silence after Deirdre's exclamation. Netty had instinctively started to shake her head, but it was too late, the game was up. She sat down and looked at her hands, lying with a semblance of normality in her lap. She let Gerald talk.

'Deirdre, we did hope really that no one would recognise us. After all, that was the point in coming out here. Oh, I like the house we've bought and all that: it's a distraction. But the main aim was to get away from ... everything.'

'My dear, you've no need to explain. We quite understand — don't we, Felix?' Sympathetic silent nod from Felix. 'And it goes without saying this will go No Further than this room. Will it, Peter?' said slightly more forcefully.

'God no. Wouldn't dream of it. Don't know what to say, really. Just, deepest sympathies, and so on ...'

Rettlesham-Carey looked acutely uncomfortable. Netty wondered why bereavement should be so embarrassing: metaphorically speaking, it made everyone shuffle their shoes and stare at the carpet.

Claudine took over. 'Madame Feldwick, allow me to offer my sincere condolences. I have no wish to upset you any further. We will talk no more of this if you do not wish us to.'

'Of course not,' added Deirdre, 'we wouldn't dream of it. From what we know, it was quite ghastly. Of course, we only gathered this and that from the newspapers, and we know how inaccurate *those* can be.'

Felix said, 'And there was that *Crime Time* programme.'

'Oh yes, there was that too. I forgot. Gerald,' her voice dropped a dulcet octave, like the Prime Minister at her most concerned, 'they never caught the ... eh ... perpetrator, did they?'

'No,' answered Gerald. 'No, they didn't.'

'But, don't you still hope they might?'

'There is still that chance. But it's unlikely.'

'We're scaling down the operation, Mrs Feldwick. It's unlikely any new evidence will turn up. I'm sure you'll appreciate we made the greatest efforts to apprehend the killer.'

'How awful! Oh, Felix, not to know who did it! Gerald,' hand on arm, 'how awful for you, how *awful*. Words fail me, Gerald. I know Felix and I just couldn't imagine, in a thousand years ...'

Netty watched Deirdre hold centre-stage, as if she and she alone had been granted a revelation of just how awful the business of murder was and it was her duty to impart this to the insensate masses.

'And you, Netty, oh my dear, my heart goes out to you. Tell me, how old was he, your little boy?'

'Three.'

'Three! Oh my God, how could anyone? It's sick. It's so sick.'

'He'd have been eight, now,' said Gerald. Don't stoke the fire, thought Netty. Claudine offered more coffee by way of a distraction, but no one heard.

'I'm sorry,' said Rettlesham-Carey, 'but I've been out here a while, and the jungle-drums don't exactly throb between me and my family, so I don't know anything about this. What happened, exactly? That is, that is, if you don't mind ... if it's too painful, I mean ...'

'Our son Daniel,' answered Gerald, saying the words that had been said so often they were almost by rote, 'was abducted in the late summer of 1984 by person or persons unknown, was abused and murdered by him or them, and his body was not found for weeks. That's what happened.'

Even Deirdre was silent for a moment.

The floodgates were opened. Netty recognised it all. She had hoped never to see this performance again.

'Netty, there, was incredible. She still is, aren't you, Net? She held firm — she was my anchor. I don't mind telling you, I went to pieces. All those weeks of not knowing, the police, the reporters, the hoax calls ...'

Shocked intakes of breath.

'Yes, hoax calls — there are some very sick people in the world. Some claimed they were holding him, one even got a child to squeal "Mummy" down the phone at us.'

Mummy, Mummy, Mummy.

'There was a clairvoyant, too, kept pestering us.' Deirdre looked uncomfortable. 'Said she'd talked to our little lad on the other side, and that there was lots of white light and we weren't to cry as he hated seeing us cry, and that nothing was hurting any more. Well, it may have been true, for all we know. I keep an open mind and I hope he's happy wherever he is, but it's no good to us, not really, he's not here for us to hold.'

'We saw photos of him, in the papers, at the time,' said Felix, gently. 'He was a lovely little boy.'

'He was, Felix, he was. Lovely nature too, let me tell you. He was special. But if he'd been as ugly as sin, if he'd been Quasimodo, no one deserves what he got. His looks have nothing to do with it. It's the evil that was done to him that matters.'

'You must have wanted to kill ... whoever ...' said Peter.

'God yes. Still do. In some ways, we're better off than others; at least Daniel was found in the end. We were able to bury him and to grieve and now we're just trying to get on with our lives.'

Don't talk about it as if it's over, thought Netty, still staring at her hands.

'Some families,' Gerald went on, 'never know. They never find out. Their loved one disappears and just never comes back. Could be dead, probably is, but there's still that hope, year after year, that they'll walk back through the door. We had six weeks of that hope and it was killing us. No, it's better to know, however terrible the news is.'

Is it, thought Netty. If only I could still dream of his return. Coming up to nine now, getting long in the limb, the last babyness gone.

'What's been so awful, though, to get back to what Peter was saying, is that we'll never know who did it and we can't look that person in the eye and ask *why*. And we can't exact the punishment — though no punishment would ever equate ... But still, if there were just *some* level of retribution possible ...'

Deirdre shuddered. 'To *think* that such a person is still on the loose!' She leant back into the crook of Felix's arm. Netty looked up, looked down, unwilling to catch anyone's eye, for fear that she should be asked to contribute. The Professor, she noted, had stayed silent throughout, somewhere on the periphery.

She noticed a fine embroidered firescreen standing a few feet away. It was nowhere near a fire, and on a summer evening no fragile female complexion needed shielding from the flames. She began to study it. It depicted a bunch of lilies and roses, beautifully shaded. The finest of stitches and many different hues of embroidery silk had given it that quality of depth and dimension. She wished she could go up to it and examine it more closely. She was dimly aware of Gerald's litany: 'And when I saw the police car I knew something was horribly wrong, only they wouldn't say... and all sorts of things ran through my mind ... they took me home and Netty was sitting there ...'

She wondered how old the firescreen was, who had embroidered it, what stitches she had used, what she had been thinking of as it took shape under her hands. Had it belonged to an ancestress of Claudine's, or had she simply bought it as a piece of set design for this chocolate-box house?

Minutes went by. Gerald hadn't yet completed his recital.

'Yes, it was just on the outskirts, by the road that leads from Marston to Summertown. There's a busy link road with a cycle-path beside it, and open fields leading to the River Cherwell. They found him in a little grove of trees by the cycle path. We couldn't believe it,' sighed Gerald, not for the first time. 'People going up and down there all the time — joggers, horseriders, kids cycling home from school, cars all up and down — and there he was, just lying there ... just his little sweatshirt still on him ... lying there all alone ...'

As always happened, Gerald's voice broke at this point.

Silence fell. Netty, with a jerk of her stiffened neck, found herself meeting a compassionate look from Madame Bellenger.

Netty loathed this milking of sympathy and the words her

husband used; the tale of horror that had become a pat ritual, trivialising the event. Words could not approach, could not touch the hem of this horror. Therefore, to Netty's mind, they should not be uttered at all. Daniel had been hers, the loss of him was hers to bear, her grief unique as he had been. He was not to be put on display, as those hideous pseudo-sympathetic tabloid reports had done: *'Tragic tot's last hours'*, *'Grief-stricken mother pleads for son'* and so on. For Gerald, Daniel's father, to talk in such a brazenly self-pitying manner was sacrilege. Netty hated him for it, for his self-indulgence, and she sent him a look that told him so, only he didn't see it.

Madame Bellenger did, though, and nodded slightly to herself.

Half an hour later, the Feldwicks left. Netty stared fixedly out of the front windscreen as the car turned down the drive and away from Bel Arbre. Gerald glanced in the driving mirror; they were all still standing there on the grey stone steps. Deirdre's perfume seemed to have got into the car with them. Netty suddenly shrugged violently, to dislodge the memory of that cloying embrace. Her nose had been pressed suffocatingly against Deirdre's shoulder.

'My *dear*. My *dear*,' was all that lady had said, and then emotion had got the better of her and she had turned to the comfort of her husband.

Netty realised she had failed to say goodbye to Fred. She had been aware of his presence, but she could only remember the cold firm grip of Claudine's hand and what had almost been a comic military salute from Peter Rettlesham-Carey.

They turned right out of the great gates, passed down to Figueil, through its grey streets, and the moon came to attention through the trees to light them on their way 'home'.

Netty unclenched her jaw and turned to Gerald.

'How *could* you!' she said, furiously.

Twelve hours or so later, and she was saying it again. They were having lunch at the Coq d'Or. The Quiberons were delighted to see them and asked many questions about progress at Le Sanglier, so it wasn't until the cheese course, after an excellent *potage de legumes* and *entrecôte,* which Netty enjoyed (the Quiberons, having got used to their little ways, had given the meat a decent grilling), that he was able to say what he had to say.

'Oh *God* Gerald, how could you?'

'Now look, Net, I'm sorry, but what else can I do? I knew you wouldn't like it.'

'Too right I don't!'

'I know, love. But he's a mate, and he's in a fair amount of trouble and he needs me.'

'But the whole point of coming out here — *you said* — was to leave everything behind us. You even made me throw out ... things that I wanted to take with us. No left luggage, you said, no clutter, no ... memories. And I went along with it. I thought you had a point — but you sold that business, Gerald. It's nothing to do with you any more. Leave it alone.'

'Don't you see that I can't? Come on, be fair, you have to admit Roy and Sheila did right by us, now, didn't they? They stuck by us through it all, you couldn't find better friends anywhere. Admit it, Net.'

'I suppose so.'

'You *suppose* so! Where would you be now without Sheila's shoulder to cry on? Where would I be without Roy's hand at the wheel when Danny died and I wasn't fit to cope? They did right by us then, and they did right by us in buying the business off us. Well, it's a two-way street, is friendship. Or don't you think so, wife of my heart? Do you just take and not give? Eh?'

'Of course not.' Monsieur Quiberon was taking away the cheeseboard. He was about to lament their lack of appetite: only little shavings taken off a couple of the cheeses and that particularly fine Bleu d'Auvergne not even touched. Then he sensed the atmosphere. All was not well. He recited the French hotelier's stock-in-trade of desserts: *crème caramel, tarte aux pommes, glaces ou sorbets,* and took himself off to cut the *tarte aux pommes,* requested with such little enthusiasm.

During this enforced hiatus, Netty stared out onto the street,

Gerald stared at her. He had begun the conversation defensively, but offence had turned into the best protection. Bombast and sententiousness could always turn the tables on his hapless wife.

The *tarte* arrived. It was delicious.

'Well,' said Netty, 'now I know why you insisted on coming out for lunch. You just wanted to make sure I wouldn't throw a plate at you.'

Gerald could afford to be generous in triumph.

'OK, I admit it. I fancied a bit of neutral territory. I knew you wouldn't be pleased.'

'Right again.'

'But look, love, you do see don't you? Roy's in a pickle — he's got the VAT man on his back, he's got trouble with the suppliers in Newcastle and that big order that went to Excelsior Fabrication? Well, they're quibbling over payments and that's affecting the cash-flow. He still hasn't found a suitable Assistant Manager to take some of the strain. It's too much for him to handle. I'll just nip back, push a few buttons, have a few words in the right ears, sort it out for him. He's a good man and a good mate. I can't see him go under — I can't see our business go under. I can't just switch off from it all. You do see that, don't you?'

Gerald's hand reached out and covered hers. Monsieur Quiberon, approaching with two tiny cups of coffee, felt relieved. It restored the equilibrium of the restaurant.

'Yes, Gerald, I do see it,' she sighed. 'Of course you must go — but try not to be gone long. It'll be difficult for me here on my own. After all, we've hardly been here that long and I don't exactly feel settled in, and my French is still very limited. I'm going to feel very isolated, stuck in that house all alone. Unless,' she looked directly at him, 'unless I come with you.'

'No, Net, not a good idea. Look, love, I'm only going because it's business and I have to. It's not a holiday.'

'I realise that, but surely I could keep Sheila company while you and Roy ...'

It was as if she had not spoken.

'Besides, it'd be a right pain to go through the rigmarole of shutting up Le Sanglier. We'd have to get that Professor of yours or somebody to keep an eye. And I've arranged for the plumber to come Tuesday. No, Netty, it'd just be a load of botheration and it's not worth it.'

She didn't answer.

'Netty, remember, Le Sanglier isn't "that house". It's our home. Take the time to ease into it. It's a bit like breaking in new shoes: a blister or two at first, but in time like a second skin.'

'Gerald, it's a trifle more significant than a pair of bloody shoes! Don't patronise me! I do have a mind, and on occasion I do *know* my mind. I miss Oxford and I don't see any reason for staying here — not now that everyone knows.'

'Everyone does *not* know! Don't exaggerate.'

'Yes, but the point...'

'The point is that I'm going to scoot across, sort Roy out and be back before you know I'm gone, so stop grousing about it, for God's sake.'

Bitter silence.

'I tell you what, Net, we'll have a proper trip, later in the year. You wouldn't enjoy it just now, really you wouldn't. It'd just unsettle you. We'll go over later, make a holiday of it — stay in London, maybe take in a show. It'll be much more fun. Just hold hard till then, eh?'

She nodded, her throat tight.

'There's a good girl. Now let's pay the bill and get out of here: there's a lot to do. Time's pressing.'

On the way back up the hill, a man suddenly stepped out in front of the car, flapping his arms and forcing Gerald to hit the brakes.

'What the bloody hell!' said Gerald. 'Ah! *Bonjour* Augustin!'

He wound down his window as the portly figure came round to the side of the car and leaned in to shake hands. His face was brick-red, like Indian leather.

'*Ça va*, Augustin? *Voici ma femme.*'

Augustin Lelouche leaned across to grip Netty's hand. She winced, but smiled tentatively at the farmer.

'Net, this is Augustin Lelouche, Mathilde's brother. I met him when I went to the baker's the other morning and we had a glass at the local *tabac*.'

'*Bonjour, Monsieur.*'

'*Bonjour, Madame.*' The bulk withdrew itself somewhat, letting light back into the car. Augustin leaned on the sill, mentioned how fine the day was and asked them again when they would come to the farmhouse for dinner. Gerald had to explain with greatest regret that it was at present impossible as he had to return to England on urgent business. Monsieur Lelouche seemed to regard this with respect and understanding.

'*C'est pas grave,*' he said, waving them on. '*A la prochaine.*' His lumbering figure dived into the woods to the left, presumably on a shortcut to the farm.

Three minutes later, as they emerged from under the canopy of the forest, they saw two more figures up at the house, one leaning against the door, the other sitting facing the view.

'Christ, no one can say we live the life of hermits here,' said Gerald. 'Who is it? Not that Professor, I hope. Him I do not feel up to, God's honest. No, thank God,' he added, peering forward as they drew to a halt. 'It's Pete, my old mate Pete! Oh, and Mr Smooth.'

He leapt out of the car to greet Peter Rettlesham-Carey. The tall figure at the door pulled itself straight, bypassed Gerald and Peter, and came round to Netty who was still getting out.

'Annette,' he said, holding out his hand, 'let me assist,' and held out a hand to balance her.

'Oh, thank you, *Monsieur*. I seem to be ...' Her heel had got entangled in the strap of her handbag lying on the floor. She was flustered and knew that it showed.

'Not "*Monsieur*", I insist,' he chided. 'Edouard. Here, allow me.'

He bent down to unravel the long leather strap. For a moment she looked down at his thick dark hair and felt a desire to run her hand through it. She felt his hand just brush her ankle as he straightened up.

'There. You are free.'

'Oh, thank you.'

Gerald and Peter had already gone into the house. She and Edouard followed them to the Salle de Chasse where Gerald was pouring out drinks with a liberal hand.

'Netty! Great to see you again,' cried Peter. 'Cheers mate,' as Gerald passed him a tumbler of whisky. 'I was just telling your worser half here that there's a *Fête Champêtre* Teddy and I are going to tonight and do you fancy coming?'

'What's a *Fête Champêtre?*'

'Oh, it's a sort of village gala, held outside. It'll be in the woods near Nonpeyron, by the Château de Hayemet. It'll be a giggle — do come. Less rarefied than last night.'

'Will Felix and Deirdre be going?'

'Doubt it. I think Claudine's got something else lined up for them, and this sort of village thing is definitely not her scene. Not Lady of the Manor enough for her I daresay.'

Netty looked enquiringly at Gerald.

'Do we want to go, dear? When do you leave?'

Peter looked surprised.

'Off somewhere, Gerry?'

'Yes; I've just got to pop back to England. Business, you know. It's a pain, but there you are. I shouldn't be gone long. Hang on for a minute: I'll just make a couple of calls.' He ducked out into the hall, taking his drink with him.

'So you will be on your own, Annette,' said Edouard. 'Unless you too are going?'

'No. No, I'm not going.' She tried to conceal the still-present resentment. 'I'll stay here and hold the fort.'

Edouard seemed non-plussed by that phrase.

'Good for you, Netty!' said Peter, draining his glass. She refilled it for him. She had the feeling that Peter was the sort who called girls 'fillies' and was resisting the desire to slap her on the haunch and give her a sugar-lump.

'Will you be all right on your own?' asked Edouard. She looked at him gratefully. Gerald re-entered the room, grinning.

'All set. Flight from Bordeaux tomorrow, ten thirty. Let's *go* for it tonight — paint the countryside red!'

Cars were parked all along the sides of the road and in fields on the approaches to Nonpeyron. They all groaned at having to leave the vehicle and walk so far but in actuality none of them minded for it was a warm night and the people they passed among seemed happy and relaxed. Overhead, there were the stars.

They did not enter the village itself, which lay to the right, just over the ridge. They bore to the left, following a narrow track which ran between the Château and the woods. The Château itself was floodlit, splendidly highlighting its chunky round towers, corbels and crenellations; a heavyweight Gothic fantasy. The mighty towers looked as if their weight had carried them partway into the ground.

From the ridge Hayemet overlooked the great plain in the centre of which lay Bourdonne, straddling the broad river as it ran towards Bordeaux. Behind the Château, straight rows of crooked vines ran back into the small wood; beyond that Nonpeyron, so small as to be more of a hamlet than a village.

They were drawn into the shade of the trees, following the sound of music. In a clearing stood long lines of trestle tables. People were already queuing for food, which was being served to them on metal trays, as if they were in a works' canteen. Joining the queue, they received portions of melon, *pavé de boeuf* served with bread and cheese, and finally profiteroles. They found a place to sit by the side of a wooden dance floor, laid down in the centre of the glade. A rickety stage, empty at present, stood at the far end. Blurred French pop music was being emitted from speakers perched on the branches of beech trees. Ten yards beyond the stage was a shrunken fair: a small merry-go-round, a couple of stalls, and a little electric car track.

Whole families took up entire tables: parents, grandparents, relatives to the nth degree, greeting, drinking, eating. Their voices competed with the raucous music.

And children. Children scurried everywhere, followed by barking dogs. Children clamoured for the fair and were taken there, to hurtle round the track in the tiny go-karts. Several toddlers were pirouetting on the dance floor, arms outflung with total unselfconsciousness, until the time when the adults should reclaim their territory.

Netty made an effort not to look too much at the small dancers. She hated looking at children: either they were the age Danny had been or they were the age he would have been if ... Far better to drink lots of the rough red wine which came with the meal, a bottle per person. Better to look at Edouard in his sleekness and grace. Far better to enjoy looking at a man for once. Better to relish the warmth of the air, and as you get drunk, the way the trees seem to tilt in, to listen to human conversation, and the way the warmth gets to the core of you and your husband seems more foolish and that man seems ever more handsome and you might even want him, supposing you could ever feel desire, ever again.

The evening fled on towards midnight. A local band took the stage. They had an accordion player with them and Netty found herself giggling at this. Peter and Gerald had become deeply embroiled in a conversation about guns. Peter had started it, saying that the woods they were now in were excellent for game birds — woodpigeon and so on. She was amazed to hear Gerald encourage him on that track. What *was* he thinking of? Man the hunter and all that crap. Well, if it made him feel big, let him get on with it. She turned her shoulder and dismissed him. She wanted to hear nothing about death and blood. Just wine and nature and music — even with accordions — and dance. She started tapping her foot.

'Annette,' said Edouard, rising in the assumption that her answer would be 'yes', 'would you like to dance?'

Her answer was yes.

The dance floor rang hollow under her feet, echoing the gap between it and the leafy debris of the forest. Dancing on dead trees, culled from the living. The music was very loud in her ears. She felt his hand on her waist and she liked the way he was so tall. She saw the tight line of his jawbone, the slight upturn of his lips at the outer edges, the length of his eyelashes.

'I've died and gone to Mills and Boon land,' she said.

He looked down and smiled. 'I do not understand you, Annette.'

'Don't worry about it!' She giggled and nuzzled her head under his chin, pressing up against him as they shuffled round the floor to the sound of a lugubrious love-song, surrounded by broad-beamed women in skirts of just the wrong length, and middle-aged men who looked as if they'd like to be anywhere else on earth. She felt Edouard's body stiffen slightly, then relax. She felt she could mould herself to him, like Plasticine.

They drifted for what seemed some time. She wondered cloudily how many animals Gerald had verbally killed by now. The tempo changed, and the whole circuit of dancers speeded up, like a merry-go-round just getting going. She found herself laughing and laughing. It was like *The Red Shoes*: she couldn't stop dancing, didn't want to stop dancing, not with this lovely man in her arms. Oh, wouldn't Deirdre be jealous! She saw the pleasure and admiration in his eyes. It was true — she could. It was real, she was still real, she had a body and it could feel pleasure — and give it, if it wished. With the right man. That was it. She needed the right man. Not Gerald. Sick of Gerald. She looked at her spouse and all their shared past was written on him and she didn't want to know. In a way he'd been right: get away, forget, start again. But the only way, the only real way to do that would be to get away from Gerald himself.

The crazy dance grew crazier and wilder. The trees were orbiting in a frantic circuit. Faces, limbs, musicians, all a blur. She gripped Edouard's arms as the only solid things in the universe. He gripped her back, he spun her round. Her heel caught, she swung and teetered, still spinning, still clutching.

The whole kaleidoscope tilted sideways and kicked backwards as down she fell, helpless, off the wooden floor, bouncing onto the soft dark turf. Edouard fell with her, landing partly on top of her, winding her. As she sucked in air she breathed the smell of him, of crispness and tobacco and clean sweat. She felt her body for an instant able only to perceive through touch and scent, for one heady instant, then the drumming music pierced her consciousness and she looked up past Edouard's shoulder into the scandalised eyes of an old peasant sitting on a chair. She laughed herself breathless, still lying there drunk and glorious as Edouard stood up, loomed down, gave her his hand and pulled her to her feet.

'My Sir Lancelot,' she said. Then the fireworks started, at midnight, great plumes and blooms and sprays of fire bursting and shooting over the valley and lighting faces with garish colour. A silly little brass band marched along the road from the village, to the bangs and whistles of rockets in the sky above Bourdonne, and hearts swelled with the pride and pomp of France.

At some point later she remembered wandering off to the vineyard to have a pee, her bare feet in the soil as she tried not to fall over. The Château loomed over her, the lights off now, a great bulk sensed more than seen. The vine leaves, the grapes, the sense of growth, the sense of richness; a long way from the potholes and pavements of Cowley.

Later still. Gerald's angry expression. Another tense drive home. Well, hell, she didn't care. She couldn't wipe the smirk off her face.

He saved his speech until they were home and sitting in the kitchen. He was all the more aggressive for having let his resentment mature.

'So, what was that performance all about?'

'Performance?'

'Oh come on! You really laid it all out on display for him, didn't you? You were all over him like a rash. Now the question I ask myself, as I watch my wife — normally so cool, so sober — as I watch her drink like a fish and throw herself at her Frog Prince and land on the ground with her skirt up round her neck ...'

'It was not!'

'You didn't see yourself. You were a disgrace. The question I ask though is, was this performance for him, for the French oily rag? Or was it for me, her better and worst and nearest and dearest?'

'Shut up Gerald. What was I supposed to do, listen to you and that upper-class twirp talk shootey-guns all evening? I wanted to have a good time and I did.'

'And you looked like it. Like the original Good Time Had By All. I couldn't believe it, I couldn't believe it was you. Just as well it wasn't Malignac. We wouldn't be able to walk down the street.'

'Don't be ridiculous. God, where's the paracetamol? Have we got any?'

She hoisted herself out of the rocking chair and stumbled around the kitchen, pushing her hair out of her eyes and pulling drawers and cupboards open. The pleasant vague goodwill she had felt in Edouard's arms had changed to a throbbing at the temple and behind the left eye. Fragments of leaf-mould still clung to her hem and between her shoulder-blades. She had kicked off her shoes and there was dirt on her feet as she padded about on the quarry tiles.

Gerald poured the coffee and brought a mug to her.

'Netty. Net. Look, I'm sorry. Part of me was glad to see you laugh. It's been a long time. And you looked beautiful, you look beautiful. But tell me, was it just for him? You can't fancy him, Net — he's not for real.' He put his cup down on the worktop and slid his hand round her waist. His gaze had dropped from her eyes to her breasts. With his free hand he stroked her fine fair hair back and then inscribed tiny circles on her forehead with his fingers, to soothe away the incipient hangover.

'Netty my love, I'd forgotten how lovely ... Say it. Say it wasn't for him, say it was for me. Because it worked. I was jealous. I was *so* jealous.'

His embrace tightened and his mouth closed on hers. Netty willed herself to respond. There was still a residue of alcohol-induced lust in her. She tried not to think of Gerald and Annette, of arguments and tension, of reporters, of Danny ... She tried to think just of he and she, of breast meeting hand, of thigh meeting thigh, of her back arching and her head tipping back and her mouth opening under his. He picked her up and carried her through the dim hall and dark hunting chamber, through to the fantasy bed. She closed her eyes, let him pull her dress away, felt his brief departure to divest himself, then his hot skin on hers. If she kept her eyes closed, it would work. Think of the wine and the grapes and the wildness. Think of Edouard dark and suave as a matinée idol. None of it real, none of it as real as Gerald panting in her ear and pushing between her legs.

'Oh Net, oh Net, oh God ...' he gasped.

A few minutes later, 'I'm sorry it was too quick. It's been too long. I couldn't help myself.'

'It doesn't matter, Gerald. It was lovely.'

He was already asleep.

In the morning his attitude was a strange mixture of tenderness and wariness. He was grateful, but grateful in a resentful way, as if he knew he'd been granted only some crumbs from the table and who knew when he'd dine again. His appetite had been whetted, not sated.

She drove him to Bordeaux and had a quick coffee with him at the airport before he caught his flight. They talked superficially, like strangers. She said she'd miss him, but what she meant was him as a male presence round the house, not Gerald himself.

Responsibility

There was an extraordinary sense of freedom in being without Gerald. As Netty drove homewards from Bordeaux, she toyed with the idea of following the signs to Montaigne's tower or visiting the Roman villa at Montcaret. In the end, however, she didn't stop until she reached Bourdonne.

She parked in the Place Gambetta under the shade of plane trees and just wandered. Strolling down the narrow lanes, she looked into the windows full of Belgian chocolates and *foie gras* and wines: Montravel, Pécharmant, Bordeaux. She felt no desire to buy. That was the difference made by living in the area. If she had been a tourist there would have been the pressure to buy the pointless presents and souvenirs that would have verified the experience along with the obligatory snapshots. What a relief it was to be disburdened of that duty. Sending those postcards had been effort enough.

She ended up down by the old quay where once barges had loaded and unloaded goods transported up and down the Dordogne, a river now given up to pleasure craft and a myriad canoes. She ordered a drink at a small café and gazed dreamily at the river, the most placid she had ever seen, its tranquillity inducing a state of meditation. A skein of swans flew downstream, flapping heavily, necks cantilevered out, and ducked under the round-arched bridge. A figure passed, stopped, turned.

'Madame Feldwick?'

Damn, she thought, looking up. Madame Bellenger, cool in cream linen, slid into the seat opposite her.

'I am so glad to run into you. Peter told me at lunch that your husband was going to be away and I am concerned that you may be a little lonely. Will you come to dinner?'

How to get out of it?

'That's very kind of you, Madame.'

'Claudine, I insist.'

'Claudine. But to tell you the truth, we were out last night, and I still feel a bit fragile.' She touched her sunglasses delicately to indicate how fragile she felt, when in fact her hangover had long since evaporated. 'Would you mind if I left it to some other time?'

'Not at all. It is not serious. You're quite right to have a rest — and I don't think Deirdre would be good for you in this condition.'

A smile of complicity. She's no fool, Netty thought. Deirdre's no more to her than the court jester.

'But,' Claudine continued, 'you will come to tea, perhaps, tomorrow? We have not had a proper chance to talk — and we are neighbours, are we not?'

Netty capitulated. 'I'd be glad to come. Thank you.'

'That is good. Tomorrow at three, shall we say? I shall show you Bel Arbre properly. It is my joy and pride. Now I will leave you. *A la prochaine.*'

Netty was beginning to feel like one of the Ladies-Who-Lunch. It was because of having no routine any more. Accidental meetings led to invitations which led to more invitations. It was quite extraordinary.

She came home to a pleasing silence, and set about filling the fridge and the store-cupboards. In Leclerc on the way back she'd grabbed anything that took her fancy from jars of olives and mild gherkins to sweet, creamy desserts in cartons. Easy food to pick at when she liked, no preparation involved. Couch potato food. If only there were something worth watching on the box. As far as she could see, the French viewing public revelled in inane slapstick, adverts full of gratuitous nudity, and pompous post-existential debate. Only the tits on the nubile girls seemed comprehensible to her and their total unsubtlety put paid to any faint aura of sensuality. The language was a meaningless rattle, a music-hall parody, bearing little relation to the carefully paused and crisply enunciated language tapes with which she'd been working.

She poured a glass of Muscadet and toasted her absent husband, thinking of the Lists which normally dominated a tour of duty in a supermarket. Carrying her glass, she mounted the stairs to the tower room and, for the first time in Le Sanglier, her sigh was of pure contentment.

The room was creamy white, cool as muslin drapery in an Indian palace. It was bare, but not stark. It was full of freshness and light. If she had been an artist she would have called it her studio.

Packing cases lay here and there. She had concentrated so hard on sorting downstairs out, partly because of 'guests' seeing it — the housewifely need for approval — that she had scarcely begun up here.

No need to sit in the red dark of the Salle de Chasse. Here she would sit in this chamber of light and sew. Sew herself into serenity: the modern equivalent of those medieval women who had retreated into convents when the world became too much for them, not so much out of piety as a desire for peace and solitude.

She sipped her wine meditatively, standing at the left-hand window, which gave onto the long wavy tiles of the kitchen part of the house, a segment of patio and the woods, held at arm's length. She saw a path lead from the side of the house and duck under the trees and made a note to find out where it led. Really, in spite of having been there for virtually four weeks they hadn't got to know the place at all. Gerald saw only practical problems: get the plumbing seen to, replace that glass, repaint this, rewire that. He had no sense of the spirit of place: how else could he fail to shudder in the Salle de Chasse? And she had been too busy being nervy, resentful and homesick, she saw that now.

Gerald's bluster had been like interference on the radio. Her own thoughts had been cancelled out or distorted by bursts of his static.

It was getting on towards three o'clock, and the sky was shimmering, but when she flung the windows open the woodland air seemed cool and smelt of greenery and sap. Swifts were darting in the air in uncanny swoops.

Netty rummaged in the tallest packing-case, unpacking the hand-frames and the tall floor-frames, the padded bag containing a magnifying glass on a stand, magnetised pattern-holders, embroidery scissors and needlecases. Shoe-boxes full of skeins of thread — cotton perlé and silk — and hanks of tapestry wool carefully sorted and numbered. She liked to run the wool through her fingers, she liked to order it properly, she liked the slight prickle of raw yarn running through canvas to build to denseness of texture and pattern.

From another case she picked out her collection of needlepoint and embroidery pattern books. She turned the crate upside down and lined up the books on it, as a makeshift bookcase.

The third case contained her previous work; years of industry in Oxford had resulted in an array of pot pourri sachets, bookmarks, samplers, pictures, cushions. She'd tried cross-stitch, crewel work, drawn thread work, cutwork, shadow-work and tapestry — most of all tapestry, rich and solid. She was an expert. All her friends and relatives said so, thanking her for yet another handmade Christmas or birthday gift, and saying how refreshing it was to see someone make an effort with a present, make it personal. Christmas is so commercialised, they'd say. She'd smile and she always knew that the bookmark, sachet or pincushion would be salted away in the bottom drawer of the dressing table in the spare bedroom, along with other such clutter — lace hankies, bath salts, fiddly cosmetic brushes in satin roll-up cases — and never see the light of day again.

She sorted through the tiny lace-edged fripperies she had made and the framed pictures of garden-arbours and children in bonnets on swings and cuddly teddies carrying hearts.

It wouldn't do. She sat back on her heels and sighed. These pictures suddenly looked too precious, too sweet and tidy, too Women's Institute. She put them back in their box, carefully folded into protective layers of fabric. As she laid the box back in the packing-case, she allowed the tips of her fingers to settle, just for a moment, on that other box, resting there at the bottom: the special box. 'Leave it all behind,' Gerald had said. Impossible to do so. Although they had sold the house and much of its contents, there was a trunk in storage back in Oxford, and here, nestling in this packing-case, was her personal reliquary. She couldn't leave all of Danny behind her. She needed to know there was still something of him to touch. The box contained photographs, crayon scribbles from playgroup, his birthday cards, his blue pram-bunny, his baby shoes, various cherished items of clothing, a lock of his hair, the plastic hospital-bracelet from when he was born. She didn't remove the lid. She rarely did: it was always too painful. It was enough to resist the horrible temptation, to let her fingertips gently graze the surface of the box. It was sufficient to know that some totemic essence of him lay there, waiting for her to be desperate enough and strong enough to turn to it.

Her glass was empty. She clattered back down the wooden stairs to refill it. It was ripe late afternoon and lethargy possessed her. She'd go and sit in the garden. She didn't want to sit out front; somehow it felt too exposed, too formal. The lawn always seemed to be beckoning one to play croquet, which seemed absurd in a foreign land. She'd be conspicuous out there and easily caught out by any passing visitor.

Netty gathered up a fat airport novel, the bottle, the glass, a patisserie and, bearing all of these on a tray, sallied out through the kitchen door. She made herself believe the intense heat was pleasant. The British were sun-worshippers, after all. One worships the mystery so rarely seen.

She set up a folding chair on the patio, put on her sunglasses, sipped some wine, tried to read. Within minutes she felt her sunglasses slipping on the greasy bridge of her nose. Sweat gathered in the creases under her breasts and the valley between them. Her bra pinched.

The whole of the Périgord had sucked in its breath and held it. Leaves hung limp on exhausted trees forced to stand bare-headed before Apollo. Madness, she now realised, to sit here out in this stone oven when she could be up in the cool box of the tower room. Madness. But she lacked the energy to do anything about it. The book sagged and fell away. The wine grew warm as soup in its glass, and was unpleasant. The weight of heat pressed her into her chair.

When she took her glasses off to wipe her wet forehead the brittle glare of sun on white stone wounded her eyes, making her flinch.

In Oxford, she thought heavily, in Oxford on a hot day there were sprinklers in people's gardens and distant ice-cream vans jingling 'Greensleeves', and there were sparrows and there were bees ...

Her chin sank down as the sun pushed at the nape of her neck.

The ice-cream van played 'Greensleeves' as it turned out of Divinity Road onto the busy Cowley Road. Netty thought, as ever, of the incongruity of a Tudor love-song being used to attract people to scoops of 'often licked, never beaten'. Daniel tugged at her hand and whined a little.

'Don't be silly, Danny. You've only just had your breakfast.'

'But Mummy, please!'

'No!'

She hoped he wouldn't argue. He often did, his face set in lines so like Gerald's. She had a lot on her plate as ever and she just didn't have the time or patience for another wrangle in the street. There was the shopping to be done at Tesco's, the dry-cleaning to be picked up, and get that home before taking Danny to the surgery by eleven forty-five, sore throat again. In my day, she thought, they just whipped your tonsils out.

'Danny, come on, get in your chair.'

He had leapt out of his pushchair at the sight of the ice-cream van. He was now hanging heavily back, knees bending, his little left hand in hers while the fingers of his right hand picked at her grip, trying to get himself free.

'Stop it, Danny! Come on!'

Abruptly he capitulated and settled himself in the buggy. He wouldn't be fastened in, though. He was really too old for it, she knew: he was virtually four, and his legs had stretched so much lately that with his feet on the rest his chin and knees seemed to be on a collision course. But it made the supermarket trip so much easier; she could hang the shopping bags from the handles and push the whole caboodle up the hill. She wished that Gerald would run to getting a second car. But, as he said, where would they park it? Number 143 was a Victorian semi-detached villa, and stood cheek by jowl with its neighbours. There simply wasn't any scope for extending the garage and Gerald wasn't going to leave a car out on the street, not these days, with the level of car-crime in Oxford. Open invitation.

The shopping took ages — why did she always choose the wrong check-out queue — and Danny was fractious even though he normally loved sitting in the trolley, legs dangling and kicking. Not for the first time she thought 'I'm too old for this lark', although she couldn't remember how she'd felt all those years ago with the first two. She must have had more energy then, it stood to reason.

Coming out of Tesco's she realised that Gerald had said he was out of shaving gel, so she nipped into Boots for that. She glanced at her watch. Eleven o'clock. If she left picking up the dry-cleaning till the afternoon, there should be just about time. The buggy was festooned with plastic bags.

It was warm out on the pavement. Autumn hadn't yet really got a grip. Danny rocked backwards and forwards in his pushchair, singing unintelligibly. She looked down at his bright little figure in his red Mothercare sweatshirt and blue jogging pants and red-and-white baseball cap. Really, there was lots of time, and his throat didn't seem to be bothering him that much. No need to feel so tense.

They passed the little patch of greenery with benches and trees, a bus-shelter and various down-and-outs. One was pacing in circles on the grass, bottle dangling from his hand. Netty averted her eyes, looking at the shops across the street. A tap on the shoulder made her jump.

'Hi, Nets! How are things?'

Netty half-turned, her hand balancing the pushchair by the handle, to compensate for the weight of the shopping.

'Carol! God, I've been meaning to ring — but you know how it is ...'

'Do I! I was just saying to John that we hadn't seen you in ages. You must come round some evening. Bring Danny.'

'Carol, that's really kind, but surely it's our turn? Come to us.'

A little jerk of the pushchair and a lightening. The shopping swung *against her so she leaned more heavily on the buggy to counterbalance its weight lest it should topple. Danny, little rascal, must have got out — she'd better grab him — busy street — only Carol was speaking.*

'Don't be daft! It's not a profit-and-loss account you know. That's what comes of being married to a businessman. If you came to us last time, so what? Come again!'

'We'd love to, Carol. Not sure when, though. Gerald has another trip coming up. I'll have to let you know when his Nibs sees fit to tell me the dates!'

'Nothing changes, eh?'

'Nothing!'

The pushchair was now a strain, tipping in spite of her. She turned to unhook a bag or two and place them on the seat to hold it firm.

'Danny, come here — you must stay in the pushchair, darling.'

No Danny.

She looked along the street to the art-shop window. That's where he'd be, looking at the draughtsman's equipment and fine coloured pens. No. Further along, to the luxury car dealer; he loved shiny new cars. What boy didn't? But there was no small red-and-blue figure pressing against the plate glass. Faint unease suddenly blossomed into something stronger and took up residence in her upper gut, restricting the expansion of her lungs.

She turned back. Carol's anxious face panned quickly through her field of vision.

'Netty — what is it?'

'Did you see Danny?' Still her gaze was swivelling. To and fro. Too fast, you've probably gone right past him. Take it easy, look carefully, he'll be there.

'No. No, I didn't see him.'

'He must have got out of his pushchair.'

'Well, it was only just now. He'll be around.' Carol's hand touched her on the forearm, but she couldn't feel it. All she could feel was the dry heavy lump within her. She scanned and scanned. Nothing but a blur.

A screech of brakes. He'd run out into the road! No, it was a car avoiding a cyclist. Curses drifting back to her. She loaded the rest of the bags onto the seat of the pushchair and started walking, uncertainly, changing direction. She knew she was calling his name. Carol was in her wake, still reassuring her, with less and less effect.

The green ground. The tramps. The weirdos. She dashed up to them. One looked at her slack-jawed. A young one cursed and held out a hand. How many had been there before, when she had passed so innocently with her bright child? How many were still there?

Panic unfurled its wings. She was aware of scurrying up and down that two hundred yard stretch of road, the pushchair wobbling in front of her, dropping cucumber and tomatoes from a toppling bag. She returned to Tesco's. Leaving Carol with the buggy, she ran up and down the aisles. The freezers — ice-cream — he wanted an ice-cream! No, not there, hope dashed. Glimpses of curiosity and concern in the eyes of shoppers she passed. She became aware that she was sobbing. How long had passed — ten, fifteen minutes? He must be somewhere else. What was she doing, wasting time in this supermarket? He would be panicking because she wasn't there. She passed Carol and the pushchair. Damn the pushchair. She ran to Boots. She ran back. He might have gone home ... She shouted to Carol and ran on ahead, ran all the way, her lungs burning and her eyes wet. She glanced at the bouncing face of her watch as she pounded up the hill. Eleven forty-five. The doctor's appointment, they'd missed it. How absurd — what did it matter?

The door was locked and no small boy awaited.

She'd run out of options. She tried to control the crying. She couldn't think clearly.

Carol caught up with her and said she'd asked in all the shops on the way. No one had seen anything. That was very good of her. Why hadn't she thought of that?

'That was very good of you Carol — I wish I'd thought —'

Already so much guilt. Letting him go — why didn't she chain him to that chair? What kind of a mother was she? And panicking like that, running all over the place — she'd probably just missed him several times over. What was she doing here, outside her house — how stupid! She must get back there — he'd be there, crying, wanting her, and she wasn't there.

Restraining hands on her shoulders. Carol's face up close.

'Netty, look, you're better staying here — really.'

'But I must get back! Carol, he's wandering about on his own! He's hardly four ... '

'Netty, you've looked and I've looked and everyone in the area knows about it now and I saw a policeman on the beat and told him. He radioed in and they're sending a car round. We'll go inside and we'll wait for them.'

She felt the key being taken from her hand. Carol unlocked the door and ushered her in as if she were a visitor to her own home.

When the police came, one of the first things they did was to send for Gerald. Strange that she had not thought of doing so.

He came home immediately, his face grey and strained. He held her hands at first, sitting crouched beside her, stroking them comfortingly like a priest with a penitent. Hushed voices here and there in the background. The policewoman and Carol made an endless series of cups of tea destined to be sipped once and then left to grow cold.

Comings and goings. Polite uniformed concern. Lots of questions. Even to herself it seemed utterly shameful that she could have been there and noticed so little.

Gerald, now seated in an armchair across the room, exploding into rage.

'Netty! Good God, what were you thinking of, to let him get out of the pushchair?'

'But he always did! He was in and out all the time, he wouldn't stay still, it was always like that. I didn't think ...'

'You didn't think! Jesus God! It's our son's life — and you didn't think!'

Her tears stopped him. He was on his knees beside her.

'I'm sorry, I'm sorry love. I know how he is — like greased lightning — I know.'

The tall officer with the notebook loomed over.

'Mrs Feldwick, did you notice the moment your son got out of his pushchair?'

Yes, she did — that lightening of the load, the unbalanced tipping of the chair. Immediately.

Gerald's breath drawn in and held.

'But, Mrs Feldwick, you didn't actually look round at that point?'

'Well, no ... That is, I meant to, but Carol and I were talking ...' She saw in their faces how it sounded. Two dippy females gossiping and that one couldn't even be bothered to look round. Some people shouldn't be allowed to be parents. They're not fit.

Only it hadn't been like that. It had only been a moment, a sentence, that's all.

'And you didn't see anyone, anyone interesting or suspicious, in the immediate vicinity at that time?'

'No.'

She racked her brains, but all she could think of was the pushchair handle and the pressure of that doctor's appointment and how to cut short the conversation without Carol noticing. She could see Carol's beaming face, the strong cheekbones and wide mouth, and noticing she'd had her hair cut a different way, not sure whether she liked it. None of this useful.

On and on it went. Almost she expected a white spotlight to be angled at her face by the man in the uniform. We have ways of making you talk.

It wasn't really like that. They were quiet and gentle, making the effort to keep their voices non-judgemental. Only her husband had felt free to reproach her. They skilfully drew out of her what little she knew; in particular the details of those shambling figures on the green, ancient tweed coats flapping. She remembered how people like that would get on the bus down by the Social Security office, and would either reek with sodden joviality or harangue the driver with venom and paranoia. How all the passengers would sit with their eyes averted or look at each other in the communion of the respectable against the outcast. How glad one would be if the seat next to one was already filled, a solid middle-class buffer against the rotting tweed and the rank odour and the infested hair.

How many of those rambling drop-outs had there been? Who else had she noticed? No one really — just the usual mingle of shoppers and kids and pensioners and hippies with blue-painted bare feet and sorry-looking dogs.

Anyone, anyone could have seen him. Anyone could have taken

him.

When it got too much, when the questions tailed off in the face of her exhaustion and anguish, and the photo had been handed over and the description sent out, she went to the upstairs bathroom and locked the door. She sat on the side of the bath and looked at the cream Amtico floor. Danny had touched down there for a moment that morning before she wrapped him in a soft towel and bore him away to be dressed. She tried to believe that she could still see the damp imprints of his feet. She knelt down, staring at the floor, willing it to be so.

Gerald went out in his car, driving up and down in distraction. Gerald was a doer. He couldn't sit at peace.

The hours passed. They made the local news that night.

The days passed. They drew the curtains against the bevy of reporters clustered out by the gate.

A week passed, and more. The TV cameras and straining microphones. Great furry booms swaying over her head. Furious clicking of shutters like disapproving teeth.

Trying to hold back her tears, so they would think her brave. Feeling, strangely, as if she were playing a role, as if her performance would be appraised. What did it matter, if they thought her brave? But it always matters, what other people think.

The tears breaking through, a cataract of grief blurring her features, washing away the sight of those eager faces, and those tiny black boxes held out to record and edit her sorrow into sound-bites for the masses.

'Lost toddler's mother pleads ...'

'Fighting back tears, Mrs Feldwick ...'

'Mr and Mrs Feldwick braved reporters today to issue a plea for the safe return of their son Daniel, missing since Tuesday...'

'Fears are increasing ...'

'Hopes are fading ...'

'Mounting concern for the safety ...'

'Local people have been helping in the search for little Danny Feldwick, missing now for two weeks. His parents, Annette and Gerald Feldwick, have once more appealed for his safe return.'

The words she said. The hope like a pain, unbearable. If she could only, somehow, be in time. If she could only, somehow, find the right words to pierce the conscience and mind — the sick mind — of the person who had stolen her child. She ought to be able to, she was the lad's mother, she was irresistible. Soothing and reassuring words, promising understanding and forgiveness. All the while the banshee wail of hatred in her head: you bastard, bastard you harm my child I'll get you by God I swear I'll get you I'll get you I'll kill you. Empty rage, dispensed at no one. Inside her head the lynch-mob bayed for rough justice. Outwardly she conformed to society's rules, said and did the right things. She was a model mother, all through it, they said. Pity and approval. But no one phoning up to say they'd track, find, kill without trial the bastard who took her son.

The trial was for herself, inside her head. Endlessly she prosecuted herself for that moment's inattention that had left Danny exposed. Like the zebra that strolls a fatal step or two away from its tottering young when the lions prowl or the jackals circle.

All those words. Six weeks of them, and for most of that time, he was dead.

Nightmare

Something ran across her foot and she startled awake. She stared foggily around, felt the familiar constriction in her throat that meant tears and opened her mouth wide to ease it, like trying to chase a yawn away. No tears. No tears. No tears.

The patio was shadowed now, the sun had sunk so low. Her watch told her an hour had passed. She felt stiff and sick, and made a face when she tried tasting the stale wine. To the other side of her chair ants had taken up residence among the crumbs of strawberry tart.

Netty hoisted herself out of the chair. She was at a loss. For a moment she missed Gerald's chatter. The house was no refuge; she couldn't bear to go inside. It would lead to weeping. She mustn't weep. Her eye was caught by a movement at the far end of the patio. A bird of some sort hopped into the shadows. She saw the path leading under the trees. She'd go for a walk, explore. She'd go on a nature ramble, like they used to do at school.

But with no teacher there to tell her the names of plants, she soon realised she'd forgotten virtually everything. She could recognise an oak, or a birch, and holly, of course — but so many others remained nameless. It seemed an insult, somehow, not to be able to acknowledge their true identity.

The path came to a junction, where she stood undecided for a moment. To the right it curved downwards, to the left it bent uphill. She still wanted to see if there was a view; from this sort of height it ought to be possible to see over the ridge beyond Malignac, perhaps to the Dordogne itself. Up she went.

It was the wrong choice. Within a few minutes the path became narrower and less even. Hog's-backs covered with briars crossed it; she had to slither down and clamber up muddy slopes, searching for the now barely-visible pathway through. She was a fool to go on but somehow kept expecting that past the next obstacle, or the one after that, it would ease, and there would be the clearing and the panorama she envisaged.

The trees up here seemed older, darker, denser. The briars were vicious. She couldn't believe the thickness of some of the stems and cried out in pain as they hooked at her.

Going back now seemed as bad a prospect as soldiering on. At least it could be said that this was a distraction from thoughts of Danny. A coiling root took her by the ankle and threw her flat. She went wild, picking herself up to kick out at stone and trunk and branch. She hated the impassive evil of inanimate nature, sitting there, just sitting there to impede her. Its uncaringness was worse than any personal malevolence. It was like the faceless man who chose her boy out of many, who chose her life to ruin, out of so many.

'*Why me?* she screamed. A nearby bird flapped off in search of peace elsewhere.

She sat down heavily and wept after all.

Of course, in the end the weeping exhausted itself. She was left with a gripping headache and itchy eyes. It was taking her a while to gather up the energy to tackle the woods again. A kind of paralysis took hold of her and she sat there leadenly on the ground, staring at nothing.

Then, all of a sudden, there *was* something. A quick, skittish movement, and a deer stood in front of her, small and perfect, a doe. They stared at one another for a moment. She saw its quick breathing under the beige flanks, the tiny hoofs. Flies darted round the flicking ears.

Netty felt as if she hadn't breathed for several years. Her chest hurt and tiny spots danced in front of her eyes. She tried exhaling in slow motion, as if in a yoga exercise. Then she couldn't resist; she slowly reached out a hand and gently clicked her tongue. She was no longer content to watch — she had the irresistible desire to stroke its soft coat.

The little deer took a step backwards, paused, then wheeled and trotted off. Netty couldn't help but follow. Her clumsy human footsteps unnerved the creature further and it accelerated away into the gathering shadows under the trees. Netty was annoyed with herself. Why was there always the human compulsion to treat an animal like a cuddly toy? She should have let it be.

At least it had got her going again. Her watch told her it was seven o'clock, her stomach told her it was time for a decent meal. It took a good half-hour's scramble more or less back the way she'd come. Eventually Le Sanglier loomed up through the trees.

The phone was ringing. She barked her shin painfully on the rocking chair as she dived to answer it.

'Netty?'

'Oh, hello Gerald.'

'You OK?'

'Why?'

'You sound out of breath.'

'Oh, I've just had a bit of a dramatic walk, out in the woods. I've just got back.'

'You didn't get lost, did you?'

''Fraid so.'

'Net — I've only been gone a few hours! Silly girl — you can't be left, can you!' A pause, while she tried to get her breathing under control, to calm anger as well as exertion. 'Net — you still there? Look, I feel really bad about this: it looks like it's going to be a week at least; things are in a right muddle at this end. You don't mind, do you?'

'Why should I mind? I'm perfectly fine.'

'OK, OK, I believe you! House all right?'

'Yes, Gerry. It hasn't fallen down in the past nine hours, in spite of you not being here to shore it up.'

'God, Netty, there's no need to take that attitude. How many times do I have to apologise?' His hand went over the receiver; she could hear his blurred voice. Her blood boiled at the thought of his injured-husband act put on for Roy and Sheila. 'We're just off out,' he continued. 'We're going to the Beaumont for a meal, the three of us. Do you want a word with Sheila?'

'No, not really. Tell her I'll phone later in the week. I'm a bit tired just now.'

More mutterings behind the palm of his hand. She knew Sheila would understand, though.

'Well, I'll save the phone-bill. You be sure to lock up properly.'

'*Yes*, Gerald.'

'Take care, then, love.'

'You too, Gerry.'

It was a long evening, spent mostly in front of the telly, which she'd brought through to the kitchen. She was not going to sit by herself in the Salle de Chasse. She didn't care what was on, scarcely registered the flickering screen. It was just a noise to fill the empty spaces of the house.

At midnight the phone rang again, startling her out of her trance-like state.

'Mum?'

'Paul! What on earth are you ringing for, at this time of night? Not that I'm not glad to hear from you, but ... nothing's wrong, is there?'

'No Mum. Look, I'm sorry, I forgot about the time difference. I just wanted to know how you were.'

'I'm fine.'

'Only, I hadn't heard anything from you in a while.'

'I'm sorry love. It's the social whirl out here — really, you'd be amazed.'

'Yeah, Dad said.'

'You've been speaking to your father?'

'Yes. Well, he rang this evening, not long ago. He'd just got back from the Beaumont.'

'Ah, I see.'

'Look Mum, don't take offence. He was a bit worried about you, all on your own.'

'He shouldn't have left me then.'

'Mum! He knew you'd take that attitude, that's why he didn't ring again.'

'Got you to do his dirty work for him.'

'You realise that you're putting him in a no-win position? Damned if he rings, damned if he doesn't. But he does care — and besides, *I* care. You know what I thought of the pair of you galloping off to pastures new. To be honest, I'm amazed you've lasted this long.'

'It's not so bad. In some ways it's better than I expected. Your Dad did have a point about a change of scene.'

'That's good. But you seem a long way away.'

'Oh, come on Paul, don't sound so lost! We hardly saw you, when you were only sixty miles away. You can always come out and visit.'

'I just might do that.'

'You sound tired.'

'I am, Mum — nothing new in that.'

'Don't overdo it, now, will you?'

'For goodness' sake, the whole point of me ringing up was to show concern for *you!*'

'I told you, I'm fine. Nothing's going on that hasn't been going on for the past five years. Right?'

'Right.'

'How did your Dad sound?'

'Heavy. A bit the worse for wear. He didn't come back to Oxford to hurt you, you know.'

'I know.'

'I gather Roy's in the shit up to here and Dad just can't leave him in it. But he'd had a few tonight and, well, I think the memories were getting to him.'

'Poor Gerry. I didn't really think of that.'

'That's the trouble with you two — you go around hermetically sealed into your own little worlds. You've had all these years together but half the time neither of you has a clue what the other's thinking.'

'You should go into marriage counselling.'

'Sorry, I don't mean to patronise. But you will phone me if you feel down or if you need someone to talk to?'

'Of course I will,' she said. Of course I won't, she thought.

'I mean it.' A pause. 'I'm your son too.'

Before going to bed she went up to the tower room again. It was ghostly grey in the moonlight, utterly blank and still. Outside, massed banks of cloud were bearing down on the fleeting moon.

She stood at the top of Southfield Road. The pushchair slipped from her grasp and rolled away down the steep hill. Her efforts to follow were in vain; she looked down and found her feet had melted into the pavement. The buggy began to bounce and ricochet off bumps and gaps in its passage. It veered to the left, out of sight. She was on her knees, sinking down into the ground. The pavement rose like a wind-blown carpet and covered her head.

Netty shuddered awake. It was pitch-dark. Her breathing took some minutes to calm. It was horribly dark, dark as that pit under an Oxford pavement.

She turned over, reaching for Gerald. He was not there. The realisation came to her that he was far away, in England, lying probably in a snoring stupor after an evening at the Beaumont. He'd have had the rack of lamb — he always did.

Netty was alone in Le Sanglier, in the night.

She rolled back to her side of the bed. The darkness seemed to be pressing on her. She'd have been glad even of Gerald's furtive nocturnal pestering, tonight. She closed her eyes. Opened them. Why was it so dark? Normally some light filtered in through the curtains at the French windows. Outside an owl started hooting, and there was the shrill shriek of some tiny creature dying. Netty's heart began to trip.

She looked to the left. A faint green glow told her the time: two fifteen. God-awful time of night. If it had been anywhere near dawn she'd have got up. She still could, of course; she could pad through to the kitchen, make herself a nice cup of tea, see if French TV, rubbish as it was, ran through the night. Her hand clenched on the bedcovers, ready to throw them back. Then she remembered — she'd have to pass through the hunting chamber. She wasn't as desperate as all that for a drink.

She sighed, closed her eyes once more, willed herself to sleep. She was on her back, her hands clasped on her breast. Like a figure on a tomb. Her skin began to crawl and itch. It was so hot, as if there was a storm coming. She pushed aside every cover, lay there in her nightie, bare-legged. Then she felt a cool draught, waxing and waning, breathing over her shins. Irritably, she pulled her sheet back over. There was no winning.

More minutes. Her lungs didn't seem to fill properly: her breathing was too light, too shallow, too fast, like a cat's. She tried to imagine her lungs like bellows and inflate them slowly, fully. She pushed her stomach out, to draw in more air. You always read how people only breathe with the top part of their lungs. And think with only ten per cent of their brains. What a waste. What's the rest of it doing?

Exasperated, she leaned over and switched on the bedside light. By its weak illumination she saw movement in the corner of the room, over by the window. Her heart stopped, then raced.

After gazing at the corner for some moments, she willed herself to believe it was nothing, and reached for her book. She propped herself up on pillows and told herself this was comfy and cosy. The words on the page meant nothing to her, even though she stared at them resolutely. Had it been a mouse? She didn't really mind them — but then she thought of how they are supposed to gnaw through wiring and start fires. Had it been a spider? God she hoped not. Gerald had killed so many but there were always more. Maybe it had come across the floor. It could be crawling up the bed, like in that James Bond film. If she slept it could crawl on her face ...

She sat rigidly, staring at the end of the bed, expecting the first waving legs to hoist the bulbous spider body over the edge. With every sense alert, all sound was magnified, every shadow distorted. On the walls, little marks and cracks in the plaster seemed to sprout feelers and legs and waver towards her. She drew her knees up. Above her the patter of something across the ceiling and beyond the window a rustle and crunch on the gravel border.

This is ridiculous, she made herself think and applied herself to the novel. It was no use. Her eyes kept darting from the page as if to catch something in the act of bearing down on her. When she moved the bed creaked. All she needed was the sound of wind or wolf, howling on the moors.

Blue-white light strafed the room, there and gone. She leapt out of bed — never mind the spider — and ran to the window. Out in the dark, dry lightning was flickering. She counted the seconds, but no thunder came. It seemed even more frightening, somehow, without the thunder. Just cat's-paws of shuddering light illuminating a dark yellow sky. The air was charged, with no sense of the imminent release of rain.

Netty decided she'd have that cup of tea after all. She pulled her thin dressing-gown on, more out of habit than anything else, it was so warm. She opened the bedroom door. Immediately, she heard the thin unearthly whine of a mosquito drifting past, so she shut the door smartly behind her. She'd run out of those evil-smelling little tablets for the mozzie-killing device she plugged into a socket each evening, and she didn't relish spending the rest of the night with ears pricked for that eerie sound.

It was very dark in the passage-way. She felt for the light-switch, couldn't find it. The mosquito passed close by her ear, making her prickle. She swatted at it savagely and bruised her elbow against the wall. The sound of bone on plaster rang loud in the confined space and was followed by the fall of dust and debris behind the partition. She covered the sound of her heart with a loud 'Damn it!' and stepped forward, feeling her way into the Salle de Chasse. Why the hell did the kitchen have to be at the other end of the house?

There was no light. Absolutely none. She'd forgotten about the shutters. Gerald had fastened all of them earlier in the day, except for those in the tower-room, when they set off for Bordeaux. Shutters were all very well — very picturesque — but they did make locking up the house a palaver. She knew that most people just locked the doors, left the shutters open — but she and Gerald had been extra careful. Burglary was rife back in Oxford, so they hadn't yet felt like letting down defences.

On her return from the airport she'd opened up the kitchen and the bedroom. She always slept with the bedroom shutters open anyway: the darkness was too tangible, the air too dense, otherwise. But suddenly she was aware of her own vulnerability, sleeping in a bedroom in a house on a hill, all on her own.

Once more she rummaged around for the switch, this time found it. Oh, the basic human relief of seeing light defeat darkness, a relief going back to the caveman striking primitive fire in the cave, the ancient mystery of clarity conquering confusion, creation vanquishing the pit.

In the dark it seemed as if things could possess life of their own. As the light came on, the sofa, the coffee-table, the bookcase, the rug and every small thing seemed to freeze into immobility like children in a game of Grandmother's Footsteps.

Netty started across the room, feeling the presence of it, not liking, almost, to turn her back on it. She had just passed Gerald's drinks cabinet when a moth of grotesque size collided with the overhead light, there was a delicate *ping* and the bulb fused.

As in her dream, darkness thick and smothering swooped in and down. She took one more step and fell onto the sofa. Its soft covers welcomed her, she grabbed a cushion and hugged it to her. This was silly: just lean over, there's a table-lamp on the coffee-table, grope around, the switch is partway down the flex, damn fool place to have it ...

A beating on the shutters, a flurry of wings, a shriek. The flex twisted, the lamp fell away. Netty on her knees, scrabbling. The air full of movement, as if the shutters had opened to the cloud-quilted sky.

A man's voice murmuring rhythmically, passionately, the clatter of boots on the tiles, a monotonous drumming, a girl's scream, a woman's moan.

The little light went on, casting a tilted beam from under the skewed lampshade, up at the tiles. Netty stared at arrows and blood and moist beseeching eyes. This place was evil ... 'Gerald,' she gasped, getting to her knees, tumbling again as her foot caught in the hem of her nightdress. The room was suddenly full of pleading and pursuit.

The Maclaren pushchair rolled down the hill.

Netty battered about the room, blundered through the corridor, back into her bedroom.

Her child called to her from that faraway grove where he lay, face-down, mouth full of moss. A young girl in a muslin gown drifted past her. A man in uniform stood by the wardrobe and smiled at his reflection. Deep in the woods a horned beast arose.

Confusion and panic grew as vision after vision assaulted her. Desperate to escape the phantasmagoria, she somehow reached the French window. She wrenched at the door-handles, the curlicued key fell from the lock and she was through, across the gravel, across the dry springy lawn.

Her fleet steps soon took her under the arms of the trees. For a moment she feared the crackle of lightning coming to incinerate her, but the lightning had stopped, and her dread of that house drove her on, downhill, scrambling along in the dust, slithering on pebbles, away from the hill and the exposure, down into the valley scented with gently ripening grapes, fuzzy, warm still with the memory of the day. She skidded at the corner of the lane and fell on her side. There was a light. She got up and went to it. There was a door. She knocked and knocked. She could hear her own breath juddering in and out, and there was a sharp stitch in her side. The door opened. He was old and silver and safe, his hand reached out and drew her out of the night.

Tapestries

It was like walking into a temple. Dimly, after his first exclamation of concern, she was aware of him gently ushering her, like a priest into the holy of holies. She clutched her dressing-gown defensively to her. Her feet were bare and dirty. Now that her breathing was beginning to slow down, embarrassment, the true prerogative of the English, was setting in. She heard herself apologising for disturbing him.

'Don't worry, you didn't wake me up. I'm so old I hardly need to sleep these days. I was just doing a little bit of late night reading. Now, before you tell me what's happened, sit yourself down. You look like you need a nice hot cup of tea. Standard English panacea.'

'What?'

'Cure-all.'

While he was in the kitchen, she looked around. Dark oak beams ran across the low ceiling and appeared at intervals along the walls. To Netty's left was an enormous fireplace, barren on this hot night. The great stones that had given the place its solidity were here left bare.

Around the room open and glazed cases held all sorts of ancient artefacts. It was like straying into the Ashmolean, Netty thought. There were Roman lamps, potsherds and small marble statues. There were tall bookcases full of plum-coloured old leather tomes and brightly-bound modern volumes. She got up to look more closely. A whole shelf was devoted to the works of Professor R. V. J. Appleby.

The God Within Time, the God Without: Two Faces of the Zoroastrian Zurvan; Syncretism in the late Roman Empire; The Devouring Goddess: Analogues of Kali and the Mexican Eagle Mother;

Mithras the Deliverer; The Cambridge Ritualists: a New Assessment; Celtic Otherworldly Feasts; The Bronze Liver of Piacenza: New Insights into Etruscan Hepatoscopy.

Against the wall opposite the fireplace, stood a high table of dark oak. Above it was a photograph of a rock carving of an enormously obese woman patting her belly and brandishing a horn. On the table were a marble statue of a foot, cut off at the ankle, and a small bronze figure of a pop-eyed god holding a phallus larger than himself. Netty's eyes widened.

She heard the Professor chuckle behind her. 'He's a lad, isn't he!' he said.

'Well, he's not effeminate, that's for sure! Is he old?'

'Very. He's the god Priapus, the Roman god of male fertility. Hence the rather obvious appendage he's so proud of.'

'My God, they worshipped that sort of thing, did they? I thought it was all Jupiter and what's his name — the sun god, in the chariot — I remember the story ...'

'Apollo. Or Phoebus. Oh yes, they worshipped gods of the sky and the light. But they had stolen a lot of it from the Greeks and the Greeks worshipped gods of darkness and the earth as well. Gods like Dionysus, or Bacchus.'

'Wine, wasn't he? You see pictures of him on adverts for wine-merchants.'

'Yes; jolly soul with a cup in the hand and a crown of grapes. But that's a simplification. Dionysus is actually a very complex god. He's the master of intoxication, and even of madness. He can be destructive to an extreme, or he can be an innocent child dismembered by brutal forces ...'

Netty caught her breath but said nothing.

'Sometimes he comforts the dying. Sometimes he sends madness as a means of healing. Sometimes he mediates between the male and the female. He's a cryptic, androgynous figure with a smile that makes the Mona Lisa's look like the epitome of clarity.'

His guest tried to look as if she understood all this. The Professor moved on to the sculpted foot, its elegant white curves, its sandal of many thongs criss-crossing up to the ankle, the slight flex of the arch, the barely noticeable splaying of the toes under pressure as if the owner of the foot were about to spring forward. 'This is Parian marble, pure and cold as milk. Most men, I suppose, would have busts of helmed Athene or torsos of athletes on display. I think this foot is as beautiful as anything I've ever seen. It could belong to Diana the huntress herself, running through the woods up there.'

Netty could not comment, for now the shock had set in; her shoulders were heaving and she was in his arms being cossetted.

'I'm sorry ... I'm sorry. God, what you must think of me. But that house — I think it's haunted, Fred. There were voices and, and *noises* and that *room*, it was like a trap closing, so I just, just *ran*. And I can't go back.'

'No, you mustn't go back. Don't worry. Stay here tonight. A house like that is no good for anyone on their own — not if they've got any degree of sensitivity. I wouldn't fancy it myself. And you're city-bred aren't you — well, there's all sorts of strange noises in the country at night, enough to give anyone the creeps, particularly when you're not used to it.'

He led her back to the sofa. 'Sod the tea,' he said, 'you need a stiff brandy.' She sat helplessly sobbing — second time that day, how ridiculous. So much for being strong and independent without Gerald.

'I feel so ashamed. My husband's hardly out the door and I have to come running here, just because you're a man. I mean, how feeble can you get.'

'Not at all. It's not like that. Something really frightened you and I'm saying to you that I don't like the looks of that Salle de Chasse myself. So please don't apologise for being human. Now drink up your brandy and talk to me. What happened up there tonight?'

'It just sounds daft, Fred, if I try to put it into words. I woke up and things just built up from there: the sound of wings flapping, something crying out, the spider ...' She shuddered. He merely nodded and waited. 'But it was so much worse,' she went on, 'when I went into that bloody room! The main light went out and the lamp fell over and I heard all sorts of peculiar things — voices, mutterings, and this girl went past me dead-white and there was another man smiling at a mirror and I think someone else wearing a fancy waistcoat. I remember admiring the embroidery, because I can recognise good work when I see it.' She stopped. 'I'm going out of my mind!'

His gaze held hers. 'Annette, as I said, it's an old house and you're out in the country and you said yourself you were in the dark. The brain has amazing powers of creation in the night. Everything, all sensation ... memory ... is magnified.'

She nodded. 'I suppose so.'

'I remember a tree outside my window when I was a lad,' he reminisced, talking lightly. 'During the day it was a friendly old oak, home for squirrels, climbing-frame for a boy like me. But on nights when the moon came out to play, there was one branch, which was just at a certain angle, and was all gnarled and twisted. To me, lying there shivering in my bed, it was everything from a striking snake to a witch's arm reaching out to grab me. It was the essence of evil. And after every one of those petrifying fits I'd go out in the morning and there it was, just an old oak tree with dead bits and bark peeling and lichen growing.' After a moment's silence, he added, 'My dear, there's more to it, isn't there? I feel there's a lot more going on in you than you say. Please tell me to mind my own business, if you like, but ...'

She twirled the brandy glass between the palms of her hands, looking down at it steadfastly while his 'but' hung in the air and gently faded. He was patient, she'd give him that.

'Fred, you know at that dinner party — at the end of that dinner party. What was said. What came out.'

'I know I heard of a dreadful tragedy and I know I saw some fairly necrophiliac behaviour, yes.'

She wasn't quite sure what he meant by that, but responded to the restrained sympathy in his voice.

'Well, since Danny, since he died, things have been bad between Gerald and me. Not that they were perfect before, really, but the cracks could be papered over back then. But since we lost Danny, we're together and we're not together, if you see what I mean. We still have things in common, our other children, for a start, but they're grown up ... and I still love Gerald, I think, but it's a feeling that's gone away and hidden itself somewhere deep and it doesn't poke its head out much. Most of the time I just feel ... oh, frustrated and tired and cut off — most of all just cut off, when I watch him at his antics, and I think to myself — that's my husband, that's the father of my children, but he might as well be an alien from the planet Zog for all he means to me.'

The glass was warm between her hands, rolling to and fro. Then it began to shimmer before her eyes.

'Look, Fred, I don't think I can go on — I'm going to snivel again. It's just ... it's just... I'm so used to bottling it up, it's been the only way to have some dignity.'

He came across to sit beside her. He took her hand.

'I know. I understand. We're very English, you and I, and the English way of death is not to make a fuss, not to be an embarrassment to others, but it's a recent, unhealthy tradition.'

She was scarcely listening. She turned her streaming face to him and cried, 'But why me? Why *us*? Why my Danny? All those years of reading reports of other people's tragedies and you'd think for a minute "Oh, the poor things" and you would really feel it, but just for a minute, and turn the page. And then it happens to you, and you hear the talk and see the glances at you — half sorry, half gloating, and the newspaper reports are about you, and you affect someone's life for a moment, then for them you're old news, but for you it goes on and on, horribly real, there all the time and worse and worse after the drama and the attention and the funeral. You have to go on, and you don't know how you will but you do — and your own little drama turns into ... solitary confinement.'

Sobs were shaking her. 'Fred, didn't you think when your wife was ill, why her, why *me?*'

'Of course. Of course I did. But it doesn't get you anywhere. It's egotistical really, to think that because we are who we are, not a bad person, nobody important, nobody criminal, that somehow we should be protected, that awful things shouldn't happen. Innocence is no protection.

'I was so angry when Miriam was dying. I had to watch her in pain and I had to watch those awful treatments, which never had much hope of success and yet had to be tried, just in case. I had to watch her, withered and bald until she looked as her relatives in Auschwitz would have looked, as if Hitler and Heydrich had at long last struck her down ...'

'Auschwitz?'

'Yes. Miriam was a French Jew. She managed to get out and come to England, when she was quite young. We met at University. I'd never met anyone like her. She was utterly determined about life — about living life. Whenever I was with her, it was as if the whole world came into sharper focus — the smell of coffee, the feel of fabric, the sound of rain — all of it just that bit more real. I think she had this intense thirst for reality because of what her family had suffered in the war. Like us, like everybody, she thought — why me, why this life, why do some die and some survive, why do certain deaths have a logic and completion, why are some so cruel and to our human sense of order, totally unjust, utterly arbitrary?'

He sighed. He was still grasping Netty's hand; she could feel the pulses in his fingertips. Netty thought, with the usual gut-clenching hatred, of her son's murderer, the faceless bogeyman who couldn't be shut out in the darkness, who had stretched vicious fingers into her nice safe middle-class world and snatched her joy away.

She thought, briefly, before making herself retreat, as always, of her son's pain. His physical pain. His need of her. Of her not being there. No. She could not think of that. From the moment of his conception she had been there. He had floated in the dim red haven of her. The world had been filtered for him by her. Nothing got past her — until the end. There he had been, exposed, alone, and she couldn't bear to imagine what his frightened child's perceptions must have been.

She returned to the present, to the quiet beamed room and the eternal artefacts sitting calmly in their cases: the flexed white foot, the urgent little god, the shallow lamps waiting to be lit, all the relics of an ancient era, all the museum pieces which had once been commonplace possessions.

The Professor's shoulder was thin and bony against her. The tiny crisp rustle of fabric signalled the breath going in and out of him. He was alive but oh so fragile, the pulse at his fingertips as quick as a bird's heart.

He squeezed her hand and pulled her to her feet. 'To bed,' he said firmly. He guided her to the spare room and pointed out where the bathroom was. When she emerged, he solemnly presented her with striped pyjamas. She cuddled them to her. Thanked him.

He paused in the doorway, slightly bent like a narrow yew bow.

'If you need anything, I'm here.' He nodded his head at her, quickly. He was going.

Embarrassment flooded back, washing away the trancelike sense of harmony. She was going to wear the pyjamas of an aged academic she scarcely knew. She'd talked about Danny. She'd beaten at his door like a mad thing. Her apologies came stuttering out to be dismissed by a wave of his hand. He withdrew. At least her fear was gone, already so far back in the night that it seemed to belong to another time and to have been felt by another woman, a frail blonde Mrs Feldwick, temporarily husbandless, understandably nervous.

She surprised herself by waking very early. The quality of the light spoke of dawn. She padded across to the window and looked out.

The sky above was a rich electric blue, vibrant, deep. To her right stretched the downward slope of vine-covered fields, bending down into a crease then rising up over the next shallow hill.

As she watched, the sun surged up over the hill, launching warm light into the sky and flooding the vineyards. Everything sprang into definition, crisp and raw. Birds yammered their way past, and up in the woods was the extraordinary resonating sound of a woodpecker in action.

She left the curtains open and went back to the still-warm bed. In spite of the traumas of the night before, she could not sleep. She lay there in the glowing bedroom and relished the state of being alive.

It was a simple white room, not very tidy. Books stood in piles or had toppled over into colourful Giants' Causeways on either side of the bed. A frameless mirror was propped on an old dressing-table, beside a bronze statue of a god with many lively arms and legs, and a rush-seated chair held her discarded night things. A cardboard box on the floor was brimming with papers. She sat up straight in bed and leaned outwards to peer into it. The word 'Symposium' made her sink back, impressed. Another cardboard box held ten bottles of wine, shoulder to shoulder.

There was no dust. Probably stern Mathilde came in here and clicked her tongue and flicked her duster but had been warned not to interfere. Didn't all men warn women not to touch their important papers, not to approach the exalted zone of meetings and conferences and reports? Gerald always had.

She wondered if her husband was awake. She wondered if he had a hangover. She found she didn't care. She realised that yesterday's out-of-school exuberance had returned; that feeling she'd had as she had driven back from the airport, knowing she could go anywhere she pleased and choosing not to because the knowledge of the possibility was enough.

She might have dozed. A quiet knock at the door brought her back. The Professor entered with a mug of coffee. She felt rumpled and self-conscious. She never wanted to leave his spare bed. He didn't say much, just, 'Take your time, the day is young,' and left.

She luxuriated some more but then felt it was bad form to overstay her welcome. Opening the door she found he'd left some clothes out on a stool for her: cord trousers and a big beige T-shirt.

In the kitchen he prepared some scrambled eggs and warmed up some croissants. 'Yesterday's, I'm afraid. Must pop down to the *boulangerie* later.'

'Thanks for the clothes,' she said, awkwardly hoisting the trousers up; their male waistband kept sitting on the outermost points of her hips.

'Well, I realised that last night you were somewhat *deshabillée* ...'

They exchanged empty comments on the quality of the eggs; the rich gold of the yolks because the birds were corn-fed. She couldn't wait to leave.

'I'll come with you.'

'Oh no — I've put you to too much trouble already.'

'Don't argue. I'll come and exorcise the dratted house for you.'

Suddenly she remembered her fear; a wispy thing in the light of day, but still enough of it latent to make her glad of his company.

'Look, you go on. I'll just pile the dishes up and I'll be with you,' he said over his shoulder. She left the clattering and the clinking and slipped out.

Le Sanglier looked sad and dull, in spite of the light. They went from room to room and Fred swung the shutters open for her. The Salle de Chasse was stuffy, with beams of dust-laden sun playing above their heads from the high-set embrasures, like searchlights at a Stalag.

Netty picked up the fallen lamp, replaced it on the table. Fred put a new bulb in the overhead light.

'All set,' he said.

She felt so awkward, continually thanking him and hitching up his trousers. She was surprised to find that she wanted him to go.

He nodded. 'Listen, I'm afraid I have to go off to Bourdonne. Meeting at the bank to sort out transfers of cash, etcetera. Boring, but there you are. Will you be OK? Or would you like to come with me?'

'No, no, I'll be fine.'

'Well, what about later?'

'Actually, I've just remembered. I'm supposed to be having tea with Madame Bellenger this afternoon.'

'You're honoured! No, really, beneath that "let them eat cake" veneer, there's a heart of gold, honestly. Sounds like she's thawing out towards *you*, anyway.'

'She makes me a bit nervous ...'

'To tell you the truth, she makes *me* nervous too. She has that effect on everyone except the Lukers, who are impervious. Anyway, you've got my number — any problem, just ring. How long is your husband going to be away?'

'I don't know.'

'Well, as I say, anytime you need some company, you know where I am.'

She escorted him to the door.

'Look — you and Gerald, how long have you been out here?'

'A couple of months.'

'And how much have you seen of the area?'

'Not much.'

'I thought so: too busy dealing with this mouldering pile! I'd say you need to get out and about a bit. Let me show you some of the sights. What d'you think?'

'Well ... it would be a pity for Gerald to miss out. Maybe I should wait for him to get back.'

'Nonsense! Do your own thing, Annette. You can always see the places again with him. Most of the sights are so rewarding they can stand being seen twice over, or more, come to that. Deal?'

'Deal.'

'*That's* all right then. 'Bye!'

Netty had a blissfully hot shower and dried her hair carefully. The sun had gently bleached it. She amused herself by pulling it into a French pleat. 'Call me Ingrid!' she said to her reflection in the mirror.

At three precisely she presented herself at Bel Arbre, feeling as if she were there for a job interview.

Madame Bellenger served tea in the salon. It was Earl Grey tea, of course. Netty had never much liked it. It was like sipping perfume. She longed for a good strong cup of Sainsbury's Assam.

'How are Felix and Deirdre?' she asked.

'Oh, they are very well. They have taken a couple of days to visit Rocamadour. It is a famous attraction, you understand. Very dramatic. You must go to see it: the village is built on a very high cliff, and it has been a site for pilgrims for many centuries. However, my friends Luker are not particularly devout. It is in the nature of a second — or perhaps twenty-second, shall we say? — honeymoon.'

Claudine's smile was sweet and tolerant, quite unlike her chiselled voice.

'Professor Appleby,' Netty said, 'has been kind enough to volunteer to show me the sights. You would recommend Rocamadour, then?'

'Oh indeed, but it is at a distance. There are many other places much closer which deserve attention. It depends on your taste. You have a liking for history?'

'Oh yes. Well, that is, I've never been able to pursue such a thing. I was going to do a course once but ... circumstances wouldn't allow. But I do feel I'd like to get to know the area, especially as we're living here now.'

'This is good. I would be very pleased to be of assistance.'

'You're very kind. But I know it's tedious to have to keep showing strangers round your home territory. I know it used to drive Gerry and me mad in Oxford, trailing round the colleges, and punting and so on. I've *never* liked punting, it's so awkward and you worry about falling in ...'

'It is no trouble, Madame. You must realise, I lived with my husband in Paris for many years. It is only since his death that I have returned to the Périgord. It was associated with my forebears, as was this house and we — Henri and I — wished to retire here, as you have done, but *hélas,* it was not to be. I am here, as you see, alone.' She paused and sighed gently. Netty sipped some more tepid scented tea. 'But to return; it does not bore me in the least, to show strangers the delights of *le pays de l'homme.* There are the caves, the castles and *bastides,* and there is the land itself, its richness, so many pleasures it offers to the eye and to the taste. Cèpes, walnuts, truffles, tobacco, the grape ... But, Madame, I will be boring you — and along will come the Professor and he will lecture you more! Would you like some more tea? And do have some more gâteau, I insist.'

Netty accepted them both and said, 'Please call me Annette.'

'Certainly, if you will in turn call me Claudine. I think we shall be friends, shall we not?'

Netty felt it was almost in the nature of an order. The next moment, she noticed the slight swelling of varicose veins under the fine stockings covering Claudine's slender legs. Netty wondered how old she was. A decade or so more than Netty? In her late fifties, rich and alone, surrounding herself with fatuous hangers-on like Peter and Deirdre. A mixture of vanity and grace, like the best of history's aristocratic personages. Netty perceived the hollowness of it all, like an empty Fabergé egg.

'I believe your husband mentioned that you have other children?'

'Yes. Yes, a boy and a girl. That makes them sound so young! They're both grown up, so we don't see as much of them as we'd like. Lynda's in America; she's married with three children. She lives in Richmond, Virginia. It's a beautiful place, but, being so far away, as I said, I don't see all that much of her.'

'And your son — I think your husband mentioned he is a financial dealer?'

'That's right. Paul's done very well for himself. But he's twenty-five, Lynda's twenty-seven. They've grown up. They have their own lives.'

'What did they think of your coming on retreat to France?'

'They were horrified! No, I don't mean they don't like France,' Netty added hastily. 'They love it. They just don't see the reason for actually living here. They think we'll just be fish out of water.'

'Fish out of water?'

'You know,' Netty mimed gasping for air. Madame chuckled. 'To tell you the truth, I often think they were right. I can't see myself ever feeling truly settled here.'

'It will take time, Annette. I know it is strange. But already you are making friends, are you not? And you do not need your husband beside you, either.'

'No,' she answered, half-surprised. 'No, I don't.' Except in the middle of the night in that bloody house.

'Besides, it was necessary to get away from England, no? Put bad things behind you. I felt the same when I left Paris. Everyone asked me "Why do you leave your so beautiful apartment?" But, I knew. It was a part of my life that was over. I put it away.'

'I don't know, Claudine. I wanted to leave the gossip, but I didn't want to leave Oxford ...' She thought of his little room, everything in its place. It was still in her head, of course, but she couldn't walk in there and dust his toys and sit on the edge of his narrow bed and look at the mobiles gently swivelling.

'I understand. It is difficult. But I think Gerald — I am right in saying it was he who suggested this move? — I think he was right.'

Netty decided to move the conversation onto safer, more impersonal territory. 'Claudine, I've been looking at that beautiful firescreen over there. Can you tell me anything about it?'

Madame Bellenger took the hint. 'Ah yes. It is exquisite, is it not?' She rose and brought it to Netty. 'It is of the eighteenth century. It was made by one of my ancestresses on my maternal line. She was a Comtesse. She was married to the sixth Comte de Saint-Eymet. They had a castle at Lazolles; it was very famous, almost as significant as Biron or Beynac. But it was not to the Comte's taste, so he built Bel Arbre. He was immensely rich. He also began work on Le Sanglier; it was originally his hunting-lodge, as you probably know. He was a very unpleasant man, however, notorious in the district for his life of *débauche*. I think of the Countess Marie-Louise — we have a miniature portrait of her. She seems so young. I wonder if she was lonely, sitting sewing this lovely work while her master was away ...'

Netty gently stroked the screen in its gilded stand. The colours had faded with time, like ancient potpourri. The stitches were tiny, the gradations of tone infinitely subtle.

'I would have thought she'd ruin her eyes, working back then without electric light.'

'Poor lady. They lost Bel Arbre during the Revolution.'

Hortense came in to remove the tea tray. Claudine stood up. Patapon, who had been lying at her feet, rose too, anticipating a walk. Claudine patted him and told him to lie down. 'And now, Annette, I will show you more treasure. I am right in thinking that needlework interests you?'

'Oh yes, yes it does.'

'Well, we will go upstairs; there are many other examples we possess.'

In the hall, Netty pointed to the pot on the table. 'Peter showed us this the other evening.'

Claudine glanced at it. 'Ah. That. Yes, well, one must show loyalty to one's friends, no? But it does not fit in.'

Netty realised that from most angles the pot was hidden from view by the sweep of the great staircase.

As they mounted the stairs, Netty drew in her breath in awe. At intervals there were alcoves set into the wall, in which were set classical urns. At the top of the stairs a long gallery opened up to left and right. High doors led, she supposed, to bedrooms. Dark oil paintings of saturnine men and podgy women in ruffles and lace hung on the pale blue walls.

'Come with me,' said Claudine, leading the way. At the end of the gallery she pushed open some double doors and they entered another salon. It was lined with enormous tapestries, lit gently by the sun coming in through a tall window which gave onto the lawns at the back of the house. Claudine sat on a chair like a papal throne set in front of the window and patted the chair beside her for Netty to follow suit, which she did, almost in slow motion, gazing round the while.

'These tapestries are priceless,' announced her hostess.

'I can believe it,' Netty answered.

'They are the prize treasure of this house. I cannot tell you what Henri paid for them. They were his greatest gift to me.

'When we acquired Bel Arbre, it had stood empty since the war, and it was a shell. It was the task of Henri and myself to put back the pieces that had once belonged here, for, as I told you, I am of an old family, but over the years we had lost everything, as old families do. Henri dedicated his money to the restoration. He said he could think of no better use for it. That was charming, was it not?'

'Oh. Yes ...'

'My Henri was a chivalrous man. People today do not understand these things, this devotion.

'*Alors,* my mother and my great aunt still possessed some of our heirlooms which they were pleased to render to me. But for the rest, Henri and I attended so many auctions, here and abroad. We commissioned an expert in the period to trace objects which had been lost. *Voilà,* the result of fifteen years' work.'

It's like Danny's bedroom, thought Netty. On a grander scale. A shrine to the past.

Claudine was still talking. 'And the *pièces de resistance* you see here, we acquired only three years before Henri's death. We had to have them cleaned and restored. He didn't live to see them hung like this.'

She looked around with melancholy pleasure.

'It is like a green chapel here,' she said.

Netty gazed at the hangings, radiating green and gold, like paradise, in the late afternoon sun.

'It's like an indoor garden.'

'Precisely. The tapestries are of the fifteenth century, and they are very similar to the famous works in the Musée de Cluny in Paris, the Lady of the Unicorn series. Perhaps you know them?'

Netty shook her head, shamed at the thought of her naive bunnies and teddies sitting in boxes in her tower room. All those pastel colours in twee little designs. All this vibrant majesty facing her now.

'Well, you must see them. I am sure with your interest you would adore them. You must persuade Gerald to take you to Paris.'

Claudine rose and made a circuit of the room, pausing in turn in front of each of the great hangings. Netty felt she could rise from her bench and follow, that she could touch the silken cloth and her arm would vanish to the elbow, that she could duck into this other world, a world of jewelled harmony whose brightness four hundred years ago was unimaginable now.

'These tapestries depict the tale of Venus and Adonis,' said Claudine in declamatory style. 'In the first picture, we see the goddess herself descend to earth. In the border, we see the symbols of love: the doves which draw her chariot and the sea-foam from which she was born.'

The picture was simple: the goddess of love stood in the midst of a forest, each branch on every tree heavy with birds in pairs. Venus' unbraided golden tresses hung to her knees, gently waving in an unfelt breeze.

'She sees the beautiful youth Adonis. It is a *coup de foudre;* instantly she loves him, she pursues him, and who can blame her, tied as she is to the dark and sullen Vulcan?'

Netty followed the sidelong glance of the divinity to the next picture, and drank in, as she did, the taut grace of the boy, his freshness, his eagerness, his easy strength and as yet unshaken confidence. The birds had left the branches and were crowding above his head. She could almost hear their voices.

'The goddess and the mortal meet: how can the mortal resist? Her divine passion ignites him, he is consumed with desire, he forgets the world of men, he thinks only of her.'

The next panel depicted Venus reclining at ease, sated, triumphant, the boy lying in her lap. Her slender fingers coiled in his hair and curled round his white neck and held him there.

'But alas, even for gods, perfection is hard to preserve. The youth becomes restless. Like all men he finds it hard to live for love alone. He chooses to go hunting, and defies his mistress.'

A view of Adonis striding eagerly down a green alleyway, his dogs prancing at his heels. In the foreground Venus stands bereft, a dove drooping on her shoulder.

'Deep in the forest,' Claudine's voice was low, thrilling. Netty was caught up in the pace of the tale. 'Deep in the forest he meets his nemesis. The great black boar attacks.'

Violent action. One white alaunt lies to the right, gutted, its entrails in crimson disarray on the emerald carpet of the forest floor. The other hound, blood on its snout, nudges gently at the wounded youth. The boar lies dead at Adonis' feet, a broken spearshaft protruding from its side. Adonis is wavering; the bright blood courses from the deep trench riven by the boar's tusk from thigh to groin. Venus is nowhere to be seen.

'His life flows away fast, all nature mourns.'

The dog's muzzle is raised to the sky, the tiny sprinkled flowers wither in dismay, and leaves fall like ashes in the wind. The goddess, a white veil thrown over her like a shroud, once more cradles her lover's head on her lap. She bows over him in silent grief.

'Oh, to be a divinity, to have that power. Venus in love recalls his life to him. She confers on him immortal life, which is both penalty and reward. She creates for him an exquisite garden, safe from the world, safe from all risk, a delicate prison from which he can never stray.'

Venus and Adonis stand hand in hand while around them the birds flutter, the flowers bloom, the creatures gambol and grin; monkeys and dogs, lions and rabbits. But is that a yearning look in Adonis' mortal eye?

Netty reached home at seven and while daylight lasted, it wasn't so bad. She went through the usual bedtime routine. She opened the bedroom window and stood there, listening to the loud white noise of insects. The owl's mournful hoot seemed sad, not frightening. The night air was as warm as a bath. The rustles and movements were still there; the flicker of a bat, the blind nosing of a giant beetle toiling across pebbles as large to it as the mountains of the moon.

I'm OK, she thought. I've had a good day. Claudine couldn't have been nicer to me. Those glorious pictures! If only I could do something like that.

She even went into the bedroom and started to undress. Fifteen minutes later, though, she was knocking on his door. He didn't demand explanation or apology. She slept under the eye of the dancing god.

'Where the hell were you?' Gerald's voice the next morning was strained and aggressive.

'Now, Gerald, where would I be? I suppose I just didn't hear the phone.' She found she was really enjoying lying to him. And oh, the relief of not having to explain or justify herself! She was glad when he said it would be at least another week, maybe two ... She exchanged superficialities with Roy and Sheila, but she felt distant from them, all of them.

The next night she asked the Professor to stay with her, so she could answer the phone, if it rang.

Getting Things Done

Rankle. That was a good word. Even when Gerald arrived in Oxford, putting all that distance between them, Netty's attitude to him rankled. The way she cosied up to the Professor. The way she threw herself at Edouard. Her frigidity towards him. The way she looked sniffily at every suggestion he made. It was rotten, it smelt rank, it worked its way inside him and festered.

So, he threw himself into work. If a job's worth doing, he said, it's worth doing *bloody* well. Watching the expression on Roy's face change from anxiety to relief felt satisfying. It was good, for once, to be appreciated.

Inevitably he found himself working with Camilla again. Camilla Thorneycroft. Bold, self-sufficient, guarded. Familiar, and yet very unfamiliar. She'd been on the sales team for seven years and considering the environment she'd really made her mark. She wasn't exactly selling Avon products, was she? Bloody great boiler-systems for factories, that was what. Gerald had been uneasy about taking her on, but Roy had been in favour; in this day and age you were supposed to give the girls a bite at the cherry. So he did. Give her her due, she'd passed all the tests: she didn't cry when criticised; she mastered all the technical specifications so she wouldn't be caught out, and she'd swig a pint with the rest of them down at The Bowler and Bulldog, and laugh when Martin Ramsden, the bugger, got on the table just before closing time and pretended to be shitting a Mars Bar. Not many women would see the funny side of that. And if she was putting on an act, it was a bloody good one.

Looking back, he could see how he'd always been aware of her.

Not in a specifically sexual sense — or at least not any more than the normal male's automatic registering of good and bad points in a female. She had good tits but poor legs; her hair had a gloss to it, but her hands were too mannish. Her lips tightened too much but when caught unawares her eyes had a soft sheen in them, like unshed tears, so that she reminded him of one of those liqueur chocolates; sweet heady fluid held braced within crisp walls. She dressed well, but dauntingly; whenever he clapped a hand to her shoulder, he felt the padding under the fabric and wondered where the living female shoulder lay, under the power armoury.

The Victorians had loved women with smooth white shoulders sagging submissively, flowing unstoppably into round white arms and plump tender hands clasped in their laps. Today's women presented the silhouette of an inverted triangle and their hands reached out to stab computer keys or to point accusingly at men like Gerald.

So, he had joked to Roy about how she must be a dyke, but secretly he was daunted by her, unwillingly he admired her, continually he was fascinated by her. Home he went to Netty each night, and ended up feeling assaulted on two fronts because his wife, after her ordinary education and what he had thought of as a satisfying married life, was suddenly making noises about taking some sort of course at the College of Further Education or the Open University. History, she said. Maybe a job afterwards, though what kind of job he couldn't for the life of him see. Get keyboard skills, he advised. Always useful. Then it all came to nothing anyway; most unexpectedly, at the age of forty, she'd fallen pregnant.

God, the ribbing he got at work. 'Thought you'd have known what it was for by now!' crowed Marty Ramsden — and that was the most innocuous of the jokes. Netty's dazed look was all too soon replaced by a horrible anxiety. At her age, the baby could potentially be Down's. They had the tests done. He watched the long needle go in and out of her belly as she clutched at his hand and then, more than at any other time — even at the height of labour, when everything was out of hand anyway — he admired her courage, as she lay there and let them draw off the precious fluid while on the monitor the fuzzy outline of what would be their son stopped somersaulting to cower deep in her womb.

Three weeks of waiting while the baby jigged in her stomach; three weeks of trying not to respond to that because they'd discussed it all with the geneticist and they'd looked at the graphs and termination seemed the best thing, if what they feared was true. He remembered that the hospital staff had always used the word 'termination'. It had always made him think of a computer program, an abstract clinical affair of wires and terminals, whereas 'abortion', now, that was different: a word of horror, connoting freakish flesh, blood, distortion, corruption.

Netty must have felt it worse than him: after all, she'd had the kicking and the weight inside and she'd have had to go through the process of purgation of the unfit child.

Maybe that made her love Danny even more, in the end. Danny, the son who was perfect, after all. Nevertheless, her relationship with her youngest, gift-from-heaven child had begun and ended in guilt.

On August the third, he'd finally sorted out the Excelsior Fabrications order for Roy, so they all went out to the Beaumont to celebrate. He was not as drunk as on his first night there and he was more relaxed. He decided he wouldn't phone Netty when they returned to Wheatley, just to get his head snapped off. Instead he took the time to relish his wine and rather enjoyed the sight of Ms Thorneycroft getting tipsy at another table. He watched her. He liked the way she laughed uproariously. He even found himself not minding that she swore like a trooper. It made her seem straightforward.

'You've got an asset there, Roy,' he said, watching her rise from the table and weave her way to the bar. Her skirt was pleasingly short and tight. 'And one *with* a nice asset!' he finished, winking.

Roy shook his head at him. 'I don't play away from home and you know it, mate. Sheila's enough for me.'

'*More* than enough for any man, I'd say,' he laughed and would have said more but for the tightening of his friend's jaw. He'd say this for the Bensons, they were a loyal couple, seemed to see the best in each other, and twenty-odd years of marriage had never shaken that.

'Anyway,' Roy added, 'even if I *was* tempted — never have an affair with someone in the firm. It causes nothing but awkwardness all round.'

'Shitting on your own doorstep, eh?'

'If you want to put it that crudely, Ger, yes.'

'Sorry mate, sorry I'm not *refeened* enough for you. But you know what I mean.'

'Certainly do. It all ends in tears and one or other has to leave the company. Usually the female.'

'Ah, but Roy, you forget — I'm no longer strictly speaking *with* the company.' Camilla was on her way back. The power jacket had been left draped on the back of her chair. Damn thing was so solid it could probably stand up on its own. Without it he saw her shoulders were narrow, he saw the moving plane of collar-bone and the hollow at her throat darkening and dappling as she moved under the lights. She had a chest worthy of Jamie Lee Curtis.

Roy was speaking. 'Gerry, this is just the drink talking, isn't it? I mean, you wouldn't *really* do the dirty on Netty, would you?'

He dragged his gaze away from Camilla as she tucked that neat behind into her chair. 'Well, that's another quaint turn of phrase, eh, Roy? No,' he sighed, because he knew it was true. 'No, I wouldn't do that to Netty. She's had enough to contend with, without that. I know I talk loud, but I don't really mean it. We all look, don't we? The women know that. They put it all on display because they like us to look. But as far as I'm concerned it's behind plate glass. Look, don't touch. There you have it.'

Roy looked relieved.

'Apart from all that,' Gerald finished, face and heart heavy, 'I still love her. It's a mess. It's all gone wrong, God knows, and everything I do or say makes it worse with her, but I do love her. Even when I could wring her neck. So there you are.'

In the end, then, it wasn't lust, but grief that did it.

The next morning, he sat with Camilla in her car on the Cowley Road. In spite of leaving Feldwick & Benson's early, the traffic had already congealed, just past the Bingo Hall.

'I'd forgotten just how bad this bloody town is,' he said to her, wanting to make conversation and not enjoying being the passenger. The power shoulders, he noted, were back in place, along with shadows under her eyes. She must have been suffering the ill effects of the previous night's spree but to her credit she didn't whinge.

'I suppose the Dordogne is like the prairies of the West, is it? Great open spaces?'

'No, it's not like that. It's hilly and wooded, full of cosy nooks, old places tucked away; but compared to this ... One of these days it'll all just *lock* totally and everyone will have to get out of their cars and walk away. Finito.'

'Oh, I think they'll just end up banning cars entirely. You can't have all these roadways feeding into one tiny area.'

He grinned and opened his mouth to answer; he liked a conversation of such predictable banality. It'd be the weather next. For once he felt he knew where he was with her.

It was the red sweatshirt that caught his eye. Back at school, yonks ago, he'd learned that the human eye reacts first to the colour yellow coming into its field of vision. Not so with Gerald. He was haunted by red.

There it was again: a small red sweatshirt, small blue shorts, a bright baseball cap on springy, badly cut hair. The child looked straight at him as they inched past in the Maestro. Gerald felt his heart stop and surge with longing. Just the right height, just the right build, though the hair was too dark and the eyes brown, not blue. He bowed his head for a moment. Camilla, thrumming her fingers against the steering wheel, glanced sideways, then the roof of the car ahead dipped and its tail-lights went off, so she eased the handbrake off and slid another tantalising couple of feet forward before creaking the brake back on once more.

Gerald looked at the child again; at first he craned round, then he used the wing mirror. His heart, after its bounce, like a faithful dog keen for loving, was now pounding. Surely the boy was too close to the kerb? And why was he standing there alone? What was his mother thinking of? Just as well the traffic was virtually immobile, if he were to step off the pavement ...

The car jerked forward, halted. Gerald reached out and altered the angle of the mirror slightly. In that moment of losing sight of the boy the man had appeared. Transfixed, Gerald watched the hand take hold of the boy's wrist. The child's mouth went square in protest. Faintly Gerald could hear the cry. The man's black coat rippled heavily as he began to pull the protesting boy along the pavement. Gerald was out of the car, running back along the verge. He stumbled on one of the notorious Cowley Road potholes, he got onto the pavement. His arm was out, he heard his own voice yelling. He passed a bus-queue of open mouths. It was as if the world had frozen in its tracks and he was the only person still with the power of movement. Why did no one react? Why did they just stand by? This wasn't New York, where they let you die in the street, scream and all. His breath hurt his lungs and sweat broke out: he wasn't built to be a vigilante. Is this what happened, Net, he wondered, did the whole world just watch our lad be taken? Well, not *this* lad. I won't have it.

The man turned, his face a glower under dark stubble, the boy now gripped by the upper arm, still squealing in protest. Gerald tore up to them.

'Just what the bloody hell do you think you're playing at?' he shouted.

The man's face registered astonishment. 'I might well ask the same of you,' he answered, his voice belying his appearance; a gentle tenor. 'What's your problem?'

The boy peered upwards. 'Who's this, Dad?'

Gerald took a step backward as if pushed firmly in the chest.

The man's hand left its grip and gently turned the baseball cap, which had turned sideways to make the kid an American cartoon-character. 'Don't know, Paddy. Just some nutter, I suppose. Which is *why* your Mum said to wait for me or your brother to take you to the shop, now, didn't she?'

'Yes Dad.' The voice was a low sulk.

'Yes Dad. Sorry Dad. I don't know — what'll we do with you?' The baseball cap was removed for a quick tousling of the hair, then splashed back on. The man looked Gerald in the eye. Gerald quailed with embarrassment and said 'Look, I'm sorry about this, I thought ... that is, well, it looks as if I had the wrong end of the stick. Sorry.'

The man continued to stare at him, while the boy became increasingly restive, tugging for departure. Gerald waited for a mouthful of abuse. He lacked the will to resist or to explain further. The man spoke. 'Kids, eh?' he said amicably. 'Give you a heart attack every hour of the day.' Gerald smiled weakly in the amity of parenthood. Father and son strolled off. He heard the man saying, 'Sorry I had to lose the rag, Paddy, but you've got to watch for the cars ...' The rest of the warning faded into the early morning hubbub.

He stood for a moment longer then stumbled back past the bus-queue. The people there studiously avoided his eye, in the way people do when they see you trip on a paving stone and nearly go flying. You wrestle with your dignity, they wrestle with their mirth.

Camilla had pulled the car to the side of the road, to the annoyance of cyclists who had to skirt it at some hazard. The springs dipped heavily as he got in. Vision in the wing-mirror was clear; his dramatis personae gone. 'So what the fuck was all that about?' she asked, but quietly, which was good of her.

Tears pricked his eyes and he felt himself tremble all over in the aftermath of it.

'Oh, just me being stupid.' He fought to keep the tremor out of his voice. 'I saw a little lad — I thought someone was bothering him ... bloody fool that I am.' She had the grace not to reply; just put the car in gear and edged back into the traffic. Then, to his own surprise, he burst out, 'It's just that ... it was around here, that Danny ... Danny disappeared.'

The tramps on the green plot gave them the evil eye as they passed. A couple were already propped against the DHSS building waiting for the doors to open. Foolish for him to blame them but he always did; he needed a focus. They represented the sickness of a society in which children could disappear. He took a breath to steady himself. The car at last reached the Plain; the roundabout at the end of Magdalen Bridge, the Checkpoint Charlie between proletarian East Oxford and the patrician colleges.

'I should have taken the ring road,' was all Camilla said. 'Silly bitch.'

They turned right, climbed Headington Hill, left the city behind. Gerald thought, 'I was right. I was absolutely right, going to France. We just can't live with this.'

She drove them back again that evening. Gerald was tired. It had been a long day: meeting after meeting in London, an extended business lunch, an artificial veneer of energy created by frequent coffees but underneath the unplumbed depths of exhaustion. That little episode in the morning hadn't helped either.

The sky was light still as they bowled along the M40. He liked summer evenings. He settled back in his seat, content to let her bring them home. In the silence above the thrum of the engine, he sagged into slumber, sucked down into it so far that he felt himself no longer to be pushing along the surface of the road, but, like a mole, burrowing a resonating path back to Oxford.

When he woke it was nearly night and the car was still. He groaned because his neck had cricked; his jaw must have been bouncing on his chest for quite a while. His mouth felt vile. Bleary, he noticed she was looking at him, her hands still on the wheel.

'We here?' he asked foggily. 'Good. Mouth feels like the bottom of a budgie-cage. Need a drink.'

'Well, come in for one,' she replied.

He realised they were not outside the Bensons' mock-Tudor with its leaded lights and double garage. Where the bloody hell were they?

'We're at my place,' she said. Her voice was flat-calm, giving nothing away. Bloody hell, he said in his fuddled brain, what's going on?

'Why?' is what he said.

'I thought you might like a drink and a talk.'

'I'm a bit tired, really.'

'But we're here now. You were sleeping like a ... sleeping sound, you were. And you said your mouth was like a budgie-cage.'

'That's true,' he admitted. 'Well, thanks, OK — I'd love a drink. I'm gasping.'

Her house struck him mute at first. It was a Victorian terraced house on Osney Island; fashionably accessible for the railway station, but horribly cold and damp in winter, with old Daddy Thamesis rushing from weir to eternity at the end of the stunted garden. Inside he found pine everywhere: stripped floorboards, skirting, banisters and stair-treads, a Scandinavia of yellow glossiness, echoing unmercifully under the foot. Her bed was on a platform over the long living-room, continually forcing itself into his awareness as he sat on the unyielding Chesterfield sofa.

'This must be a killer to heat in the winter,' he said to her.

'It is. But I can afford it.'

'Roy pays you enough, then, does he?'

'Oh, what's *enough*? It's never *enough*. And I deserve every red cent.'

He spread his hands wide, submissively. 'On today's showing, I wouldn't argue with that.'

She gave him some mineral-water as a standby while she brewed up some coffee in a cafetière. He took no alcohol: that was the strangest thing. Later, he didn't even have the excuse that he was drunk — that old cliché; the blowsy hiccup of 'my wife doesn't understand me', the beer-sodden fumbling embrace, the hangdog shame of the morning.

No, he wasn't drunk, except on her strangeness and newness to him and her willingness to listen, not in strained tolerance or pseudo-maternal cossetting, but purely and simply out of *interest*. It was colossally flattering, that interest in *him*, Gerald, how *he* felt, in all honesty, no putting on a show of what was expected.

She didn't waver, even when he started to cry and sobbed out Danny's name. She didn't twitch in embarrassment or dissolve into tears herself. She was strangely detached, but not coldly so. Her detachment carried with it implicit respect. She was a marvel.

'You'd think,' he said, 'that grief would bring us together, wouldn't you? But it hasn't. It's just broken us. I know she feels guilty and she thinks I blame her.'

'Do you?'

For the first time he admitted it. 'Yes ... yes, I suppose I do, but not all the time. It changes. I mean, you've got to find a focus, haven't you? For the blame. Otherwise it's all just so meaningless you'd laugh if you didn't have to cry. So sometimes it's Netty. Sometimes it's God, giving with one Almighty Hand and taking away with the other. Sometimes it's me — though God only knows — I mean, I was at work, what could I have done? It's just that I feel I should have done *something*. It's just about the worst feeling there is: to feel helpless, to feel that things go wrong because they're bigger than you or out of your control. Just a huge bloody lottery, which you could stand if it didn't involve flesh and blood and love and ... and innocence.'

The tears started at that point, part self-pity; oh poor Gerald victim of cruel fate, lived a decent life and did his best by all, but look what happened to him. Part the dreadful crucifying love for his son so that his arms trembled with the need to be wrapped round that fragile body. Then his fists shook in their turn with the familiar assault of hatred, driven by love and testosterone.

'Oh if I could just find him, I'd, I'd kill him.'

'And would that solve anything?'

He pushed his face angrily up to hers. 'Too bloody right it would! Don't give me all that *shit* about how capital punishment wouldn't work. I'm Old Testament, me — an eye for an eye. I'm with the mother who would murder Myra Hindley if ever she got out. At least *she* knows who she hates! I *need* it — I need my focus — I need to get rid of it. I'd bloody *kill* him. Slowly too.'

His face was gorged with hate. Her answer was to put up her hand and cradle his cheek. Her touch turned the hatred into need. He collapsed into her arms; she cherished him dispassionately, like a vet soothing a bitten dog.

'Come to bed,' she said.

'What?' He couldn't believe it; she was making all the moves, her motivation cryptic to him.

'Come on. Look, we're both knackered. You're a man who needs a cuddle — and more. Talk all you like. It won't go any further. Just get it out of your system.'

So they clattered up the egg-yolk varnished stairs and fell into her bed, draped entirely in white, like the Snow Queen's bower. He talked until she knew all there was to know, but she was still a mystery to him, even when with shaking hands he traced the outlines of her lean body and sucked her nipples and sank into her depths like an explorer into a snow-hole. Blizzard-free, snow-blind, content, alive, asleep.

What was astonishing was that he felt no sense of guilt, nor of awkwardness even, as she watched him pull on his clothes in the grey of six a.m., her hands clasped behind her head as she reclined against the pillows. He could hardly take his eyes off her. He wanted to memorise her before meeting her again at the workplace, where he knew it would all be different.

It was: she was as snappy and jibby as ever; she was an excellent actress, or indeed she had no heart. He didn't care to find out; it wasn't necessary. He felt like a balloon which had been about to ground before ballast was dumped. He soared up buoyant into the ether. He solved all Roy's immediate problems with vigour and panache.

It wasn't until he was on the road to Heathrow, mission accomplished, that he considered his wife. Netty had been a pale sliver of a ghost in his consciousness, like the moon in daylight. But now the guilt took hold and he spent the whole flight to Bordeaux planning how nice he would be to her.

Chevalier sans Preux

1420

The Battle

As dusk fell, they passed under the grey gleam of overhanging limestone
at the base of the hill. They were weary, returning from an assault on the
French positions near Sainte Foy la Grande. Soon they would camp for
the night, and on the morrow reach the fortress of Castelnaud, perched
on the rough heights above the Dordogne. Castelnaud, which had been
French and now was English, almost opposite Beynac, which had been
English and now was French. So the great sway of power crossed from
one bank of the river to the other, time and again.

Richard had just exchanged a joke with Lionel de Merton, smiling
to hear his friend's hearty laugh ring out, when those great guffaws
were drowned by the thunder of hooves in the rock-fenced pass behind
and before them. Shouts of warning and alarm and the ambush upon
them before there was time to prepare. A whirl of hammer-blows,
sparks striking from sword and shield, the cloudy sky spinning above
him as he tried to wheel his horse away from the attackers and come to
the rescue of Lionel, sore beset. A glimpse of Lionel, arms thrown wide,
toppling. Geraint of Monmouth speeding past, mouth a black hole,
blood on his shoulders. William Durward falling, an axe embedded
in his back. Percival Norreys, stricken to his knees, arm raised to ward
the blow.

Richard tried to control his horse. It screamed and backed, head tossing. A shadow loomed: a French knight, sword raised. Turning, Richard saw his chance, ducked under and felt the satisfaction as his own weapon ground past chain-mail under the man's arm, piercing him. The enemy fell, dragging the sword from Richard's gauntleted grip. He fumbled for his battle-axe. A blow caught him on the back of his helmet. The world clanged and rang. Another on his right forearm, numbing it. He tried to raise his shield. The blows fell thick and fast. He felt the horse sag beneath him, sinking onto its haunches, then over. His left leg was imprisoned as it fell, as he fell, as the sky tilted into woods, into dark moist earth. Where were the others? 'Rescue!' he called. His voice was thin, the breath knocked out of him. Scarcely a sound seeped out of the visor grill. Then the dreadful blows again. Hammer and axe and sword. On an anvil of pain, beaten to death. Fire in his upper arm, his right thigh. The horse dying, its blood drenching him, its spasms twisting his trapped leg all the more. He bowed his head and gave up, surrendering to the filthy death the Almighty had ordained for him.

It must have been hours before he woke. Thin strands of night mist had already coiled their way onto the battlefield; ghostly fingers pointing and poking at the dead. The carcass of his mount was rigid. It took some time to wrench himself free from under it. Its hide felt damp, rough and stiff.

He crawled a few feet, his own breath hot as the wounds that had carbonadoed him. His hands felt the first body. Under the fitful moon, Percival, eyes and mouth and throat agape. The black blood already crusted in the cold.

They were all there, immobile as images on tombs, but in frozen contortions so unlike the peace their eventual effigies would possess, back home in England, in country churches. William, face in the soil, arms wide, hands clutching the grass. Geraint recognisable only by the device on his dented shield. And finally, Lionel, the great wound cleaving his skull.

The Dream

Calvary. Via Dolorosa. Oh Lord God, oh Holy Virgin save me. Holy Mother, weep for thy son. Dew dripped on his head from the branches he brushed in his passage. The Virgin's tears, cold and pure as ice. Blood on the grass, black on grey in the moonlight. I walk in blood, blessed in suffering. Save me oh Lord. Sweet Jesu.

His steps grew more wavering. Branches and twigs, cruel fingers, plucked at him. They mock me, my Lord, they spit on me and pull at my raiment, they call for my life and I walk towards the tree of my salvation. He fell over and waited to be raised. But first the demons were sent to torture him with fire and sulphur and molten lead. A long night of woe before redemption.

Coolness of tears on his brow. Holy Mother, he breathed, opening his eyes. Fairer than the Madonna, the girl wept for him. A peasant girl, but high of brow, eyes grey as a goose, hair of spun ash-gold.

She took him to the forester's hut and hid him. She told him her name was Genevre and she would heal him if she could. She cleansed him and gave him to drink.

There was a dream, fairer than he had ever had. He strayed into a garden, enclosed by high hedges. The air smelt sweet and small birds sang in rejoicing that it was May. Daisies sprinkled the turf with merry eyes. He wandered the winding ways into the heart of the garden. There was a pavilion of silk and a statue of Venus. The statue beckoned to him. Nearby a fountain sprayed silver music, dropping through the air. He knelt at Venus' feet. She raised him up and offered him a gift. He looked and saw it was a rose. Dew lay on the bloom of its curved petals. He inhaled its heady fragrance. He bowed to the Goddess and took the stem of the rose in his hand. There were no thorns. He heard Cytherea say, 'Welcome to my court, fair Sir Amor.' He buried his face in the cup of the flower. Deep deep into the red velvet of it.

He awoke, and the dream was true: fair as a flower, Genevre was in his arms, warm in the sunlit glade, and Venus' benison on them both.

The Hunt

A blackbird shrieked and scuttered through the trees. A twig snapped. Sudden silence. Richard, smiling, looked up. His beating heart chilled at the sight of their spears and bows. Six huntsmen emerged from the shadows of the woods. Richard rolled and rose into a crouching run. He dived behind the hut as the first spear drove quivering into the turf. Then he was into the woods, scuttling through bush and brake, his breath loud. He heard their voices calling openly to one another. Briars tore at his bare hands, roots tripped him. He tried doubling back, but they knew of that trick: they knew all the tricks of their desperate prey.

His scarcely-healed leg broke open again and bled freely. Soon he was limping, then he was staggering. The trees were high towers, the bushes solid walls. No way through. On hands and knees he scrambled up a bank, over, into a ditch, like a dry fosse round a castle. He cried out as his knee struck an old mossy stone, hard-edged, planed by the hand of man.

Crouching there he looked up to see their heads rise above the ditch-wall. His hand went automatically to his belt, but there was no knife there. For a moment they stared impassively at him, then they were cresting the ridge, they were dropping down, they were on him.

The girl, Genevre, panting, reached him just before he died. She cradled his broken head to her, then sat with him as his body grew cold. The men, unable to move her, cursed her for a whore and left her. She remained, her dead love in her arms, and a new love springing silently within her womb.

Route Touristique

Netty woke to the sound of hammering. Drat that woodpecker, she thought, before realising that even a demon woodpecker could not be producing that noise.

It was Saturday. At least, she thought it was. Gerald had been gone nine days.

She stumbled through to the hall, pulling her dressing-gown around her as she went. The sound was echoing up the stairwell. She opened the inner doors, unbolted, turned the key.

'Paul!'

He stood there in the early light, a hire-car behind him, a supple leather bag at his feet.

'God, Mum, you were sleeping the sleep of the just!'

'But Paul, what are you doing here?'

'Thought I'd come and see what all the fuss was about.' He picked up his bag and came in. She backed away into the hall. He looked around and up the white stairwell. 'So this is what Dad fell for?' He poked his head round the kitchen door, taking it all in with one swift summary glance. 'Well, for once I'll give him credit. It's lovely, Mum.'

'Why didn't you ring, Paul?'

'Thought I'd surprise you. Succeeded, eh?'

A pause.

'Look Mum, I'm sorry — I just took it into my head ...'

'That's not like you.'

'I know. And I know I ask you to give me lots of warning when you come to me. I apologise. I just felt like doing something rash, out of the blue.'

'*Definitely* not you!'

They laughed. He turned to the left, she scurried to be at his side.

'Wouldn't you like a coffee or something? You must be tired.'

'What's through here?' he asked simultaneously. 'The great Baronial Hall or what? The Minstrel's Gallery? The ...'

He fell silent. In the russet gloom of the Salle de Chasse stood the Professor, dressed in an old T-shirt and boxer shorts. He was barefoot. His legs were long and wiry. His white hair was ruffled and tiny white dots of stubble had pushed their way through his morning chin.

'Good morning,' he said.

'Paul, this is our good friend Professor Appleby. He lives down the hill. Has Dad mentioned him at all?'

'No, Dad hadn't said. Pleased to meet you.'

'How about that coffee?' said Netty brightly, as the men's hands met briefly and fell away. 'You too, Fred — you must be gasping.'

She trotted to the kitchen and bustled about, leaving them to follow at their leisure. Paul entered first.

'He says he's just going to get dressed.'

'Oh good. I'll just put the kettle on.' More than that I will not say, she thought fiercely to herself. This is not a Brian Rix farce. I am not going to explain myself. Paul can think what he likes.

The cups chinked as she put them on the saucers. Paul sat on a high stool and regarded her thoughtfully. His light brown hair still flopped too much over his forehead and she had to resist the urge to push it back with her fingers. He wore jeans and a light jacket. He looked very pale, as if deprived of light, and there was a podginess to his cheeks and jawline that spoke of Gerald's genetic input.

When Fred came into the kitchen, Netty poured the coffee and took hers off to her bedroom, wishing to shower and dress.

She left them to it. She knew Fred would be unfazed. Fred could handle anything. She could hear their voices in the distance.

Just as she finished putting on her make-up, the phone rang. Her heart gave a thump at the thought that it might be Gerald. She answered it quickly.

'Mistress Feldwick!'

'Pardon?'

'Peter Rettlesham-Carey. Gorgeous day, don't you think? Teddy and I were wondering if you fancied going out and about, if you've got nothing on.'

'Well, actually, my son's just arrived from England.'

'Excellent! The more the merrier! We'll be with you in about an hour. Remember your sunglasses. It's a blisterer out there!'

He rang off. She didn't know whether to be irritated or amused. Then she decided she was relieved. With company around, she wouldn't have to deal too personally with Paul.

She returned to the kitchen. 'Paul, we've just been invited out on a jaunt — but do you feel like it? You can stay here and rest, if you like.' Either way, you don't get to bother me. You can sit and think your own thoughts, or you can come with us and find out for yourself how nice Fred is, and what a jumped-up crank your father has taken a shine to.

But don't watch me watching Edouard.

She hadn't seen him since the night of the *Fête Champêtre*. Lovely Edouard, falling through space with her, entangled in her arms.

'Well OK Mum, I'll come along. A quick shower will freshen me up, if you show me where everything is.'

While he was about his ablutions, she said to Fred, 'I'm sorry about that. He thinks the worst — it's mortifying.'

'The young usually do. They judge their elders by their own shenanigans. Anyway, you should be flattered that he thinks you're still up to it, even with an old poop like me!'

Half an hour later she heard a toot on a car-horn and the slam of a car-door. The front door swung open and in breezed the Honourable Rettlesham-Carey, bottle in hand. As Peter embraced her, Netty looked over his shoulder to where Edouard came prowling in behind. A drink was insisted on before departure, which gave time for introductions to Paul who had emerged damp-haired from the bathroom. Netty felt concerned: the darkness under his eyes seemed so pronounced.

'Are you sure you wouldn't prefer to stay and have a snooze?

It would be more sensible than traipsing over half the French countryside.'

'No, Mum, I'm fine. Honestly.' A shrug and a grin to his all-male audience. 'I'm really looking forward to seeing the area. Dad's been going on about it so much.'

'That's rich!' snorted Netty. 'Considering he's hardly seen anything but hotels, antique shops and this old place!'

'Right, now, I'm in charge!' called Peter. 'First stop, drinks at Trémolat. You coming, Prof?'

The Professor answered Netty's mute appeal. 'Yes, yes, of course. I've been fusticating and rusticating far too long. It'll be nice to get out and about.' Suddenly Netty felt the same way and rushed off to find handbag and camera while the men were on shutter-closing drill.

On the long drive south in May, Netty had been too tired and resentful to look at the countryside properly. It was Foreign: that was all she knew, and Foreign in a different way from Torremolinos or Tenerife. It was not donkeys with sombreros and shell-encrusted ashtrays. Gerald was asking her to regard this as Home. Well, home was Number 143 and the gently turning mobiles in Danny's silent room. Home was Pledge spray and *Neighbours* at lunchtime and polyanthus in the garden and Tesco just down the road. It wasn't Johnny Hallyday and *pain au chocolat* and Monsieur Propre and giant fields of droop-headed sunflowers.

Once in the Dordogne she had been limited to the hotel and the hill, with little forays to Bourdonne. Even on the drive back from the airport at Bordeaux she had seen — yet not seen — the landscape flowing past her. Now, as they drove to Trémolat she began to understand why Claudine had adjured her to explore a little of the area. Périgord. *Le pays de l'homme. Y vivre. Festoyez.*

How green it was. Woods everywhere, rolling over hills, crouching in deep valleys. Folds and ribbons and carpets of trees. Yet also, a sense of openness, even of starkness where the age-old limestone broke through the verdure, like a war-torn dragon's bones through its scales. Elsewhere, red earth, a hint of the Mediterranean, echoed by the forty shades of terracotta on the roofs of the houses.

They drove to Lalinde, then climbed up the hills to the Cingle de Trémolat, with the Dordogne idly meandering through the great fertile plain below. Waterskiers buzzed on the water, grand houses stood on terraces and gazed at the sun. Peter's car darted along in front of them like an ardent beetle. Netty followed with the Prof beside her and Paul in the back, and Paul's tacit disapproval just behind her headrest. She was glad her dark sunglasses meant that she could see Paul in her driving mirror every few moments, but that he couldn't see her, the eyes being the windows of the soul. She followed Edouard in the car ahead, resenting the separation, drawn after him as if by a tow-rope.

They raced down through Trémolat: quick view of cars parked in the shade, the tricolour above the Mairie, parasols outside a cafe, a church with frighteningly cracked masonry. Then they crunched through a gateway on the outskirts of the village and rollicked up an uneven gravel drive to face Peter's palace.

Its owner leapt out of his ancient Citroën. Netty wondered if he ever did anything slowly or with restraint. He was at her door-handle almost before she had switched off the engine. As he bore down on her, she noticed how narrow his shoulders, how immensely long his arms were, like an ape's. The Professor, who had kept up his customary gentle banter along the way, went speakingly silent.

'Netty! Humble abode and all that. I'm just going to crack open a bottle of the good stuff. Drop of fizz OK by you? Wonderful! Just prowl around — Edouard will show you.'

Monsieur Chevalier was indeed approaching. Netty's eyes rested on the catlike sinuosity of those hips as the Professor muttered, 'I keep forgetting where Edouard lives. All that white shirt, black jacket stuff — he's so manicured, I shouldn't wonder if he took to sleeping in a box by day and avoiding garlic.' Netty laughed obligingly.

'Well,' said Paul, standing beside her. 'It might clean up nicely.'

They looked at the building in front of them. It seemed to totter towards them, drunk as a skunk, the roof so uneven as to make them take an involuntary step backwards.

Peter emerged, swinging a bottle by its stem. 'Come on!' he cried. 'Or are you just transfixed by the beauty of it all?'

'Does it have a name?' asked Netty.

'God no. Well, at least, not as far as I know. Perhaps we ought to christen it. Rettlesham Park Mark II? The Drunken Dive? The Betty Ford clinic? Ha! Actually, it's a dear old dump and I love it madly.'

The Drunken Dive was built of unrendered stone with shreds of ivy clinging here and there like a woman taken by surprise in the shower and vainly trying to cover breasts and groin with her hands. The canal tiles on its wavering roof were tilted every which way, and loose. A bedspread hung airing from one of the upper windows. The shutters thirsted for a coat of paint. A lone chicken pecked scraggily on the drive.

'Lunch!' joked Peter, veering the bottle towards it. 'No — it's a stray. They flutter in from all over the place, can't think why. I'm a bloodthirsty bastard really. You'd think they'd sense it. Chickens, pigeons, even a couple of goats.' He strode off to the left, past a wooden garden bench stained with mouldy green. 'Come and see my atelier!'

They followed as Rettlesham-Carey swung open two heavy doors, arching high above their heads and opening onto a huge barnlike extension at the side of the house. He darted inside and started flicking switches, lighting up the interior. The walls had been whitewashed unevenly and were already peeling with damp. A long wooden workbench ran along one side of the room. It was strewn with sherds of pottery, ripped sketches, knives and brushes, jars of glaze, empty beer cans, and glasses encrusted with the tide-marks of red wine. The place smelt of charcoal, damp earth, grape and, suspiciously, a faint undertow of piss.

The Professor had found his way to a low chair of unravelling rattan. In front of it was a mottled coffee-table, also laden with glasses. How many glasses did Peter have, wondered Netty. Did he never wash them, just buy new as required? He could have a glorious time flinging them all at the fireplace, Russian fashion. Fred picked up one of various clay-stained, dog-eared art books on the table: it was of Roman and Etruscan antiquities — craters, libatory and funerary cups and jars. Peter leaned over him, showing him a double-handled drinking vessel he'd picked off the counter.

'Of course, the shape isn't *quite* right yet, but I'm working on it. What I want, and I've discussed it with Hermione at my gallery, the Mnemosyne, is to maintain the forward momentum of the whole Prehistory thing — you know, Venus figures and the like — and I also want to introduce the classical aspect, but classical with a twist, nothing *too* neat or predictable. I'm just playing with various ideas — the only prerequisite is that I keep the Muse married to Mammon!'

'I'll drink to that,' said Paul.

'Oops! God, *where* is my mind?' Peter scrabbled on the worktop, selected some glasses marginally less rimed than the rest, rinsed them perfunctorily under a tap near the tank containing his clay, popped the cork and foamed their glasses full.

'Here's to the bloody Dordogne and to the British invasion thereof! And here's to the inspiration of Roman colonial art! I tell you, I'm going to do for ancient times what Morris and Pugin did for the Gothic.'

'I think William Morris, at least, had a rather more idealistic view of what he was doing.'

'Granted, Prof, granted. But you'll have to agree Morris also wanted to *popularise* what he saw as beautiful. "Have nothing in your houses that you do not know to be useful or believe to be beautiful," etcetera.'

'And your display of derivative mugs and bas-reliefs in a Bond Street gallery selling to the nouveau riche of Thatcher's Britain in their over-priced renovated properties, is your idea of popularising beauty, is it?'

Peter put a forefinger on Fred's sleeve and mimed drawing it away with a hiss. 'Ouch, I surrender! Fred, dear man, lighten up! I'm not robbing a crust from you, am I? It seems to me you're rubbing along *very* cosily, retired as you are from all the hurly burly of the Cambridge cloisters — *also* well known for bringing art and culture to the Philistine masses!'

Edouard was leaning against the workbench alongside Paul; they looked like two cowboys at the saloon bar. 'Peter, does your house contain anything but drink, damp and pretentious art? I am keen on eating — is anyone else?'

'Absolutely! Dreadful host you've got here. Let's go raid the fridge — you can have a proper look at the old dump.'

A swift passage across the now baking gravel and into the cool dim house. It smelt as Le Sanglier had smelt on the first day Gerald and Netty had opened it up: of wood and dust. Oak beams, dark as shoe polish, were slung across the ceilings; the brown weight of them seemed to compress the stale air. The living-room was dominated by the obligatory stone fireplace, a beam across it as a mantelpiece, so high Netty would have had to stand on a chair to dust it. On various cupboards stood examples of Peter's Art: bulbous vases with the usual murderous scenes on them. On the walls some ragged tourist posters, along with sketches which in their slapdash way were executed with some flair.

They crossed to a poky, ill-equipped kitchen by way of the central hall. Skeins of sacred cobwebs wafted from its upper levels. Peter obviously lacked a Mathilde to come and 'do' for him. Along one wall hung a vast array of weaponry, arranged geometrically. A lozenge of arrowheads, flint and metal, all pointing upwards like little rockets. A fan of daggers with hilts of wood and bone and gilt. A circle of swords all directed inwards as if bent on mutually assured destruction. Finally, stepped oblongs of guns, side on as if in flight; from ancient splay-mouthed muskets to long carbines and double-barrelled shotguns.

They all surveyed this armoury: Netty and Paul with muted horror, Edouard impassively, Professor Appleby with an ironic twist of the mouth.

Opposite the weapons, the slaughterhouse. A shelf of stuffed creatures preternaturally poised among the dusty leaves of their habitats. Three owls, a moorhen, a duck, a fox, a stoat. Above these effigies, lines of trophy heads worthy of a Scottish baronial hall: stags' heads with magnificent twelve point antlers, a couple of snarling fox masks, and, spaced evenly, three boars' heads, also snarling, tusks to the fore, black snouts wrinkled, little piggy glass eyes buried in coarse bristles. Sad and mothy, yet impressive after-images of the force and vitality that had once been. Three little piggies, thought Netty. And along came Peter the Wolf.

'Not bad, eh?' said the proud owner. 'Of course, didn't kill all these myself; swiped quite a few from Rettlesham Park and from Auchindourie, our place in Perthshire.'

In the kitchen stood an ancient, boxy fridge. Peter forced it to disgorge various fragments of cheese, some ham and another bottle. The ham was curling a little at the edges. 'Not brilliant catering, I'm afraid. Shall we call it a day and head off for a restaurant somewhere?' said their host.

Edouard sighed. 'I might have known better than to waste time here. Peter, your priorities are all wrong.' He came over and placed an arm negligently over Netty's shoulders, the other he draped over Paul. Netty tingled. His shirt gleamed in the crepuscular kitchen.

'These good people will have no fine opinion of us, particularly this poor boy here, who has only just arrived from England and must be exhausted. What did you have at the house of your mother, Monsieur Feldwick? Coffee only, was it not?'

'Yes, I'm afraid so. If I get any hungrier some of those animals will be vanishing off Peter's walls!'

'Oh, it is not so grave! We will make a little expedition, beyond Limeuil, to Le Bugue, where we will dine well.'

Three hours later, over coffee in the restaurant, the Professor turned to Paul. 'You see how the days go here? You have breakfast, you linger over it, you converse, you plan, you have lunch, you linger over it, the heat strikes you down so you think you'll rest till dinner, over which …'

'You linger,' finished Paul. 'Yes, I get the picture.' He took his mother's hand and squeezed it, much to her surprise, as he was not given to demonstrative acts of this order. 'If you ask me, it sounds just the thing. Mum needs a long rest. God knows, I could do with it too.'

A harsh beam of sunlight fingered his face and she saw how tired he looked. Strained. More than a long journey warranted. She half-opened her mouth, wanting to speak. All day she had taken refuge in the company of others, to preclude an inquisition from him. Now suddenly she wanted to shoo them away like flies. She wanted to know, she wanted to sweep away years of careful empty exchanges.

She noticed Edouard looking with concern at Paul, and she warmed even more to him. Any warmer, and she'd come to the boil.

Peter was resting his chin on one bony hand: several glasses of red were beginning to take their toll. The Professor seemed to have retired into himself and he had that sardonic look on him which Netty didn't particularly like if she felt, as she did now, that she was included in his appraisal.

Edouard took charge. 'We do not wish to tire Paul further, but we would like to amuse him. If you want to, Paul, you may return with your mother and sleep, this afternoon. Perhaps it would be right. But if not, perhaps you will like to make another excursion? I can recommend the caves near here: they will be less crowded than those at Les Eyzies. After which,' he continued, now wholly master of ceremonies, 'we can go on to Lalinde, where there is a fiesta tonight.'

'Oh, you'll like that Paul! Your Dad and I went to one with Edouard, at Hayemet, nearly two weeks ago. They had the most brilliant fireworks, and dancing ...' She could feel a blush coming on.

'Indeed, we had a superb evening. At Lalinde it will be similar, with *feux d'artifice*. Also there is a casino, of a sort. You are an *habitué* of such places?'

Netty started to shake her head, then realised the question was directed at Paul.

'On occasion,' he answered, surprising her.

'*Alors*, it is settled. We will make a night of it. First the caves ...'

Whereupon Peter's chin jerked upwards from the cup of his hand. 'Count me out, mate! Bit of a busman's holiday, don't you see, for me to go prowling around the caves *yet* again!'

The Professor also stirred. 'Perhaps I could prevail upon you, Peter, to give me a lift home. I think my old bones have had enough for one day.'

Netty was astonished, not only by his departure but by the fact that he was even prepared to sit for an hour in the same car as Peter, to get away. Perhaps he was being tactful. Perhaps he realised she needed time with Paul. Perhaps he was what he said: tired. She felt guilty about the past nine days of exploiting his assistance: she hoped he didn't see it that way.

The party split up. 'Might catch up with you in Lalinde, folks,' called Peter, dancing like a feisty boxer round the Professor's measured path. 'Once I've seen old Father Time here back to his bathchair. Haven't been to the Casino in *ages!*'

'OK. *A bientôt,*' they chorused.

They crunched to a halt on a gravel-strewn platform half a mile out of Le Bugue and clambered even higher on foot, up a wooden stairway to the entrance to the Cave of Bara-Bahau, a name which seemed as if it ought to have come from some Polynesian adventure. Around them were fuzzy reaches of birch and bush where darted butterflies of a furious blue. The heat was stunning.

The cave itself was carefully managed with an anteroom filled with postcards and glossy books and a prim-mouthed guide with a belt full of keys like a prison warder who gave them the set-piece tour in French. The predetermined pauses at the highlights: a deep archaeological trench, carefully spotlit; an immense rock slide; strange striations and scorings pinned to the rock by her torch-beam, which, she assured her followers, were lifelike pictures of bears, bison and ibex, transfixed there for fifteen thousand years. Netty felt her imagination on the rack, both with the effort of picturing that passage of time and with trying to make what seemed to her random scarring of the rock fit with the images she was being so dogmatically told they represented. Like Rorschach inkblots, anything could be true.

Paul was by her throughout, shepherding her along narrow walkways and steep slopes, near her when they halted to listen to the guide. Edouard gravitated inwards to translate now and again, then swooped off into the outer darkness, leaving only a vestige of his presence, a hint of white linen sleeve beyond the outermost circumference of the group. Netty imagined him darting off even further, to hang upside down, batlike, from the roof; a cape folded, in defiance of gravity, across his breast. She shook herself slightly, reinstating the image of her Rosencavalier, irritated that the Prof's casual remark about Edouard should so have taken root. But, she thought, what did she know of him? How did he live? Then again, mystery, surely, deepened attraction. Such a contrast to Gerald — realising on a gasp that that was the first time she'd thought of her husband for ages, and that she hadn't phoned Sheila as she'd promised, and what would they be thinking of her ... ? A slight click from Paul's jaw as he yawned brought her back to herself, here, down metre upon metre of passageway shafting into the rock, with a son so obviously shattered he could have lain down on the cold stone and slept.

The place had the most extraordinary atmosphere. It was like a church of an ancient cult, it had the air of reverence, of small sounds magnified into a significance greater than they could bear. The presence of the guide and her weedy torchlight seemed like a coarse intrusion at which the *genii loci* must shudder in distaste. The glass case near the door containing bones and teeth of cave-bears and such sad detritus seemed a futile taming of what once had been wild and raw.

Above ground the shadows of flame and war had flickered and passed and men from Ausonius to Montaigne and Montesquieu had thought their thoughts about the place of man in the great incomprehensible scheme of things, but all that shrank and withered away under the speculation of this great blind eye of ancient stone.

As the yellow beam probed from scoured rock to frozen stalactite, Netty tried hard to imagine who had inhabited this place and so many others in the limestone honeycomb of prehistory, the valley of the Vézère. She had heard the terms and titles from the industry of excavation: Mousterian, Aurignacian, Gravettian, Solutrean ... They were called men — but what relation had she to the creatures who had scrabbled away in this cool dry dark? No relation except through the desire to defeat death in some way. Her son stood breathing beside her, her little piece of immortality, though it didn't look as if her genes would find further perpetuity through any fruit of *his* loins. There were her grandchildren; Chelsea, Eden and Lincoln, who, as they reached adolescence would each wear metal tramways concealing incipient All-American smiles, white teeth lurking behind braces like butterflies in the chrysalis. There was Danny, silent and fading fast in his little tomb.

Here, there was rock where once had been sea. Here was solidity where once there was verdure. Here there was the dustiness of preserved air in a tank of rock. Here were the scratchy cravings for order and beauty and eternal life, of a species which thought itself so old when really so new.

She shuddered and Paul's arm came round her instantly, protectively. It was reassuringly solid, running slightly to fat. She leaned against him, as she had leaned so often against Gerald. She could scarcely believe that this transmogrified adult had once been hers so entirely, in the womb, in the cot, in the shelter of her arms.

'Had enough, Mum?' he asked. 'It's a bit of a poky old hole really, and my French just isn't up to following what Madam there is saying.'

'I'm all right, Paul. It can't be much longer. Anyway, we can't get out: we're here for the duration.'

He chuckled. 'Captive audience, that's the technique, eh? Always a winner.'

Over their shoulders streamed the darkness. Ink. Pitch. Eternity. Impossible to grope one's way through that back to the light of day. They would have to wait for the guide's torch to carve its way through the solid banked dark like a stonecutter, and follow in its narrow wake.

'Like Aeneas in the underworld,' said Paul, dredging up long-forgotten memories of the classics. 'If it was anything like this I wouldn't blame Dido for having a fit of the sulks.'

Netty hadn't a clue what he was talking about and that pleased her. It had always pleased her to think that her son knew more than she did, as if he were carrying the baton of knowledge one stage further in the great human relay race, as she fell back, her stint complete, winded and breathless and cheering him on.

At last they were released and emerged like Lazarus to a sun which seemed to sear their eyeballs. Edouard had glided back into their orbit and was already talking of Font de Gaume, Rouffignac ... She caught a speaking look from Paul. She wasn't sure if she could cope with any more of these places — too chilling by half, too morbid. Why should she think of queuing up at Montignac before nine in the morning to see Lascaux when it was only a copy anyway, however clever? And, as Gerald had so often reminded her, they were residents here now. They could go to these places at any time. As was usually the case this would result in *never* getting round to it because you took it for granted that It and you would always be around; like a friend you were always meaning to write to and remembered from time to time with a quick twinge of conscience.

She said as much to Edouard as they made their way down the hill. Once Paul slipped on loose scree and quick as a flash Edouard reached out and grabbed his elbow, balancing him. Netty caught a heart-surging glimpse of lean muscle flexing on Edouard's forearm. Paul nodded his thanks and they reached the car without further mishap.

It was by now the interregnum between late afternoon and early evening. In less than an hour they were sitting in a café bar in Lalinde, a town geometrically laid out beside the Dordogne. Not far away blazed all the fun of the fair. As dusk gathered, children walked about sporting necklaces of fluorescent green or pink tubing, to be worn like hula-hoops for the neck or straightened out and whipped through the air, leaving electric after-images on the retina. Klaxons and music blared constantly. Netty felt a headache coming on. They started eating around eight though she felt no appetite. She felt herself sinking without trace beneath the surface of the conversation, which had become suddenly and surprisingly animated between Paul and Edouard. She felt an absurd double pang of jealousy, that Edouard should be poaching her son's attention, and that Paul was so quickly at ease with Edouard. They talked as men and she drifted idly on the outskirts of their conversation, metaphorically trying to thumb a lift to whatever topic they cared to discuss, but always being left stranded.

The meal took an eternity, as meals always seemed to do in France. Netty tried to make herself relax, to take things as they came. But she had never been successful at this. She ate each course too quickly, not savouring the food, and found herself with nothing to do but will the waiter to reappear so that *something* which might be said to concern her would be happening. She could of course have swilled down more of the Merlot than she did but that headache was still there. Instead, she drank lots of water, and rubbed the pads of her fingers together in memory of the cool grainy texture of the rock surface in Bara-Bahau. She thought of that darkness, now that the guests had gone and the guides had locked history away once more.

In Bara-Bahau not the faintest of glimmers would illuminate the enamel on the tooth of a bear, millennia old, in the wood-framed glass case. Would there be silence? Would the aged rock sigh in relief as it returned to solitude, much like a man who has swatted a fly away? Would there be the faintest liquid creak as the thinnest sliver of calcite slid down a spike of stone; rock dissolved in itself, creating itself?

'We must go to the Gouffre de Proumeyssac some time,' she said suddenly, thinking of a brochure showing forests of stalagmites and stalactites, a cave like a stony Venus fly-trap, fringed with spears.

Edouard and Paul looked at her in surprise. They had all but forgotten her and were engaged in an arcane discussion of how to work the system at the roulette table.

Netty gave up. She looked around, idly. The dining-room was sparsely populated. Napkins stood like fabric ice-cream wafer fans, waiting for someone to shake them out. In the long straight street outside, distorted music blared. She thought of leaf-mould and warm earth up on the hill by Hayemet. She thought of the Professor selecting a heavy book and sitting in his cosy room, reading, the quirk on his lips as he shot someone else's theories down in flames. She thought of Peter, arms flailing, slapping clay onto his potter's wheel, sculpting money for himself, red wine coursing through every vein.

A strange thing happened. A woman stood in the doorway and stared, quite hard, at Edouard. As if her gaze had the force of the sun directed by a magnifying glass onto the back of his skull, Edouard seemed to become aware of it. He was very still for a moment, then with a murmured apology he pushed back his chair. It screeched nastily on the tiled floor. He loped over to the entrance and stood there, his head lowered slightly to listen to her. She was short and rather stocky, but well turned-out. Jewellery. Spiky heels. Why did so many women round here, Netty thought, wear such uncomfortable, rather tarty shoes, all heels and thin straps licking like snakes' tongues round insteps and ankles, imprisoning the poor hot flesh and bone? The woman looked at her watch. Her mouth was a thin red gash. She pushed slightly at Edouard's sleeve. He moved as if soothing her. Then, as suddenly, with a quick taut smile, she was gone.

Paul looked at him. Netty waited for him to explain. He did not. He pulled his chair up and remarked that after one more *digestif* it would be time to go to the casino: the conversation about gambling techniques restarted.

As they made their way along the street half an hour later, the long-awaited fireworks began. Paul smiled upwards, and she had a sudden vision of a whole procession of little Pauls strung out on a sequence of Guy Fawkes' nights, with that same smile and only inches of height marking the passage of the years. Gerald, hunched in his heavy jacket, would dash to and fro with his cigarette lighter, to prop rockets in lemonade bottles before their milliseconds of feeble glory. Always he moaned about the price. With Danny they gave up and went to the civic bonfire: impressive, but joy spread too thin among so many thousands of people. Organised public joy.

As this was. At the tail of the brief pyrotechnic tempest, Netty saw a bright red sign, large letters on a white wall. Casino. A temple of delight for losers.

'This it, then?' she asked.

Edouard laughed, his eyes gleaming pink, purple and green in the last flurries of coloured fire.

'Oh no, dear Annette! I'm afraid not! This is a supermarket.'

Paul began to laugh too. She felt silly. It confirmed her resolve. Curiosity had waged war with exhaustion and had lost. She had felt alone in spirit all evening and wanted to be alone physically as well.

Which was strange, but necessary.

'Where is it then?'

'The nearest — ah — *official* casino is at Arcachon, on the coast beyond Bordeaux.'

'If only I'd known,' said Paul, 'I'd have turned west instead of east when I came out of the airport!'

More laughter. 'There are certain *private* casinos, one might say,' continued Edouard. 'I happen to know one locally, which I will be happy to take you to, as my guests.'

Is that how you make your living, thought Netty in a sudden access of bitterness. Are you on commission?

'Well, I'm zonked. You'll have to count me out,' is what she said.

She left them there, surprised. She was relieved and betrayed by Paul's decision to remain. Edouard had assured her he'd make sure Paul would get home safely. As if he were fifteen again.

She dreamed that Edouard smiled at her and spread a cloak around her. Then he picked her up and rolled her into a tight ball. He threw her onto a glittering roulette wheel where she bounced and jiggered and felt sickness in her throat, not knowing if she would land on black or red. Edouard flew off up into the corner of the room to await results. She caught glimpses of his teeth gleaming white as a sabre-toothed tiger's, as she whirled frantically in the land of chance.

The green digits on her clock told her it was three a.m. as the door banged. She got up and met Paul standing in the hall. He looked sheepish, as if she were about to say, 'What time of night do you call this?'

'What time of night do you call this?' she said, smiling to defuse his sense of guilt. 'You are daft — and you so tired too. Look at you, you can hardly stand.' She bustled off ahead of him. 'Look, I've sorted out bedding for you. You'd hardly credit it, would you, that a place this size would have so little in the way of bedrooms. Still, your father was just looking for somewhere cosy for the two of us. Cosy!' she snorted, as they left the Salle de Chasse, 'Not *my* idea of cosy. Still, the kitchen's nice and so's our bedroom.' She held open the door to let him peek at her symphony of lilies and gold, before beckoning him into the dim box of the spare room, tacked on behind.

'Here we are, then. There's a couple of blankets and one of those funny bolster-pillow things — can't stand them myself.' She stopped, anxious, and looked at him. 'Of course, if you'd like, you could bed down on the sofa in the Salle de Chasse. I just didn't think you'd like to be surrounded by all those horrible tiles. If I had my way, I'd have them off the walls.'

He seemed dazed. The look of guilt was still there. 'No,' he said, distantly. 'This'll be fine. Thanks Mum — you're so good. After all, I wasn't invited.'

'Silly! Take it as read — any time. We see so little of you. I've put your bag on the chair there. You know where the bathroom is. Would you like a cup of tea? I know it's late and all that ...'

'Thanks Mum — that'd be nice. Too much wine tonight. But, am I keeping you up?'

'Don't worry about it. Believe me, this house on its own is quite capable of keeping me up. Gives me the creeps — but don't tell your Dad. It's different when there's someone about.'

She paused in the doorway. 'That's why the Professor was here,' she said, wishing the moment she said it that she hadn't broached the subject. That morning already seemed long ago and Paul had said nothing, perhaps thought nothing about it. Stupid then, to focus his attention on it. But, having begun, she had to flounder on. 'The thing is, I had a bit of a funny turn here one night and I've spent a few nights down at his cottage — it's just at the foot of the hill, by the farm — just for company's sake. He's so nice about it. And last night he came for dinner and he just kipped here to save the effort of tottering home. There's nothing ...' She trailed off.

'Untoward?' said Paul. 'I didn't think it for a moment. It's not you, Mum.'

She felt slightly miffed, to have any charge of brazenness so easily dismissed.

'Anyway,' she began.

'Don't tell your Dad!' he finished, and they laughed and she went to make the tea.

He followed her through to the kitchen. 'By the way,' he said, as she stirred two oblongs of *Daddy Suc* into his cup, 'I met a couple of friends of yours at the casino. Felix and Deirdre Luker.'

'Oh, them,' she said. 'Well, they're not friends exactly. We met them at Bel Arbre, Madame Bellenger's place.'

'My, you are moving in exalted circles,' he said. 'She's the widow of Henri Bellenger the banker, isn't she?'

'How did you know that?'

'Oh, the Lukers were careful to mention it. Anyway, I know these things. He was in line for presidency of the Banque Communale de Bruxelles; prestigious EEC appointment. Poor sod snuffed it, though.'

'Nicely put! So, what did you think of the Lukers?'

'Oh, he was decent enough. She's a bit of a tart, though.'

She chuckled. 'And Edouard — don't you think the film-world missed out on him?'

'He's pleasant enough. A bit bland,' he replied.

'Oh come on! He couldn't have been nicer to you — he's charming. And he's sensitive too, he notices things.' She felt the colour rising; she was babbling like a teenager with a crush.

'Mother, we're not talking about Stewart Granger. We're talking about a small-town gigolo.'

'Paul!'

'Wise up, Mum! Who do you think that woman was at the Fleur de Lys? His Aunt Mabel? I think not! It looks like he'd stood her up — and happy she was *not*. No doubt she'll dock his pay!'

'You're talking rubbish!'

'Well, has anyone told you how he makes his living?'

That thought kept her awake for what little remained of the night.

Too Bad, My Son

'How long have you got?' she asked, next morning.

He looked up, startled.

'What did you say?'

'I only asked how long you could stay.'

'Oh. Well, I'm not sure. I've got about ten days left of summer leave. I don't know whether I'll stay here or push off to pastures new.'

'Don't worry: *c'est pas grave,* as they say round here! It's not as if *I'm* going anywhere. You know you're welcome to stay as long as you like. It's really lovely to see you.' She went over and hugged him. Still holding him, she added, 'And your father should be back any day now.' She felt the tension flood into his muscles. 'Anyway, drink your coffee. I'll just pop down to the *boulangerie* for some croissants and *pains au chocolat*; they do really good ones, you know. Makes you *not* miss your Shredded Wheat!'

And so three days passed. August began. They saw nothing of the Professor. Netty was rather hurt by that. She thought of him as her special friend and had expected he would want to get to know her boy. They called at his cottage on the second afternoon but there was no one in. Toiling up the hill, they exchanged nods with Augustin Lelouche, lumbering, and Norbert, slouching.

'*Ça va?*' asked the farmer.

'*Ça va,*' she answered, still hollow from the echo of knocking at Fred's door.

She waited patiently for Paul to talk. He did not. She did not wish to force the issue. Each evening he set off in his hire car to meet

Edouard. A few bars, the casino, he said. She was always awake when he returned. It was always late.

Three days, and Paul looked, if anything, more exhausted than when he had arrived. Topics of conversation, like paper wood-veneer on chipboard, had worn away. Things were becoming rough.

Netty had never thought she'd be glad to see the Lukers roll up to her door, but when they did so, on the fourth morning, she felt quite uplifted.

'God, Netty,' cried Deirdre, '*What* must you think of us? Did you think we'd quite deserted you?'

'Well, I got by.'

Deirdre laughed, turning to look up at her husband, like a flower searching for the sun. Today she wore marine blue and large silver earrings, her lush hair caught back in a too-youthful alice-band.

'It's my fault,' said Felix. 'I whisked Deirdre off to Rocamadour for a little bit of tender loving care.'

'Yes,' said Netty. 'Claudine told me. Was it fun?'

'My dear! It was *heaven!* You must persuade Gerald to take you away from it all. After all, who *deserves* it more than you?'

'Actually, Gerald did take me away from it all — that's why we're here.'

'Of *course* it is! And I'm sure it's doing you good too.' Paul at this moment emerged from the house. 'And here's Paul! He's a credit to you, Netty. But why doesn't he take you to the casino? Shame on you, young man! Take her out and about!'

'People will think I've paid for his company — like Edouard,' said Netty daringly.

'Oh! You know about that, then? Well, I always say — in this age of liberation why shouldn't the oldest profession be followed by both sexes? If it weren't that my husband here is so drop-dead gorgeous I'd be inclined to slip a few francs Edouard's way myself!' Deirdre pealed with laughter. Netty swallowed hard.

'How's Gerald?' Felix asked. 'Is there any word?'

'Yes, when's Gerry coming back to us? He'd better make it soon, or he'll miss us!'

'Well, he's phoned a few times, but our friend's business problems have been quite tricky, apparently, and Gerald's not one to leave a job half done.'

'I'll bet he's not,' Deirdre smirked. 'Still, you've got your lovely son for company, so it's not so bad. It must be a lonely house for you, when you're on your own.'

There followed the obligatory aperitifs and a guided tour of the house. Paul bore with the pawing and cooing very well, as Deirdre scouted about, Felix the well-dressed cipher following a step or two behind.

Netty knew that Deirdre missed nothing; that each room in Le Sanglier, in all its detail, was now etched on her guest's memory. She wished she'd had time to tidy up properly. Nothing escaped the attention of women of Deirdre's stamp. She also felt a sense of invasion: strange, as she felt so little love for the house. She shouldn't feel any more involvement in it than would a guide showing people round a stately home. But she did. She felt reluctant to allow Deirdre up to the tower room and tried to divert her by claiming there was nothing to see; store-room for old boxes, attic really. Her faint excuses were brushed aside as Deirdre mounted the stairs, her voice echoing down to them as they followed in her bold wake.

'Nonsense, Netty, you *must* let me see this — there's got to be the most marvellous view.' Her heels clattered across the bare wooden floor. 'Ooh!' she screamed. 'There is! Oh Felix come quick, it's delightful!' She turned from the window as Netty emerged into the room. 'Netty, if ever you want to sell ... !' She turned back to the view and gave it the benefit of her attention for a full thirty seconds, then the spotlight of her gaze began to probe the interior much like the guide's torch in Bara-Bahau.

'Netty, this is *lovely*. So fresh and cool. And what have we here, *what* do I see? Oh how *sweet!*' She pounced like a kitten on a ball of string, rummaging without permission, picking out some of Netty's cross-stitch and long-stitch pictures. 'Bunnies! And teddies on a swing! Oh how lovely! Look Felix, aren't they cute?'

'Adorable,' he replied. Netty felt her insides withering. Those were some of the very works she'd felt so ashamed of lately. They were Mabel Lucie Attwell. They were twee. She'd liked them at the time. But now her ambitions were so much greater, designs unfurling in her mind like a great green banner, rippling in the wind.

'I made those ages ago — I don't really do that sort of thing any more ...' she said helplessly, not daring to hope she'd be believed.

'But why not?' Then light seemed to dawn. 'Oh, I *see!*' It was more than Netty could. 'Of course! They're kiddy pictures. Did you have them in the nursery?' Her voice dropped an octave and several decibels. 'In *his* nursery?'

Netty couldn't reply and that was taken as answer enough. Deirdre placed the little pastel pictures down as if they were the holy relics of Saint Amadour himself. 'Come on, Felix, we must leave.' She tiptoed away as if from a shrine. Clearly she thought it was.

Back downstairs she took one of Netty's hands and covered it with hers. Two palmsful of sincerity. 'I'm *so* sorry Netty, barging up there that way, when it was clear it was so special, so private. You must have so many memories ...'

Paul cleared his throat to break the syrupy morbidity of the moment. Felix seemed suddenly to come to life.

'Netty, Paul, the reason we came here in the first place was to invite you for lunch.'

'Yes!' cried his wife, returned to the land of the living. 'We know this lovely place. We've arranged to meet Edouard and Peter there. You must come — you didn't have anything else arranged, did you?'

And so they left behind them the odour of sanctimony and swept off to lunch, expensively, near the ramparts of the hilltop town of Domme, with a magnificent view of the Dordogne wandering off towards its distant rendezvous with the Garonne.

The conversation was, unsurprisingly, monopolised by Deirdre. Netty found, between the *brochette de saumon* and the *gâteau basque,* that she could just drift off. She had acquired a carrier bag of goodies on their way up to the restaurant, having purchased in one of the tourist-trap shops a bottle of walnut oil, a tub of chestnut honey, rich, dark and resinous, and a couple of jars of *confit de canard,* reddish thighs swimming in yellow grease. Paul had looked at the *confit* with distaste. 'It's good, really it is,' she insisted. 'Your father and I had it several times at the Coq d'Or when we were staying there during the renovations.'

'It looks like a real artery-clogger,' he replied.

'No, it's not greasy, not really. They put it in the oven and it sort of dries it off. It's rich though, I will admit. You wait till you try the potatoes sautéed in goose fat!'

'Vegetarianism not really in round here, then?' he smiled.

'No, not really!'

The onslaught of heat began to slacken as they walked back from the ramparts, past the central square and the entrance to another descent to the Underworld — caves *everywhere,* Netty thought, like holes in a Swiss cheese — past the tower where once the Templars had languished in the last tortured phase of their Order's existence. They loaded themselves back into heat-filled cars and eased off down the congested hill.

They paused for half an hour at La Roque-Gageac, an extraordinary gaggle of houses with steep brown roofs strung out under a huge pitted rock-face, like a Dulac illustration for the brothers Grimm. 'How can people *live,* knowing there's all that weight of rock perched above them?' asked Deirdre. 'I wouldn't be able to sleep in my bed.' In front of the spectacle, the narrow ribbon of road, seething with August traffic, hung on grimly as it skirted the shore of the river.

On they charged, the Lukers, Netty and Paul in one car, following Edouard and Peter in Peter's Citroën. It was like watching Sir Lancelot ride a Shetland pony, thought Netty, seeing Edouard fold his elegant limbs into the tinpot interior of the 2CV.

Beynac was suddenly upon them. Literally, Netty felt; the huge fortress, overwhelming, overpowering, so high on its crag as soon to be out of sight from the car as they met the trickle of rust-red roofs and mouse-brown walls of the town, but its presence felt, just as a vulture is sensed by a wounded antelope. They edged their way along under the stone ambush of it. The river ran right beside the road. Tiny pleasure-craft were out on the green-brown water: it seemed the only way to get some perspective on the vertical grandeur of the place.

A flurry of ice-cream signs and T-shirts on stands, as the road hoisted them up through the town's higglety-pigglety into the hinterland. Green fields, spread-out car-parks, wobbly lines of cars and pilgrims, the narrow road ducking and diving, a mile inland, a wavering mile back on itself. The castle came into view once more as they reached the cobbled outreaches and parked. Craft shops, more ice-cream, more postcards: romanticised photos of balloon-flights over rose-pink battlements swathed in early morning mist.

The effort of reaching the castle by such indirect means had robbed them of the energy to enter the gate. They followed the ramparts instead. Even Deirdre's chatter had faltered into inconsequential spasms.

On the path by the ramparts, Peter pointed out a sign leading to a modern troglodytic dwelling. 'Fellow artist lives there,' he said, 'Can't say I fancy it much myself, must be bloody chilly in winter. Brass monkeys, I should think! Better off at old Dun Tremblin, bless it.'

Silence fell for a moment. They gazed up and down the long still river. They were as high above it as if in a creaking balloon-basket. Adrift above it all, coasting through history. A view of modern campsites: serried ranks of tents like tawdry imitations of the pavilions of Crusaders. Rows of canoes, drawn up on the shore, like an invasion of the Pawnee. All of it fenced in by protective lines of poplars with upward-pointing branches like hands beseeching heaven.

Across the river stood Fayrac castle. Further to the west, Castelnaud, proud and stately, taller than Beynac, seemingly less sprawling, less lumpen. Real warring castles swapped again and again by England and France in the war of a hundred long years.

Paul was leaning over the low wall to the right, as if to peer straight down at the river. Netty watched him idly. She hoped he'd stay in tonight. Surely this jaunt would have been enough excitement for one day. He needed his rest, really he did. As she watched, Edouard came up very close behind Paul, to contemplate the view as well. Paul turned his head slightly, acknowledging his arrival. He said something, Netty couldn't hear it. With an air of preoccupation, Edouard took another step forward to stand, not beside, but right behind Paul. His legs were apart. He bent slightly, and slowly, deliberately, shamelessly, put his hand on Paul's right buttock, then slid it down, just as slowly, in between Paul's legs from behind. She saw the muscles on his arm move, as they had back at Bara-Bahau, as his invisible hand clenched and squeezed.

Netty saw all this.

The drive back was a torture to her. Her mind batted around crazily like a panic-stricken bird. She brained herself against the solid reality of what she'd seen. She was horrified to find that her self-vaunted toleration of what she had guessed to be Paul's lifestyle simply did not exist in the face of such incontrovertible evidence. She was sickened. Aghast. Bereaved. Another son had died. Another son had died. That is how she thought on the long drive home, while Deirdre trilled and Felix complained that Peter, in spite of the decrepitude of his vehicle, drove too damn fast: 'He'll be right up our backside if he doesn't watch!'

Edouard and Peter had headed for Bel Arbre, where the Lukers were to join them after dropping Netty and Paul at Le Sanglier. Home at last, Netty took a glass from one of the kitchen cupboards and filled it with wine. She walked through to the Salle de Chasse, Paul a shadow at her heels. She felt the shaking begin at her ankles and knees and rise to her very spine, to her nape, to the top of her skull. To camouflage the shaking she put her glass down and started plumping up the cushions on the sofa. Plumping and patting and stroking.

'Paul,' she said casually over her shoulder to where he stood, 'how was it that you got here?'

His own personal radar may have told him something was in the offing. 'A flight to Bordeaux, Mum. You know that. And I picked up a hire car. It's that thing with four wheels standing out on the drive, in case you hadn't noticed.'

'Oh, I'd noticed. I've also noticed that you're lying. No flight to Bordeaux would bring you in at that time. You got here pretty early in the morning.'

'A bit too early for *you*, it looked like.'

She stopped patting and stroking. She came to stand in front of him. 'Don't try to turn the conversation. I'm wise to it. I'm wise to a lot, so don't bother lying to me. Why did you come here?'

He was sullenly angry. He might have been a schoolboy again. He was inches taller than her, close to her as if to challenge her tardy authority.

'Mother, just mind your own business. I won't bother you any longer. I'll pack my bag.'

'No!' she found herself shouting. 'No!' As he began to move she tugged like a frantic beggar at his upper sleeve. Her voice rose and rebounded from the oak beams. 'I won't have it, do you hear? I won't have it! You'll bloody well *talk* to me.' She was still plucking and riving at his sleeve. He was amazed.

'I told you to mind your own bloody business! I don't know what the hell's going on!'

'I'll tell you what's going on! What's going on is that I saw that tart Edouard with his hands between your legs. You didn't tell me he swung both ways, did you? Well, I know now, and it makes me *sick*. My God, have you no sense of self-control, no self-respect ...'

He was suddenly, threateningly, still. His voice was quiet. 'It seems to me that you were pretty keen on him yourself, mother dear, always gabbling on about him. *That* was disgusting — a middle-aged woman like you drooling all over him, and anyone with half an eye could see what he was. Had *you* no self-respect?'

They were both suddenly silent, staring at one another. Paul sat down, his head lowered. She stood over him, fighting the shakes, wondering what to say next. Then she noticed that what he was doing was weeping.

'I'm sorry, Mum, that wasn't fair.'

Netty stood nonplussed. She'd worked herself up into a state ready for combat, not this. She sat beside him and said nothing and waited for his tears to stop. It seemed to take a long time. She was half in a daze, and there in the darkening room she seemed to hear a woman's cries and her own tears, and Danny's shrieks, so often imagined, pulling the heart out of her each time. She looked at Paul's hands, clenching and unclenching. The fingers looked so massive, the sinews strong as wire. How could he be weeping?

'It's all Stephen's fault,' he muttered, finally.

'Stephen?' she said, tentatively, fearing he would retreat into himself, lower the portcullis, raise the drawbridge.

He sighed deeply and leaned back. She bit back the words 'nice cup of tea?' She wasn't sure that having set all this in motion she wanted it to go on. She wasn't sure she wanted to hear what he had to say, to have made explicit what had hitherto been tacit.

'You were right, Mum,' he said heavily, tiredly, each word costing him effort. 'I didn't fly into Bordeaux. I was already in France, in the Luberon, and I hadn't originally any intention of visiting you.' He looked up; those sheepish schoolboy eyes. 'I'm sorry, Mum.'

'It's OK. What the eye didn't see the heart wouldn't have grieved over, eh?'

Another sigh. 'I suppose so. Truth is, well, I've been having a bit of a sticky time of it over the past few months.'

'Because of this Stephen?'

'Because of Stephen. He was my ... partner, you might say.'

'Come on Paul, there's no need to beat about the bush. I've known for ages.'

'Does Dad know?'

'No, I don't think so. I think we'd know about it if he did. Best not to tell him.'

'God, I agree! I can't believe that *you* know about it. It's hard to talk about something I've kept secret for so long. When I went up to London first I — well, I had quite a time of it, you might say, looking for affection.'

She knew what they called it. Cruising. Like blue-rinsed Americans wearing Bermuda shorts, on vacation. An incongruous term.

'It wasn't the most satisfactory of lifestyles, not in the long run. I just didn't know what to do with myself. I couldn't help myself. Then I met Stephen and it all seemed OK. With him, I thought, I'll have stability, loyalty ... it'll be like a marriage.'

Marriage isn't always so full of trust and togetherness as you seem to believe, Netty thought, glumly.

'We were both in corporate futures, though with different firms. We've had more than a year together. Not that we've set up home or anything: we each have our own place.'

He went on talking, reminiscing. Netty thought of his flat, sterile in black and grey, never anything out of place. A tiny seed of fear took sudden root within her and sprouted at an alarming rate. She believed she knew what he was going to tell her and she had to resist the urge to flap her hands wildly in front of his face to shoo his confidence away.

'Anyway, to cut a long story short, I found that Stephen ...'

Oh God here it comes: Stephen has AIDS, Paul is dying.

'Stephen was involved in some insider dealing.' She looked blank. 'On the Exchange, if someone trades on information received from a privileged source to make money for themselves, it's illegal.'

She let her breath out quietly. She didn't give a shit if the unknown Stephen went all the way to Jail, do not pass Go, do not collect £200. Just as long as Paul was all right.

'What did you do?'

'Well, I didn't know what to do. I didn't want to find it out. I wasn't checking up on him. I trusted him. I was in the most horrible moral quandary. I hated him for that: that he put me in a position where I did more soul-searching than he obviously ever did on his own behalf.

'We fought and argued for ages. It was all a power-trip to him. He loved it. He knew I wouldn't report him and I hated him knowing me so well. Then, after all this, he comes to me and he says "Oh by the way Paul, thought I'd better tell you — I've been for the test — *the test* — don't you think you should too?"'

Netty's heart bounded like a hare flushed out of covert. God, she thought, I was right the first time.

'So I said to him, was there any particular reason why I should have the test, or was he just being super-cautious. And he laughed in my face and said "Oh Paul my dear, you didn't actually expect faithfulness, did you?" "Well, yes I did. I didn't think it even needed saying," I answered. "Till death do us part?" he asked, and then I hit him. Several times and there was blood on his face but he seemed to like it. It was all control you know. He liked to hold that threat over me, just as I'd held the threat of going to the police. Even though he knew I wouldn't do it, he had to take revenge on me for having had the option. For having had the balance of power.'

Netty's throat was tight. More than ever she wanted that cup of tea, or something stronger. 'And did you ... did you take the test?'

'Had to. You can see that, can't you? I had to know. He was sure of that.'

'And was it ...'

'Oh Mum, I'm sorry. No, no, don't worry. It's all right: it was negative. I should have said that straight off.' He enfolded her in his arms, and she thought of the blood pumping clear and clean in his veins. Oh thank God, she thought; unsullied, saved.

'So how come you were in France?'

His grip tightened and he laughed harshly. 'Oh, wait till you hear this one, Mum! This is the *pièce de resistance,* or the *coup de grâce* or whatever you want to call it. I was on holiday with Stephen — would you credit it? We'd hired a villa. With pool. It was supposed to be our great reconciliation scene. We lasted two days: he was off down to the coast to pick up rent boys: said did I fancy coming? You know those times when you put your foot out at the end of a flight of stairs, thinking there's another step to come and there isn't? And you slam down and it judders all through you, the shock of it? Well, it was like that. I thought there was someone there, that Stephen was someone — but he wasn't really there at all.

'So it's over. We had a blazing row and I left. I expect he's still laughing. I bet he tormented cats when he was a little boy.'

He smiled ruefully at her. 'So I came running to Mummy.'

'But why, why after all this, Edouard ... ?'

'God, I don't know, Mum. I just felt bitter and wild and I couldn't stop myself. And with Edouard there was no false illusion. You just put your money down. No smiling face making you love it and then laughing at you for doing so. Just a business transaction. Just insider trading.'

'Would you ever have told me all this on your own?'

'No, I don't think so.' A heavy sigh. She contemplated those masculine hands of his. Hands inherited from the Feldwick side of the family. Not wispy weedy hands like hers, hands that failed to keep hold of things. The awful words she'd heard, the kind of words Gerald himself used, were running through her head: grotesque, brutal, explicit. Brown-noser. Shirt-lifter. Chocolate-stabber. Her son. Why had this happened, why was this so?

'Oh Paul, surely you knew you could come to me, tell me. Why didn't you tell me?'

Those hands, Gerald's hands, began to shake. Paul looked fiercely at her and she quailed.

'Jesus, Mother, Jesus *Christ!*'

He rose and strode about the room, his words attacking her from all angles.

'Are you quite of this world, or not? You sit there and ask me why I didn't talk. When I've got a father who cracks jokes about queers and tells me not to bend down for the soap in the school showers. A father who runs away from what he can't cope with, and drags you off on this magical mystery tour — and you, you bloody *let* him! A father who weeps into his whisky, whining for his little boy and doesn't even look around to see that I'm here. I'm still here — and Lynda too, though neither of you seem to credit it.'

Netty felt breath going from her in a sequence of little gasps, as if she were a punchbag and must take these repeated blows. He came right up to her; she sank back into the cushions. His look was wild and inflamed.

'Christ, look up from your Mother of Sorrows bit and look at *us* — we're your children — think what it has been like for *us* Can you imagine? Can you possibly stretch that obsessed brain of yours and imagine that Lynda and I have feelings too?

'We were never jealous of Danny. When he came along, we loved him, we loved him too. But we're jealous now, we're jealous of him in death, because he's got your entire attention. You feel so bloody guilty, don't you, because it was you who lost him, that day.'

She began to cry. 'Paul, don't, don't. I can't bear it. Don't talk this way.'

'Don't talk, you mean. Don't let anyone talk about this. Private property. Trespassers on Mrs Feldwick's grief will be frozen out.

'You're so damn *proud* of playing the martyr, but deep down you *know* it won't redeem you. You *know* you're the one who let him go and you just can't live with yourself for it and you won't let any of us come near. Lynda and I talk on the phone. That surprises you, doesn't it? We were never that close, but I tell you there's nothing like shared rejection to give siblings a common cause. And you're a bitch to her, Mother; it's just as well she's so far away. You look at her as if she turned into a Stepford Wife one weekend. You don't give her credit for any feelings at all.'

'I do! I'm proud of both of you — your father and I are always saying ...'

'Bullshit! Middle-class bullshit. So Lynda's got a house with pillars and two air-conditioned cars, and I'm "doing well in the city". Jesus! Just look beneath the surface for one bloody minute! Lynda's petrified that Bradley will trade her in for a new model, and me,' he ran his hand frantically through his hair, 'me, I'm up shit-creek without a paddle.'

He bent down, stuck his face close to hers. 'You love Danny best because you know where and what he is. He's neatly labelled and filed away under "Innocence, death of". Nice and safe, nice and tragic. And you can carry the signs of your grief like the stigmata through the rest of your life and expect tact and understanding from others. They won't dare enter the holy of holies, Netty's sorrow — no. It would be sacrilegious.'

'Cruel, you ... cruel!' She rose and slapped him. Her turn to sob. 'Believe me, believe me, I love you, I really do, I just ... Danny was so little ...'

'That's it, isn't it. That's what makes it so clear-cut. He was little, he was utterly innocent; he did nothing to deserve his death, other than trust a stranger. There's nothing there to complicate the issue for you: just his innocence, little white flower nipped in the bud, and your guilt. Your little ewe-lamb and the big bad wolf — as obvious as a fairy-tale. A boy too young to be made of frogs and snails and puppy-dog tails. Not like the rest of us.'

How had it all come to this? She'd started the evening in control, challenging him, expecting him to defend himself. She sobbed and sobbed, turning away. He grabbed at her shoulder.

'There you go again. You hang onto your grief, mother, as if you patented it. It's all yours, finest quality. No one else can ever match it. Why don't you add a little disgust and revulsion? Come on, say it. Stop the Samaritans act. You saw Edouard feeling my balls. Come on, come on — how did that *really* strike you? Come on, tell me!'

'All right!' she shrieked, at bay. 'All right! You *disgust* me — you *disgust* me — what you do sickens me. When I think of Danny, how good and pure and untouched — and what that bastard did to him ... You come along and tell me of *lovers* and expect me to understand and all I can think is that the things you do, the things you delight to do, are the things he did! Perverted, murderous ...' Her breath wouldn't let her go on.

'Oh good,' he panted. 'So that's how it is. That's how you see me. You rank my dirty deeds with the worst of child molesters. Well, thanks Mum. Thanks a lot. At least we've cleared the air. So don't worry, I'm off now. It's finished. It's a relief.'

And then she was throwing herself at him, holding him, gripping him to her, exhausted with melodrama. 'No, don't go, you mustn't go!'

'I have to.'

Power. It was all about power and control, this caring about people.

'Don't go out there: it's dark.'

'Don't be stupid. We've had our say.'

'God, I'm sorry, I'm sorry. I didn't mean ...'

'*Au contraire,* I think, deep down, you did.'

The telephone rings to the exhausted air. She is astounded to find it is still only half past nine. She goes out into the hall to answer it.

Returning, surprised to find him still standing there, she says, 'That was your father. He'll be home tomorrow.'

'Then I'm *definitely* for the off.' He turns in the doorway, his shadow cast in wobbly exaggeration behind him. 'Oh, and Mum, whatever you do, *don't* tell Dad, eh?'

Aristo

The blade was sharp. The deer lay, its flanks heaving, foam and blood dappling the pale coat. The dogs had been whipped back to stand panting and whimpering with excitement.

Charles Auguste Joseph Vimarin, sixth Comte de Saint-Eymet, nodded to his chief huntsman, Martin Cabochard, who had just handed his whip to one of the others in order to draw his thick short knife.

The deer's breathing was stertorous in the quiet glade, louder than the rasping eagerness of the hounds. On a whim, the Comte told Cabochard to stop. His huntsman stepped back. Vimarin took the knife from him and strode forward to the wretched animal. He looked down into the liquid eyes, darkest brandy. He could see how its heart agitated its frame, how the small hoofs twitched in an effort to rise, scrabbling at the leaves and mould.

He felt the familiar tightening of the groin. How often at Versailles, honoured to be one of the king's party and as addicted as his sovereign to the sport of the chase, had he longed to take the knife himself and release the creature. The glorious hesitation on the threshold of eternity, the transformation from animate existence to mere dead meat: the very reversal of the mystery of the Eucharist. It was a philosophical as well as a physical pleasure.

He fingered the knife, exerting just enough pressure to feel a slight thrill at the imminence of metal piercing skin, the pad of his thumb like *a ripe grape squeezed to bursting point. So near to death, the life within one's veins, pumping in contained canals, so easily breached.*

He held the deer's eyes in a sweet communion as he knelt and pulled the knife towards him, slicing its throat with the efficiency of a practised slaughterer. Breath and blood bubbled into the cool air.

The Comte sighed. He placed a hand on the still-warm head, as if in benediction. The hair was dense and springy. A spatter of blood was on his lace cuff. The moment was over. He turned swiftly away and out of the dell, leaving his men to paunch the creature and reward the dogs with its entrails.

His horse took only a few minutes to make its way up the green and amber rides, out from under the canopy of beech and chestnut onto the broad shoulder of the ancient hill. Once or twice the sound of stone rang out from under the hoofs. He had heard tell of fragments of road and dwellings from centuries long gone, evidence of generation after generation coming and going, the flux of life speeding like shadows, flitting into death beyond the sombre shade of the slowly growing trees. How many of these branches had arched across the path since the passage of the Roman or the armoured knight or the rebellious Croquant? How many Huguenots had fled the wrath of the true church, perhaps by the skirts of this very hill? How many had passed this way since his own ancestor had built the Château de Lazolles in celebration of the nobility granted him by Charles the Fifth in the wars against the English?

His horse gallantly crested the last steep slope. There in the sun, still early, still palest gold, stood the rawness of the newest Vimarin possession. His hunting lodge, named for the wild boar living deep in the forest.

His houses stood for the aspects of his nature. The Hôtel Vimarin, in the Faubourg St Germain, for so many years locked up or let, as life in Paris was so prohibitively expensive. Now, in the late dawn of his fortunes, ready to blaze again with the glitter of its Bohemian chandeliers and rococo gilding, whenever its master chose to grace the salons of the capital.

The ancient stronghold, Lazolles, fit prize for nobility of the sword, nobility of ancienne race, *stood for the staunchness of his blood-line and the well-held loyalty that kept pride high through all the vicissitudes of the royal descent from Valois to Bourbon. He was proud of it, but disdainful of its lack of comfort. The Vimarins had progressed, and so must the quality of their habitations.*

And so Bel Arbre had come to be the jewel; the ruination of his father, the perfection he had completed, albeit at the price of marrying beneath him — the daughter of one of the Farmers General. Nobility was a matter of blood, but survival was a matter of practicality. Marie-Louise was insipid, silently reproachful, well-trained but lacking in grandeur of spirit. However, her father's coffers were well-filled, thanks to his farming of the tax on tobacco. Bel Arbre was grey silk and Valenciennes lace. It was a minuet in the mirrored halls of Versailles. It was courtliness in the heart of impoverished Périgord.

Now, Le Sanglier. The hunt, the chase, the kill. All male.

She was waiting, as instructed. He dismounted, his excitement still upon him. Seizing her wrist, he pulled her into the lodge. The high hall, too grand for the rest of the building, was cold and unfinished. The floor was only half-tiled and the chill air came through the as-yet unglazed casements. There was the smell of raw wood and damp. A far cry from the embroidered hangings of his sumptuous bed at Bel Arbre.

Her eyes were as dark and fathomless as those of the deer. She matched his gaze as he took her, watching him impassively as he sank into his little death and was resurrected to the smell of blood as his men toiled up the slope and dumped the body of the slain deer outside the chamber window.

He ordered her back to Bel Arbre before him and stayed awhile in the serenity of fulfilment. A good morning, a good day, until latent desire should stir again.

Marital

Gerald rang her again, from Heathrow. 'Listen love, no need to come all the way to Bordeaux for me. I know how hot it is out there. Bit of a trial for you.'

'Actually, it's not that bad today.' The sky had changed from cerulean blue to whitish grey and every so often a dispirited drizzle fell, tepid like tea.

'No, no, it's OK. I'll get the train from Bordeaux and I'll give you a ring from Bourdonne. You can come and pick me up there.'

'Well, if you're sure.'

'Absolutely! Look, they're calling my flight. See you in a few hours. And Netty ...'

'Yes?'

'I'm looking forward to seeing you, love.'

She gazed in surprise at the receiver in her hand, before putting it gently down.

By five o'clock he was with her, sitting with a cold beer in the Salle de Chasse. He looked around. She'd had time to tidy up. The bed stood, stripped and forlorn, in the spare room.

'Paul was here,' she said, wanting to say it quickly. She knew that if she didn't tell him, someone else would.

Gerald looked startled. 'Good God, what brought him here?'

'Oh, he was just passing through,' she replied. 'On his way up from the Luberon. He'd hired a villa down there. I think he wanted to make a bit of a tour of it — said something about visiting the Loire.'

'Shame I missed him.'

'Yes. He said he needed to be back in the office by Monday, so it gave him three days to drive up to the coast and visit the sights on the way. We had a lovely time: I took him about, showed him various places. He went, oh, late yesterday afternoon.'

'Pity I didn't ring earlier.'

'Yes, bad timing that. I'm sure he'd have waited if he'd known.' She felt the bile brewing at the bottom of her gullet. 'I thought you'd be in Britain a bit longer. It all sounded so complicated.'

'It was. It was.' He sighed and stared at the empty fireplace. He looked tired. She went over to him and kissed him gently.

'I'm glad to have you back.'

'I'm glad to *be* back. You were OK, were you, when I was away? I mean, you sounded a bit funny that first time I rang.'

'Yes, yes,' she said. 'It's been fine. Everyone's been so nice to me and I've been getting to know them.' She prattled inconsequentially about Fred, Claudine, Peter, Edouard, the Lukers. She made him laugh. She saw him visibly unwind and she was touched that he had been so tense for her sake. Her whole attitude towards him changed. Wounded by Paul, not daring to dwell any more on his words, she burrowed into the comfort of Gerald's solid presence. She understood him; he really hadn't wanted to leave her. She'd been awful to him. He was glad to be back. She'd make him even gladder.

They spent the next few weeks like newly-marrieds setting up house together for the first time. They spent a day in Bordeaux, where she bought tapestry wool and twelve-point canvas. She tried experiments on little scrap pieces; combinations of colour and stitches. Gerald found hanks of numbered Persian yarn and rough sketches lying about the place. Finally, she set about making charts. Gerald found himself admiring her, and said so.

And all would have been well, but for the dreams.

Some were of Edouard, bending over Paul, sucking the blood from him, like Christopher Lee in one of those shrill Hammer horrors. Each time, Paul would rise, the puncture wounds dripping, and dip into his pocket to give Edouard a coin which, cloak whirling, Edouard would immediately spin onto a roulette wheel which said LIFE/DEATH/LIFE/DEATH.

At least these occult little numbers were something new. The other dreams were familiar; a ghastly reprise of the aftermath of Danny's death.

The hunt had been scaled down, and she couldn't bear it. Often she prowled up and down the Cowley Road, reliving that ghastly calvary. She knew the shopkeepers recognised her and pitied her. She resented it and she feared any blame, any further blame. 'Look — that's the woman who let her little boy be carried off and didn't even notice. Well, I ask you, how could she?'

There was no relief to be found there, so she started her pilgrimages out to the fields by Marston. She would turn the car off from the busy link road, cross the cycle track and park in the farm track by the little grove where Danny had lain, waiting to be found.

In front of her would be a stolen car: some joyrider had taken it, burned it out, left it. A Ford Capri, bonnet and wheels gone, bodywork bright orange with rust. A huge expanse of broad field opened up beyond it, on towards the University Parks and the heavy blocks of the Science area and in the distance the airy pinnacles of St Mary the Virgin.

She'd sit there, not letting go of the steering wheel. If she felt strong enough she'd get out and stand in front of the thicket of bush and young trees, lavish with growth.

And once, a man rose from the undergrowth, beside the wrecked car.

This, she dreamt about.

Long long ago, Paul had played Ariel in a school production of *The Tempest*. He had sung:

Full fathom five thy father lies
Of his bones are coral made:
Those are pearls that were his eyes:
Nothing of him that doth fade,
But doth suffer a sea-change
Into something rich and strange.

She had always thought how clean and pure that transubstantiation was, a transformation smelling of ozone and kelp, the biting persuasion of sea-salt. Better than mould and clay, heavy and cloying. Better the scoured bleak bone swirling with the tide. Danny's spirit could have gone wandering the seven seas, like an ethereal Hornblower. Instead, he was stuck under the turf at Kidlington, his muffled cries still coming to her. She wished she could have made a little raft for him and shot it full of burning arrows, her baby Viking, and let him roll on down the sweet Thames adrift in ash and flame to sink into the clean grey sea.

In late August, the Feldwicks dined at the Lelouche farm. Netty was glad her French had improved: as long as the conversation limited itself to mundane affairs she felt she could hold her own.

They dined on a terrace at the back of the farmhouse. Rich scents hung heavy on the air. The *vendange* would soon begin.

Mathilde, thought Netty, as she sat at the long trestle table and the first insects sawed the air and the first barber-shop chorus of frogs began to gulp and bellow; Mathilde is, in her own way, as stately as Claudine. Look at her, carrying dishes to the table, and serving and pouring and eating with precision and taking things away. She's so self-contained. I don't think that it's just that she's wary of us. Look: she hardly gives a smile to the rest of the family. Augustin there, sinking Pécharmant in a way that must impress even Gerald. Norbert down by the corner, what a shambles; he looks like he's done something he shouldn't and expects to have to spend the night in the kennel. Albert, wiry as a whippet, bare feet thrust into flip-flops, toe-nails in a disgusting state. His wife Solange, brown and shy, limpid eyes, looking cowed as the men talk and Mathilde ignores her.

Fred was there too. Netty made a point of being lovey-dovey with Gerald. She felt let down by the Professor: he was wise to the ways of the world, he must have known about Edouard. Why hadn't he warned her?

The meal began with soup, rich in garlic. They were instructed by the Lelouches to *faire le Chabrol,* which involved swilling red wine into the dregs in the bowl and drinking it as if from a cup.

Home-made pâté followed, sealed into pots with yellow butter. Netty dreaded to think of the cholesterol levels or of the poor geese with funnels down their gizzards to force-feed them. So far, so good, she thought: no hen's feet or tripe sausages.

The main course was a relief: the familiar *confit de canard,* served with green beans and yards of bread. By the cheese course, the conversation was really motoring. Even Gerald had to admit that the Professor was useful as a translator. He was feeling the benevolence of the Pécharmant and was coming round to the view that the Prof wasn't so bad after all.

They talked about wine, about regulations, about the Arab problem. 'An Arab?' snorted Augustin. 'That is not a person.' Embarrassed, the English guests smiled tightly and went on.

'It is so hot,' volunteered Netty in French, with courage born of good red wine. She nodded towards the great wolf-like farm dogs panting in the shade. 'One would need a tail in this heat.'

They looked at her in silence, and she felt her frail smile evaporate. The men laughed. 'Annette,' said Fred, 'the word for tail in French is the same as the slang word for penis: *la queue.*'

She went scarlet. Gerald patted her hand benignly. 'Well, that's *one* way of breaking the ice!' he said, and laughed and nodded at Augustin and Albert.

When Netty next felt able to pay any sort of attention to the conversation, they were talking about the war. Mathilde had abruptly left the table and could be heard washing dishes indoors. Netty wondered if she should offer to help; she didn't know what the rules were. Perhaps Mathilde would take dreadful offence and fix her with a stony glare. Better to leave it. Norbert had shuffled off at some point, his presence having struck no one with any more force than if a bundle of old rags had been piled on a chair. No one could have pinpointed the moment of his departure.

'I remember hiding in a cornfield,' Augustin was saying, 'and watching the armoured cars and lorries go past. They were all over the place — bastards. They used to get their bread at the bakery in Malignac.' Netty tried to imagine it: jackboots clouded with dust and flour in the *boulangerie, pain de son* and *pain de campagne* tucked under uniformed arms.

'Of course,' said Gerald, 'we English just can't imagine how that felt.' She agreed with him, but in his efforts to show sympathy, she felt he ran the risk of sounding patronising, implicitly saying to the French, 'Well we *English* of course don't really know what an occupation is like. Haven't had such a thing since 1066.'

'Some of the bastards were even up at your place for a while,' added Albert. Augustin shot a look towards the kitchen window, from which the clatter of china came echoing.

Netty chilled at the thought. 'What happened?' asked Gerald, curious. Fred sipped his wine quietly.

'They were trying to flush out some of the Francs Tireurs — part of the Resistance. They were in the woods up there. Some men from the village included,' said Albert.

'And did they manage it?'

'They shot people,' Albert shrugged. 'This is what happened: Mouleydier, Sarlat, Périgueux, here. It happened. It was the war.'

Augustin took hold of the conversation and turned it into another channel. Little Solange trotted out in the wake of Mathilde, carrying bowls of fruit and a huge apricot clafoutis.

Around midnight, after protracted farewells at the farm, they had coffee and brandy with the Professor. Netty half-dozed in the little sitting-room, familiar and yet strange to her now, while Fred showed Gerald round.

'Blimey! She's a big girl!' said Gerald, looking at the photograph of the Venus figure.

'Steatopygous,' said the Professor.

'What?'

'Big-arsed. Good word, isn't it!'

Gerald laughed, and laughed even more at the rampant little Priapus.

That night she had an orgasm with Gerry, her first in — how long? As the tremors died away she became aware that he was weeping in her arms. Touched that he should be so moved by her response, she gathered him to her and soothed him to sleep.

The phone rang. It was Deirdre. 'Netty dear, do come over, and bring Gerald. You realise we haven't seen you since he got back?'

'I know. I'm sorry.'

'Oh don't apologise! Just come and see us. Claudine misses you too.'

Deirdre sounded fine, at the time.

In the hall at Bel Arbre, Felix was on the phone, talking volubly. He raised an arm to them as they passed by.

Claudine and Deirdre were in the salon. Patapon lay dozing at Claudine's feet. Deirdre jumped up to embrace Netty and then Gerald. She started to speak, then seemed to have an obstruction in her throat, like on the night of the dinner party when she choked on her sweet.

Claudine came forward at a more measured pace, with a smile of genuine welcome. She planted two kisses in the air at either side of Netty's face. She smelt, still, of lilies, penetrating in their acrid purity.

'Oh Netty!' Deirdre burst out, the bronze of her tan looking sallow against the eau de nil of the walls. 'Oh Gerald ... !' and she reached out her hand in a trembling faint-maiden gesture.

'Deirdre, what's wrong?' he asked.

'Everything!'

Claudine shook her head slightly and called for Hortense. 'Tea,' she ordered, firmly.

'Gerald, I'm so glad to see you again, and it's so *sad,* so unfair! Here you are just back — and you didn't come to see us *immediately,* shame on you, and now we're leaving.'

'Leaving?' asked Netty. 'But I thought you had at least another week or so.'

'If I'd had anything to do with it we'd have had more than *that.* But no, we have to go, immediately. It's all falling apart!'

If this were a Georgette Heyer novel, thought Netty, we'd be sending for the hartshorn and the burnt feathers by now.

'What's falling apart?' demanded Gerald. 'Come on, tell us!'

At that moment Felix entered. His clothes were as dapper as ever, but his hair was ruffled and on end. He moved quickly across the room, as if something were snapping at his heels, and shook hands with Gerald. 'It's damned ironic, this whole thing,' he said. 'There you were back in England, sorting out your business ...'

'Well, not *my* business, strictly speaking.'

'The business you sold to your best friend, wasn't it?'

'Roy. Yes. He was in a bit of a fix, as it happens. Couldn't not lend him a hand.'

'Right. Loyalty: that's what it's about, Gerry, loyalty. Well, while you're there doing the decent thing, here's Deirdre and me sunning ourselves and enjoying Claudine's excellent hospitality,' — a nod to his hostess, acknowledged — 'and all the time ... God, it makes me want to ...'

'*What,* for God's sake!'

'Back at DeLix, our best friend, Deirdre's cousin in fact ...'

Deirdre bridled. 'Now don't you go blaming me, just because I happen to be related to him.'

'And who, may I ask, just happened to bring him into the company? Who but Madame Nepotism, sitting not a million miles away.'

'Felix, don't you dare — it was a joint decision ...'

'Joint decision,' he repeated bitterly. 'Just when did we ever make a joint decision? Eh? Not since my balls ended up in your clutch.'

'*Felix!*'

Netty was fascinated. Gerald held up a hand. 'Would you two say truce just for a moment, just long enough to tell me what exactly has been happening?'

Felix held his wife's gaze as he spoke. 'Deirdre's cousin, our much trusted third in command, Harry Baxter, has been quietly or not quietly enough cooking the books at DeLix Properties. Especially while we enjoyed our little jaunts abroad, fruits of our labours. Now we're up to our necks in it — the Revenue, the VAT men, the Serious Fraud Office — for non-declaration, embezzlement — you name it, our Harry's dabbled in it.'

Deirdre began to cry into the silence. Neither Netty nor Gerald knew what to say. The tea arrived. Claudine went over to place her arm round Deirdre's heaving shoulders.

'You must be calm,' she said.

'Calm!' shouted Felix. 'When that ferret of a cousin of hers ...'

'You see?' sobbed Deirdre. 'He's always going to blame me. All I've ever done is try to help him, support him.'

'Push him around, you mean.'

'Only when you needed it! Where would you be without me, I'd like to know.'

'Not heading for bankruptcy or the clink I wouldn't be!'

Over Deirdre's sobbing Claudine said, with a streak of iron in her voice, 'It is useless to have these recriminations. It is necessary to be practical. Thanks to Henri I have friends in the financial world. I will do what I can.'

Felix simmered down. 'Thank you Claudine,' he said. 'You're a friend. Deirdre, for Christ's sake stop bawling.'

Netty sat and watched and felt herself shiver. She remembered the day in La Gabare. She remembered Deirdre's confidence. Nothing was safe in this world. Nothing was ever safe. The tea grew cold in the pot and the two men exchanged glances over the head of Deirdre of the Sorrows.

Netty watched the man rise up from the hollow in the grass where he had couched like a pheasant. Up he rose and confronted her. She looked at him, she looked him in the eye. She came round the car, brushing orange rust off onto her skirt as she did so. She moved forward. She knew he would not be able to move away. The knife cut through the shabby filthy cloth with ease. Half-rotten, the fibres fell away. Dirt. He wore dirt. He was dirt. He was shit.

The knife paused. His cock was tiny, coiling away from her, curling into retreat. She smiled. He was so exposed.

She stared at him, at his pleading. The knife arced swiftly into his heart, into an explosion of red, then, as the body fell, she cried out in rage at her own mercy and bent to slash wildly at his genitals as he crumpled to the ground. He lay on the green altar where he had sacrificed Daniel.

She woke. The dream again, the dream that gave the killer a face. She shuddered with hatred and regret. She always made it too easy for him.

Debate

It was autumn, and the hills were alive with the sound of gunfire.

'They'll shoot anything,' said Gerald, coming into the kitchen. Netty looked up from her mid-morning coffee, sipped, French-style, strong and milky from a big round bowl. 'I know,' she answered. 'The sound of it's driving me mad. Can there be anything left alive in the woods when they're done?'

'Probably not!'

'Poor little songbirds!'

'By the way,' he said casually. 'Peter's coming over later. He's bringing Ed.'

'Ah.'

'Ah indeed. Look, Net, what's got into you? I seem to remember you were quite keen on the oily rag a while ago. Gone off him, have you?'

She tried to turn it into a joke. 'Yup — like all crushes, it's burnt itself out. I was the same for Elvis, once.'

'Like the greasy ones, don't you.'

'I suppose I must. What're they coming over for?'

For a moment she thought it was his turn to look shifty. 'Oh, chat about this and that. You know.'

'I suppose they'll want lunch,' said Netty, mentally reviewing the larder and fridge. Outside another gunshot ricocheted in waves of sound from the hill.

'No, don't bother. Thought we'd pop down to the Coq d'Or, put a bit of trade René Quiberon's way. Don't suppose you'll want to come?'

'Actually, I quite fancy it.'

'Ah.'

'And I think I'll give Fred a ring and see if he wants to join us.'

'Well, if you must.'

'I thought you'd changed your mind about him. You were quite friendly with him that night at the dinner party at Grand Caillou, and you drank enough of his brandy afterwards!'

'Yes. Well. I suppose he's OK. In small doses.'

Six weeks. This is how it had been: Netty and Gerald, caring and careful. Stepping on eggshells, frightened to disturb the fragile equilibrium. He had been affectionate, tentative; not inflicting on her the overpowering lust and need that had so besieged her before his departure for England. In return she had been sunny and positive. Her songs drifted down to him from the tower room where her floor-frames bore her canvases. She spent hours up there, slowly filling with rich warm wool the outlines she had traced. She wouldn't let him see what she was doing. She didn't talk of the past, or of dreams, or of Danny. Neither did he.

Down at the Coq d'Or the Feldwicks were on their second *apéro* when Peter came breezing in, carrying a long canvas bag and trailing a rather weary-looking Edouard in his wake. Been working hard, have we, thought Netty.

When he greeted her he held her eyes for that one significant second more than necessary. 'Annette,' he said, and the voice was still a caress.

Was it someone like you, she thought, in the private jurisdiction of her mind, who bent down to my little son and carried him away? An unfair bitter thought, born of frustration and despair, because, like Gerald, she longed for a target. As unjust as her treatment of Paul had been — Paul, who might as well have dropped off the face of the earth since their quarrel. Inside her overcrowded secret self, the pain of that silence barged into all her other pains and guilts.

Peter was rabbiting on. 'Gerry, you must come over and see Dun

Tremblin. Your lady wife was quite impressed!'

She raised a smile, she raised a glass. 'It was certainly full of *character*, Peter!'

'Absolutely! And the new *chefs d'oeuvre* are coming along *beautifully*. Had a first firing of the ceramics last week. My gallery's going to love them, even if our friend Fred doesn't.'

Friend Fred only sloped in as they took their seats after making their selections from the vast *buffet campagnard*. Not for the first time Netty found herself wondering how on earth small businesses like the Coq d'Or broke even, let alone made a profit, when they catered so lavishly for so little recompense.

Looking at Fred, she felt suddenly nostalgic for those nights at the cottage while Gerald had been away; their long free talks.

'Any word of the Luker drama?' he asked, sitting down with a plateful of *crudités* and *terrine de campagne*. No one could say very much. Claudine, the primary conduit of information on this subject, was in Paris.

'Could be banged up in Pentonville,' said Peter brightly.

'Not Deirdre, she's a woman,' replied Netty.

'Well, knowing Deirdre, she'd *prefer* a men's prison!' Gerald guffawed.

'Poor Deirdre,' said Netty, and was surprised to find that she meant it. 'It must be awful for her.'

'Oh, don't you worry about *her*,' answered Peter. 'She's a fighter. Lay you a bet she dumps Felix in it and takes off.'

'Done,' said Fred.

'Anyway, Fred old stick, how's life at the retreat? Buried yourself away a bit there, haven't you, you old fossil?'

'Had some work to do, actually, Peter. I've been writing an article for *Genius Loci* on Gallo-Roman worship of Dionysus in this region and how it might have been synthesised with earlier mother-goddess cults, as, for example, at that temple we know to be up in the woods. I tracked down a depiction of the Etruscan version of Dionysus, rejoicing in the name of Fufluns Pacha, who had been placed in conjunction with the tutelary divinity Vesuna, some kind of vegetation goddess. What I'm considering is whether there's any link with our local goddess Vesunna, up at Périgueux, and whether the worship of Dionysus and Vesunna could have co-existed amicably in the Gallo-Roman era. Would there have been any interchange between them? Female power, for example, could have been given expression through the frenzies of the Maenads.'

'Sorry I asked,' said Peter in a stage-whisper to Gerald. 'Fred's got the bit between his teeth. Typical academic — they never stop bloody lecturing!'

'Who were the Maenads?' asked Netty.

'Female worshippers of Dionysus, who worked themselves into a transcendental state, whereupon they were visited by the god. Legend has it that they would hunt down some creature in the woods, maybe even a man, and they would tear it apart with their bare hands.'

'Ugh! That's horrible!' shuddered Netty. 'To think that women ...'

'Ah! You feel, do you not, that the fairer sex should be incapable of such aggression?'

'Well, yes, I suppose so. It's certainly how *I* am,' protested Netty. 'I've never wanted to tear anything apart in my life.' It's a lie, her inner self cried, I'm a one-woman lynch-mob, looking for my victim. If only I knew who he was.

The Professor looked at her piercingly. He saw that she lied. 'Ah, but Annette, the Great Mother, in spite of her huge breasts and gargantuan hips, is a ruthless force of death as well as life, demanding our immolation as individual identities in the eternal cycle of life and death, the eternal see-saw between female and male, light and dark. But we men, we little walking sperm-banks, we poor bare forked animals, we want more than to be swallowed up in the great womb of eternity. Each of us wants to say "I was here, I was *me*, I was unique."'

He paused to take a sip of wine.

'Female,' said Peter. 'Deadlier than the male. Well known fact.'

'All very Freudian,' said Gerald. 'Eh, Prof? Tell me, did you have a nanny when you were young? She seems to have left quite an impression, if you did.'

The merest twitch of his lips told Netty that Fred was angry. 'OK,' he said. 'Lecture over. Here endeth the lesson.'

Suddenly Edouard, the silent one, spoke. 'It seems to me your studies are appropriate, Professeur; for this region associates the forces of the male and the female. The Périgord is described as the cradle of man; it is the nurse of humanity. Yet its history is also of war and destruction: the Romans, the English, the Nazis.' He paused. 'Your pardon, of course — I do not wish to associate the English with the Nazis.'

'I should bloody well hope not!' snorted Gerald.

'Mind you,' said the Prof, 'during the Hundred Years' War we English committed our share of atrocities. It happens, it always happens. In wartime there is no good or bad — there is survival, that's all.'

'Now look here!' said Gerald. 'Of course there's good and bad in war. Ed just mentioned the bloody Nazis, for God's sake.'

'So you are saying that it can be right to kill?'

'Too bloody right! It was a moral obligation to get rid of that crew — where would we be if we hadn't?'

'Well, yes, Gerald, I take your point. But the point *I* want to make is that in the struggle for survival, we always need to find a moral justification for what we do. We call on God as divine reinforcement, we give our feuds titles and causes: Crusade, Jihad, Liberation. Or we euphemise: the Nazis gave genocide a pen-pushing label that put emphasis on logistics rather than morals.'

'The Final Solution.'

'Right. Anything rather than admit that it means knives in guts, gas in lungs, blood, decay, stench.'

'Stop it! Shut up!' cried Netty, shaking. 'There's no need for all this! All this morbid detail! You relish it — even you, you relish it!'

Again, she thought, I accuse others of my own sin. How many times have I pictured the process of death at work on Danny? But it is taboo, taboo to think it, taboo to talk of it. Talk instead of a nice funeral, of a lovely service, of a shiny box, brass handles, lavish flowers, a granite headstone. Beloved son, preserved in inscription.

'My dear, I'm so sorry. God, how tactless of me. I was a bit carried away, I suppose, trying to make my point.'

Gerald wouldn't let go. 'The point being, I suppose, that however much we tart it up with fancy labels, it's dog eat dog out there.'

'Yes. And worse than dog. Even the holy institutions set up to sanctify the structures of society — the Platonic idea of rising to the godlike in us, leaving the beast behind — even these institutions become corrupt, until we think it right to oppress and kill in the name of God. We kill the infidel, we torture the heretic. Look at the Cathars, and the dreadful subjugation of the Knights Templar and the mutual murder of Catholic and Huguenot in this area.'

'So it's human nature, then, no matter how we try to avoid it: that's what you're saying.'

'I suppose so. The nature of the beast — if that weren't an insult to beasts.'

'It's an insult to man.'

'So be it.'

Edouard chipped in. 'Professor, you are a cynic. Surely man is more than beast. Surely religion has lifted us above that level.'

'Edouard, I've just been telling you how religion turns into bigotry and persecution, even though it holds out the candy promise that in the great beyond there'll be comfort for it all, there'll be a point to compensate for it all.'

'So all your studies of religion have led you to being irreligious.'

'I suppose so. I know too much, and thus, like Socrates, I know I know nothing.'

'But,' persisted Edouard, 'you talked earlier of how we need to declare in some way that we were here. Can we not defeat annihilation by taking a view of the long-term? Long ago men instituted the building of cathedrals which would not be completed for two hundred years; we are bigger than you say.'

'So dedicating ourselves to great causes will help save us from our transience? It won't do, Edouard, my friend. Ninety-nine per cent of us can't defeat that anonymity, the meaningless of a brief and passing life. Think of the medieval peasant dying of the Black Death, or the woman expiring because of child-bed fever, or the Jew sitting in the transport for days on end waiting for the doors to open on the smoke of Auschwitz. It's all chance, cruel chance — there's nothing special about us. We just hope to be lucky enough to survive long enough to die in our beds. It's a lottery, as much as that roulette wheel you're so fond of, Edouard; it's just that the chances of a decent lifespan have improved, more or less, as time passes — though, even now, you couldn't say that to a street-kid in Rio or an Ethiopian farmer.'

'This is dark, very dark, Professor,' said Edouard, shaking his head. Netty was surprised to hear traffic still going past outside. Normal life, days full of petty thoughts: shall I have coffee or tea, must get to the post office before it closes, that pile of ironing needs doing.

'History is dark, my friend,' said the Professor, 'and it's a fallacy of the Age of Reason to believe that our route to the future inevitably takes us to the light.' Gerald looked as if he had indigestion. Edouard toyed with his coffee spoon. Peter fidgeted. He edged his buttocks from side to side, like a child at an adult dinner-table dying to slide off his chair and go play outside.

Netty looked at the Professor. I thought I knew you: I thought you were kindly, genial, positive. That you had everything, however terrible, in perspective, in proportion. But no, you're as bleak as I am. You're just able to express it better. On impulse she put her hand over his and felt the thin lizard skin of age sliding uncushioned over sharp bones.

'So now,' said Edouard, smiling, 'instead of hunting other men, as was the case — oh not so long ago — we go hunting the beasts of the wood and the air. N'est-ce pas?' At the same moment René Quiberon joined them, offering a digestif or more coffee.

Netty's head had snapped up quickly, as a dreadful suspicion struck. Yes, her husband looked shifty. Peter blithely replied: 'Yes, Gerry here's interested in taking a potshot or two at the wee beasties — aren't you, Gerry?'

Fred wore an expression that said all his grimmest opinions of mankind were being confirmed. Gerald said loudly, 'Yes, René, I'd love some more coffee,' and as his host retreated, 'Is he into hunting too?'

Peter said, 'Who isn't?', which gave Netty the chance to answer curtly 'I'm not.' Gerald shot her a look.

'Oh poor Mistress F!' cried Peter. 'You're not having a very happy lunch, are you? All us horrible male so-and-sos talking about killing and such!' At the same time, with exquisite lack of tact, he lifted the long canvas bag he had brought onto the table, in order to extract various articles of weaponry. Gerald's eyes shone. 'Christ, Pete, you must have a bloody armoury at that gaff of yours.'

'Oh, he has, he has,' said Fred. 'All artistically arranged.' Peter took that as a compliment and beamed.

Gerald was taking hold of carbines and shotguns. He ran his hand over smooth barrels, round lustrous wooden stocks, tickled cool metal triggers, pored over intricate chasing. 'Beautiful,' he breathed.

'Yes — oh that one's a Purdey, the best in the business,' said Peter.

'Gerald, are you really serious?' asked Netty, keeping her voice restrained.

''Course I am! Pete and me have had a few chats about it, haven't we mate? He's going to lend me one of his guns, teach me the basics.' He punched Peter's upper arm in gratitude and Peter grinned.

'So he's going to teach you the basics is he? He's going to teach you how to line up the sights of one of those ever so posh guns of his on some little furry or feathered friend of nature and you're going to blow it to pieces.'

'Nothing so coarse, my dear. Credit us with a little finesse.'

She ignored Peter. 'You're going to hold a bundle of fur, and feel it all limp but still warm and say to yourself "I did that — I chased the life out of it, just like that, and I'm *ever* so proud of myself." That how you see it, Gerald?'

'Net, don't be so bloody sensitive. You've got it all out of proportion. They won't suffer, and they're only animals, for God's sake, when you come down to it.'

'Of a lower order of nature, you see,' murmured Fred. 'God put them all on earth for us to play with: bird of the air, beast of the field. Give them their names, blast them to kingdom come.'

Gerald glared at him. 'They're *animals*, Netty. Just what do you think you've been eating here for lunch? What was in your pâté? Aubergines? You're such a hypocrite: you're glad to eat them, but you don't want to know how they got onto your plate!'

'But you're doing it for *fun,* Gerald, for *fun!*'

'And what is so wrong with that, Annette?' asked Edouard out of the blue. 'It is man's right — no, permit me to explain,' as she threw up her hands in despair. 'It is a challenge, it is right and fair. If the *chasse* is done well, it is a game.'

'A *game!* Bloody serious game for the poor creature getting the bullet in the neck!'

'A game with rules which are understood by the man and the animal. They show each other respect. There is dignity.'

Netty was virtually speechless. 'Have I just been transported to another planet or something? I don't understand you people. I just don't know how you can see it that way.'

'But it is rational, it is calm. It is in the order of things. Of course there is the wrong way to do it: to use jeeps and telescopic sights and such aids. That is not right. It gives no chance to the game.'

'A *sporting* chance!'

'Yes, if you like. We show respect. The man goes out with his dogs and a good gun and his knowledge of the habitat and the customs of whatever *gibier* he is hunting, and he gives the animal the chance to use its natural talents: its strength or agility or cunning, and it may get away — *voilà*, he salutes it, he respects it. Or he may win and *voilà*, he gives it a death which is a mercy, and he preserves it, which is its own little glory, or he eats it, so it is part of the cycle of life. It is natural, all this; it is not correct to resist it. The creature will die anyway. There is always death.'

'There is always death,' she repeated, hypnotised.

Peter nodded, by now quite convinced that in killing animals he was giving them the equivalent of a Roman suicide: death with honour. Poor little birds of the air, poor little beasts of the field, how much they would prefer their tiny anonymities to the false mercy and glory of Peter's gun.

'*Nature red in tooth and claw,*' intoned the Professor.

Gerald downed the last of his coffee and waved away the offer of another refill. 'Shit, let's stop talking about it. Let's just get *on* with it!'

Netty opened her mouth.

'Probably won't bag anything, anyway,' he added quickly, 'just get

some fresh air in the lungs and stretch my legs. So don't go *on*, Net.'
He patted her hand.

The veneer of cultivated affection cracked and fell away. She hated
him. She hated them all.

Body and Soul

1831

Bertrand du Blenier wooed Thérèse Vallet for three years. His devotion inspired amusement among his friends, 'Les Sages', whose meetings in a smoke-filled room in the Rue Marmande in Bourdonne were originally constituted as artistic and philosophical forays into the mysteries of Inspiration and Liberty, but in reality were more likely to lead to opium-ridden trances or the achievement of nirvana in the paid embraces of local filles de joie. So, gradually, Bertrand's attendance fell away. He dedicated his life to the pursuit of the feminine ideal he had found.

A poet should not gain reciprocal love too easily: how else is he to write his poetry? The lady was shy and modest. Her father, a wealthy local wine-farmer, had planned to marry her off to the nearest vineyard as represented by the portly son of his neighbour, Monsieur Gabon.

During this period, Bertrand poured out his passion in a flood of letters and poems. Thérèse Vallet was quite overwhelmed; flattered and confused by classical invocations for which her limited education had not prepared her. Her father was rather less struck, because of Bertrand's financial insecurity and, as he saw it, posturing. The death of a rich maiden aunt and Bertrand's consequent inheritance, however, changed his attitude; he duly bestowed his daughter on the poet and began speculating whether the Gabon boy couldn't be persuaded to settle for Camille, who was almost as pretty as her sister.

Bertrand could not bear to take up residence among the bourgeois chatterers of Bourdonne. After much searching he settled on the small hunting lodge near the hamlet of Malignac. He bought the place for the view: the house itself at that time was not at all satisfactory. It had stood empty for well-nigh forty years, since the exile of the notorious Comte de Saint-Eymet.

He could see no other purpose in his life than to pour his money out in a river of shining gold for the pleasure of his fair one. The sanctity of her presence would purify the house and exorcise all the profane memories of the Comte. He was a courtly lover of old, a vassal to the proud demands of his idolised mistress. Not that Thérèse Vallet, bewildered and passive, ever made any proud demands. She was a dutiful daughter and it was in the nature of things to marry, and she was marrying money, which pleased Papa, and Bertrand was different and rather glamorous, which gave her a tickle of pleasure, along with a faint sense of superiority to all the other demoiselles of her acquaintance, destined to marry farmers and lawyers and doctors, not ardent poets.

With fine extravagance, Bertrand had the shabby accretions of the lodge knocked down, preserving only the Salle de Chasse. On either side of that room he added well-proportioned chambers, filled with light, and he built a little tower above the hall, a symbol of his poetic and amorous aspirations. Furniture was brought by carrier from Bourdonne. Damask and brocade hangings were paid for out of Bertrand's then seemingly bottomless purse. Old Monsieur Vallet came to see and approve and Thérèse herself expressed timid delight in Bertrand's taste. She contributed some spidery embroidery and dilute watercolours to the ornamentation of her future home. However, she sometimes sighed for the dark oak dressers and homespun simplicity of her father's farmhouse.

And so they were married. The poet brought his bride in triumph to Le Sanglier. Days passed into weeks, yet the nights remained chaste, for Thérèse expressed reluctance and Bertrand felt a reverence for his wife that, initially, quite cancelled out desire. But the nights passed, approaching months. The sun reached the zenith of the year, and he was a man, after all.

Day after day he read to her, long tracts from his own works or from

Lamartine or Rousseau, with the passion for language and thought thrilling his heart and deepening his voice. Thérèse listened carefully. Day after day the heat increased and the crisis advanced.

In the garden on a sultry afternoon in late August, he watched her as she read. The contemplation of such beauty seemed to take him out of time itself, desire muted by an aesthetic trance. She wore a white muslin dress with a pale blue sash drawn neatly under her small breasts. Puffed sleeves ended scarcely before beginning, leaving her delicious arms bare. Her dark hair was drawn smoothly up, but tender little coils of it escaped to cling to her forehead and behind her ears. Her head was bent over her book and she frowned slightly but prettily; she was a slow reader. However, the most beautiful thing about her was the gentle curve of her nape, taut and pure, inviting a lover's kiss. She was careful to protect her fair skin from the sun; her parasol was propped up to cast a blue shadow over her, as if she were a creature gliding under a summer sea. The whiteness of her fingers made the pages of her book look yellow, like a mummy's cerements.

Bertrand was a man at war. The reverence he felt for her deepened and darkened, like a swirl of blood in clear water. His passion was holy, but it was passion none the less. She talked of duty but begged for time. He had given her time. Her father had called her his 'little nun'. It was distasteful. She was meant for love, he knew it, as a flower, even a pale lily, must blossom and unfold to the sun. He had a sudden hot vision of her sprawling upon sheets, or on the dark tiled floor of the room behind him, her hair spread out, her legs apart, her mouth red now, oh red as sin, opening to him.

The walls of the house exuded damp, like sweat. Drowsy birds and insects had scarcely the energy to pursue or be pursued. Dust spun under footsteps.

For weeks her defencelessness had been her best defence. But on that August night he grasped her arm, white as frost, and left his livid mark there as he pulled her to the bedroom. Despair and pleasure mixed as he plunged into her and into an all-too-swift release. He shuddered and collapsed. Thérèse lay under him, her eyes closed. She had not resisted, pleaded or whimpered. As dutiful a wife as she had been a daughter, she accepted that her husband had exercised unnatural restraint hitherto *and that such rough treatment was no more than her due.*

In the morning, and on all the mornings after, he saw the look on her face: closed and wary, careful not to displease him, but desirous of escape. Like a trapped fox, not biting, not fleeing, just watchful — and never to be tamed. His desire was crushed by shame.

She had her escape. In the autumn a severe chill settled on her lungs. Even when seeming to convalesce, the racking cough would shake her thin frame and she would gaze at him apologetically. The doctor, summoned at some expense from Bourdonne, shook his white head and pronounced her consumptive. Bertrand wanted to take her south for the winter, but she would not go. She denied that anything was seriously the matter and hid the blood-soaked handkerchiefs.

His pain was of course very great when she died. He drifted about the house like a ghost and spent long hours up in his tower, scribbling poems to her which were eventually published in Bordeaux, in a slim volume which was the only child of his sterile marriage. He received some praise, but for him poesy no longer worked: bleached images and overworked metaphors, like elaborate carvings grey with dust. He only wished he could have captured her as she was, blue and white, pure and serene, on that summer's day before he profaned her.

His money was virtually exhausted. He sold the house on the hill, left the woods and the chattering birds and returned to the bustling world of men. Parnassus had too rarefied an atmosphere. It was time for life to be a little more mundane.

Beast

'I'm for the off, then,' he shouts.

'Fine.'

'Aren't you going to wish me luck? Big adventure, this!'

Silence.

'Suit yourself, then.' The door shudders behind him. She hears his booted feet on the gravel, she hears the greetings, and the heavy thunk of car doors; all the footsteps and male voices go round the side of the house, across the back terrace, then the footsteps go silent as they hit the forest trail, but the voices drift back for a few moments.

It is early and cool. Already she is in her tower-room, sailing high above the morning mist as if in the crow's nest of an old galleon, the green forest waves surging around her. Needles, threaded with various hues of wool, are lined up at the side of her canvas, ready for use. But she sits for a while, with her hands folded in her lap, as if for a school photograph.

Gerald plunges on down the path, leaving the heat of his resentment towards his wife behind him. She can sit back there and stew, as far as he is concerned.

This is *la chasse en battue*. There are two teams of four men and they have ten dogs with them: a mixed pack of griffons, *Bleus de Gascoyne* and beagles. Gerald wonders if Claudine would have lent out Patapon for the occasion — but no, although he is a beagle, Patapon is a citified type, an aristocrat. These are working dogs, tongues hanging out with eagerness, noses working overtime.

Gerald is with Edouard and Peter and Jean-Jacques Maturin from the village. In the other group are Augustin and Norbert Lelouche (Albert wanted to come but could not spare himself from farmwork), René Quiberon and Gerard Fayolle from the next farm along. They have a pretty fair idea where the wild boar may be, and both teams make swift and purposeful progress.

The path rises for a while, then starts to fall away and curve to the left. Gerald begins to be aware of the vastness of the Colline, the sheer acreage of untouched peaceful woodland, how little his house and garden impinge upon it. His breath comes fast and rough; partly from unaccustomed exertion, partly from schoolboy excitement.

The sound of his boots — worn in case of snakes, rather than because of mud — is muffled by the resilience of the dark, almost peaty earth. He is surprised at how easy and open it is. True, there are certain areas which are a bit of a scramble, where Jean-Jacques takes out a short machete and hacks away at briars or pulls overhanging branches aside to let Gerald through. There are dense areas of waist-high bracken, sprinkling him with dew, but there are also clearings patched with pale autumn sun, great vistas of brown earth and perspectives of endless hornbeams, launching out like slender rockets from communal roots, graceful lances which seem only to require stripping and sharpening for use. Chestnuts, oak, hawthorn, fir, shivering birch — a Périgordine arboretum.

It seems to Gerald that he has never truly looked at *green* before: pale and silvery on the birches, darkly varnished on the holly, edged with fluorescent lime against the moving sun. Old tired dusty green, remnant of the draining heat of summer, mixed now with flame red and burnt ochre and old gold; the treasure chest of autumn.

After a while he doesn't trust himself to *see* anything. Jean-Jacques, child of the land, tramps ahead of him in brown corduroys and a checked shirt, half-open. He carries his gun, his knife and a stout stick he uses to prod the ground or hold branches back for their passage. His voice is deep but low, his accent so strong that it loses Gerald and Edouard has to translate. Here, he says, the tracks of roedeer. There — that circle of white mouldy dots in the soil? — a mushroom is coming up. Up in that tree — nest of a buzzard.

By your foot — the droppings of a weasel. He knows the names of everything, the significance of every sign, and dispenses information casually. He takes it all for granted. Gerald feels at the same time privileged and patronised. If ever I was stuck on a desert island, he thinks humbly, I'd be dead meat. Provisions could be right under my nose — I'd never see them. I know about mobile phones and how to set the video. Mother Nature didn't foster me.

From time to time he asks a question: he asks Jean-Jacques to identify something for him, and the man gives him a measuring look, like a doctor in an asylum assessing how much the patient is capable of assimilating.

It strikes Gerald how quiet the forest is, hushed as a green cathedral beyond the rasping of his own breathing. His questions come out in short phrases punctuated with grunts and pants. There seem to be no birds: no calls or coos or twitters, no flapping or rustling. Stupid, Gerald: they're probably out there, watching you with a beady eye, waiting patiently until you lumber past. But when he asks Edouard he is told that indeed there are not many birds, not right in the heart of the wood.

Heart of the wood: heart of oak and chestnut, heart of bush and briar. There may be no birds, but there is a population there. Insects totter on and off leaf-mould and twig; voles run their snuffling channels, gleam and glimpse of velvet coat; sinuous swayback of weasel; neat clipped scutterings of gentle deer. And somewhere, snorting and whiffling in odoriferous undergrowth, is the beast you seek, Gerald, and are half-afraid to meet — the slope-shouldered boar, glaring at you with his piggy eye, wild and feared since the days of Meleager in the ancient woods of Calydon.

The morning marches on into full maturity. It is quite warm. She knows — everyone has told her often enough — how lovely autumn in the Dordogne can be. Around her the roof of the forest is caped in rich velvet colours; amber and russet and tortoiseshell. People can sit outside for Christmas lunch, she's been told. A far cry from British drizzle and damp and slush. If snow falls at all — and will it? — it will be crisp and virginal, white as snow should be, white as Christmas cards have always claimed it is.

All these thoughts run through her head as she sits. Once she reaches out tentatively for a needle, but she hasn't the energy or will to pluck it from the canvas. Her hand sags back onto her lap and cossets the other, nervously.

The worst is, she thinks, the worst is not being able to talk to him. Not properly. Not with a half-phrase, a word or two in the ear of her soulmate, who will turn and smile and raise his hand to halt her stumbling sentence and say, 'It's all right. I know. You don't need to explain.' Never that. Instead, the blank look, the bemused stare, the sneer, the contemptuous put-down. What *are* you drivelling on about, woman?

She saw the relish on his face, last night, talking about it; this morning, downing his coffee in great gulps, prancing from foot to foot in eagerness, tomcat on a hot tin roof. Sickening.

So now he is out there, hunting the poor creature — not a particularly pretty creature, not a cutesome Walt Disney creation, but a living being, as yet unaware that it is singled out for oblivion.

Can't he see? Can't he imagine? Her identity lies with the hunted, not the hunter. She remembers thrillers of the seventies, films that opened with the crosshairs of telescopic gunsights trained on the head of some unsuspecting victim, who walked about, bent and straightened, laughed even; and the gun bobbed and ducked but never lost aim, and then the moment was right and the victim was no more. Cue titles.

That is how she sees Danny's last morning. The hunter prowls the urban street, vacillates as so many innocent creatures pass him by, going about their mundane affairs. His eye moves, scans, is caught by the tired-looking mother chastising the boy as he clambers back into his pushchair. The boy's hair glints in the sun. The sights are lined, the aim is true. A small matter to bypass the distracted mother. Her guard is down. The boy comes easily into his grasp. At first there is uncertainty, on realising that his mother is no longer there: 'Mummy ... Mummy?' Later, though.

She shudders when she comes up against this thought. It is the worst of all. Not the image of his small lifeless body or even of the corporeal blasphemy of the grave. It is the image of his panic, his realisation, his need of her. Of him going through that pain at the hunter's cruel hands, with no one there to protest or help or save him. It is an agony to her that she betrayed him by her absence. It is a pain she very nearly cannot live with.

And Gerald, her husband, father of that boy, has allied himself with the hunters.

It is a Browning. It is a beautiful object. Its stock is glossy, its muzzle fairly short, stubby, matt black. Underneath is slung capacity for five cartridges. Five opportunities to blow life away, before reloading. Above the trigger is a delicately chased panel depicting ducks in silvery flight.

It has potential. That is what is so attractive about it, he thinks, hefting it into a more secure position. It is loaded. He has fingered the tight neat beautiful cartridges, twelve calibre. At one end of each he could see the solid grey ball, held compactly, in readiness to be set murderously free. Potential, that's what it is. Death held in stasis, subject to the impetus of *his* will.

It is a thrill. In the distance he can hear the other team. They're all getting closer. The dogs are panting and weaving to and fro. He feels more and more distant, though; he's retreating into an inner space where sounds are magnified but tiny. He can hear Edouard pointing out the muddy banks and the black-looking pond. Yes, the boar like to drink there and roll there. To the right a thicket of low grasping bushes of unbelievable density. Surely only a viper could worm its way through that. But no, he is told, the dogs are eager, the *sanglier* is closeted there by day after a night of rooting and snuffling with its sensitive snout.

In his inner space Gerald is alone with his victim. His wife is not the only one: he too has projected time and again onto the screen of his mind the image of the killer. And he has wanted to kill that

210

killer. He has beaten his head against the incompetence of the police. He has raged, he has wept. But now he has a gun in his hand, he has tracked, he can kill. He has power.

Don't worry, Edouard said: when? The other day? So much talk prior to the event. Don't worry, he said, they're not really dangerous. They're shy. They don't want trouble. They'll do anything to run away — that's all they want — to be left in peace. Unless we come across a *laie* with young. Yes, it's possible I suppose. If she lost her first litter early in the season, it's possible for her to come into heat again. Even in October there could be the little *marcassins*. But it is not likely. Why, there is every chance we will find no *sanglier* at all. Much easier to shoot woodpigeon — they are all around!

There is a roar of noise. Crashing. Blood pounds in his ears. The other men are — where? For there it is: with miraculous swiftness it has appeared across the glade and stands eyeing him with a knowing amber eye. Somehow he knows he is registering it all, in one glance: the ridge of black bristles running like a Mohican haircut down the back, the short high shoulders held tight like an over-muscled body-builder, the tiny haunches, the whole animal a tetragon of force. The silly tail, suddenly held high, the quick bruising bombastic trot — not a trot, a run. The sight, half-buried in the grey-black pelt, of the tusks: not gleaming white, he thinks, surprised. He thought they'd be white, like an elephant's tusks. But they're a sordid mottled yellow and brown.

The gun is, somehow, against his shoulder, the weight bracing him, the heavy muzzle up and ready, well trained.

There are shouts. The animal circles, stiff-legged, jumpy, and sees nothing but shirts and trousers and dogs. Its nostrils are in revulsion, flaring, sensing too much hostility. Persecuted, seeing or scenting no escape, its own hatred bellies up and bursts from it in a furious squeal. Still squealing it races towards Gerald.

Now is your chance: take all your hatred, Gerald, and ball it up and send it down that muzzle, spiralling into a velocity that will kill your enemy in the blink of an eye. Now's your chance.

'*Tirez!*' he seems to hear. The animal is crazily near. The gun jerks against his shoulder. But not because he has fired. He cannot fire. He cannot, after all, kill.

The beast knocks him to one side, he falls, winded. Tears in his eyes. He curses. He hears the shot. And another. Peter and Edouard, his friends, pump death into it on his behalf.

Forest

'Was it a mother?' she asked later.

'No, it was male. The females don't have tusks.'

'Was it young?'

'Youngish. Just past the stage where they call them *bêtes noires*.'

'But not really very mature.'

'No, not really.'

'There you are.' She bandaged the graze on his thigh which he had received from his scouring tumble on the ground. She stood up and moved away, constrained. Words were of no use at all.

The next day she went to visit Fred.

'You didn't go to the hunt.'

'Well, no. My old bones weren't quite up to it — nor my heart, I don't think.'

'I'm glad you didn't go. I didn't want Gerald to go. I didn't want him to ... *enjoy* it so much.'

'Are you sure he did?'

She looked at him.

'Well, you know boys,' he continued. 'It could be bravado. Maybe he was a quivering wreck inside.'

For the first time in forty-eight hours a thin smile touched her mouth. Fred popped into the kitchen to fetch the coffee. She strolled idly round the room. As he came back in she was running her hand over the instep of the marble foot. The cup he offered her shuddered on its saucer and the coffee slopped over. He was breathing fast, as if he'd run from the coffee plantation in Brazil.

'Oops. Sorry,' he said, proffering the cup, islanded in brown.

'That's OK.' She held it sadly, still looking at the foot.

'Right — get your coffee down you: we're going for a walk.'

'A walk?'

'A walk. You're in a sad way and maundering about here in this foreign outpost of the British Museum isn't going to help. Let's make a picnic of it and go commune with old Mother Nature.'

She brightened. 'Yes. Yes, I'd like that.'

Climbing the hill was much easier now in the cool of autumn.

'I had a stroll up here in the summer,' she said, panting. 'Got myself thoroughly lost. It put me right off.'

'You haven't bothered since?'

'No. As I say, it put me off. I got all caught up in briars and couldn't find the path. It was a bit frightening. I don't think nature rambles are really my thing.' I remember that deer, though, she thought, and how I wanted to stroke it. How, in a funny way, I wanted to *talk* to it. Silly bitch, Gerald would say. 'It was that night that ...'

'The night you came knocking at my door? Ah. You had a busy time, didn't you!'

'You could say that! No sooner is my husband on the plane than I start running around like a headless chicken!'

'How are things with you and Gerald?'

A silence.

'I'm sorry. Just tell me to keep my nose out.'

'No. No, it's not that. I can't really answer. I can't really say how things are. When he first came back from England, I'd have said we were getting on better than we had since ... well, for years, anyway. But all this hunting business — let's just put the tin lid on it all as far as I'm concerned. It turns my stomach.'

'Why is that? I mean, why do you feel so strongly? You obviously do: I saw that at the Coq d'Or.'

'It's because of Danny.'

Fred took her arm to help her over a fallen tree-trunk. As she crossed it she saw the twitch of leaf and twig as hidden tiny creatures went about their chores. 'Do you know, I think when I came here before what frightened me most was not being lost; I knew as long as I went downwards I'd come out somewhere at the foot of this bloody hill. It was the sense of all the life around; it made me feel clumsy and alien.'

Furtive life, minding its own business, following the impulses of chromosome and hormone. Hunger. Fear. Aggression. Heat. Birth. Nourishment. Desertion. The tree expands into its next ring. The sap fades from the reddening leaf. The insect spirals a mating dance and dies. The fish bobs over the gleaming clutch of eggs. The mammal is milked by her young. The predator paces through the wood, hollow-gutted, nostrils quivering. The prey shivers under shelter or pokes its nose out into mortality. The bird lets fall feather or dropping as it flies the nest. The worm gleams wet in its tunnel. The spider abseils from top storey to basement. The lichen adds tiny grey cell to tiny grey cell in growth of infinitesmal patience. Neurons pulse, chlorophyll collects, corpuscles churn, stone weathers in false stasis.

'Look,' said Netty, and showed Fred the underside of her shoe. Embedded in the tread of it, a still life of squashed beetle and soggy leaf. 'It's so easy, to wipe things out. I don't like it. I know nothing I'm saying is original — but I *do* know that I hate being reminded of how easy it is to die.'

'As an individual, you mean?' he answered, as they entered a high glade and settled themselves on a blanket. 'What I'm saying is that you squashed that particular beetle, with whatever limited perception it had of itself and its world (and God knows what that was — can beetles be said to think?) but that genus of beetle was unaffected by its demise: on a wider perspective that beetle's death is negligible, it's a barely measurable event.'

'Yes! Yes, that's it. That's what I can't stand, because, at least for humans, it's got to be more, mean more. We're not just statistics. When people think of Danny, he's a statistic. A newspaper report. It happens all the time. We look at the event, we forget the person. I saw Danny through birth and colic and potty training and *Postman*

Pat and finger painting — all just to let him die like that, to let him be a newspaper report, soon forgotten.'

He put his arm around her.

A sudden scurry and scattering of leaves, panting, a yelp. The dog sprang, stiff-legged, eager, from side to side, his eyes bright as shiny buttons. He triumphed over them, his play-prey. Then his owner came toiling into view, hissing 'Patapon, *Patapon! Méchant — viens ici!'*

Netty was amused that Claudine, who managed people in her own little domain so well, seemed to find it impossible to control a pet dog.

Claudine's shoulders went up in a shrug of mingled embarrassment and exasperation. 'It is all the fault of Felix and Deirdre, you understand? They had him first, they quite spoiled him.' Kisses and greetings were exchanged. 'You know, I think I am lost? I was lost in thought at first, I suppose, and then suddenly I look around and the path is unfamiliar. After all this time, I *still* don't know my way about the hill! Why, I remember one time, Patapon, oh the naughty one, he ran off, just like today, and he took me all the way to your house, Annette. *Such* a long way!'

'Really! When was that?'

'Oh, it was before you moved in.'

Claudine turned suddenly, her voice sharpening from indulgence to anger. *'Patapon! Come here!'* The dog seemed to know that this time she was serious, and grovelled to her. Patapon's mistress relented and bent to pat the gently-domed head. Netty noticed that her face and neck were quite red. It must have been quite a toil, pursuing that dratted hound. She hoped Claudine's coronary arteries were in better shape than her husband's had been.

'So Claudine,' said Fred, 'how does the Luker case progress?'

Claudine sighed. It was like an echo of her exasperation with Patapon. 'Deirdre telephones often, but it is difficult to understand how matters are progressing, even though our conversations are long. This cousin of hers is in custody and Felix is ...'

'Helping the police with their inquiries?' said Fred.

'Yes, he is helping in the investigation. All the records have been confiscated. I think he feels he can divert extreme penalty by being as helpful as possible. Of course,' she added hastily, 'it is unquestionable that he is utterly innocent in this affair.'

'Poor Felix. He's been dumped right in it,' said Netty.

'And how's our Deirdre?' asked Fred. 'Bearing up heroically?'

Claudine's normal discretion failed her, ambushed as she had been, night after night, by the shrilling of the telephone. She made an expressive gesture; clearly she felt Deirdre was letting the wifely side down. 'Oh I try to persuade her, to advise her that she should support Felix in this so-difficult time. But she is irrational about it, quite hysterical, you understand. It is,' with a weary expellation of air, 'tiring.'

'Tiresome,' muttered Fred, but none too quietly.

'Your pardon — did I say the word in error? I try so hard to be precise in my English. *Tiresome.*'

Netty and Fred shared a silent smile.

'Anyway,' said Fred, 'Annette and I were just about to have a late autumn picnic: *déjeuner sur l'herbe* or *sur les feuilles mortes,* at least. Care to join us?'

Fred perched on a boulder nearby, Claudine and Netty shared the blanket. The wine was uncorked. Patapon made quick forays into the undergrowth, like a scout checking for Indian activity near the wagon train. Several slices of *jambon du pays,* and a baguette, a bag of *Blondes à Croquer* and some *cornichons* later, Claudine said, 'It is so long since you came to Bel Arbre, Annette. When will you come again? The tapestries are still there, if you need more encouragement!'

Netty answered, 'It's been difficult since Gerald came back. I don't know where the time goes, really I don't. We keep busy, but what we keep busy *with* it's tricky to say. The days just pass somehow.'

'I hear Gerald has been out hunting.'

'Yes. But it's not my kind of thing.'

'Ah, I understand. But it is admirable, is it not — the local people will see that he takes part in their pursuits; it will help the process of adjusting. And I am sure it is good for his health.'

'It's not very good for the health of his targets!' flashed Netty.

Claudine spread her hands. 'But *bof!* It is life — you must not fight these things, Annette. It is how it is.'

'*Why?*'

Fred interposed. 'Now Annette, don't get all het up again — it gets you nowhere. You're not going to make any converts, so you might just as well save your breath.'

Netty resisted the impulse to sulk. 'All right. What I meant to say, Claudine, was that I'd love to visit Bel Arbre again, with or without Gerald. But I feel you really must come over to Le Sanglier for dinner. You've been so hospitable to us: I would like to repay you.'

To her surprise, Claudine seemed less than enthusiastic, merely saying vaguely, 'Well, perhaps ... some time it can be arranged ...' before turning the conversation into other channels. Why was it? Had she taken a dislike to Gerry? In her present mood with regard to her husband, Netty wouldn't find it hard to believe. Didn't she trust Netty's ability as a cook? God knows that could be a justified fear: the moment the invitation had left her mouth Netty's brain had jangled a panic warning — what could I cook for her? Oh God! Gerald's business dinners in Oxford had been bad enough.

Or was it that Claudine liked to reign, queen bee, over her own little empire, Marie Antoinette in a shrunken Versailles?

Patapon's bored whine eventually reminded them of the passage of time. Netty's bottom was cold from the inadequate protection afforded by the blanket.

'Not so much *déjeuner sur l'herbe* as *rhumatisme sur l'os,*' groaned the Professor, unfolding himself like a Swiss army knife and limping over to help Netty up. Only Claudine preserved some litheness.

Goodbyes were formal and friendly, invitations left open, times undefined. Claudine soon disappeared from view among the glossy brown palisades of hornbeam, but Patapon's crashes through the bracken echoed back to them in the still autumn air. Air which smelt of peeled bark and leaf-mould and mushrooms and the faintest whiff of woodsmoke from the farm beyond Petit Caillou.

Netty shook out the blanket with some difficulty; the damp leaves adhered like appliqué. Fred rolled it up and tied a leather belt round it, leaving a loop to carry it by, like one of those old-fashioned parcels of books boys used to carry to school. A breeze was rising and he turned his collar up, whistling thinly between his teeth, a sound that set Netty's on edge.

They headed for the circumference of the glade, negotiating tussocks and tree-roots as they went. Abruptly, Netty went sprawling, all her length, helpless, hands splayed; a whole-hearted fall, like a child in the playground. Still lying on her front, her hands scrabbled round automatically to pull down her skirt as the Prof bent over her in concern. It was utterly graceless, utterly humiliating.

'My dear! Are you all right?' He pulled her gently into a sitting position. She encircled her left wrist with the fingers of her right hand. Her brain, on automatic pilot, had instinctively sent her left hand forward to cushion the weight of her fall.

'Ooh,' she groaned. 'I hope I haven't sprained it,' as she touched the joint lightly, gingerly, with the pads of her fingers.

'Good job you're not left-handed. You're not, are you?'

'No.'

'Thought not.' His fingers joined hers. 'It doesn't seem too bad to me. How about your ankles?' Before she knew where she was, those bony fingers were encircling each ankle, like ancient knobbly bracelets, then his forefinger lightly ran up and down each instep, over the arch, round to the twin hollows by the Achilles tendon. In an instant, like a play of light.

'You'll live,' he said, helping her to her feet. 'No great damage done.' But he was breathing fast again, so she must have given him a fright.

'What did I trip over, anyway? It must have been a giant *cèpe!*'

They turned to look and in a moment the Prof had dumped bag and blanket and was crouching to look more closely.

'Come and see, Annette, my amateur archaeologist! This fragment of the past is an old friend of mine. I first came across it years ago, with Miriam.'

Carefully he brushed leaf and moss away to reveal a worn, speckled stone. Leaves were piled up against it and as he ploughed them away the stone became deeper, its real height more manifest. It had bulges at the corners, faint whorls and grooves channelling up the edges and, blurred as could be, like pressing a finger into bread-dough and watching it spring back, Netty could see the outlines of writing and a worn head, a cup, a dagger.

'What is it?' she asked impatiently. 'Apart from a lethal sprainer of limbs?'

He took her hand and guided it gently, like a blind person reading a face, over the tired gritty contours of the stone.

'Is it a gravestone or something?'

'No. It's an altar.'

She drew in her breath and her hand. 'An altar! Human sacrifice!'

'No, no,' he laughed. 'We're not in the land of the Aztecs! This is Roman: it's a bit of the temple I've told you about. This lady under our hands — can you feel her? — he guided her fingertips back to the relief, 'could be Cybele: one of the many forms of the Great Goddess, and a much travelled lady too. And here we have a cup: libatory vessel, or possibly for receiving the blood of sacrifice.'

'But you said it wasn't for sacrifice.'

'Not for *human* sacrifice. A bull most likely. Damn, I can't get round to the other sides. It seems to have sunk more deeply than when I last saw it. Look, let's get back, before my joints seize up completely like the Tin Man! I need hot dry weather to be any sort of field archaeologist these days. I'll bring you back to examine it properly in the spring, if you like.'

In Le Sanglier the air was stale after the fresh circulation of the hill. She went through to the bedroom to make sure the shutters and windows were open.

She found Gerald like an actor in an American TV movie, stuffing clothes into an open suitcase on the bed. She almost expected him to say 'I need some space.'

She knew he was aware of her. Even his shoulders looked shifty, but he went on bending and turning, selecting and rejecting, folding and packing. That at least was a step up from the TV movie, where characters seem to know instantly *exactly* what they'll need for the trip or the trial separation and shovel it all indiscriminately into the bag, a bag which seems to weigh nothing when they carry it downstairs to the waiting limo.

'What is it this time?' she asked, trying to keep her voice light.

'Big game hunting in Africa?'

He turned. 'Don't be silly, Net.'

'I thought you were getting totally carried away on blood-thirstiness.'

'No. No, it's nothing like that. You always get things out of proportion. Just because I like to take a pot-shot or two. I don't have to apologise to you about it. I needed to go on that boar-hunt.'

'It was what Linda would call an affirmative experience, was it?'

'Christ, don't be so bloody sarcastic. Who d'you think you are, sitting in judgement over me all the fucking time? The lads would have gone out and killed it anyway.'

'So that makes it OK then.'

'I give up. There's no talking to you these days.'

'Well don't then.'

'Fine!' The packing degenerated into an ill-tempered scrimmage, with muttered execrations as clothes wouldn't fit or fold, and he couldn't find his travel-alarm and where was the mini-hairdrier, for God's sake. She watched him work himself into a lather.

'So, I take it, it's back to Blighty, is it?'

'Right.'

'Again.'

'Yes, *again*.'

He was going to make her ask. 'Well, am I allowed to know why and where?'

He rammed the top drawer of the chest home. 'Of course you are. I was just going to explain but you come in here like the Spanish Inquisition ...'

'I did not!'

'... and get my back up the way you do.'

'Gerry, calm down! I can't believe you're laying into me like this. It's not like the last time: I've settled in here a lot better than I had then. I don't mind — at least, not much.'

At this moment, she thought, I don't give a tinker's curse, husband mine.

'As long as I've got good reason — want a note from teacher do you?'

'Don't be so snide!'

He sighed and flopped onto the bed, patting the duvet beside him. 'Come on, sit down.'

She sat.

'I had another phone-call from Roy, while you were out. I don't know. Maybe it was a big mistake, him buying F & B. He just can't get a grip. I need to go back.'

'But Gerry, isn't this just going to keep happening? You go over and sort things out, then a couple of months later it's all a mess again so back you go. You can't go on like that and Roy shouldn't ask you.'

'I know, love, I know. And give the man his due, he *hasn't* asked me. But I could hear it in his voice — panic. I volunteered. I can't let him down.'

She opened her mouth to protest further, even though she knew it would be no use. Loyalty in friendship was one of Gerry's better features. He raised his hand to cover her parted lips.

'And before you say another word, just listen to me. I think I can get it sorted, this time, permanently. The mistake is in having Roy running the company, hands on, General Manager. My first idea was to get a deputy in to carry some of the workload: I'm going to suggest to Roy that we take that a stage further. I'm going to put it to him that he should step down from the day-to-day running. He'll still own it, of course, but he'll work more in an advisory capacity. He's not getting any younger. I think he looks at me in retirement and he envies me. I've still got some good contacts, and there are those head-hunting set-ups as well. We'll scout around, find someone really efficient to put in as front man.'

'That sounds constructive. Do you think Roy will go for it?'

'I hope so. I really hope so.' He rose from the bed and made for the bathroom to pack his toilet bag. 'Because Net,' he turned in the doorway and she saw the slump of his shoulders. 'I'm really worried,

I'm *really* worried.'

She sat on her bed of lilies and honeysuckle, gazing at the empty doorway, all the fight out of her.

Two days later, with Gerald gone and the house blessedly silent, Netty treated herself to a solitary tourist excursion, south of the river to the *bastide* town of Monpazier with its cloistered market-place, then on to the abbey of Cadouin, nestling in a green wooded cup with lazy smoke rising into the autumn air. Her nerves, for once, were at peace. A whole day with no one to talk to, no one's judgement to defer to, no pretence. She could get used to this.

In Lalinde, she stopped to stock up at the supermarket. She had loaded the car and was in the process of clicking her seatbelt into place when someone rapped sharply on the window. She jumped. It was Peter Rettlesham-Carey. Her tranquillity fled.

'Mistress Feldwick!' he cried, as she cranked down the window. 'How serendipitous: you've just saved me a trip. Now, don't move! It'll be worth it!'

He leapt like Jeremy Fisher, all legs and elbows akimbo, over to his Citroën and extracted a large package from its battered interior. Back he came.

'Open the door, then, open up!'

Bemused, she obeyed. He leaned in and dumped the package on her lap. It was heavy.

'For you, Mistress Quickly! And your esteemed husband too, of course.'

Mistress Quickly? What was he talking about? He was virtually hopping from foot to foot. She began to pull the thick brown paper aside, revealing a Leclerc carrier-bag. A smell arose from its contents; an animal smell. 'Go on, go on!' he urged. 'It won't bite! At least, not any more!'

The wrappings fell away and Netty sat aghast. Nestling in her lap, the great black head of a boar, glass eyes atwinkle, tusks agleam. The smell of it was rank, a blend of musk and dusty hair and taxidermist's preservatives. The ears were pricked, the snout ready to wrinkle and snort, the jaws part open to reveal the tongue.

'All he needs is a Cox's Pippin in the mouth,' crowed Peter, 'and he'd be suitably festive. Wassail and God rest ye!'

Netty was speechless.

'Like it, Mistress Quickly? Get it? Boar's Head Tavern. Education at Filkin Hall *not* wasted, you see!' He reached in and patted the head; dust rose. 'Of course, this isn't the creature your best-beloved helped despatch. Old Quiberon went off with that. But I saw this fellow in a *brocante* shop a couple of streets away and I thought "just the thing"! Gerry will love it, don't you think?'

'I'm afraid Gerald's just gone back to England.'

'What, *again*? Business, was it?'

'Yes.'

'Shame — I was really looking forward to seeing the expression on his face! I'm a bit busy myself, just now: I've got the new exhibition coming up soon, lots of organising there, though Amandine Verwoert, who manages the Jules Clicquot Gallery, is doing most of it. She's a real stalwart, but there's always a few niggles to be ironed out, so I need to be on hand. Then I'm off to England myself, afterwards. Got to discuss the transfer to the Mnemosyne, and then to the Museum of Modern Art in Oxford, and then Liverpool and Glasgow. My grand tour! I feel like one of the Rolling Stones!

'Anyway, since I'm not really available, tell you what: you get Norbert Lelouche to put the boar's head on the wall for you. He's a bit of a handyman, I'm sure he'd oblige. Then it'll be a nice surprise for Gerry when he gets home. Any idea how long he'll be away?'

'No,' she managed to answer, while resisting the urge to roll the dreadful weight of the head off her. 'No, it's a bit up in the air at present.'

'Well, get in touch as soon as he's back, and we can have another hunting expedition. That's if I haven't gone back to Blighty myself by then. Must go. I'll get Dutch Mandy to send you tickets for the opening. The Jules Clicquot gallery's in Périgueux so you won't have too far to travel. You must come — and bring that old connoisseur Fred with you!'

As soon as Peter's car had turned the corner, on its merry way to Trémolat, Netty dumped the boar's head on the floor and pulled the plastic and paper over it to hide the glint in its false eyes.

Terminus

Gerald picked up a hire car at the airport. Roy had offered to come to Heathrow to fetch him but he'd refused, although it had taken some persuasion. He needed time to think, as much time as he could get. He needed to work out how to handle this ... this *mess*. No other word for it. Bloody mess.

Part of his brain dealt with the practicalities of driving the car from M25 to M40. Certain brain cells were registering, as they had done just a few weeks ago, that the traffic congestion was worsening. Horrible. Fumes. Claustrophobia. The Dordogne: clearest air in Europe, he was proud of saying, validating his choice of residence. Now in the metallic muck of southern England, he knew how true it was.

The rest of his brain, which should have been engaged in lucid analysis of the problem, remained paralysed.

They were lined up in Roy's dining-room on high-backed Ercol chairs. It was like being in church. Sheila's attitude was what he would have expected. They hadn't often seen eye-to-eye over the years.

While Sheila loaded the dishwasher Roy asked him what his plans were. He tried to smile confidently, but of their own volition his hands spread themselves wide in a helpless gesture. Sheila came stalking back in. Every sound she made seemed exaggerated, probably deliberately so.

Before he slept, his last thought was: I'm sick of apologising. To women. They always see things in black and white, and it's not like that. In his sleep he set sail on grey seas of grief, fog-shrouded, rolling, confused, his ship of dreams ultimately wrecked.

He spent the next day going from pub to coffee-shop; froth-smeared glasses and cooling cups sat in endless succession in front of him, as he laid his buzzing forehead into the sustaining clasp of his hands, and wondered, and wondered. Roy was at work. He couldn't stay in their house in Wheatley, alone with Sheila. It wasn't on.

At five he was sitting in his car outside the factory gates. The gates looked both familiar and strange. To pass the time he tried to work out how many times he had passed through those gates over the past thirty years — no, less than thirty: when was it that he'd bought those particular premises? Twenty seven years ago, was it? His daughter Lynda would have called this displacement activity. He called it putting off the evil hour. Putting off *thinking* about the evil hour, because all it did was give you a sick feeling in the guts and a horrible sense of helplessness. That was it: helplessness. He'd put his finger on it, at last. He wasn't in charge here and he wasn't sure he'd manage to *take* charge, either.

The workers started emerging soon after the hour. He almost got out of the car to shake one or two by the hand. He wanted friendly contact. He wanted respect — he'd always had that, he was that sort of boss. He'd prided himself on it. He was a philanthropic Victorian: do right by your men and they'll do right by you. The firm father of the Firm.

Instead he had to lie doggo and let them pass.

At half past, Roy came out, looking shifty, as well he might. For a moment Gerald wanted to laugh. The moment passed. Roy caught Gerald's eye and jerked his head very slightly: a signal of imminence. Gerald shifted in his seat. The car felt suddenly hot and airless; he wanted to wind down the window, but felt any movement would destroy his camouflage. Roy scuttled off out of range.

No more time to register anything. The gate clanged once more and Gerald's gaze shifted, his focus shortening from Roy Benson's retreating back. The key turned in the padlock, the body turned, the gaze drifted past the unfamiliar car, then froze and sharply met his. He opened the door.

'Get in,' he said. 'I want to talk to you.'

In his head he scolded 'No, not like that, you bloody fool! Too bossy by half. You've got to coax, you've got to handle this with kid gloves.'

Too late. She was turning away, her pace quickening, her heels snapping out indignation with each step.

'Damn and blast,' he muttered and hauled himself out of the car. 'Camilla!' he shouted. She went on, but she heard. 'Camilla!' he called again, more loudly. Heads turned. He realised there were other people around. They might recognise him. 'For God's sake ...' He started pounding along the pavement after her. Almost immediately his breath started to catch. Beer and coffee swirled abominably inside him.

Miraculously she halted. Half-turned. He kept lunging onwards; he didn't dare stop.

She wasn't as pretty as he'd remembered. He found that strange; somehow he'd imagined it would be the other way about. She stared him hard in the eye.

'I suppose Roy told you,' she said, wearily.

'You suppose right.'

'I might have known.'

'Maybe you wanted him to tell me.' Bloody hell, he thought, here we are out on the pavement, haven't even said hello, and we're in deep water already. I want to sit down. I want a drink. His shirt-collar felt starchy to him, like it used to do forty years ago at school. Her foot was swivelling to and fro on a spindly heel: in, out, in, out, heel, toe, heel, toe, as if preparing for a Highland dance. She could take off on me at any minute, he thought, and I don't think I'm up to charging after her again.

'You're wrong, Gerald. I didn't want Roy to tell you. I didn't want him, of all people, to know. It was that bloody Joyce Hudson — caught me with my head down the toilet one morning just after I'd come into work. The woman has a mouth like a whore's legs —

always open.'

'Cam!'

'What?'

'The language you use!'

'Got used to your mealy-mouthed wife again, have you? Can't
stand a bit of salt?'

It was true. He'd forgotten how different she was, how unapologetic.
How shocking it had been. How refreshing.

'Don't bring Netty into it.'

'Oh dear — I've trespassed again, have I? Really, Mr Feldwick, I
don't think you're in the best position to dictate to me what I should
or should not do, eh? Christ, I need a drink. Several drinks.'

'But, we will discuss it, won't we?' he said, finding himself trailing
in her wake. Not in charge. Not the firm father of the Firm.

'Yes, but not now. I'm tired. I need to think. Ring me.' She stalked
off. Gerald felt the worst possible thing would be to give her time to
think, but couldn't find the words to hold her back.

'Have you had much of a talk with her, since you found out?' he
asked Roy later. Sheila had gone to bed. The TV was on with the
volume turned down: *Newsnight* analysing the political gaffes of the
day. Pundits mouthed silently at the two men as they sat nursing
their drinks.

Roy shrugged. 'Not really. There didn't seem to be much point.
You know Camilla: she'd just tell me to mind my own beeswax, and
she wouldn't mince her words either!'

'True,' Gerald replied, his chuckle turning into a sigh.

'She'd have been right too: it *is* none of my business. It's between
you two.'

'Also true.'

'It's up to you to sort it out. After you'd told me about your fling
with her, I just thought you had a right to know that she was ... she
was ...'

'Up the spout? Yes. Yes. I had a right to know; I appreciate it, mate. But Christ, Roy, I'm in a right hole here.'

'So have you thought — have you decided what to do?'

'What *can* I do? She won't let me near her. I just want to *talk*, that's all. For the present. I mean, I need to know how she's taking it.'

'Not very well, by the look of it.'

'You can say that again! I need to *know*, though, what she's decided. That's what it boils down to. I mean, is she going to ask me to take care of her and all that?'

'She's pretty independent.'

'I know. I *know*. I respect that. But well, a woman in her situation, she needs a bit of TLC, doesn't she? Even the most women's-libby types do, I mean, don't they. It's the nest-building whatsit.'

Roy laughed. 'Still can't see our Ms Thorneycroft going all Laura Ashley on you, mate!'

'Stranger things have happened, stranger things! And I'd stand by her, if it came to it, I'd do the right thing. After all, it's my child: you said she admitted it.'

'What about Netty in all this?'

Gerald leaned forward and shook his head, just as a miming politician wagged his finger in remonstrance on the box. 'Oh God, Roy, I just feel so bloody *guilty*. Net doesn't deserve this. I don't ever want her to know. But if Camilla wants to sue me for support ...'

'Well, most probably it won't come to that,' said his friend calmly. 'Most probably Netty will never have to know. What the eye doesn't see the heart doesn't grieve over. Most probably Camilla will get rid of it.'

Gerald's head snapped up. In all his mental blunderings he'd somehow failed to come up against that particular brick wall. 'Abortion?' he whispered. 'Oh *God*.'

Roy sighed. 'Oh Gerry, how did you ever get yourself into this?'

Gerald now looked back on his affair with Camilla with a kind of awed fascination at the inevitability of it. Free will must have been involved, on both sides, but their meeting had seemed as programmed as the interlocking of yin and yang.

At the time, and for some time after, it had definitely done him good. He'd fulfilled his intentions towards Netty; he'd been more obliging and understanding. In return she'd been wary and polite but he'd sensed the will there too, like his. She wanted to rebuild. She'd found a proper interest: he didn't mind in the least all that sewing, up in the tower. At least she was doing something positive — better than all that morbid brooding. And she seemed to have made some friends: good for her. Paul had been with her. She'd been out and about, seen some of the sights.

It had all gone so well until that bloody business with the hunting. She'd gone all Joan of Arc on him, preaching all the damn time. She hadn't understood what it had meant to him. She hadn't seen that he needed interests and distractions too, now that Le Sanglier had been more or less sorted out. That he needed to find a way to settle in and become part of the region. And he'd needed that focus he'd described to Camilla: an outlet for his bloodlust.

So — he grinned bleakly to himself — he'd stuck to his guns, as it were. Until that moment when he confronted his enemy. He should have been its nemesis, but he had looked into that eye and had heard the breath and had seen the flanks judder under the heavy pelt. He had had the sudden perception of its life, its unique life, under the false invulnerability of hair and hide. A life he couldn't take, not face to face.

'So, it *is* mine, is it?'

'What the bloody hell do you think I am?'

'Sorry. I said as much to Roy — that I was sure it was mine.'

'Oh, so you discuss me with him, do you? Charming! Very discreet! And does his anally retentive lady wife put in her two-pennyworth as well?'

'Actually, she's on your side. I'm cast as the villain of the piece.'

'I'm much obliged for her support — I *don't* think.'

'Grow up, Camilla,' he said curtly, exasperated by her endless touchiness.

'Grow *up?* What I'm fucking doing is growing *out,* out beyond all my waistbands. You going to pay for a new wardrobe?'

'I'll pay for anything you like. Just calm down.'

'Careful, Monsieur Feldwick. You don't want to commit yourself to unspecified expenditure, even verbally. You should know that.'

'Don't take it that way. Don't twist everything I try to say ...'

'I don't! I'm watching my back — bit late in the day, I'll admit, but there's no one else to watch out for me.'

'But that's the point, for Christ's sake, woman! That's why I'm here! I want to help. Don't you think that if I wanted to wriggle out of this mess all I needed to do was to stay in Froggie-land. Eh? I *chose* to come back. Give me a bit of credit!'

'Gerald, you blind git, I'm not going to give you credit for something I never asked you to do in the first place! I didn't get on my knees and pray for holy St Gerald, patron saint of fallen women, to descend from the sky and bless me with his healing presence, did I?'

'Don't be so sarcastic. Christ, you've got a tongue on you.'

'Oh, you remember!'

He winced with embarrassment.

'You may also remember this,' she continued, 'or age is addling your brain: I didn't *ask* for you. I didn't even want you to know. The grapevine did that. Not me.'

'But what are you going to do?' he almost wailed. The prolonged tension was all too much, like a discordant orchestra trying to tune up, endlessly, fractiously, with no sign of the concert beginning.

'That's my business!'

'*No!* No — just shut up a minute — don't you walk away from me, madam!' He grabbed her elbow, pulled her down none too gently, back onto the bench. They were at the Victoria Arms, a pub overlooking green fields and the River Cherwell. It was her choice of venue, not his. Never his. Only a few hundred yards away, across the ceaseless drone of the Ferry Link Road, lay the rustling, yellowing autumn grove; Daniel's penultimate resting place.

She sat, sullenly. It was chilly and raw, a prelude to the vile freezing fogs that would later rise from this river and its big brother the Thames.

'It's *my* business too. You hear? It's my business too because it's my baby, as you were so keen to make clear. So I have every right to be involved.'

'Oh, who says?' God, she really did sound so childish. He turned his head to look at the punt-free landing stage. He remembered summers of tipsy parties, poling along erratically, punts rocking and disgorging people onto the lawns or into the water. And he had had no shiver, no premonition of how dark and blighted this place would become to him. He counted to ten. He mustn't lose the rag; she would just take off on him. It had been hard enough getting her to agree to this meeting. He sighed. If only it could have been The Trout up at Port Meadow, or The Perch out at Binsey, or The Head of the River down by Folly Bridge. All perfectly good pubs, if she was so keen on frostbite by a river. But no, it had to be here. Par for the course.

He finished counting to ten and then added another ten, for safety's sake. He looked at her. Her stance was erect, as if pulled against a Victorian back-board, her clothes were as immaculate and stiff as ever, but almost hidden from view, through the slats of the wooden table, he could see her twisting a massive ring on her finger, over and over, round and round, in jerky sequence, like a screw-top that wouldn't come off.

'Let's start again, and take it slowly. First of all, can I ask you, just how did you manage to get pregnant in the first place? You did tell me you were on the Pill.'

'Why so I did.'

'Well then, if you were ...'

'I was! You not going to take my fucking word for it? Do you really think I'm that stupid, or are you vain enough to believe that I'd not only risk but *want* a baby of yours?'

Jesus, her hormones really did have her jiggered. He'd thought Netty's antenatal tantrums had been bad enough, but they were nothing compared with this level of aggression. Sexual McCarthyism: guilty of everything charged, guilt by reason of being accused, accusation by reason of paranoia.

'Surely I have a right to know.'

'Oh, we're back to *rights* again.' She paused for a moment, then capitulated. 'OK. I'll tell you. I didn't plan this. I didn't plan any of it. I was sorry for you. I saw you go through a lot, we all did, at work. I respected the way you hung on in there. I saw it from your point of view; at least I tried to. I knew you fancied me. I wanted no strings. I knew you'd be going back to the arms of your loving wife, so I thought, where's the harm. I saw how cut up you were that morning, when you thought you were saving that little boy. You meant well, even though it was a bit farcical. I've never been the kind of woman who goes goo-goo at every pram and cradle — ironic, eh? But that night, when you talked to me and told me how it felt, to lose a child, I think I did see how it could be, and I just wanted to give you a bit of time-out from it all, nothing more than that. I never gave you the impression, did I, that I wanted more?'

'No. No. I was confused about a lot of it. I mean, I couldn't work out why you would want to bother with an old fart like me, but I did feel clear that you weren't trying to make it more than it was.' At last, he thought, a conversation. A two-way street, traffic flowing freely.

'Good. I'm glad. I'm not one to sleep my way to the top, even with the ex-boss. It was part Good Samaritan, part curiosity, part just a good fuck, a less-than-lonely night.'

He felt a warm glow in his belly. She'd called it a *good* fuck!

'So there we were: ships that pass. Then I got seasick. I was horrified. I didn't lie to you, Gerald, I was on the Pill. But the week before, I'd had a stomach bug; I threw up for a day and a half. It must have been just at the wrong time for the hormones.' She suddenly left off her ring-twisting and struck her fist against her forehead, theatrically. 'I just can't believe what a *fool* I was! I mean, I *knew* if you're sick like that, you're supposed to take extra precautions. I *know* it, so how could I have forgotten? And don't give me any cod-psychology on my secretly wanting a child. I've had enough of that from my doc. It's a load of crap.'

Gerald stayed silent. He wouldn't presume to trace the mazes of Camilla's mind. People did do daft things, just blanked out now and again, and all sorts of consequences followed. No need to call on

Doctor Freud. People just weren't with it sometimes. Look at Netty, taking her eyes off Danny for a second ...

Camilla was still explaining. 'Anyway, Gerald, there you have it. I've been had, well and truly, and there's no one to blame but myself. So, as I was trying to make clear, there was absolutely no need to come tooling over here. I don't need you to hold my hand — and *you* don't need this hassle, God knows. You've got enough to deal with.'

To his astonishment she took a last swig from her drink and began marshalling handbag and jacket together. His interview was over. She held out a hand; he gazed at it bemusedly. Her voice, at least, was less strident now. 'Look, I'm sorry I was such a prickly cow. I always was. I'm just worse now. You wouldn't think it possible, would you?' She laughed. 'Anyway, I do appreciate the gesture. The age of chivalry is not yet dead. But there was absolutely no need: I've already given Roy several pieces of my mind about it. I got into this mess through my own stupidity and I'll get myself out of it. It's my responsibility.'

She was leaving. Somehow he defeated the paralysis of the past few minutes. 'But it's not a mess — it's a *baby!*' he blurted out.

She stopped in her tracks, looked at him gravely, sat down. 'Gerald, get this. It's not a baby. It's just a bundle of cells and some over-active hormones.'

'You're going to get rid of it, aren't you,' he said slowly, facing it at last.

She bit her lip, nodded, looked down at her hands.

Gerald felt a rush of pain, a geyser of it, spurting upwards from his guts to his cerebellum. His eyes filled. 'But you can't!'

'*Can't?*' Her voice had that ominous calm to it. There wouldn't be much time. He reached out to her. Her hand lay still and heavy in his shaking grasp. 'Cam — Cam, listen to me. Look, I'm not religious, I'm not condemning you ...'

'Bully for you, Gerry.'

'Oh, *please!* Look, there are other options.'

'Don't you think I know that? Christ, Gerald, did you really think I woke up one morning and said "Oh deary me, I seem to be preggers — never mind, I'll just flush it down the toilet".'

'God, Camilla, don't, don't talk like that!'

'Jesus, I never met such a squeamish crew as men are. You all sing your rugby songs and threaten to give us a good poke or a good slap, but you are just so *soft!* What do you know about blood and basics? Fuck all! But women do. Women have far more to do with the real world that you lot.'

God curse Germaine Greer, thought Gerald, trying to keep hold of his temper. He wanted to pin her in a strait-jacket so that she wouldn't harm herself. Or the infant. For the first time he let himself really look at her breasts, just pulling at her blouse. He felt desire. He felt horrific tenderness. Half-hypnotised he put out his hand to touch that roundness, that Venus-figure. She froze, then slapped him away, rose, made off. He scuttled after, half-expecting ironic applause from the other customers. It wasn't far to her car. A cutting wind was rising from the Cherwell. Cows in the field across the river looked hunched and stoical, haunches turned into it.

She was giving out mixed signals: on the one hand, she had headed for her car at a cracking pace; on the other, once there, she hesitated. She fumbled for her keys. She was not a fumbler. He was given time to catch up. Out of breath, aware of his clumsiness.

Gerald chose honesty. It was the only policy. Guile was not his forte, and anyway it wouldn't wash with her, as jumpy as a cat, whiskers quivering to the slightest current of deviousness.

'If you want to get in that car and drive off, you can. I don't know what to say, I don't know what will work with you. I just can't bear it if you leave it like this.'

Without looking at him she made a curt gesture and unlocked the car. They slid into the front seats simultaneously. It was good, as the doors *woomped* shut and the world beyond was instantly muffled, to be out of the wind. The mournful cows eyed them enviously.

In their metal and plastic cocoon, Camilla sighed. Silence stretched between them like a tenuous rope-bridge. He was frightened to speak. Silence brought them together, talk would alienate them. She never interpreted words the way he meant them, as though somewhere in their brief journey through the air they transmogrified themselves before meeting her ear. Words which were meant as soothing were to her patronising. For persuasive, read coercive. For opinion, read male dogma. For emotion, read domination.

How could he get through to her? Many's the business meeting he had chaired, as a commercial equivalent of *One Man and his Dog*. He knew all the whistles and cries that would shepherd his fellows into an enclosure of his making. Here was a meeting more crucial than any of those had been and he was bankrupt. No reserves of fluency.

Gerald kept his voice low and carefully distant, as if she had her hand on the button of an ejector seat and could zap him out of the car in an instant.

'How many weeks gone are you?'

A pause. Any moment now he'd be two hundred feet up and falling to the soil. Silly. Silly. She couldn't *force* him out. He could stay here, wedged in this mock-tweed seat, for as long as he saw fit. She wouldn't be able to make him budge.

Finally, 'Nine.'

He took a moment to assimilate this. Nine weeks. He glanced sideways at her stomach, tried to picture the infant within. He remembered Netty on the hospital bed, the needle, the ultrasound picture. Daniel fully formed, sucking his thumb, bright fluorescent backbone, fragile limbs waving in the amniotic sea. Nine weeks; not fully formed yet, this one.

'How long have you got . . . to get it done?'

'In theory, quite a while. Up to week twenty-three, I think. But that's really for mothers who've had tests and want to get rid of damaged goods, or dimwit schoolgirls who take all that time to admit they're pregnant.'

Her words were as brutal as ever. No need for it.

'So what you mean is, you'd need to do it fairly soon.'

'Yes. If you leave it too late they don't just hoover it out, or do a scrape. You have to go through labour. A hiding to nothing, that is.'

'Oh Jesus, oh Jesus God oh Jesus God.' His control broke. Tears burst out. One hand gripped and gripped his knee, rhythmically, as if to crush the cartilage. 'Oh Jesus Christ!'

Their eyes met. She was crying too, but not convulsedly, not like him. Water just went down her face in flat washes, as if running down glass. His own face felt contorted.

'Jesus, you *bitch!* How can you, how *can* you talk, talk like a surgeon or Doctor bloody Mengele or somebody, some bastard? To hell with your talk of cells and time-factors and all of it! Inside you is a child, it's a being, it's alive!'

'*I know!* I know that.'

He shook his head from side to side as if there was water in his ears too, as if he were an old mongrel fetched out of a canal, shaking water in all directions.

'In the hospital, when Netty was pregnant with Danny, we had to think about the possibility. They called it termination. Termination! It's *killing.*'

'No it's not.' But the tears were still there. 'Look, it's *not* alive, not really; it's not viable. In the normal course of things Nature herself gets rid of a quarter of all foetuses.'

'Oh good Christ, Camilla, you've done your homework, haven't you? You've got the whole vocabulary off pat.'

'Of course I've read up on it. I had a reasoned decision to make.'

'But reason doesn't come into it!' He reached across and planted his hand on her belly. 'Do you feel the presence of it in you? It needs you. You wouldn't drown a kitten, I bet, but you'll let them — how did you so choicely put it? — *hoover* it out of you.'

'Shut up! What are you trying to do, Gerald, campaign to be Pope? I had a choice between being emotive and being practical. What kind of life could I give it?'

'A bloody sight better a life than those poor cows could, out on the Blackbird Leys estate! Don't give me that crap, Camilla. It wouldn't ruin your career; you've been with F & B long enough to know that. Roy would bend over backwards to help. You can afford childcare, everything ...'

'I've thought it all through, Gerald. It just wouldn't work. If I were in a stable relationship ...'

'Crap again! How many stable relationships do you know? What you are is *selfish.*'

'OK, I'm *selfish.* We all are. Don't sit in *judgement* over me, you have no *right.*'

'*You* have no right to kill.'

'Stop using that word.'

'No right to take another life.'

'Oh *Christ!* This is getting us nowhere! Look, the bottom line is it's *my* body and it's my right to do what I like with it. You have nothing to do with it.'

'Yes I bloody have: it's *my* child too!'

'You just want me as an incubator for your precious infant!'

For a moment he sat stunned. Beyond the windscreen some of the cows had lain down, perhaps to ruminate. Heat died out of him, sweat cooled, to be replaced by a cold crackle of electricity. Excitement charged him up.

'That's it! That's the way out.' He grabbed her arm, talked fast. 'Camilla, have the baby, *please!* I'll do anything and everything to make it easy for you. Then Netty and I will take the baby — you can see it of course, any access you want. But you wouldn't have the burden of it, don't you see? Your life can go on as it was. It's the perfect solution!'

To his horror, even as he spoke, he saw the jawline tense, the determined set of the mouth. He wanted to shake and shake her.

'No.'

'No? Why not? What have you got against it?'

'Plenty. But even if I hadn't, once again we're back at the same basic point: I don't need to explain myself to you because you have no jurisdiction over me.'

'I don't believe this! We're not talking as employer and employee here, we're not talking about tea breaks or company cars: we're talking about *life!*

'So, you want me to go through physical agony, ruin my figure and quite possibly develop an emotional bond to a child I never wanted in the first place? No. I'd *never* be free.'

'Camilla, freedom is a myth. Aren't you old enough to know that? You're going to have to commit yourself to something, someday.'

'I'm committed to my job.'

'Fuck that! You should be committed to an asylum!'

'Right. That's it. This has gone far enough. Just get out of the car,

Gerald. Right now.'

He found he was obeying her. The electricity had earthed away. He was hollow. He was beaten. Before he could properly take it in he was standing on the gravel, the car was revving, moving, gone. He stood in utter desolation, remembering only that there had been tears on her face again; the only sign, he felt, of her common humanity with him.

He found himself walking along by the river. He bludgeoned a shivering path through dry brambles and withered nettles. He reached the Link Road, crossed it like a sleepwalker. He reached the grove. He felt the soul of his child calling to him. Bizarrely, irrationally, he felt that Daniel's soul was now latent in Camilla's womb, and calling to him not to be murdered again.

He could not accept this, not any more than he could accept the injustice of Daniel's end, the vicious violation of that one life, and the sneering freedom of the killer.

She hadn't done it yet. She could have done it as soon as she found out. Women found out about pregnancy early these days. Here she was, nine weeks gone. She'd let time pass. She had mentioned no appointments. There must be hope. He would have to try again. He must not let his child down.

Alles in Ordnung

Spring 1944

Ewald Sigehart was a decent man. All he asked was to be able to do a decent job.

Of course, things could have been worse. It could have been the Eastern Front. Some commanders might even have welcomed this sort of posting. Ewald did not. All that remained was to take comfort in the ideals of duty and order.

He had never felt so alone. His deputy, Strücker, he didn't trust. The man was too alert and his attempts at camaraderie did not ring true. His eyes were watchful, his movements abrupt and unpredictable.

At night Ewald lay in the darkness of the bedchamber and felt the weight of that darkness and the greater dark beyond. He felt the solid impassivity of the wall of trees beyond the house. He felt the night listening to him, even though its hollows were broken by the movements and greetings of soldiers.

Ewald came from open country near the sea. His wife Traudl waited for him there, and little Albrecht and Cosima. In Nordhafen you could smell the tang of the sea and the salt marshes and white gulls came yodelling overhead.

He could not like this place, this brooding green hill and its blanket of trees, the brooding village and its smothered resentment. He suffered the, for a soldier, fatal desire to be liked. This could not be. It was not how it was meant to be. The individual could not manifest his individuality in the greater presence of war. They looked at him, they saw the enemy.

He looked at them, he saw cunning and wilful obtuseness.
Try as he might, Strücker would not find anything wrong. Ewald
ran a tight ship. The only way out would be to do the job well. But
this was not proving easy. He knew that a group of the Francs Tireurs
was hiding out somewhere on the hill. Rumours reached him of hidden
caves, but even caves were not necessary; the forest was dense enough
and large enough to hide an army.

He could have lodged his men in the great château on the other side
of the hill, but he had left it undisturbed. He preferred to be near the
village. The answer lay there, he was sure.

Time was short. Two weeks had passed since the bridge at Lazolles
had been blown up. They knew of his presence, there was no doubt
about it, as there was equally no doubt that something was planned. If
it were not prevented, then it might indeed be the Eastern Front, after
all.

Tactics. Only tactics would work, not open force. Blackmail, really.
So he had every tenth man in Malignac arrested, with the threat that
they would be shot within the week if someone did not come forward
and talk.

Now he lay and smoked in the darkness, hearing the great silence
pressing on the walls, as he waited for someone's nerve to break.

It was a woman. On the third night after the ultimatum, Strücker
showed her into the Hunting Chamber with the kind of smirk Ewald
would have liked to strike off his face. With a brusque nod he dismissed
his underling. He decided he would behave with scrupulous politeness
to her. He looked at her in curiosity: how was it that she was prepared
to betray her friends?

She wasn't. Her name was Mathilde, she stammered, twisting a
battered hat nervously in her hands, and her lover, Didier, was one of
the men arrested. Would he not have mercy? No one in Malignac knew
anything, she was sure. No one could help. In the name of God, let him
go. He has done nothing. Please, please ...

The night was hot. Ewald felt a sudden thrill within him as he
looked at her. The room spoke to him of power. All around on the walls
were the trophies and signs of the hunt. His blood began to course, red
and dark. Slowly he went to the door, bolted it, slowly returned. The

heat and stillness grew.

When he spoke, he scarcely knew his own voice, scarcely understood what he said. In the shadows of the room he thought he saw a figure, a faint glitter of embroidery and lace, a bow of approval and encouragement.

He must be ill, he must be fevered. He saw the shock on her face, the momentary spark of refusal, then the dumb assent, like that of a cow in an abattoir. In the dim glow of the lamp he saw her undress, he saw the spasms of shuddering that took her even in the warmth of the night, he saw her body emerge in surprising fragility from the layers of coarse armour: the sagging jacket, the awkward skirt, the heavy lace-up shoes, the thick brown stockings.

She stood, her roughened hands twisting together. He stepped forward. He felt the stunning pleasure of her fear; that millimetre of flinching away from him, as if her flesh shrank within her skin, wishing to retreat to the very marrow of her.

Ewald seized her roughly, pulled her to the desk, bent her forwards over it, holding her wrists down. He wrenched at his own clothing, set himself free. He heard her belly hit the edge of the desk. He looked down at the curve of her haunches and himself going fiercely into her. He looked up over her shoulder and stared into the eyes of a deer, pierced by an arrow, in one of the ornamental tiles. He held that gaze, his own face stern. Then it was over. The pinned creature fell, to her knees, to the floor.

In the shadows, an echo of distant laughter, like the steel-wire plucking of a harpsichord.

Ewald came out of his daze to find her dressed and clutching the rim of her hat once more in two childlike fists, held close and high to her chest, like a squirrel holding a nut. Her voice was high, strained, but she had to know. He would let Didier go now, wouldn't be?

The door was unbolted, Mathilde was gone. He sank into a chair. Bile rose within him. That he could have done this! Thank God no one would know. She would not talk.

Strücker knocked all too discreetly, entered all too tactfully. Ewald quelled his hate as best he could, but barked at him all the same. Strücker in all patience replied that the man was waiting, as arranged, outside.

Ewald sent Strücker out and sat alone for five minutes before going out to negotiate with the 'mauvais Maquis'; the man who had infiltrated the local group and would betray them to him. It was always as well to have more than one way of achieving one's objective.

He would have the prisoners shot, though, as well. It had to be. Even Didier. Especially Didier. Get the job done. Get out of here. Alles in ordnung.

Reverie and Revelation

Something was happening to Netty. The days passed, composed of hours and minutes and seconds; slow and serene like the swinging of a pendulum. The days composed themselves into weeks. The weeks became a month. Still Gerald did not return. She did not care. His phone-calls were jangling reminders of his nature, making her think of those manic old alarm clocks with brass bells on top, jumping all over the bedside table.

She shut him out, as she shut the world out. She felt like one of those time-lapse films of a flower blooming, but in reverse: she folded herself away and slept at the heart of herself.

Her blood slowed to the rhythm of the pendulum, a long pendulum, swinging ever more slowly in massive dignity. She spent her days up in the tower, sewing, the pendulum echoed by the steady piercing and plucking of the canvas as the blunt needle went through, pulling skeins of colour behind it, reducing the world to a textile.

One morning Augustin Lelouche brought her a brown paper bag with two gigantic *cèpes* in it, fresh from the woodland, russet as Spanish leather, smelling of mould and moist growth. Norbert loitered in the background as his uncle made the presentation. Netty thanked him profusely. In the kitchen that evening she beat some eggs for an omelette and sliced one of the massive fungi. Then she could not eat it. She sat on a high stool by the worktop and prodded the strange whitish-yellow flesh of it under its healthy tan.

Augustin, at least, expected little reciprocation. The others were more difficult. Claudine arrived one day and left a note shoved under the door. Netty saw her drive off as she emerged from the sheltering canopy of the woods. The note was tricky: unlike a ringing phone, she felt she could not ignore it. She ended up calling Claudine and agreeing to a visit to Bel Arbre.

Fred, of course, was more persistent. Twice in the first week she saw him in the village. Each time she drove past him with a friendly wave but drove quickly, as if hastening to an appointment, making no attempt to stop and talk. After that she took to driving all the way to Bourdonne; she shopped on the further side and loaded up the car each time with enough food to keep her going for several days. All to avoid the *boulangerie* and the *boucher* and the small *marché* in Malignac, and the *comment ça va, Madame.*

Fred came to the house, more than once. He rang the bell, he waited as patient as a cat. It pleased her to look out from her high shuttered window under the pagoda-eaves, down onto the brown disc at the top of his white head, and know he was there and he couldn't get in. Once he stepped back abruptly from the doorway; his heel crunched in the gravel and his long bony hand went up to his brow as he peered upwards. But she was too quick for him, gliding back into her sanctum and the silken prisms of her tapestries.

'Rapunzel, Rapunzel, do us a favour,' she thought she heard him say. He was a wise old bird. She looked out again at his lean shoulders turning in the aftermath of a shrug as he went off down the hillside.

The first of November. Netty sat in the car until her hands felt chilled as they grasped the steering wheel. What is happening, she wondered. What is happening to me? Her heart beat slow and thick with longing; she wished to return to the room, to the colours, to the pattern of her pictures, the world schematised and ordered in her designs, her grief and desire made sense of at last.

She craned her neck to peer up at the tower. Le Sanglier sat, unwilling to let her go. But go she must. She started the engine, put it into gear, eased the handbrake off, slowly crunched down the drive and away.

At the bottom of the hill she turned left for Bel Arbre. The trance-like state began to depart from her. She began to anticipate the visit. The country lane was almost free of traffic. The woods hung drooping under the weight of heavy drizzle. Autumn's fires were virtually out. The bones of the trees were visible through the last of the curled foliage, the hill was wreathed in the smoke of fog. She drove slowly, just in case. It was hard to see clearly and a lumbering tractor or trailer could be just around the next bend.

Bel Arbre's sharp roof-line and geometrical windows looked, for once, fuzzy in the mirk. However, Claudine herself was as crisp and defined as ever in a suit of aubergine wool with a high-necked blouse.

At Claudine's suggestion they spent the afternoon on a trip to Lazolles, the ruined castle twenty miles away, once owned by the Comtes de Saint-Eymet. The sad redundancy of the structure depressed them both and they were glad to return to the warmth and light of Bel Arbre. That evening, Netty felt at the same time comfortable and ill at ease as they dined at the long table under the cherub-strewn ceiling. She seemed to hear echoes of Peter's ebullience and Edouard's urbanity and Gerald's bumptiousness at that first dinner party. She thought of Gerald. How did she feel about him? She could no longer tell. At times she missed him, but mostly she felt unburdened and joyfully silent about her motives and behaviour. She didn't even need him as a male presence to banish the spooks of Le Sanglier.

The meal was, of course, delicious: dainty fish quenelles, followed by medallions of beef, and then *tarte au citron*. Netty drank slightly too much wine and blessed the fact that the police were scarcely likely to be lurking on the road home to Malignac. Claudine talked of the history of her family and of her marriage.

'Henri and I married rather late. We never had children. Bel Arbre, I suppose, is our child. I love it and I am kept awake by it at night — thinking of all the rooms and the treasure about me and wishing I could lay my hand over them all, like a giant, and hold them safe. It is bad to go through life like this, striving to gain and hold, fearing to lose. Our Comte, Saint-Eymet, he had scarcely finished Le Sanglier, and he loved Bel Arbre as I do; it is the one area where I feel affinity with him. During the Great Fear he was in terror that one day the mob would come to his gates and rip out the marble fireplaces and burn the great tapestries and tear down the golden weathervanes from the roof. But the mob, perversely, chose Lazolles. The Comte fled to Germany — he may even have gone on as far as America. His properties became *Biens Nationaux,* his wife died young. His mistress, who had been a maid at Bel Arbre, and with whom he had assignations at his hunting-lodge, bore him a son. She called him Lazare. Lazare Lelouche.'

'You're saying my neighbours the farmers ...'

'Yes. So Fortune's wheel turns, does it not? Now, let us have coffee. Would it please you to visit Venus' garden once more? You said you would like to see the tapestries again.'

'Yes please, that would be lovely.'

The phone rang as they reached the foot of the stairs. Claudine stopped to answer it, signalling with an imperious wave of her hand that Netty should follow Hortense as she carried the coffee things upstairs.

In the tapestry-room, Hortense placed the tray on a low tulip-wood table. The massive door shut behind her and Netty was left to steep in the green light of the mythical forest. She wandered round the room, from page to giant page of the textured manuscript, marvelling at tiny details of design. In awe she stroked the heavy fabric, to feel the density of it; the imprisoned dust, the prickle and dryness of the wool.

Claudine's entrance scarcely ruffled her reverie. Her hostess stepped quickly to the table and felt the silver coffee-pot with the back of her hand. She uttered an exclamation of annoyance and hurried back to the door to call for Hortense.

'I am so sorry, Annette, the coffee is cold. What kind of hostess must you think me? We will have fresh. Hortense, Hortense!'

Netty had opened her mouth to say something polite about it being quite all right to have cold coffee. The slight shrill edge to Claudine's voice took her by surprise. 'It's not a problem, Claudine. I'm sure it's not that cold ...'

'Of course it is! I have been gone an age! It could not be helped. Oh, the demands that are made of me — endless, endless! Hortense!'

The maid appeared and was sent away with the pot. Claudine and Netty seated themselves on the grand thrones. Claudine pulled at the cuffs of her blouse; alternately right, left, right, left, staring hard at them, seeming to measure to a millimetre the degree of exposure of the fabric beneath the aubergine sleeves. 'It is so difficult to achieve balance,' she murmured.

Hortense returned and Claudine busied herself with pouring the coffee. She mentioned her plans for another trip to Paris. Netty talked of Lynda: her latest letter had threatened that she and her all-American brood would come to visit in early summer.

'Does that not please you?'

'Well, there are practical problems — I mean, Le Sanglier is a big house in terms of space, but not in terms of accommodation. We'll be tripping over camp-beds all the time. The kids will want to sleep up in the tower.' She stopped, realising this would be the case, in a moment of visionary clarity: Chelsea, Eden and Lincoln, romping around her room, poking about, giggling, *touching* things. 'The other problem is Lynda. It's just that, well, we don't really get on.'

'Does that make you feel guilty?'

'I suppose it does. I had dreams of having some sort of "girly" relationship with my daughter, and it just never happened.'

Netty rose to go to the window. Darkness had long since fallen: a thick, wet, cloying darkness, bearing the full weight of winter and the death of light. Her mind darted forward to the balmy days of summer: the children's feet would hammer in the room above, Bradley and Gerald would talk earnestly about wine as if they *knew* anything about it, and Lynda would be welded to Netty's elbow, haranguing her mother to *get a life*.

When she turned back from the window she noticed Claudine fiddling with her cuffs again.

'Claudine, is everything all right?'

'But of course! We have had a pleasant day, have we not?'

'Oh yes — I want to thank you. You were right to bring me out of my shell a bit! I was turning into a proper hermit!'

But Claudine's attention seemed to have wandered.

'Claudine?'

Hein? Oh, *pardon,* Annette. I have a little headache, that's all.'

'I'll go then. You look tired.'

Claudine abruptly squared her shoulders. 'Annette, you are right, there is something. That phone-call ...'

'I thought so. You were fine before. Who was it?'

'Deirdre.'

'Ah.'

Claudine clicked her teeth in exasperation. *'Alors,* I might as well tell you. It is over. We argued. I have told her our friendship is at an end.'

'Why?'

'I cannot condone her actions, that is all. She has left Felix.'

'No!'

'I am afraid it is so. Felix is in such trouble, but she thinks only of herself. She is not listed as co-director, she bears no official liability. She ignores the moral liability. She protects herself. She has no sense of duty, of loyalty, of honour ...'

Claudine's voice trailed off. Feeling *de trop,* Netty gathered up her handbag and scarf and headed for the door, words of farewell ready on her lips. Her friend spoke again. 'No! Annette, you must not go.'

Netty turned. Claudine stood under the trees of Venus' garden, her hands convulsing against one another.

'Annette, there is something else. If I talk of duty, who am I to do so?'

Netty could think of no sensible reply.

'All these months, I have not said, I have not told you ... but I must. I *must.*' Claudine took a step closer, her patrician face haggard. The draught from the partly opened door sent a slow ripple along the line of tapestries, a waxing and waning of bird and beast and flower and leaf. The golden hair of the goddess undulated in possessive coils.

Claudine reached out and took Netty's hand. 'Before I speak, you must believe me, my silence was born of friendship. Respect. You and I, we have had an understanding. Silence *is* respect. But now I have a responsibility, I feel I *must* talk. I am not Deirdre. I must not think merely of my own ease.'

'Claudine, what is it? What are you talking about?'

'Please, sit down again.'

Netty allowed herself to be led, like a blind woman.

'What you must know is — before you bought Le Sanglier, it was owned by another English couple. They only owned it for a short time. I never met them, not really. But a terrible thing happened. The man, he ... he killed his wife. In Le Sanglier. In your house, Annette. No one has told you — how could they tell you ...'

Netty had scarcely seated herself in her chair. Already she was rising. Claudine tried to hold her back, but the leaves were swirling and the dogs in the tapestry howled and the goddess pulled her veil over her head.

'Annette ...' Claudine cried.

Netty paused only for a moment. 'How could you not tell me? How could you claim to be my friend? You even encouraged me to get used to living there!'

As she ran along the corridor past the brandy-toned portraits of long-dead people with prim mouths and folded hands, she heard Claudine's voice again, but she would not listen. There would be self-justification but it would not be enough. There were words but she would not decipher them.

Ars Gratia Artis

Netty spent the night, another long dark night of the soul, up in her tower. She had thought of going to Fred's cottage again, to be away from this polluted house. But she felt compelled to go back to her tapestries. They were the only things that made sense. They were her silent refuge. She stitched furiously, shutting out thought as best she might; longing for, yet dreading the completion of her pictures. She gazed at the richness of ochre and jade, at penetrating cobalt blue and shimmering gold, she peered at her charts, at the eye of her needle. The night passed and the sun rose in a twinkling of sudden frost.

The phone rang, several times. Each time, on hearing Claudine's voice, she hung up without a word. Like a drunk who preserves a weak inner voice of sobriety, some part of her protested at her treatment of her friend. Deep in her brain, Claudine's reasoning, Claudine's justification had taken root. But her conscious self took vengeful pleasure in rejection. She wanted to regain the peace that had been hers only the day before.

At ten in the morning someone knocked at the front door. Sighing in exasperation, she opened it. To her surprise, the shambolic Norbert stood before her.

He put down a small wooden case he was carrying and held out his hand for her to shake.

'Bonjour, madame. Ça va?'

'Bonjour, Monsieur Lelouche. Ça va bien ...' she answered, a query in her voice.

'I have had a telephone call from Monsieur Rettlesham-Carey,' he explained in French. 'He said to me that you have an object you would like me to hang on the wall for you. I am happy to do this, if it is not already accomplished.'

Netty stared at him in utter blankness, long enough to see a dull red flush creep up under his skin. The hand she had shaken went to his upper trouser leg and unconsciously clutched at the thick fabric. Her eye followed the action. Then she remembered.

'Oh! The boar's head! Thank you. You're very kind. Come in.'

Cursing inwardly, she led the way into the house. She would have preferred to forget the dratted thing. Dammit, she *had* forgotten the dratted thing. No doubt Peter meant well. No doubt Gerald would like it.

Out it came from its carrier bag, silently snorting. She realised that the creature was not going to improve on acquaintance.

'Perhaps you would like this to hang in the hall here?' Norbert asked, taking the hairy head from her and weighing it in his hands. Netty felt the prickly aftermath of the bristles she had touched.

'No, no, in here's fine. More appropriate, don't you think?'

He halted on the threshold of the Salle de Chasse, taking a good look, then came in slowly. They chose a place fairly high on the wall opposite the great fireplace. Norbert knelt and opened his box of tools. Netty fetched him a beer from the fridge, then left him to it.

He was a fast and silent worker. In no time the dust was cleared and the hairy black head presided over the creatures on the wall-tiles.

He was almost as silent and fast in departure, as if afraid that she would offer him money. When she shook hands with him at the door, she was amazed to find that his big rough paw was trembling.

As if 'Exit stage left' and 'Entrance stage right' had been explicitly dictated, the Professor appeared at the mouth of the lane which led down to the farm and his cottage. Netty was caught lingering in the doorway of the house.

'Well, well, Rapunzel. Down from your tower at last?' he said genially as soon as within earshot.

'Hello, Fred. How are things?'

'Things are just dandy with *me*. Usually are. Was that Norbert

Lelouche I just saw leaving?'

'Yes. Peter asked him to do a favour for me, which I could well have done without! Come and see — you won't believe this!'

A minute later they stood under the boar's dead malice.

After a moment, Fred murmured, 'Have you noticed — the eyes follow you about the room!'

'Don't! Don't make it worse, for goodness sake! Come on, let's have a drink in the kitchen.'

'Good idea. And then we're going to leave Pigling Bland to his own devices.'

'Are we?'

'Yup. We're going to grab a bite to eat and head off to Périgueux.'

'Périgueux?'

'You've forgotten, haven't you? You're in danger of turning into the Lady of Shalott, cooped up here away from the world. And nothing good happened to *her!* Out in the real world, where us ordinary mortals dwell, today's the day the Honourable Pete opens his exhibition.'

'Today? My God, I've completely lost track ...'

'Didn't you get an invitation?'

'Oh, probably. It'll be out on the hall table, I suppose.'

'Well then, in spite of everything, I think it behoves us to show a little English solidarity and turn up. Plus, I have to admit to being curious: what new levels of monstrosity can the Honourable attain?'

In Périgueux, they left her car on the Boulevard Montaigne and made their way to the Galerie Jules Clicquot in the Puy Saint Front quarter. The manager, Amandine Verwoert, was stationed at the plate glass doors. She was dumpy, dressed in black in an effort to streamline her silhouette, with many-stranded amber necklaces picking up the henna tones of her hair, hair which was so dry it looked as if sparks might crackle from it at the slightest touch. A tall young acolyte bore a tray of glasses beside her.

'Poor kid!' the Prof whispered in Netty's ear. She nodded and took a gulp of wine. 'They've got him up as Ganymede the cup-bearer, poor soul. He must be about ready to sink through the floor.'

'He must be frozen too; this is hardly the season for shortie-togas!' she answered, as Amandine with her thick Dutch accent bullied a way for them through the slight throng.

To the left and right rose enormous blown-up photographs of Vesunna's tower. Then they emerged into the main body of the gallery. In the centre of the room a huge Roman standard had been set up, the eagle's beak etched against the light. Halogen spots on trapeze frames lurched, swung, arced, dived, like birds of prey themselves, locking onto the various precious objects of Peter's creation. Above it all a huge purple banner announced:

ARS DERIVATUS EST

Against the right wall the first array of exhibits was titled LIBAMUS: a colony of jugs and goblets was set against a daubed imitation of mosaic, such as a child might achieve with finger-paint. Roughly painted on the goblets were images of a jolly Bacchus, face agleam, astride a goat.

'Looks for all the world like Mr Pickwick, doesn't he?' said Fred.

After some bas-reliefs of happy drinkers, festooned with garlands and parading with all manner of Sileni, satyrs and nymphs, they came to a large statue depicting a youth reclining on a couch. His head was tipped back to drain the last drop from his cup. His eyes were closed languorously, his neck-muscles standing out as he swallowed.

The rear section of the exhibition, ornamented with plaster doves and muslin draperies, was labelled LUXURIA VINCIT OMNIA. In the centre stood a statue of Venus: pure white, graceful, appealing — until one noticed that her face bore a smirk of licentious triumph and that her right hand was buried between her smooth thighs, the sinews on that hand flexed with working.

'Good grief,' said Netty.

'Well, it's different,' said the Prof, bending to read the little card stapled by the statue's plinth. '"Venus Masturbaria". Oh, *very* witty. God, Peter's such a bloody adolescent.'

Turning to the left, Netty was confronted by a waist-high sculpture of a snarling dog, three-headed.

'Cerberus,' said Fred, 'guardian of the gateway to the underworld. Well, give Pete his due: he's trying to be pretty comprehensive. Booze, sex, death. Centuries of art and philosophy try to come to terms with the eternal mysteries and our Honourable Pete the Puberty-Struck sums it all up in one roomful of tacky derivations and sub-garden-centre statuary. Down, Rover,' he added, patting the hound's ugly centre head.

A black banner on the wall announced in letters of gold MORITURI TE SALUTANT. Beneath it, on a stone couch, lay a youth, head back, arms outflung: the mirror image of the young man imbibing his wine at the other side of the room. But this time the outstretched throat had been cut and the nerveless hands were limp. After an array of funerary cups and urns, the final exhibit was a funerary stela, a copy of one from Vesunna itself, commemorating the death of one Aurelianus Felicianus, the preciseness of the carved angular letters and figures somehow disciplining the mystery of death itself.

Fred and Netty found themselves standing, silent, under the secateur-beak of the Roman eagle.

'All human life is here,' remarked the Professor gloomily, and twirled his empty glass. A sudden hubbub by the door. 'God, here we go — I was hoping we might get away without seeing the artist himself.'

The crowds parted like extras on the set of *Ben Hur* and there they beheld Peter, wearing a crumpled beige linen suit.

'Nettles!' he cried and rushed forward. Kisses exchanged. 'Did old Norbert turn up and do the deed for you? I suddenly remembered the boar's head and gave him a ring yesterday, in case you hadn't got round to it.'

'Yes,' she answered. 'He came this morning. He was very efficient about it, too. It was kind of you to arrange it.' She was careful to avoid meeting Fred's eye as she spoke.

'Not at all, not at all. What else are friends for?' said Peter. 'It'll be a surprise for Gerald when he comes back.'

'*I'll* say,' she heard Fred mutter.

'I don't see old Edouard around,' said Peter, scanning. 'In fact it's all a bit dismal, no Gerry, no Lukers ...'

'I believe Edouard's abroad,' Fred said. 'He and a lady friend have taken a trip to America. Las Vegas, I was told. Seems appropriate.'

Yes, thought Netty. Tacky glamour, just his thing. I hope he weds some rich and wrinkled old bat at a drive-thru' chapel with rhinestones glittering all around and Tammy Wynette songs playing and neon light glancing off his smooth smooth hair.

'I'm surprised to find so much sculpture here, Peter,' Netty said. 'I thought you specialised in pottery.'

'No, actually I started with sculpture. It was my first love. Came to ceramics later. But it's nice to get back to it — like riding a bike, I suppose, you never forget! I'm bloody exhausted, though! Still, it's such a lot of fun. And then there's all the galleries back in England. You know, I think this is going to be my year.'

'You having your fifteen minutes of fame, then?' asked Fred. 'Which period you going to rehash next? The possibilities are endless. Satin-stuffed dummies and a real working guillotine? That'd be good.'

'Ha bloody ha. You are such an old hypocrite: you've built a career out of the past too, haven't you? It's given you a good living, hasn't it?'

Netty hastily interposed. 'How long is the exhibition going to go on here, Peter?'

'Oh, less than a month. Then we've got the fun task of packing it all up and transporting it to London. The Mnemosyne show runs from late January. I discussed it all there with Hermione when I was over in England. They're going to call the show *The Past is Present.* Good, eh?'

'It's just that I wouldn't want Gerald to miss it,' Netty continued, eyeing Fred who had wandered off to stand in front of the gravestone of Aurelianus. She saw him raise his glass as if to salute the departed Roman. 'It shouldn't be long before he's back. I mean, we're nearly in the run-up to Christmas, if you come to think of it.'

'Oh, he said late November to me.'

'What?'

'Bugger me, I didn't say, did I! Mind like a bloody sieve. I saw him when I was over in England! Total coincidence. You know I said I'd be popping up to Oxford to make arrangements with the Museum of Modern Art? Well, I ran into him there! Actually, I nearly ran him *over!*'

Netty felt confused. 'But Gerald didn't say when he rang last ...'

'Probably doesn't remember! He was pissed as a fart!'

'Was Roy with him? The friend he's been helping out?'

'Nope. He was on his ownsome — and a bit *lonesome* at that. Probably missing *you,* Nettles!'

'So, *where* did you say ...'

'Well, I'd had a meal at Gee's and I was driving down St Giles, and I saw him at the taxi-rank. In fact he had his arm stuck out and he was virtually toppling off the kerb. So, as soon as I registered that it *was* him I hit the brakes and reversed and said "Fancy a lift?" D'you know, he didn't recognise me at first? Well, the state he was in, and not knowing I was in Oxford and it being pitch-black and brass-monkey weather, it's hardly surprising. He gets in and tells me this address and I think to myself, "Blow me, he thinks I'm a taxi-driver!"'

'So, he got you to drive him all the way out to Wheatley, did he?' asked Netty, smiling. 'That's a fair way. I hope you asked for a good tip!'

'Actually, it was even further, because at first he sent me off in completely the opposite direction, down past the railway station and under the bridge. Osney something.'

'Osney Island,' said Netty.

'That's it. Foreign territory to me. Said there was someone he had to see, didn't care what time it was. He was muttering away like one of those winos you see in the gutter. Then we get under the bridge and he looks at me. And I think at last he realised it was me and it was weird because there were tears in his eyes (the booze probably, it gets to me like that, sometimes) and he tells me to turn the car around and off we go, all the way to Wheatley and I end up having coffee in the wee small hours with those friends of yours.'

'Roy and Sheila.'

'Yes. *He's* nice enough, bit on the quiet side, but I wouldn't want to go a couple of rounds with *her!* No wonder Gerry's out boozing!'

'Oh, Sheila's OK, really. Once you get to know her.'

'Well, I'll have to take your word on that one.'

At this point, Amandine came up. 'Peter my friend, stop this gossiping! I have here Maurice Saussignac and Honoré de Prigonrieux, waiting to talk to you. You want good reports, do you not? Then come!'

'OK, OK, if my public need me! Catch you again, Nettles. Oh, but have you heard the latest about the Lukers?'

'Yes, I have. Deirdre's left Felix.'

'God, but news travels fast! Didn't I always say she'd bail out? Highly developed instinct for self-preservation. Leaves poor old Felix for the high jump, though. If I hear any more juicy details when I'm in London, I'll let you know. 'Bye Fred! See you in the spring, probably! Claudine, I was going to pop over the day after tomorrow to say goodbye. You *are* a sweetie to turn up!'

Netty, released from Peter's bear-hug, turned to see Claudine now standing beside Fred. Although she was as *soignée* as ever, there was pleading in her eyes.

'I'll see you back at the car, Fred,' Netty said, put down her glass, and left.

It was a good half hour before Fred opened the car door and got in beside her. As she drove she was conscious of his surreptitious looks and his careful restraint. His tact incensed her.

On the outskirts of Périgueux he said, 'You know, it beats me how Peter's managed to produce so much, given that most of his waking hours he's steeped in booze. Maybe it steadies his hand.'

'Maybe.'

Five minutes later, on the N21, he tried again. 'I wouldn't have thought that MOMA would have been keen on Pete's kind of art. I thought it was all photo-montage and installation-work there.'

'I've never been, so I wouldn't know.'

'What — you lived in Oxford and never visited MOMA?'

'There's a lot I haven't done, Fred. I've led a sheltered life.'

Silence lasted for another ten kilometres.

'Annette, what's this about Claudine? She's upset, you know.'

'It's between Claudine and me.'

'Come on, it isn't fair of you not to let her explain. I gather she told you about the nasty business up at Le Sanglier.'

Netty took her eyes off the road to glare at him. 'My God! You knew too!'

'Of course I do. Everybody does. The event had a certain notoriety. Hardly surprising. When you first moved in, I assumed you knew, but when you came down to my cottage that night and you were having the screaming ab-dabs, but you didn't mention the most obvious reason for having them, I realised you weren't aware of what had happened.'

'But you should have told me. We had a right to know. The *immobilier...*'

'Annette, the estate agent was hardly likely to think a recent murder a great selling-point for the house, now, was he? Old Lupin kept his lips zipped for professional reasons. Now, what are you going to do? Are you going to cast me into outer darkness, like you did poor old Claudine? My, but you're a judgemental woman, Annette. You don't make a scene, you just shut down. You just stew in your own juice.'

Curiosity defeated resentment. 'OK, then, Fred. Give me the details.'

'You didn't give Claudine the chance to tell you?'

'No.'

'Well, it's a short, sad little tale. About two years ago, an English couple bought Le Sanglier. Brits with Utopian dreams of the Dordogne — how unusual! He was an architect or something. Big barrel-chested fellow. About fifty-odd, not in the first flush. She was dark, gipsy-ish, a bit wild round the edges. They hadn't been married long. He used to watch her all the time and she moved as if she knew it; she basked as if in front of a log fire. I thought it was rather touching.'

They had arrived in Malignac. The familiar sequence of buildings passed: the Coq d'Or, the church, the *boulangerie*. Netty's mind was up ahead, in the house deep in the forest. She could picture the scene. That dreadful room; the room she hated so. 'But — he murdered her?'

'Yes.'

'Was she having an affair or something?'

'Not as far as I know. The story is that they were given to various sex games; a few minor and not very original perversions, nothing hugely depraved. But he killed her during sex. Strangled her. Dreadful. When they took him away he kept crying that he loved her. The house was shut up. Monsieur Lupin asked Mathilde to go up there and clean it every so often, but she wouldn't go.'

Netty halted the car in front of the main door. She made no bid to get out or to invite the Professor in for coffee. 'It was that room. The Salle de Chasse.'

Fred reached over and patted her hand. 'My dear, it's not so neat. I'm afraid the murder took place in your own bedroom. Claudine saw it.'

'She *saw* it!'

'Of course, she didn't know at the time that she was witnessing a killing. She'd been out for a stroll with that delinquent hound of hers, and the mutt took off. She caught up with him here and somehow ended up looking in. Hard to think of our Claudine as a Peeping Thomasina, but there it is. I daresay she couldn't help herself. So she saw them rollicking about in the bedroom. Patapon went quite frantic, she told me. She had a hell of a time getting hold of him and she was mortified — even though, obviously, they were never aware she was there. Imagine how much *worse* she felt next day when Hortense told her the latest news: the Englishman had killed his wife. She was appalled, she was guilty. She had done nothing, she had said nothing.'

'Poor Claudine.'

'Now can you understand why she didn't tell you? She had no desire to dwell on it, she's a woman of discretion, and when she heard about your son, there was even less reason to broach the subject. She thought she was doing the right thing.'

'Yes, yes, I appreciate that. Oh God — it's just, all the lies and the feeling that something's lurking out there and ... and that the world is just *sick*.'

'Annette, the world is cruel but it's good too. It isn't totally blighted.'

'That's not what you said at the Coq d'Or that time, when Gerry was talking about hunting. You felt like I feel, that everything is out to get everything else. So please Fred, please don't do the wise old uncle on me. I'm not in the mood.'

He shrugged, opened the car door, levered himself out. She took the keys from the ignition, gathered up her handbag and got out as well. There was a pleasant smell of woodsmoke in the air. The breeze stirred his white hair. He stayed at his side of the car but his gaze was intense. 'You mustn't let these thoughts obsess you so, they'll lead you nowhere. Now, will you be all right here, on your own?'

'You mean now I know there's been murder and mayhem in my house? Yes, I'll be all right. I might camp up in the tower. I might go into the woods — strikes me it's safer.'

His brow was furrowed. 'You know you're very welcome down at Petit Caillou. Any time.'

'I know. Thanks. But I'm OK. Really.' She looked directly at him, her face hard. 'Think of it, Fred — back in England there's a man who killed my child. He's on those streets. He may seem to lead a normal life. He shares a pint with a mate. His house might have double-glazing and a three-piece suite. He's there. He's everywhere. So it doesn't matter where I am. He's here.'

Netty sat like a Viking queen on her *lit bâteau*. The room was dim after early sunset. She had been proud of this bedroom, but her territory within the walls of the sullen old house was being eroded. She sighed, picked up a couple of bags into which she had stuffed night-things, as if called on an urgent business-trip, and climbed to her tower. She had already hauled the single mattress upstairs: it would be comfortable enough.

Bad Dog

The cry came in the heart of the night. Netty started awake, her heart juddering. Then she was out of bed, befogged still in sleep, acting on instinct. The night-light was on, but the dream still persecuted him. He sat up in his cot, feet facing one another like a frog, fists in eyes, cheeks aflame. She lowered the drop-side of the cot, reached in, lifted, ignoring the protests of her sleep-stiffened back muscles.

He was in her arms, clinging, his hot head on her neck. She sat in the slipper chair in the corner and crooned to him in the dimness. Idly the mobiles swung above her, steadfastly his teddies' black eyes stared her out. He muttered about the bee, the dreadful bee, that buzzed only in the night round his sleeping, tormented head. With her words she shooed the bee away and restored him to peacefulness.

In the cool heart of the night he was hers entirely. Gerald slumbered, alone in the bedroom. Netty cradled her son and thought of that first cradling, the night he was born and his eyes, dark and solemn, had held hers in their first and everlasting encounter. After all the nausea and agony and blood, she had looked at him and thought 'It was you, it was you, all along', with a wonderment that had renewed itself in spite of the births of her two previous children, so long ago.

Danny stopped muttering about the bee. She kissed his hair and smelled the unique smell of him. He grew heavy in her arms. Her back still ached, but she felt no desire to ease her discomfort by returning him to his cot.

The first bird cleared its fluty throat, the night-light suddenly looked yellow in the growing light. She thought 'I'll never leave you. You're mine alone. I will always protect you.'

What foolishness. What idealism. He was not hers. He was separate. Possessive tenderness and the investment of years of energy and emotion would, eventually, be powerless when he was alone with his destroyer.

The cry came in the heart of the night. Heart racing, Netty jolted awake. She was confused for a moment, then the familiar griping pain took her by the heart and tears flooded her eyes. The smell of her son, his heat, his presence, faded. As always.

Dawn was approaching. She lay flat on her back on the single mattress. Then she raised herself on her elbows as if she were lying on a beach, gazing out to sea. In the grey light her tapestry-frames stood, a rigid guard of honour. Colour did not exist, just shadowy shape and substance, objects gaining reality as the light strengthened.

The thought came to her that she had heard a cry. She stood up and went to the window. The valley below, where Malignac lay invisible, was a sea of mist. A few dim stars were winking out, bowing off-stage after the moon. A figure stood on the lawn. Her heart thumped, scurried, steadied. Curiosity warred with fear. An awful fascination possessed her.

It took merely a moment to shrug on a heavy sweater, trousers and boots. The clean cold air assaulted her lungs as she stepped outside and she gasped.

At first, she thought the figure had gone, but as her eyes grew better accustomed to the deceptive gloaming, harder to penetrate than darkness itself, she saw he was still there, immobile, out on the grass. She went towards him.

He acknowledged her with a slight nod, as if they were acquaintances passing on a village street. The briefest recognition of fellow-humanity. Then she stood beside him, turning so that she too faced the grey bulk of the house, its edges coming into focus like Brigadoon after a hundred years.

He looked different. His head, for once, did not look as if slung between his shoulders, conveying fear of the world and of men's eyes.

He stared up at the house like a questing hound. Now he looked at her; starlight caught the moisture on his eyeball. For a moment he gleamed like Oberon. Then the posture changed; the head came down, the shoulders lifted protectively. He smelled of earth and dust. She almost put her hand on his arm to reassure him, but there was still an element of fear. Local loner slays ex-pat. Her body would be found later with the dew upon it and nobody would have heard a thing, officer.

Suddenly he cleared his throat, muttered, guttered darkly in curt phrases. She saw his hand clench and open. Desperately she tried to make out what he was saying, but her mind was still foggy and his accent too pronounced. Words she caught: 'This house ... that room, I should not have been in that room ...'

She thought of his silent labour as he hung up the boar's head. It had to be that room, that bloody room. But why did it upset him so?

Embarrassment caught up with him. She felt him leaning away from her. The incomprehensible utterances dried up. In the carrying air of uninhabited morning they heard slow footsteps, the powdery crunch of pebble and dust. Turning to the left they saw a figure appear from the farm-track and take up position at the edge of the lawn. A short, dark figure, unmoving. Mathilde had come for her son.

Norbert begged her pardon, as if he had trod on her toe, not haunted her house and scared her half out of her wits. He was shambling off with his peculiar loose-kneed, heavy-bodied gait, scuffing dust into the cool air, before Netty realised that she had said nothing to him. The mother claimed the son; their figures shrank and died in the descent. Netty found she was chilled to the bone.

'Poor sod,' said Fred at Petit Caillou next morning. They were having coffee and pastries. Every time Fred bit into his *millefeuille*, his eyes closed dreamily, like an old turtle's.

'All I could make out was that he was going on about the Salle de Chasse. It seemed to unsettle him.'

'I dare say it would. I hate to bring you even more bad tidings about your house, but Norbert's mother was raped there, and he's the result.'

'Oh my God!'

'Yes, it was a nasty little war-crime. You know the Nazi soldiers were quartered at Le Sanglier late on in the war?'

'Yes.'

'The officer in charge was trying to capture the local *Francs Tireurs* and he arrested various Malignacois men, threatening to kill them if no one blabbed. One of them was Mathilde's lover.'

'So she spoke.'

'No, apparently not. But everybody did think so after the war. She had a very bad time from what I can gather. They thought she'd betrayed the Resistance to save her man, which is ironic as the German officer had had her lover shot anyway. Later they found out a *mauvais Maquis* had done the evil deed. He'd been in cahoots with the Germans all along: anti-Communist type, probably thought he was doing the right thing. Dreadful mess, all in all. So, Mathilde lost her love, her honour, had her head shaved and was reviled, *and* ended up with an illegitimate semi-Teutonic son.'

Netty absorbed all this. 'But why didn't she leave? I would have.'

'She's just not that type. Many of these rural French are very parochial; they're not gypsies like the Scots and Irish. It's not in them to up sticks and move, just like that. Plus, I think she just wanted to face her enemies down. She'd have thought it cowardly to run and it would have confirmed their notions of her.'

'But Norbert ...'

'Yes, poor bugger, I agree. It's been tough on him to live his life as a living emblem of his mother's pride and shame. He must wonder about his father — I mean, was he sadistic by nature or was it that *power* that went to his head. Rape is power, isn't it? Maybe he went back to Germany and married a nice girl called Liesl and forgot he'd ever been a monster. Who knows?'

'What I know is that I've had it, Fred. I can't live there anymore. I lurk up in the tower all the time as it is. I can't go on. There was a little while where I thought I could grow to love the place. There was a time in the summer when I got quite possessive about it, quite involved ... but now ...' She was stopped by a sudden hammering at the door. Before the Professor could rise from his armchair, Claudine came in, out of breath.

'Annette ... ! *Professeur*... !' From her gloved hand dangled a thin strip of brown leather.

'Claudine, what is it?' asked Fred.

'It is Patapon — he is lost! We were having one of our promenades and I was tired. I called him to me — you know how he is — and when I attached his leash, you see what has happened.' She held the broken lead out for them to see. 'He was excited ... he was gone. I came this way: he knows the path. I have passed Le Sanglier. I must ask at the farm. You have not seen him?'

'Sorry, Claudine, I haven't been out this morning.'

'Oh! Oh, the *méchant*. He is such a fool, if he runs down onto the road ...'

Netty saw the tears in Claudine's eyes. Fred put an arm round her shoulders and ushered her to the chair he had just vacated. 'Come on, Claudine, have a drink and then we'll go looking. I'll turn the soup off. We can have some for lunch after we find him. Annette, could you pour Claudine a coffee? I'll just nip across to the farm and see if anyone can help us look for him.'

The door banged behind him. Netty obediently fetched a cup from the kitchen, poured out the coffee, passed it to Claudine. It was hard to shake off constraint. For a moment, their eyes met. 'Don't worry,' she said reassuringly. 'He'll turn up.' In her bitterness towards Claudine, she couldn't help thinking *it's just a bloody dog, after all. A dog. A creature of a brief life-span. Not a child, even though to Claudine it was the approximation of one.*

Fred soon returned, with Norbert and Alexandre, one of the farm-workers. 'Don't worry,' he repeated. 'Dogs have a kind of homing instinct haven't they? Remember *The Incredible Journey?* The pooch is probably on Madame's doorstep right now, howling for his Winalot or whatever the French equivalent is. *Gagne-Beaucoup,* no doubt.'

Two hours later they stood in the clearing by the last remains of Dionysus' temple. They were all chilled by a wind that had harried them, darting up sleeves and down collars, nipping and worrying.

'I'm sorry, my dear,' said Fred to Claudine. 'I don't see what else we can do. We're all worn out.'

'I will look for a while longer,' volunteered Norbert.

'You are kind, but the Professor is right,' answered Claudine. 'We have searched everywhere.'

Netty spoke, softened slightly by the suffering beaten expression Claudine wore. 'Maybe, as Fred said, maybe he's found his way home. Let's go back to Petit Caillou and have some soup to warm us up. You can call Hortense or Guillaume from there.'

'Perhaps I should go straight to Bel Arbre.'

'No you won't! You've walked far enough!' said the Professor. 'Annette's right: get some soup inside you, then one of us can run you home.'

The weary little procession set off, the Professor's arm round Claudine's shoulders. The clearing was left in silence. Damp soil, dormant or dying vegetation, brown light, the darting wind. The flurry of a dry leaf like the scrabble of paws. The whine of air through a crevice like a canine lament.

After a brief lunch and an unproductive phone-call to Bel Arbre, they adjourned to Le Sanglier, on the grounds that there was an outside chance that Patapon might turn up there. Minutes of fidgeting unease passed. Netty was still finding it hard to unbend towards Claudine. They sat in the kitchen, nursing coffee they did not wish to drink.

'Annette, what about the famous tapestries? They finished yet?' Fred asked.

'Pretty well, I suppose,' she answered, diffidently.

'Well, can we see them? Weeks you've been lurking up there, Arachne.'

'Well, I ...'

'Oh, come on! You're among friends.'

She remembered Deirdre, oozing false sympathy. She looked at Claudine and realised how great the difference was. 'All right,' she said. 'Come on.'

They clattered up the wooden stairs, Netty fighting her reluctance all the way. Claudine raised an eyebrow at the mattress on the floor, with its turmoiled linen. Behind it, in a wooden phalanx, the floor-frames stood.

'A triptych,' murmured Fred. 'My dear, how clever.'

'Such work!' cried Claudine. 'Let me see your hands, Annette. Ah! I knew it! Such wounds, such scars. Why give yourself this pain?'

'I had to. I didn't notice half the time. Of course, the one on the right isn't quite finished,' she said, 'but the other two are.'

'Exquisite.'

'Beautiful, Annette,' nodded Fred. 'Beautiful, my dear.'

Three pictures. None of them large, but intricately shaded, in densely-textured petit point.

In the picture on the left a slate-grey sky loured over the dark mourning tones of yew trees, spiced with red berries. A chalk-white path meandered through the shadows and the shadows were not those of the trees but of the creatures of the woods. A small child had tripped headlong and fallen on the path, his little arms splayed out, his face unseen. He wore a red sweater; he was a living lure for the glooming threats around him. His smallness, his vulnerability, cried out for protection. Netty watched Claudine step forward involuntarily, impelled by a desire to embrace that frail torso.

On the right, a different set of tones. A sky of navy, studded with beige stars. The entrance to a cave, grey standing-stones like sentinels marching from the portal into the distance. In the foreground a figure, hunched and grey, swathed in veils, head lowered, distinctly female. The essence of grief; lamentation given woven force. Right at the centre, on the figure's lap, the eye was drawn to the hands, febrile and nervous, the white hands endlessly clutching and caressing a fragment of soft red fabric. Under the veil the shadow of a mouth, soundlessly blaring in unbearable grief.

Even the Prof looked shaken. Netty found herself wanting to fill the silence. 'Don't look at me like that. I'm not sure how I came up

with these notions. I know they're morbid. You *did* ask to see them!'
The third picture. On either side of it, worlds of nightmare. In the
centre, the dream.

Once more the palette changed. The sky was cobalt, the soil rich
agate and topaz, the verdure jade and emerald. In a garden a fountain
sprang. Behind it ran sweet box hedges in frisky mazes, enclosing
topiary pleasures; bunnies and kittens and doves. The fountain fell
into a basin out of which sprang friendly fish, radiant in golden
mail. A goddess gowned in white and crowned in gold and sapphire
trailed her hand in the water and tickled the fish for the delight of
the infant she held on her lap. The child was naked and pure. White
wool caught the glint of the baby eye, pink and white were the shades
of the soft flesh. The child laughed straight out of the picture at the
observer.

'You see,' said Netty, 'all I ever wanted was to think of him as
safe. Like a fairy tale. Like he got lost in the wild wood but the fairy
godmother would look after him. I wanted to believe it, because it
wasn't true. No one saved him — least of all me. God only knows
where he is now, or what he thinks of me. So this is all I could do:
offer this to him.'

As they turned away, Claudine laid her hand on Netty's arm.
'Annette, you must understand, my silence was meant for the best.
Sometimes it is right to be silent, some things are better not talked
about. *You* must know this.'

'Claudine, I know you meant well, whether it was right or wrong.'
Wrong, wrong. She put her hand over Claudine's and squeezed.

On her return to Bel Arbre, Claudine found herself weeping, and
it wasn't just for Patapon, the dissolute and disappeared.

'If you keep this up,' Fred had said, 'you could have an exhibition.
Give the Honourable Pete a run for his money.'

Alone in the tower room after her friends had gone, she thought
of this. She thought of Peter's exhibition, and of Peter's casual, joking
words. Osney Island, he had said. Osney Island. What had Gerald to

do with Osney Island? Why had that not registered at the time? Eaten up with resentment towards Claudine, and shaken by the revelation of murder in Le Sanglier she had failed to see the implications, but now they were starting to strike home. Stupid woman, stupid *stupid* woman, she thought, hurrying downstairs.

It was early evening in Oxford. Sheila answered the phone promptly.

'Hi, Sheila, it's Netty.'

'Well hello, stranger! What a pleasant surprise!'

'How're things?'

'Oh, we're fine. Well, one of the drains has backed up again — Roy's out there just now with the man who's come to see it. And I've been to the doctor with my veins again: I'll have to have them stripped, he says, but it just puts a shudder right through me, the very ...'

'Sheila, I'm sorry to interrupt, but is Gerald there? I really need to talk to him.'

'Hasn't he rung you then?'

'Not for, oh, about a week, I think. Was he supposed to?'

'Well, he did say he would, before he left.'

'Left? Left, where?'

'He's staying at Paul's. You'd better try there.'

'OK, I'll do that. Right now. Sheila, I'm sorry ...'

'Never mind — we'll have a good natter some other time. It's long overdue!'

'I know, I know! Sorry! Bye!'

Paul had just got in from work. His voice was immediately cagey.

'Come on, Paul, I've just phoned Sheila. There's something going on. Why's your Dad staying with you?'

'Can't a father come and see his son?'

'Paul!'

'All right, then. Apparently things were getting a bit sticky with the Bensons. He thought it would be better if he left.'

'Let me speak to him.'

'I can't. I don't know where he is.'

Netty let out a sigh of exasperation. 'Just what is going *on* over there?'

'I'm telling you the truth, Mum. He was with me a couple of nights, then he said he needed to be on his own. He's in some hotel or other — he wouldn't give the name. But he did tell me that if you rang I was to say he was fine and that he'll be home on the twenty-first.'

'And that's supposed to reassure me?'

Paul was silent. She decided on a bold gamble.

'Was it his affair that caused problems in Oxford?'

Paul gasped, 'How ... how did you ...'

'Oh, somebody said something to me yesterday. I didn't twig at the time, but I've been putting two and two together, since.' How horrible that it should all fall into place so easily. She was amazed at her own calm reaction. Why was she not weeping? Why was she not beating her breast? Didn't she care? Was there nothing left, between Gerald and herself, worth salvaging? 'Who was it?' she felt obliged to ask.

'Er ... I wouldn't know.'

'Oh, I get the feeling you do.'

Another silence, then he capitulated. 'OK. Someone at F & B. Her name is Camilla Thorneycroft. Do you know her?'

'I think we've met. I think so.' She knew so, her suspicions confirmed. A house-warming party, years ago, in Osney Island. Domineering type. Did Gerald appreciate that sort of thing after all? Should she, Netty, have worn leather and cracked the whip, on occasion? Did they all, secretly, crave punishment and want to come whining and licking?

'Well, Dad admitted to me that he had a bit of a fling with her in the summer,' Paul continued.

Oh, she thought, *that's why he was so nice to me.* Anger, at last, began to rise, bobbing up from below the shock. Anger, born of hurt pride and a sense of betrayal. She had no love left, she was sure of it. None.

'Listen Mum,' said Paul, more urgently. 'I know we haven't seen eye to eye all that much, me and him, but you've got to feel sorry for him. He's in a state.'

'*He's* in a state.'

'He's lost it, he's a lost soul. He's not as strong as you think. It's eating away at him. Anybody with half an eye can see he's really sorry.'

A voice, almost subliminal, in the background.

'Are you sure he's not there?' she asked suspiciously.

'No, Mum. That's Stephen.'

'Stephen! Don't tell me ...'

'We're back together. Well, till the next time!' His laugh was awkward, the laugh of a shuffling schoolboy.

'Paul ...'

'I know. Don't worry. I have no false expectations this time.'

'Why should expectations of loyalty and faithfulness have to be *false*? Don't set your sights so low. I did, and look at what's happened. Your father's walked all over me.'

'Mum ...'

'Just don't let Stephen do the same to you.'

'Mum, I feel lousy about this. I don't like being piggy in the middle, you know. I agonised about whether to tell you. I've seen the state Dad's in, but I'm really worried about you too. Nothing justifies what Dad's done to you. What are you going to do?'

'Not much I *can* do, until I see him.'

'Are you going to be all right? I don't like to think of you, all on your own.'

'I've got used to it.'

'I'll come over, if you like. I could bring Stephen.'

'No, Paul. Let me sort things out with your Dad first. Stephen will keep.'

'I hope so! Look, I just wanted to say, sorry I was such a screwed-up petulant berk when I visited you.'

'I'm sorry too. I didn't mean those things I said. Not deep down.'

'I know. I knew at the time. I just felt . . . let down.'

'A feeling I'm familiar with.'

'Oh Mum ... just ... take care. Love you.'

'Love you too.'

She put the receiver was back on its cradle. Thank you, Peter, she thought. Thank you for being such a tactless blab.

'Girding your loins, are you?' asked Fred over dinner at the Coq d'Or.

'What do you mean?'

'Well, I know Gerald's returning in a couple of days and you haven't said what the problem is, but I can see you revving up for something, that's for sure.'

'The Oracle strikes again.'

'I knew it!' he crowed.

'Fred, can I come home with you tonight?'

His face registered a passing shock. 'Well, blow me, I didn't see *that* one coming. Should have, though: you don't want to be in that nasty old place on your own.'

'No, it's not that, Fred. I've got used to that. I just fancy the company.'

He paid the bill and escorted her to Petit Caillou. They shared a serene hour of coffee and triviality; a subdued implicit wooing, then he took her in his arms. He had the sense to be silent, she thought, relaxing in his bony embrace, hearing his old heart bounding. That was all she wanted; a little gentle, reverential comfort. Then, to her amazement, he had slipped to the floor and he was removing her boots and socks. His fingers slid over her instep, into the hollow by her Achilles tendon, down under the ball, darted between her toes. 'Such beautiful beautiful feet,' he murmured.

'Fred, get up!'

He knelt and placed her feet on his thighs and gazed and gazed. She tried to pull them away, but his grip tightened. Then he stood, grasped her wrist. 'Come here, come with me.' His mouth was working spasmodically. In his bedroom he wrenched open the double doors of the wardrobe and out they fell: a cascade of shoes; red and sinful, patently gleaming, lustrously buffed, purringly velvet. All fiercely heeled, naughty, impractical, archly sexual.

'Choose. Choose! Try these!' he scrabbled on the floor and held up a pair, black and shiny. The feet within them would be held at an impossible angle, contained only by dainty ankle-straps.

Netty backed away. 'Fred, there's no way ... My God, what are you playing at?'

'That's it, Annette. It's just playing. Miriam used to. Please, won't you? I can't explain it, I've never been able to. She understood. Please, for me.'

'No. No, it's disgusting! I may have led a sheltered life, but this ... it's just creepy!' She looked at him: the genteel tweed jacket and the beige moleskin trousers, the brushed cotton shirt worn thin at the neck, and the perverse shoes held out to her. The antiquated Prince offering shoe, sex and safety to his Cinderella. The wounded look in his eye, and the growing resentment.

He stood up. She shrank away from him. 'Don't be afraid. You've made your feelings clear. You're not into this.' He piled the shoes back into the wardrobe and shut the door on them. 'I'm sorry I ever mentioned it. I got a bit carried away, I suppose. Don't worry. It was just my little game. I wish I'd never ...'

She had thought to let him touch her, soothe her, lie with her, in the hours before Gerald's return. But like the rest, he had let her down. Back at Le Sanglier she watched the dawn come up from her wintry tower-room and thought what treachery there was in men. How their games were no games at all. How the best of them were selfish and the worst of them dangerous vermin. The fountain played silently and the infant laughed in the safety of the garden, but Netty looked out on a world in which wolves prowled, tirelessly.

Coup de Grâce

She would play a waiting game. She was witchfinder general. She would prick him and watch him bleed.

'Good God! What the bloody hell's that?'

'It's a gift from your friend Peter. Don't you like it?'

'Well, it's a wicked-looking brute, isn't it? Look, the eyes seem to follow you about the room.'

'Fred said that too.'

'For once I'm in agreement with him! Puts you a bit on edge, doesn't it. I'm surprised you've got it on the wall, Net.'

'I thought you'd like it, after your hunting trip. It's not the same boar, but it's a kind of memento. Peter was *sure* you'd love it. I could hardly say no.'

'I suppose not. He meant well, the old bugger. Funny not to have him around.' Gerald slumped into a chair by the dead hearth. 'Pour us a drink, love.' As the whisky gurgled into the glass Gerald found himself relieved that he wouldn't have to explain to Peter that he no longer wanted to take any pot-shots at the beasties, large or small, furred or feathered. He just couldn't hack it any more. He was absolutely sure of that, if of nothing else in his benighted life. But he hadn't relished trying to convey this to Pete or resisting his jackrabbit enthusiasm. 'I'd been looking forward to sinking a few at the Drunken Dive. Ah, well. What about poor Felix — any more news of him?'

Netty handed him the glass and watched him swallow. He looked the same, he wasn't the same. The tone of bonhomie was pitched just a little too high. 'No,' she answered. 'Apart from his lady wife leaving him, not a sausage. Maybe Claudine will know.'

'And how's Madame these days?'

'She's a bit upset, actually. Her dog's gone missing.'

'Hardly the end of the world. Neurotic brute.'

'He means all the world to her.'

'He may well do, but you've got to feel sorry for anyone who focuses their whole life on a *dog*.' The whisky was going down well. 'Any more news?'

'Not really. I see Fred every so often.'

'Nice for you.'

'Yes, it is,' she answered lightly.

'Paul's hoping to come over in the spring. It was good to spend some time with him,' Gerald said. 'Mind you, I didn't much like the look of that lad he's sharing his flat with. Self-centred bugger, if you ask me. Couldn't pass a mirror to save his life.'

Netty decided not to follow this line of conversation. The problems with Paul's secret life would have to wait. 'If I'd known you were going to be so long in England, I would have come over myself. I feel totally out of touch: I know there's a real world out there, and I keep thinking of it hurrying along, like one of those speeded-up films, and here I am, just ticking over. I feel guilty about not talking very much to Sheila lately, and she's been so good putting you up — although of course, you were there to do *them* a favour, weren't you. Anyway, I've had this great idea: why don't we ask Roy and Sheila over for Christmas?'

Ah, she enjoyed that, she enjoyed that look on his face. She relished his fear.

Gerald tried to tell himself it was all going well. They settled into a kind of routine: they went for walks in the woods, they shared rather too much to drink in the Salle de Chasse of an evening, they ate out frequently, they nodded hello to Augustin and Mathilde and Norbert.

The Professor visited, but Gerald noticed Netty was cooler towards him than she used to be. Paradoxically, he found himself warming to the old coot; he was genial company, in default of any other.

There were other changes: he noticed that she never went to bed ahead of him, the way she used to. He noticed also that she drank more, and that she visited her tower a great deal less than she had done in the summer. Too bloody cold, no doubt, too draughty. The Salle de Chasse could be quite cosy after all, now that they'd got Charbis in to sort out the chimney. A roaring fire on a frosty night, a full glass, goodwill to all men.

Goodwill to all, except himself. Often as he sat with the malty glow of good usquebaugh within him, he'd feel the sudden swelling of memory and grief.

A couple of times Netty almost caught him on the phone to Roy, telling him to keep his wife silent, at all costs. He'd hear Netty's footsteps on the gravel and he'd slam the receiver down. The visit was all arranged for the festive season, and Sheila, that bitch, his nemesis, was coming. Panic lay pregnant within him, like that horrible thing in the *Alien* movie, waiting to burst out of John Hurt's chest.

If she should find out.

Midwinter. Once she would have taken Danny to visit Santa. Once she would gleefully have found places to hide his gifts.

'Get plenty of booze in,' said Gerald. 'That friend of yours drinks like a fish.'

'She does not! Anyway, you're a fine one to talk.'

'I know,' he admitted, to her surprise. 'I look down at my hand; there always seems to be a glass clamped to it these days. I don't know how it gets there. Not enough to do, I suppose.'

'Well, get over here and help me with these decorations.' From her perch on the chair by the boar she looked down on him and saw the sag of the burly shoulders and the matching sag of the mouth.

She must not pity him. She must not.

The forced breezy bumptiousness was tiring him. It drained him, like a vampire, night by night. If she had patience, in time he would tell, he would have to confess, and then she could exact her penance.

Roy and Sheila arrived on the twentieth of December.

'Sheila! You found us!' Netty embraced her friend, then turned to hug Roy.

'A couple of wrong turnings on the way. All Roy's fault, naturally!'

'But of course!'

'Anyway, nothing too drastic. Hello, Gerald.'

'Sheila. Greetings. Come on in. Like a drink?'

'Gasping.'

Netty took the jackets. Roy and Sheila gazed round the hall and were led into the Salle de Chasse.

'Good grief! Lord and Lady of the Manor, eh?' exclaimed Roy, accepting a generous tot of Glenfiddich.

Gerald laughed. 'Sit yourself down, mate. Take the chill off.'

'No need; it's really mild down here, like you said it'd be. Still, there's nothing like the look of a real fire, eh? Nothing to beat it.' Netty noticed Roy lifted both hands to the baldness on the top of his skull, unconsciously smoothing it with his palms, as if to check the few shreds of hair still adhered there. Years, she'd seen him do it; methodical, nervous Roy. Bit of an old woman, Gerald had always said, with the bluff superiority he enjoyed. Roy to Gerald was like the plain girl at the pretty girl's side at the Saturday dance. The perfect foil.

'What'll you have, Sheila?' Netty asked.

'I'd love a coffee! I'm flagging a bit after that journey. If I touch anything alcoholic, I'll just conk out!'

After showing Sheila the double bedroom where they would sleep, the small room now allocated to Gerald, and the tower eyrie which was her domain once more, Netty ushered her friend to the kitchen. Sheila was loud in her appreciation.

'Oh, it's so *roomy,* Netty, and so rustic! The only thing missing is an Aga.'

Netty showed her the bottle of gas lodged in its metal cupboard beside the oven. 'We're not on mains here, of course, and these bottles are amazingly economical. It's just a hassle changing them over: you have to buy them at Leclerc's petrol station, and you need a spanner to loosen the connection. It's a lot of botheration.'

I'm prattling, she thought. The truth was that she felt disconcerted to see Sheila sitting there. It was incongruous. Netty visualized her friend back at home, her living-room cluttered with Lladro and Royal Doulton figurines on little mock-Georgian tables. The tiered mahogany pot-plant stand. The gold-rimmed china, the gold-plated taps. And Sheila herself, with her rasp of a voice and her welded curls, brooches like shield-bosses on her wool-mix jackets, and blue veins lurking under support-hose.

Netty carried two big mugs through to the Salle de Chasse. The men were deep in business-talk. Back in the kitchen, Sheila told her of the shops that had opened and closed, the horrors of Oxford's traffic, the holiday she was planning: Florida next year. A vision of Roy, shrunken and timid behind the wheel of a Buick, came to Netty's mind.

'So,' said Sheila, inevitably, 'what happened that night, ages ago, when you rang me, wanting to talk to Gerald? We've been so caught up with making arrangements for this trip, you haven't filled me in.'

'I told you: I phoned Paul's flat,' she answered, knowing full well Sheila would not be satisfied with so little.

'And?'

'And nothing really.' Netty made a show of tasting her coffee and adding more sugar. She felt reluctant to confide in her friend: Sheila's sympathy was too blunt an instrument, too easily manipulated. Private jurisdiction, that was all that mattered.

'Oh come on! I want to hear the gory details. What did Gerald say?'

'He said nothing. He wasn't there.'

Sheila drew her breath in sharply. There was a silence, then she spoke with unaccustomed hesitation. 'Netty, maybe I shouldn't ask, but you *do* know why he left our place, don't you?'

Netty, in turn, debated with herself. But Sheila was her friend, her long-term, concerned friend. She deserved her trust.

'Yes. I wormed it out of Paul. Well, that's not strictly true: I had twigged, I suppose, what was going on before I rang him — before I rang you, actually. It was something somebody had said to me. I had a gut feeling and I was just looking for confirmation. It was awful, though, having to quiz my son about his father. It felt like treachery, but I had to know.'

'Of course you did. Whoever said ignorance is bliss was a fool. Ignorance is humiliation.'

Netty sipped some more of her coffee and offered Sheila another *Petit Écolier* biscuit. 'In the end,' she continued, 'Paul was more concerned to tell me how sorry Gerald was.'

'I'll bet! Oh yes, he did a lot of being sorry at our house, too. It turned my stomach. You're my friend, and it's a *disgrace*. He was under my roof and we all knew he'd betrayed you with that hard-faced little madam. I didn't know where to put myself. Why, if Roy ever ...'

'He wouldn't dare, Sheil!'

'Well, I know he wouldn't. I've no worries on that score. But for Gerald, knowing what you'd been through ...'

'Maybe he thought enough time had gone by.'

'Anyone who knows you knows better than that. It's a disgrace! Has he said anything?'

'Not a dicky bird. Look, these things happen. Our marriage has been under strain for so long ...'

'Oh good God, don't start making excuses for him! You're angry — I know you are, you have to be.'

'Of course I bloody am!'

Sheila came to her and put her arm round her shoulder. She gripped like granite and smelt of Avon's *Occur*. 'I could kill Roy for even letting Gerald know about it, keen though I am to see a man face his responsibilities. Little Miss Independence should have been left to her own devices. But Roy, once he knew there was a baby involved ...'

Netty felt herself, for a second, leave her body, soar up to the beams of her blue kitchen and look down at herself: at her thin hunched body, at her defeated face, at the sudden look of shock she wore. She saw her own lips form the word: *What?* She saw Sheila recoil, saw the guilt on her well-meaning face, saw her lips move in reply.

'You didn't know? I thought ... Oh my God, this just gets worse! I thought you ... I was sure you knew. Didn't Paul say?'

Netty was back in her dry arid bones, under her desiccated flesh, with acid for blood, corroding her veins. 'No. I suppose he thought I'd guessed that too. I sounded so confident. I thought I knew the worst. But you never reach the worst, do you? Not while you can still believe you're at rock-bottom.'

'Oh God, Netty, I could shoot myself! I wanted to tell you, really I did, as soon as we knew, but Roy was adamant that Gerry should be given a chance to sort it out. It was his job to tell you.' She paused. 'I take it he hasn't said anything.'

'No. He goes around looking shifty and sorry for himself, but I'm supposed to be the little woman living in blissful innocence.'

'He just fell apart on us when he couldn't persuade her to keep it.'

'That's what he wanted, was it?' Netty, by an effort of will, held on to herself; she mustn't fly off again, out of her body, out of the room, the house, the world. Things had to be faced. Her child had gone and he had thought to replace him with another. What shallow roots his love had. She became aware that Sheila was gazing at her, questioningly.

'What are you going to do, Netty?' she asked.

'I don't know.'

'But you must be feeling ...'

A bellow from Gerald, from across the hall. 'Any chance of more coffee, Net? Jump to it, ladies!'

Her voice, strangely, didn't quaver. 'Coming!' She took Sheila's hand. 'Look — I need time to think. Just, just don't say anything, will you.'

Sheila sighed. 'All right. But it'll take some doing.'

'I just need to handle this my own way.'

'As long as your own way doesn't mean lying down like a dog.'

'Oh, it won't. No.'

The Chase

Three days passed quickly with Roy and Gerald in a boozy huddle, Netty and Sheila bustling about in preparation for Christmas. The segregation prevailed even on car-trips: Roy sat in the front passenger seat, Gerald drove. Netty did her best to point out the sights but found Sheila, hip to solid hip with her in the back, was far more interested in gossip than scenery. She let her friend's gabble wash over her and gazed out at the passing countryside, drably beige in mild December. She felt so distant from the summer and the white heat of it all. She was dead. No. No, not that. On the surface, a strange trance-like state had taken her in its embrace, but beneath, lay the molten anger.

They visited Bourdonne and strolled on the cobbles of the old *quai* beside the Dordogne. Netty picked up her newly-framed tapestries and listened to Sheila's extravagant praise and Roy's, 'Very nice dear. Very clever.' Back home, Gerald looked at them for long silent minutes. 'They're not your usual style, are they? Where are you going to hang them, love?' he asked, his tone of voice not encouraging their display in any public place.

'Oh, I don't know. I'll just pop them up in the tower-room in the meantime. I'll think about it after Christmas.'

Her precious pictures. Her precious love. Deirdre had been right, paradoxically: here in the tower was the shrine to her precious child.

'We're going to have a French-style Christmas,' announced Gerald. 'When in France, do as the ...'

'It means that most of the celebration is on Christmas Eve,' said Netty. 'Would you like that? I mean, do you mind?'

'As long as the alcohol's flowing, Netty love!' answered Roy.

'I might have guessed,' said Sheila, making eyes at heaven. 'Now, why do I get the feeling that whether it's Christmas Eve or Christmas Day, Britain or France, it'll involve us poor womenfolk labouring in the kitchen!'

'Just as long as you know your place, Sheila!' Gerald said.

Netty spoke quickly. 'Now, Sheila, I've got it all in hand. You're on holiday. You just enjoy yourself.'

'As if I could, knowing you're all alone in there, slaving away.' Sheila shot a look at Gerald, who steadfastly withstood the ocular onslaught. 'No, I insist, Netty. *Somebody* has to help you and it might as well be someone who knows what they're doing.'

'So, that's agreed then!' said Gerald, clapping his palms together. 'Roy and me'll do the washing up — if we're still capable!'

'Well, we might be by the twenty-eighth, so hold hard, ladies, we're your men!'

Guests were duly invited. With some trepidation Netty sent Gerald down to the farm to ask Augustin and Mathilde. She felt guilty never to have reciprocated after the dinner party at Grand Caillou. At the same time, she dreaded the traumas of making conversation with them and of cooking for them. However, the invitation was declined: they had other arrangements; a big family party. Of course; stupid to think they'd accept at such short notice.

Only later did it strike Netty that Mathilde would have refused anyway.

Edouard was still abroad. Peter was in England, perhaps roasting a whole ox at Rettlesham Park.

Fred and Claudine agreed to come.

The morning air was mild but they lit the fire anyway and watched it roar. Smoke drifted up the chimney and out over the dim forest. They were determined to be festive.

Claudine arrived, bearing quietly expensive gifts and wearing a dress of claret velvet with a black bolero jacket. Sheila's patter dried somewhat in her elegant presence and Netty noticed her friend's hand often going to the pussy-cat bow of her blouse, twitching it, adjusting it, the turquoise polyester in blaring contrast to her florid face, patched with spider naevi. Claudine was older but definitely wearing better.

Netty herself wore a caramel silk blouse and matching skirt which went well with the pale tired gold of her hair. Most of the time no one could see the effect, however, as she wore a huge plastic apron to protect her as she cooked.

Gerald sported a red waistcoat and a green bow-tie with little flashing lights on it, which he'd bought a couple of years previously for the office party. Putting it on triggered a seemingly endless series of office anecdotes; Gerald and Roy capping each other's stories, to no one's amusement but their own.

Fred arrived last, making no concessions to the season other than to proffer them two better-than-usual bottles of Saint-Emilion. As with all their meetings since Gerald's return, Netty camouflaged her constraint under the trite phrases of hospitality.

They began eating in the mid-afternoon, when the brief brown winter light was already in retreat and the temperature was starting to drop.

The huge kitchen table had been manhandled through to the Salle de Chasse. Netty had covered it with a red cloth and used her best white china. Bunches of holly and mistletoe snaked among the dishes and everything gleamed, burnished by the firelight. On every surface candles glowed, prompting dire warnings from Sheila about conflagration. Gasps of appreciation as Netty brought in a huge platter of oysters.

'How extravagant!' cried Sheila.

'Are you sure they're OK this time of year?' asked Roy, gingerly selecting one, pallidly gleaming in its shell.

'I asked the Quiberons for advice about French festive food,' said Netty, 'so don't give me any credit.'

'Of course, you realise that if Doctor Johnson had been here, he'd have been disgusted with you: in his day oysters were the poor man's food,' said the Professor, already on his third.

'Cheers, Prof!' said Gerald.

'No offence, of course — they're delicious,' added Fred.

'None taken,' answered Netty.

Claudine managed her slippery customers with grace, accomplishing the consumption of each in one easy swallow. Sheila was less able to manage the co-ordination of tip and swallow and brief tight smile. She fingered her blouse again nervously and left a briny stain.

'My father,' commented Claudine, after dabbing her upper lip, 'was an inordinate consumer of *fruits de mer*. I have seen him eat six dozen oysters at a sitting.'

'Seventy two!' exploded Gerald, 'Bloody hell! And lived to tell the tale?'

'But of course,' answered Claudine, serenely.

Roy, having managed one, sat back in his chair and pretended to be fascinated by the flickering of the fire. His expression was that of a man who has never wished to venture beyond prawns soused in sweet pink Thousand Island dressing.

Confit of goose followed, served with sautéed potatoes and a *mélange* of mushrooms and fine beans redolent with garlic, gleaming in goose fat.

'I know the French tend to just serve meat with a simple vegetable, but I felt we just had to have potatoes,' said Netty.

'OK Net, own up,' said Gerald, spearing a little speck of black on the tines of his fork and holding it up, 'what have we here, and, more to the point, how much did it cost?'

'It's a truffle, Gerald, or a bit of one, as well you know.'

'And how much did it cost?'

'Gerald dear, don't show me up in front of our guests. It's Christmas. I went to town a little.'

'It's delicious,' said Fred loyally.

'It's a bloody rip-off,' said Gerald glumly. He stuck the fork in his mouth. Chewed. 'They look like rabbit-droppings. Net, my love, you've been had.'

'*Gerald!*'

'These tend to appeal to a sophisticated palate,' said Claudine.

'Pity Paul isn't here to enjoy all this,' said Gerald, 'Talking of sophisticated palates.'

Netty shot him a quick look. Yes, she was sure now. He did know.

'Yes, it is a shame,' she answered.

'I wonder where he's spending Christmas.'

'I think he's visiting Stephen's parents in Norfolk.'

'Oh. Well, it'll be bloody cold there, I should think. He'd have been much better off here.'

'He'll probably ring tomorrow. Lynda too.'

'Yes. That'll be nice.' Gerald sighed and stared at his drink. Netty, who knew him so well, knew he was thinking of Danny and that maudlin reminiscences could well be brewing. She felt the rage rise within her. She struck it down: it lay, paws in the air in mock submission, but it snapped and snarled. To cover the sudden heat of antagonism, she cleared the dishes with a great rumbustious clatter.

Out in the kitchen a salt tear dropped onto the amber skin of a wedge of Port Salut. She wiped it off carefully. Sheila appeared.

'You OK, Netty?'

'Fine. I'm fine.'

'You're not, are you my dear. I suppose, this time of year ... it's always the hardest. Bound to be.' A pause, then, 'He hasn't said anything to upset you, has he?'

'No, no, he hasn't said a thing. Now, go back through. Take those plates, if you would.'

Sheila went, sighing a massive patient sigh. Netty leant against the kitchen worktop, the snarling now loud in her head; gutteral, blood-curdling, slavering. She hated him. She hated him sitting there with his twinkly bow-tie and his self-pity and his treachery.

She put the sharp cheese-knife on the board and went through.

'Cheese before dessert,' she announced. 'The French way.'

After the cheese, they consumed plum tart and chocolate roulade with *crème fraîche*. Netty received the compliments of sated guests. The fire was refuelled, the glasses replenished. The dishes were stacked in the kitchen, the table pushed back to the wall under the boar's head. Gerald had tried to insert an apple in its mouth, but it kept falling out, so he stuck it on the point of one of the tushes. This gave the boar a rakish air.

Outside, the world was quiet. Netty wondered if Norbert stood silent out on the grass thinking of Teutonic molestation. Talk echoed from the beams. She remembered her first night alone in this house, with the mysteries of the past glancing off her like bruised moths.

Claudine and Fred sailed the ship of conversation deftly through channels of blandness and straits of prejudice, skirting the rocks of bumptiousness and skimming the shoals of boredom.

Netty's head felt hot and heavy. She sat under a pool of lamplight and watched Gerald's face, even redder than usual in the fireglow, and the snarling creature muttered and grumped within her. It gradually dawned on her that Gerald was aware of her intentness, that, self-conscious, his movements became clumsy; this put down to drink by the others.

Roy's head gleamed. He was happy. His nervous fingers went less often to his pate. Sheila was beaming.

Some time around the opening of the second bottle of port, the carol-singing began. Claudine listened as the others sang, astonishing themselves with their repertoire: 'Hark the Herald Angels Sing', 'O Come all ye Faithful', 'The Holly and the Ivy' ... Out they all came, with their tinsel images and their blowing trumpets and their solemn fields of snow on a hushed supernatural night.

It was while singing 'Once in Royal David's City', that Gerald broke down. He stumbled on the words *Where a mother laid her baby* ... His voice shot into an absurd falsetto register for a moment, then thickened and sank into sobs.

Claudine looked embarrassed. The Prof clicked his teeth and strolled over to the drinks cabinet. Gerald sat, mercifully saying nothing, his large shoulders heaving, both hands round his glass. He stared down at it as the sobs came, like a schoolboy under rebuke.

Netty said, 'I think we could all do with a coffee,' and made for the kitchen. She went past Gerald, saw one hand reach out to her; it nearly touched her leg. She forced herself not to veer away like a rugby-player avoiding a tackle. The fingers brushed her thigh. The muttering grew to a snarl again inside her head.

Sheila, of course, followed her.

'You can't let this go on. *Say* something to him.'

'I can't. Don't nag me, Sheila. Anyway, we've got guests.'

'They're talking of going. I think Gerald has successfully put a dampener on the festive cheer.'

And so it proved. Coffee was drunk hastily. Claudine embraced her. 'I will see you soon?'

'Soon.'

'It was a lovely meal, Annette. I appreciated it so much.'

'I hope Patapon turns up.'

Claudine shrugged. 'I do not think it possible now. My hope is that, whatever happened, he did not suffer.' Another embrace. *'Joyeux Noel,* Annette.'

Madame Bellenger was gone, driving clear-headed back to the steel-grey embrace of her château.

Fred lingered a little longer. 'Come for drinks tomorrow, all of you. But don't rush — I think we all need to sleep off the booze! At least we won't have to endure the Queen's speech!'

Quietly, on the doorstep, he said to her, 'You all right, Annette?'

'Perfectly.'

'Hmn. Look, I'm sorry about that last time you came to Petit Caillou. You needn't worry that anything like that will happen again. I misjudged the situation. I hope you can still ... that if ever you need to, you can knock on my door.'

She was almost too preoccupied with her antagonism towards Gerald to feel grateful, but nevertheless, she thanked him. She let him hug her.

'Merry Chrimble,' he said.

'Merry Christmas, Fred.'

At the turn of the night, as the Nativity approached, Sheila helped Netty wash up, then whisked Roy off to the big double bedroom. Gerald still sat, silent, by the cooling grate. Netty paused in the doorway of the Salle de Chasse, looking at the silhouette of his thick neck and heavy shoulders. The twinkle of his bow-tie cast a tiny gleam, a flickering red and green nimbus round his head.

'Netty?' he said, without turning his head. She didn't answer. She turned and climbed up to her tower room.

She was aware that she was cold. As a child she had adored Christmas Eve; she would look out at diamond stars in a holy sky and feel that the universe was charged with excitement and love.

She stood at her window, long enough for the waning moon to rise from a counterpane of cloud and march in splendour across the hollow dark. The first fingerings of frost felt their way across the lawn. No sign of Norbert. Probably he was snoring at Grand Caillou after the gathering of the clan.

Tears pricked her eyes. On this night, of all nights, she missed him most. Even more than on his birthday. On this night, all should be well with the world. The only concern ought to be the silent filling of a stocking, the only lump in the throat, that caused by anticipation.

She laid her forehead against the glass and wept, wearily, tired of all the times this had happened; the harassment of memories, the tugging of the heart-strings, the bleak knowledge that every year it would be like this. Danny, Danny in his sleepsuit, thumb in mouth. Danny, surrounded by rustling paper. Danny clamouring for batteries for his latest toy, chocolate smeared lavishly round his mouth. Danny, lying dead in an autumn copse. Danny lying dead in his grave.

Gerald's voice startled her, even though he kept it hushed.

'Net? You not in bed, then?'

She turned to see his face, white and full, weirdly disembodied, behind the banisters as he stood near the top of the stairs.

'No,' she answered. 'Clearly not.'

'I just ...' He cleared his throat. 'I thought we could have a nightcap together.' He was as awkward as if it were their first date and he didn't know whether to come in for a coffee.

'I don't know, Gerald. I'm tired.'

'I bet you are. You've worked like a Trojan. It was all much appreciated. But Net, please come down, I'd like to talk to you.'

'Can't we do it here?'

'Well, it'd be cosier down below, don't you think?' He looked around and shivered. 'I mean, doesn't this room give you the creeps? It doesn't seem part of life, somehow, cut off up here, nothing but trees to look out at.'

'Actually, it's that room downstairs I have trouble with.'

'Oh, come on Netty, come on down to the warm.'

'All right,' she sighed.

Downstairs was scarcely warmer. The night temperature was plummeting like a stone. Gerald leaned forward to stir the fading ashes of the fire.

'I'll put another log on, shall I?'

'It hardly seems worth it to me; we're not going to be here that long, are we?'

'Well, actually, we might. I've got something I want to say.' He made a fuss of fuelling the fire, bending to blow sparks into conflagration. She sat and watched. The boar with the apple on its tusk watched. The rising fire glinted on its glass eyes. It was waiting, like Netty, for Gerald to spill the beans, to spill his guts.

At last he had settled again. 'Thing is, Net, I've had something on my mind since I got back. I didn't intend to say anything: I just wanted, *really* wanted, to put it behind me. But I can't.' He looked up at her. 'It seems that we just can't put the past behind us, can we?'

'I've never claimed that we could.'

'That's true. And I've always accused you of not letting go. That's why I brought us here. Sheer escapism. All these months and we've never really *been* here, have we? I mean, we've met people, French people, but we've not impinged on their lives. We're nothing to them. We've not blended. We're still tourists. We don't live here: we still live in that house in Southfield Road.'

Netty thought of the mobiles swinging in Danny's room.

Gerald was still speaking. 'I realise it was wrong, Net, bringing you here. I know I bulldozed you. I thought it was for the best, that it would help you snap out of it.' He laughed curtly. 'As if you, as if *we* could snap out of something like that. And then, poor love,

I leave you here. I've hardly been here and you've had to cope all on your own, and you have done, brilliantly.' He put out a tentative hand. Netty sat rigidly. The hand fell back. 'So, irony of ironies, there I am, back in Oxford, passing the end of our street day after day, dying to go and have a look, hating the very idea, and angry with you.' He breathed in hard. 'Angry with you, though God knows I shouldn't have been, but you were so negative, so cold ...' He looked at her. Never had she seemed more frosty. The house was quiet. The boar seemed to twitch an attentive ear and slyly wink. Who's been a naughty boy, then? A naughty, naughty boy? Oh God. 'Netty, while I was in Oxford ... something happened. Back in August. And ... and it got worse and worse and I can't stand living with it and I've got to tell you.'

'I know.'

'*What?*'

She met his gaze. 'I know all about it.'

'But ... but how? How?' Light dawned, and rage with it. 'Sheila! Sheila: that's it, isn't it. That bitch! Interfering cow!' Relieved to transfer some of the load of guilt to another party, he rose and made for the connecting corridor through to the bedroom. 'I'll show her! I'll tell her!'

'No you won't. Sit down Gerald.'

The very calmness of her words stopped him in his tracks. He stared back at her. Her clothes were the caramel colour of the placid cows, out there in the fields in summer. He looked into her face and saw the absence of the wife he knew.

That he should have worried about hurting her! That he should have cried before their guests! Gerald pulled up a chair, not caring that its feet screeched protestingly on the quarry tiles. He sat facing her.

'You're unnatural,' he told her, rejoicing in his own righteous resentment. 'I don't believe you! I don't believe that you could sit there and say you know what I'm going to say and show no emotion. It isn't on. Have you any *idea* what I've been going through, bracing myself to tell you, worrying about hurting you?'

The sound came from her throat, distorted by the clenching of throat muscles in a paroxysm of rage so great she thought she felt herself swelling, growing tall as the ceiling, towering over him, ready to strike. Still she sat facing him, the sound coming from her throat, intense but low, an insufficient warning to him. Obtuse, he sat still and faced her and made excuse.

'Net, look ... listen to my side of things. No doubt Sheila's been giving you *her* poisonous view of it. I can imagine what she called me. Funny thing is, though, that she can't have called me anything worse than I've called myself over the past few months. Really. You've no idea what it's been like.'

Netty's neck was now rigid. The sound had gone off into a register so high-pitched Gerald could not hear it. Perhaps Patapon, if still alive, would respond to the alarum.

'I know you'll be upset that it was Camilla. You'd probably rather I'd gone with some tart down by the station. But honestly, it didn't mean anything more than that. I don't know why she ... what she saw in me. I was flattered. But it was all forgotten by morning. It would have stayed forgotten if she hadn't fallen ...

'Not that I didn't feel guilty. I *did*. Right from the start. But I was looking for comfort, Net; you'd shut me out.'

'My fault is it, then?'

'Pardon?'

'Nothing.'

'I just wanted to feel *alive* again. But when Roy called and said she was pregnant I was desperate. I had to go back and see to things.'

'So, did she want you to leave me?'

'Bloody hell no! And I wouldn't have gone, Net. I wouldn't. I wanted ... I *want* to make a go of things, if you'll let me. We've been through so much, Net, too much to just chuck it down the Swanee.'

She could see him beginning to perk up. He thought the worst was over.

'You see, Net, I'm making a clean breast. I'm trying to make you understand. When I got back to Oxford, she would hardly speak to me. I thought I'd go mad. She said she wanted an abortion.' The easy tears filled his eyes again.

'And what did you say?'

'I begged her, *begged* her, to reconsider. I mean, Jesus, a child, a child of mine, and she wanted to kill it — that's what it amounts to, doesn't it?' Sweat broke out on his brow. 'I thought, I've got to stop her. Net'll understand. We've got to save life. But I wasn't getting anywhere. She was as hard as ... Then I had my brilliant idea.'

He had been pacing the floor, shaky and urgent. Now he came back to her, knelt before her, took her hands in his, palms pressed together.

'It *was* a brilliant idea, Net, the answer to it all! I said to her that she must have the baby, she mustn't kill it, but that if she really didn't want the responsibility I quite understood. I said we'd have it, Net! I said we'd take it and bring it up as our own — well, it *would* be our own, essentially, wouldn't it? And you could love it and in time you'd forget that it had been Camilla's baby. We'd be happy and she'd have her career. We'd have another chance ... a little baby!' His breath came thick and fast as he gazed up at her. His hands were wringing hers. She looked at him in horror.

'And you want me to sanction this, Gerald? You want me to say your idea is brilliant?'

'But it *was* brilliant! It was the solution to everything!'

'Was. Do you mean she didn't agree?'

The shining light died in his eyes. He lowered his head, laid it on her knee. His voice came muffled and gruff.

'She wouldn't have it. Wouldn't hear of it. And do you know why?' Up came his head again and his voice creaked with resentment. 'It wasn't her career; it was a man. She'd met someone, just after being with me. She wanted him. She wasn't going to risk losing him. She made all those fine speeches to me, but basically she was shit-scared of losing this guy. So no way was she going to have another man's kid. Not even to give away. She wasn't going to spoil her figure and have him go off her.'

'So ... she had the abortion.'

'Yes. *Yes!* Fucking bitch! She killed it. She killed the little baby. *My* baby. I was helpless. I couldn't stop it. It just had to happen and nothing I could do. Useless. It was like when Danny ... oh God help me, oh God, Net, you've got to understand! We've only got each other. We've only got each other. Oh, the baby. Poor little thing. It was innocent and it was alive and I couldn't ... couldn't protect it. Useless, Net. I'm useless.'

He buried his face in her lap and wept noisily.

'Gerald, calm down. Roy and Sheila will hear.'

He raised his streaming face. 'Who gives a fuck?' Nevertheless, he tottered to his feet and blew his nose. Netty still sat, motionless. He looked down at her, uncertain. 'I feel better now, now that I've told you. I hated keeping it from you. It's been awful, you've no idea.'

She couldn't answer. He sat down, facing her. 'Net,' he said gently, mucus thick in his voice. 'Can you forgive me?'

Still she could not answer. He sighed. 'I see. Well, I don't blame you. You can't think anything worse of me than I've already thought of myself.'

His wife remained silent. It was getting to him. 'Roy and Sheila must be sleeping the sleep of the just and no mistake! Just as well. Damned if I'm going to explain myself to *her*. Just to you, Net. Your opinion is all that matters. Listen, I've been thinking: I know you never wanted to come out here. I bullied you into it. I think we should just call it a day. It's not for us, this foreign stuff. We could go back. Oh, not to Southfield Road. Maybe not even to Oxford. But we could go back to England. Or America, even; be near Lynda. Would you like that, Net? You just say the word. *You* choose. Whatever you want, it's yours ...'

It was like something out of *Alice in Wonderland*. Gerald's voice had shrunk and spun round and vanished, spiralling down a long tube. She was alone, in this room, his voice merely the buzzing of a distant gnat. Or a mosquito; a thin whine, meaningless yet irritating. She rubbed her elbow. Long ago, back in the summer, when she was alone and afraid and Gerald was in Oxford, making eyes at Camilla, hadn't she cracked it on the plaster of the wall? There had been a shower of dust. There had been voices, voices, cries, music, a deep bellow. They were all here again with her now and Gerald was gone, long gone.

She spoke with difficulty, forcing her words through increasing static.

'Go to bed, Gerald.'

'But...'

'Please. Just go to bed. Give me time to think. I'm tired. I can't deal with any more of this just now.'

'OK. I can understand that. Sleep on it, Netty.'

Gerald started to leave the room, making his way to the single bed where Paul had slept. He turned in the doorway.

'You sure you won't be too cold up there in that tower?'

Slowly her head moved and she looked at him.

'You don't fancy cuddling up in a single bed?' he asked.

The dying firelight glittered on her eye, and something there made him quail.

'No, 'spose not. You need time to yourself; I appreciate that.' He began to shuffle off. 'Merry Christmas, Net.'

Her neck was so stiff. With difficulty, she turned her head back. She stared into the fire, as she sat on the upright chair, hands clasped on her lap.

The house was still. *Stille Nacht, heilige Nacht.* God made himself manifest, coasting on blood into a bed of straw, rehearsal for the blood at the end; blood and ichor and a bed of stone. Beyond it, glory and redemption.

Netty shuddered. Her head ached. Inside her brain the rising cacophony. Evil. Injustice. Roy and Sheila, like Jack Sprat and his wife, lying in that bedroom where murder had taken place. Gerald, in the little bedroom, slumbering already in guilt and release. Things were so easy for him.

Stille Nacht, heilige Nacht. Frost on the lawn, stars in the sky, out there, in space, where her cry went shrilling in an infinite vacuum.

There. There, she heard it: the dint of booted heel on the tiles. He came into the room and the boar winked slyly in recognition. No doubt about it, the uniform was beautiful. Such style. He stood in front of her. He actually had a nice face, but the clothes gave him power and he relished that, she could see. He couldn't help but stand with his legs apart, in those gleaming black boots.

'Heilige Nacht,' he murmured, and turned to meet Mathilde. As he did so, a thin white wraith drifted by. What a beautiful girl;

dark hair, pale blue skin. She held a paper to her bosom. Netty saw verses written there, written in red, and the red transferred itself to the clutching hand and flooded out over the white bosom and down over the thighs. The girl faded.

A hand fell on Netty's shoulder; she looked up at a man as elegant as a prince in Perrault. The gleam of metallic embroidery. The arched brows under powdered curls. He bowed. His smile was not pleasant. His sweeping arm, trailing scented lace, revealed behind him a pile of deer, slaughtered and steaming. The reek was cruel.

Cries beyond the window. Netty rushed out into the hall. On the lawn, the figures of hunting men, outlined in quicksilver, bent over the body of a man cruelly beaten. As they drew away, Netty saw the girl grieving over him. She wanted to go out and comfort her. The maiden looked beseechingly at her.

The ground shuddered. Shuddered again. Netty backed away as a shadow fell on the lawn, obscuring the pearly glint of frost. A shadow, horned and hoofed.

She retreated in terror, back into the Salle de Chasse. Slaver dripped from the tushes of the boar and the creatures in the tiles howled. There, above the fireplace, was the gun. The gun Gerald had borrowed from Peter. It quivered in her hands like a questing beast.

Gerald, still dressed, was in the doorway. She saw how white his face was, how he didn't know whether to come or go. The barrel was surprisingly hard to hold steady.

'Don't call to them,' she said, 'I'll kill them too.'

He wavered, the gun went off. The boar's head, ruined, fell to the floor, the red floor. She fell against the wall, stunned by the recoil. Then she was up, after him, a delighted yell in her throat. He was afraid of her. In the hall she paused. No sign from above. He would not be in the tower, under the reproachful eyes of their child. There would be nowhere to go.

Out on the lawn, she scanned from left to right. He might have thought of making for the farm track ... No, no: there he was, scuttling into the forest.

She marshalled her allies, the pallid girls and the military men, and she chased him. Lights went on in the house behind her. Roy and Sheila. Too late, she thought, you can't save him.

The forest was dark and piercingly cold. The beast's breath was warm and smoked on the air. She heard her husband's terrified gasping. They reached the clearing. A pale Roman sat on the temple-stone. He pointed to the flitting shadow that was Gerald.

The pace quickened, amid the cracking of twigs and rustling of leaves. The world was spinning on this holy, purgatorial night. She was lighter and fleeter of foot than he. When she called to him, her voice was stronger and more resonant than it had ever been. He could not resist; he stopped and turned, at bay. She raised the gun. He was the slick molester, he was the ghastly derelict, he was all the killers that have ever been.

'Netty!' she heard him cry. 'Netty, no!'

The gun fired. She saw his arms fly up, she saw him fall and disappear. Recovering from the mighty blow to her shoulder, she raced up to the place. Her foot slipped, the gun went spinning. Down went her leg, down she fell to her waist, to her neck, then she was sliding in grating darkness and falling into space, onto rock.

There was breathing, loud in the darkness. It was her own breath. Netty could hear nothing else. The voices and presences had gone, and so had the roaring of the beast and the echo of gunfire.

Bewildered, she sat up. The darkness was thick. Smothering. She fought panic. Her hands reached out, scrabbled about, trying to make sense of her surroundings, reading rock and space like braille. Her fingers touched a body. Hairy. Cold.

'I think that must be Madame Bellenger's dog. It's been there a while. Smell it.'

She jumped at his voice, distorted by the strange acoustics of the underworld. 'Gerald! Is that you?'

'Who else would it be? Just fucking keep away from me, you mad bitch!'

'Gerald! Where are you?'

'Too bloody dark to see me, isn't it! Just as well for me!'

She heard him move slightly in the dense blackness. He let out a groan.

'Gerald ... oh God, are you OK?'

'What a fucking question! You just tried to blow my head off!' He groaned again. 'Oh Christ, just let me wake up from this.'

'Gerald ... I'm so sorry ... I don't know what ... you're right: I'm mad.'

'I know I'm right. I could come at you in this dark, see how *you* like it. I mean, my God, after I explained and everything! Jesus, my ribs.' He went quiet. The silence was as thick as the darkness. Panic seized her.

'Gerald? *Gerald!*'

'Don't bloody shout! I'm not going anywhere. *We're* not going anywhere.'

'Somebody will come ...'

'You sure of that? Nobody came for that poor dog, and you can bet he yowled his head off.'

'If we could just see ...'

'Hang on. I was lighting the candles earlier — I borrowed Roy's lighter.'

A few seconds later, the wavering light revealed him to her. She scrambled over to him and after a moment's hesitation he put one arm around her.

'Jesus, it's cold,' he said.

He raised the trembling lighter higher. Its feeble illumination acted like a spell, animating great galleries of ancient creatures, ochre and russet against the rock walls, their sides quivering as if with breath, their majesty and beauty unchanged by time. Near Netty and Gerald, the red outline of a human hand, stencilled there millennia before. At their feet, the stiffened corpse of the once-lively Patapon.

The cold seized them like the jaws of a man-trap.

Hours later, the faintest of grey light glimmered down from above, and they shouted. After that, darkness ruled again.

Later still, there was the snuffling and breathing of some creature at the gateway to that underworld.

Epilogue:
The Cradle of Man

The latest attraction in the Bourdonne area is the recently discovered Caverne du Sanglier, near the picturesque village of Malignac.

Prehistorians theorise that many cave-systems exist in the Périgord which still wait to be found. As happened at Lascaux in 1940, the Caverne was first discovered by a local dog out hunting in the woods, then by an English couple who fell into the cave by accident. It is strange, is it not, that the glories of primeval art should come to light by such chances!

Like Lascaux, Rouffignac and Font de Gaume, du Sanglier reverberates with colour; polychromic cavalcades of bison, reindeer and mammoth march from cave to cave, ritual herds, it has often been believed, awaiting ritual slaughter. At the heart of the warren of caves is the cavern of the wild boar itself, painted on a shoulder of limestone with such marvellous effect that the animal, noted for its strangely sardonic expression, seems to be charging out at the visitor. The boar does not feature in any other Middle or Upper Magdalenian cave at present known in the Périgord, though of course he is to be seen at the famous site of Altamira in Spain. Boars are more familiar in the climate of the Mesolithic and Neolithic periods, when temperate conditions led to the hunting of forest game — a tradition still in continuance today.

It is intriguing to imagine how many thousands of years of human culture have gone by since our unknown ancestors ornamented this place. Looking at these paintings somehow reinforces our notions of what it is to be human; to try to control a hostile environment and a mysterious, often cruel universe through magic, through the orderly yet inspired portrayal of the wonders of nature. We feel a common bond with the unknown early man. We have sent men of our generation to walk on the moon, but still the world is too big for us. The more we understand, the more we fail to understand. To contemplate the face of the boar, the charge of the bull, the massive presence of the mammoth, is to be humbled by the essence of life itself. We are everything, and we are nothing.

Parties of tourists are strictly limited in number. Visits are permitted from March to September, every day from 9.00 to 12.00 and 14.00 to 18.00 hours. Caves closed on Sundays and jours fériés. Consult M. Lelouche at Grand Caillou, 2 km from Malignac.

Sadly, it is expected that these tours will be prohibited entirely in a few years, as the breath of visitors is already corrupting the environment: there are problems with green algae and accelerated depositions of white calcite, creating a haze over the images like the fog of time itself.

Acknowledgements

I want to thank my fantastic husband Rob and my two sons for their constant love, support and belief in me. I'm also indebted to Liz Calder and Rosemary Davidson for first publishing this novel at Bloomsbury. Especial thanks go to Linda Gillard for encouraging me to believe that *The Chase* deserved a second outing and Ali Luke for her knowledge, enthusiasm and for being my go-to person when technology throws me into a panic! I also recommend The Alliance of Independent Authors at www.allianceindependentauthors.org for anyone thinking of going it alone in the publishing world: you'll soon discover you're not alone at all. Finally, I'm so grateful to Jane Dixon-Smith of JD Design for formatting the text and creating such a wonderful cover.

About Lorna Fergusson

Born in Scotland, I studied English at Aberdeen University and at Merton College, Oxford. For seven years we owned an old country house in the Dordogne, the region which provided me with such powerful inspiration for *The Chase*. I live in Oxford with my husband and two sons. I run Fictionfire Literary Consultancy, offering day courses, workshops, manuscript appraisal, editing, one-to-one consultancy and mentoring, at www.fictionfire.co.uk. I blog at http://literascribe.blogspot.com. You can follow me on Twitter: @LornaFergusson and at www.facebook.com/pages/Fictionfire-Inspiration-for-Writers.

To be kept up to date with news and future releases, please join the Fictionfire Press mailing list at www.fictionfirepress.com.

If you enjoyed *The Chase*, I'd be very grateful if you'd tell your friends about it, Tweet or share on Facebook, or write a review on Amazon, Goodreads or your blog, if you have one. Thank you!